by Michael Malone

the four corners
of the sky

the four corners
of the sky

Michael Malone

SOURCEBOOKS LANDMARK™
AN IMPRINT OF SOURCEBOOKS, INC.®
NAPERVILLE, ILLINOIS

Sourcebooks and the colophon are registered trademarks of Sourcebooks, Inc.

The characters and events portrayed in this book are fictitious or are used ficti-
tiously. Any similarity to real persons, living or dead, is purely coincidental and
not intended by the author.

Published by Sourcebooks Landmark, an imprint of Sourcebooks, Inc.
P.O. Box 4410, Naperville, Illinois 60567-4410
(630) 961-3900
Fax: (630) 961-2168
www.sourcebooks.com

Library of Congress Cataloging-in-Publication Data
Malone, Michael
  The four corners of the sky / Michael Malone.
     p. cm.
  1. Women air pilots--Fiction. 2. Air pilots, Military--Fiction. 3. Abandoned children--Fiction. 4. Mothers and daughters--Fiction. 5. Fathers and
daughters--Fiction. 6. North Carolina--Fiction. I. Title.
  PS3563.A43244F68 2009
  813'.54--dc22
                              2008038938

Printed and bound in the United States of America
LB 10 9 8 7 6 5 4 3 2 1

For Maggie

Acknowledgments

My deep and lasting thanks to Hillel Black, Peter Lynch, Dominique Raccah, and Peter Matson.

My appreciation to the Bogliasco Foundation for the generous fellowship that allowed me to work on *The Four Corners of the Sky* in a setting as memorable as the company I met there. My gratitude to the three Annies for whom the heroine of this romance is named: Dr. Ann Hackmann, The Reverend Ann Stevenson, and Professor Ann Rosalind Jones.

Among the many who gave me advice and information about aviation, let me especially thank Captain Marion Barnett, U.S. Air Force, Retired.

Thanks to my first two readers, Sue Martin and Cathy Wagner. Thanks to Astrid Giugni for the algebra.

And, as ever, there would be no book without Maureen.

the four corners *of the* sky

July 4, 1982

In small towns between the North Carolina Piedmont and the coast the best scenery is often in the sky. On flat sweeps of red clay and scrub pine the days move monotonously, safely, but above, in the blink of an eye, dangerous clouds can boil out of all four corners of the sky and do away with the sun so fast that, in the sudden quiet, birds fly shrieking to shelter. The flat slow land starts to shiver and anything can happen.

In such a storm, on Annie Peregrine's seventh birthday, her father gave her the airplane and minutes later drove out of her life.

When thunder scared her awake she found herself in their convertible, parked atop a hill near a barn. Off in the distance rose a large white house with a wide white porch. A white pebble road curved away behind the car, unreeling like ribbon on a spool. Annie looked past two rows of rounded black trees to where fields of yellow wheat spilled to the edge of the sky. Her father and she must have arrived at Pilgrim's Rest, the Peregrine family house in Emerald, North Carolina, toward which they'd been driving all day.

Sliding from their car, she saw him, slender and fast-moving, his white shirt shimmery, as he ran toward her out of the barn and across the dusky yard.

"Annie!" Reaching her, her father dropped to his knees and hugged her so fiercely that her heart sped. "I'm in trouble.

I've got to leave you here a little while with Aunt Sam and Clark. Okay?"

She couldn't speak, could only shake her head. How often had he told her that the house where he had grown up, that Pilgrim's Rest had been for him a pit of snakes, a cage of tigers?

He kept nodding to make her nod too. "Okay? I'll be back. Just hang onto your hat." Pulling a pink baseball cap from his pocket, he snuggled it down onto her head. Colored glass beads spelled ANNIE above its brim; a few beads were missing, breaks in the letters.

Across the driveway a tall woman with short thick hair banged open the large doors of the barn. She called out to Annie's father. "Jack? Jack! Jack! Jack!"

Annie's father turned her around to face the woman but kept talking with that nodding intensity that always meant they would need to move fast. "See my sister Sam over there? I told you how nice she is." The sound of sharp thunder flung the child back into the man's arms. "So's Clark. They'll take care of you. I'll call you. Remember, you're a flyer." He yanked her small hard blue suitcase out of the convertible, dropping it onto the gravel beside her. "Give Sam the cash."

"Stop it. Where are you going!"

"Annie, I know. It's rotten." A drop of rain fell on his face like a fat fake tear. Drops splattered on the suitcase's shiny clasps. "Go look in the barn. There's a present for you. 'Sorry, no silver cup.'"

She kicked him as hard as she could. And then she kicked over the blue suitcase. "I want to go with *you*," she said. "You!" But before she could stop him, her father had run to their car and was driving away.

She raced after the Mustang, down the pebble road between the dark rows of large oak trees. It was hard to make her voice work loudly but finally it flamed up her throat and she could shout at him to come back. She was already crying, already knowing she couldn't run fast enough.

Behind her, the tall woman named Sam kept calling, "Jack! Jack!"

Annie echoed her, hoping it would help. "Dad! Dad!"

The convertible braked to a skidding stop, her father twisting around in the seat to call out, "Your birthday present's in the barn, go look in the barn! Annie! Don't forget. You're a flyer!"

She screamed as loudly as she could, "You stop!"

The wind caught his scarf as he sped off; it flew into the air behind him. Then he was gone and the green silk scarf lay coiled near her feet. She ground it into the pebbled road with her small leather cowboy boots; they were as green as the scarf and stitched with lariats. She had wanted these boots so badly that only a week ago her father had turned their car around, drove them back fifty miles to some small town in the middle of a flat state; he took her to the store where she'd seen the boots in the window and he bought them for her. "Never wait to say what you want," he told her. "It's no fun to go back. And sometimes you can't."

But now she'd said what she wanted and he'd left her anyhow. Dust and rain stung Annie's eyes shut and the world turned black. The tall woman's voice was calling again. "Annie! Annie!"

Furious, the child flung herself into the gully beside the road, tumbling down a tangle of vines and underbrush; she lay there in the rain, hiding from the woman Sam until her voice, solicitous and worried, passed by, still shouting, "Annie! Annie!"

After a while, the woman's voice faded and there were no sounds but the hard wind and rain. Annie decided to walk along the road in the direction her father had gone. Maybe he would stop for gas or food and she would find him again.

But suddenly her pink baseball cap blew off, whisking over the bank. She chased the cap onto a path that wound up to a hilltop, where it caught against a pair of closed white wooden gates. On a post beside these gates there hung a wood sign with painted letters. It said, "Pilgrim's Rest, 1859." And above that, "Peregrines" was carved in the wings of a wood hawk flying. She undid the heavy iron latch of the gates and pushed her way through the opening.

In the yard, gusty stinging rain and wind slapped at her, shoving her against the front of the barn. Its immense gray weathered doors blew suddenly apart as if she had knocked on them in a fairy tale and some invisible sorcerer with power over the elements had ordered the wind to sweep her inside.

The barn was an enormous dark empty space, with high rafters and a sweet strong smell. Outside, the storm was close and noisy, but the barn was quiet. Annie walked into the middle of the shadowy space. There, alone, sat an old airplane. It was a fixed-wing single-engine plane, a Piper Warrior painted cherry red with blazing yellow stripes and a silver propeller on its black nose. The door to its cockpit was swung open. From the seat the beam of a large red battery lantern was shining on the plane so clearly she could see the fresh footprints of her father's shoes in the thick dust on the wing. She ran over to the plane, crawled behind its wheel cap and beat her head against her knees in a shout of grief so hopeless that the noise she made scared her. She cried until she heard an unfamiliar man's voice call her name, "Annie." Quickly she bit at the cloth on her knee, quiet, listening. The voice moved away.

Above her, beneath the airplane's low curved wing, she could make out spiraling green letters curled like a dragon's tail, spelling the words, *King of the Sky*.

While they'd traveled on highways together, her father had told her about his old airplane, the *King*, how he and she could have been moving much faster back and forth across America if they'd only had the use of the *King of the Sky*, how the plane was "just sitting there in the barn" at his childhood home Pilgrim's Rest, in a town called Emerald. He'd told her that someday they'd go get the *King* and they'd fly it all over the country.

Annie had never much believed such a plane existed, any more than the lost treasures and magic elixirs and prison tunnels he'd also described.

Now she hugged the *King of the Sky*'s wheel with both arms and legs. "I'm a flyer," she said. "A flyer. A flyer."

part one

North
July 4, 2001

Chapter 1

The Bride Comes Home

On her twenty-sixth birthday, U.S. Navy Lt. Annie Peregrine Goode was speeding home from Annapolis for the weekend, going 74 miles per hour, enjoying the sharp turns and brisk shifts of well-tuned gears. As she had done since her father had left her at Pilgrim's Rest when she was seven years old, she would spend her birthday there with her aunt Sam and Sam's housemate for decades, Clark Goode.

The sky was busy with a storm coming. Clouds bunched together, swelled and darkened to a black roil that fell in shadows over the land. On the highway, a strong wind pushed the clouds scudding ahead of the young woman's fast-moving convertible. Her ponytail tucked inside a Navy cap, she raced the car through heavy air. On the seat beside her sat a container of precisely chopped carrots, celery, and cucumber slices from which she snacked. Her flight instructor's uniform was white, the pants and jacket spotless. Her gray sports car was a Porsche Carrera. She and her soon-to-be-ex-husband Brad had bought it because it could accelerate to 60 miles per hour in 4.3 seconds.

In front of her an old Volvo station wagon with long green cones tied to its roof bounced off onto the shoulder to give her room the driver mistakenly thought she needed to maneuver around him. The slow-moving white car belonged, Annie knew, to her uncle, Dr. Clark Goode, doubtless on his way home.

Tapping her horn as she passed him, Annie slowed down, calling out, "Hi, Clark! Pull over!"

He waved out his window. "Annie! Be careful!"

She stopped precisely on the shoulder ahead of him, running back to the tall, thin man as he stepped from the opened door of his car.

"Hi, sweetheart." He folded her in his arms. "Happy birthday! Weather Channel's predicting a tornado." He gestured at the clouds, then at the long plastic cones on the roof of his station wagon. "They're for the roses."

She hugged him again. "Will you stop listening to the Weather Channel?"

Behind round tortoise-shell glasses, Clark studied her. "You look a little anemic. Teaching too much?" A pediatrician, he had long been checking her health.

"I'm fine."

He felt her left land, touching the ring finger with good-humored taps. "Divorce final?"

A year ago, Annie had left her husband but she still wasn't legally divorced. "Next week, the lawyer swears."

"Hmm." Clark nodded, the quiet blue of his eyes speckled as light through an old window. "Hmm."

She rubbed his hands between hers. "Don't 'hmm' me. Let's get home before it rains." She checked her watch. "I'll be there in twenty minutes and you'll be there when, in…about an hour?"

"Ha. Don't mock the late-middle-aged." Comfortably he curled his lanky frame back into the Volvo. "You were speeding, sweetheart. Slow down."

"Clark, it's good to be home." Annie raced back to her Porsche, revved the motor, and rocketed away.

"Too fast." He shook his head, slowly starting his station wagon.

Annie's uncle never went over the speed limit; in fact, he rarely reached it. He preferred walking to driving and occasionally walked even the two miles to the hospital where he ran a pediatric clinic. When Annie was fifteen and he'd been teaching her to drive, he'd told her, "Slow down," so often that she had begged her aunt Sam to give her lessons instead. "Where are you going, you have to get there so fast?" Clark would ask the teenager. "Everywhere," she'd tell him, although there was really no place in particular she wanted to go; she just didn't want to be left behind.

Clark had always acknowledged amiably that he saw no reason for speed except to save a life. In Emerald Hospital's hallway, generations of children had heard the same old slow stories as they waited outside the ER. In the same unhurried way, he moved his cushioned rocker, one foot nudging it in a steady (and to the child Annie, maddening) rhythm of three taps, pause, three taps, pause, while he watched baseball games, with slow shadows inching across vivid green grass on the television screen. Clark loved almost nothing that moved fast, except Annie.

Now she was racing so quickly along Old 41 that within less than a minute he could no longer see her gray Porsche ahead of him. "Too fast," Clark repeated and rubbed at his hair and checked his speedometer.

As she drove, Annie glanced at her bare left hand on the wheel where once she'd worn a wedding ring. Her husband had fought their divorce; she'd avoided the fight. As a result, the settlement was still "pending final papers." It wasn't like her not to finish things. For what was she waiting? Certainly not for Lt. Bradford Hopper, a textbook example of a false hypothesis—that he loved her—on the basis of which the logic of her life had crashed into mistake after mistake.

A year ago, when she had flung her suitcase into the Porsche and told Brad, "I'm leaving you," he shouted at her, kicking at their doorstep, "Get back here! You can't leave me!" And she told him with the steely distinctness that was always her response to his fits, "Watch me!"

• • •

The fight took place at their small stucco house on the San Diego base where they were both pilots. They were not long back from Kuwait, but long enough for Brad to start an affair.

He blocked her path to the Porsche, jumping up and down on the hard asphalt as if it were a trampoline. "A, you come back here right now! What's the matter with you?"

"The *matter?*"

As always her irony ricocheted off him. "Yeah, what's the matter!" He repeated it. "What the fuck's the matter?!"

"How about, you cheated on me!" Their hands fought at the Porsche's door handle. "How about, you cheated on me in my own bed! I'm taking the cat and the car."

"What?"

"You don't want the cat and I trust the car!" She'd grabbed at Brad's fingers, feeling the wedding ring she'd put there. "Back off, Brad or I'll break your wrist, I swear to God. You won't fly for a month."

"You're nuts." But he believed her, pulled away his hand before she could slam the car door on it.

In the Porsche's rearview window, as she skidded away from the replicated row of military houses, she watched him kicking over a big green garbage can at the curb. His attack on the can looked so much like the tantrums he'd had at Annapolis that she stopped the car with a jolting bounce to watch him. Then she leaned over to ask the slender cat in the carrier beside her, "Was I crazy? Why did I ever marry him?"

The cat, Amy Johnson, ignored the question.

That was thirteen months ago.

• • •

In Emerald, Annie glanced behind her but didn't yet see her Uncle Clark anywhere on the old two-lane that led toward Pilgrim's Rest. She was almost home. On her cell phone, she called her divorce lawyer in Maryland, near the Navy Academy where she taught. She'd been postponing talking with this man,

whom she'd met only twice and who charged her for every minute of conversation. When she reached him, she spoke quickly.
He assured her that the final settlement would be awaiting her
signature and Brad's when she returned to Annapolis after the
holiday. "Enjoy the Fourth," he advised. "Relax."

"I'll relax when I'm divorced."

"I doubt it," the lawyer predicted.

She hung up, not wanting to chat about her personality at
three hundred dollars an hour.

Annie passed a field of ripening corn. She had not been
home to Emerald since early spring and she made an effort
now to notice the changes in the summer trees and farmland
as she sped by them. More often than not she was, she admitted, in front of or behind the moment, planning for the next
problem, remembering the last crisis. Her aunt Sam was always
telling her that life was what was happening in the side view.
But moving forward, Annie ignored peripherals and while she
admitted their loss and tried to remember to look left and right,
usually she forgot.

Today was, however, her vacation, her birthday, her trip
home. So she slowed slightly and as she did so, saw around her
soybeans and tobacco, wheat and corn bowing to the strong
storm wind. On both sides of the old highway stretched out
an America that nearer to Emerald had been replaced by huge
concrete box stores stretching across hot parking lots in which
high-wheeled trucks and big SUVs banged into each other. But
here on the outskirts, the world was still local. People still kept
machines and repaired them. In a yard across the road from her,
a man bent under the hood of an old truck. Here the long flat
green land was lush and ripe and empty. A boy was making his
bicycle jump in a driveway. A woman kept looking into her
mailbox, hoping for more than was there.

Annie's fingers loosened on the steering wheel as she waited
at the familiar stoplight blinking at the crossroads. Rolling her
neck side to side on the headrest, hearing the crackle in her vertebrae, she felt everything easing. Across the intersection, two

little girls ran out of a peanut field beside an orange-red brick ranch house with aluminum white columns and an over-sized door. The little girls wigwagged their arms when Annie blew her horn. She waved her Navy lieutenant's hat at them so that her hair flew out, wild and gold. She wanted them to see that the fast driver of the powerful convertible, the military officer, was, like them, a girl.

While Annie had ostensibly been hurrying to protect the Porsche's leather seats from the coming rain, the truth was—as her uncle Clark always said when asking her to slow down—she was speeding because she liked to go fast. Speed had long been the gauge by which she'd judged herself. During her four years with Brad at the Naval Academy, she'd been secretly frustrated that in aviation tests he was consistently the faster flyer. To be fastest, to be first, mattered. Now her chance was coming. A week ago, her commanding officer had told her that she had been chosen to take a test flight in a new experimental model of an F-35 Lightning II vertical-landing fighter jet; she'd be trying to break a speed record. A chance was all she wanted. "I can do this," she'd assured Commander Campbell with her infectious smile. "I'm a flyer."

"That you are, young lady," he'd agreed in the outmoded way of his that she tried to ignore. "Concentrate on flying. Don't be running off and getting married again."

"Amelia Earhart was married, sir."

He hunched his shoulders, as if nothing more needed to be said about Amelia Earhart.

She couldn't resist. "Her plane didn't crash because she was married."

He hunched his shoulders again, returned her salute, and left.

• • •

As Annie sped around a rattling tractor, her cell phone rang. The caller's area code was one she didn't recognize.

"Lt. Annie Goode," she said briskly.

"This is Vice Detective Daniel Hart." The young man had a pleasant low voice. "I'm with the Miami Police Department. I'm calling about a fraud investigation and I need to locate your father, Jack Peregrine."

The detective's inquiry took her entirely by surprise. Her response was to accelerate. She passed two cars one after the other. Their drivers looked at her, taken aback by the noise of the sports car's racing motor.

"Jack Peregrine," the young man repeated, making a strange crunchy noise. "Sorry, I'm eating trail mix. I missed my lunch."

"You shouldn't," she told him.

"You're right," he agreed affably.

"I wouldn't know my father if I fell over him on the sidewalk."

"A sidewalk? I love sidewalks but who walks anymore? My ex-wife would borrow a car to drive to *her* car in a parking garage."

Annie downshifted before the Porsche banked a curve. "Detective Hert—"

"It's Hart. Like, you know, thump, thump, thump. Sgt. Daniel Hart. Here's the thing. Your dad, Jack Peregrine. I had him under surveillance. He gave me the slip."

About to show her impatience, oddly she laughed instead. "Join the club. The 'slip' from what?"

"Well, for us it was a case of false pretenses, but now the FBI's involved. They want him for defrauding Cuba."

She laughed again, but a tight tense laugh that went on longer than she wanted. "I'm sorry? Defrauding Cuba?"

"Some swindle of a Cuban artifact. I don't know why Americans just don't leave Cuba alone."

She asked Hart how her father had given him "the slip."

He explained that Jack Peregrine had been the subject of a recent stakeout. Peregrine fled his Hotel Dorado room in South Beach, Florida, minutes before an attempt to arrest him. He climbed into the next room by the balcony and allegedly robbed the occupants of their digital camera on his way out.

Annie noticed her knuckles were white. "How'd you get this phone number?"

"We tossed your dad's room before he took off. It was on the back of an old photo in his jacket. Says 'Annie,' and has this number on it."

The news was astounding to her. "I've used this cell phone for less than a year! And I've had nothing to do with my father since I was seven."

"What can I tell you, Annie? He had your number. So, you on your way to Emerald? Bride comes home?"

The man's easygoing familiarity with her life angered her. "Is somebody playing a fucking joke on me?"

"Hey, take it easy." There was a crackling noise of a plastic bag being crunched. "This was an old photo of Jack Peregrine with a cute little girl. Says Breakers Restaurant in West Palm. The little girl's you, I figure. Bangs, pearl necklace, cowboy jacket. Great smile."

Annie fought off the vivid memory of that pearl necklace and that cowboy jacket, both gifts from her father. She turned her neck side to side, trying to loosen the tension.

"So you haven't seen him since you were seven?" The detective spoke casually, as if they were catching up on old friends.

Her hands gripped the Porsche's leather-wrapped steering wheel. "No, I saw him once. Eight, nine years ago but I didn't talk to him that time."

Hart sounded skeptical. "Why not?"

The thought struck her that Hart was a crank caller of some sort. Or maybe some other crook in pursuit of her father. It wouldn't be the first time. "Can you prove you're with the police?"

"Sure. Badge number…" He reeled off a realistic-sounding series of numbers. "Detective Sergeant, Miami Vice—" He paused.

She asked, "Are you waiting for a joke here?"

"It happens." Hart had a very engaging voice. "Sorry, let me put this other call on hold." He came back on the line. "So, about your dad's mess. Feds told me to back off. Where's the respect for locals anymore?"

Annie asked again to know what Hart meant by her dad's "mess."

"He stole a relic, alleged relic, that if it exists, belongs to the people of Cuba. *La Reina Coronada del Mar*."

The Spanish words floated up at her out of her childhood; she'd heard them often from her father. "Queen of the Sea?"

"You know it?"

Annie thought back. "…A statue?"

"Sixteenth-century. Peru. Virgin Mary."

Memories hurried in. Her father had told her long stories about *La Reina Coronada*. "The Queen of the Sea. I used to have dreams about that statue. I used to dream I was trying to save her from drowning." She wondered why in the world she had just told this complete stranger a childhood dream of hers.

Just as oddly, he replied, "Did you save her?"

"No, I woke up."

"Yeah. It's too much for a kid. For years after my dad died, I was always dreaming I was trying to pull him out from under a car wreck. He died in a car wreck. He was a cop."

Neither spoke for a moment. Then Hart asked, "So you ever get the impression your dad actually had hold of the Queen of the Sea?"

With a glance at her speedometer—92 miles per hour—she took her foot off the accelerator, breathing carefully while she slowed the car. "Sergeant Hart, I got the impression my dad had hold of the golden flip-flops of Helen of Troy and a MapQuest to Shangri-la." Her father had told her thousands of extravagant lies: that there was buried treasure in his backyard, that the neon-blue plastic sunglasses he'd given her as a birthday gift would endow her with super-powered X-ray vision. "It's what he did for a living, 'false pretenses,' lies to con suckers. He was a con artist."

Hart laughed his pleasant laugh. "Still is. No offense but I wouldn't trust Jack Peregrine if he walked on water and then turned it into wine."

"Trust me," Annie said, "If he could turn water into wine, he'd sell it."

Hart's jaunty guffaw surprised her. It was rare that people laughed aloud at her jokes. His response warmed her into asking, "So the FBI is what, shoving you aside? Federal intervention?"

"You should talk. You're U.S. Navy."

She couldn't read his tone. "You have a problem with the Navy?"

"Well, I remember the *Maine*. Listen, I'm just trying to do my job, Lieutenant Goode. Protecting people like you."

"Funny, that's my business too." Annie was accustomed to, but not particularly tolerant of, sarcasm about the military.

Hart laughed. "I gotta tell you, I was impressed, what I read about you. You and your husband flying the Super Hornet in Operation Desert Fox. I mean you guys bombed the shit out of some sand."

Indignantly, she asked if he'd been reading files on her.

"Don't take it personally. Anyhow, I need your cooperation. The FBI says this relic *Coronada*'s real, they say your dad's got it, they want it and him both."

She shook her head as vehemently as if he could see her. "You think that relic's real? No way."

Hart claimed to have better information. "FBI says it's a sixteenth-century gold statue of Mary with Inca jewels and a thorn from the Crown of Thorns."

Annie snorted. "Total bullshit."

"I figure you love your dad." Again, his familiarity jarred her. "Well, the guy's in a serious mess here and you need to tell him, come see me, turn himself in. We can work a deal." Abruptly Hart announced he had to take another call. "Fly safe, Lieutenant."

"Hello? Hello?"

As Annie hit redial, she memorized the caller's number. It was a skill she'd had since she was a toddler, a short-term photographic memory. When her father had discovered this talent, he'd used it to win bets against unsuspecting strangers who'd been sure she wouldn't be able to repeat a column of figures after a brief glance. She had dreaded disappointing him by being wrong.

Sergeant Hart's good-natured baritone sent her to his voice mail. "MPD, Vice Sgt. Dan Hart speaking. Keep it brief. Thanks."

"This is Lt. Annie Goode. Call me back, Sergeant Hart!"

To her puzzlement, she felt so shaken that she had to pull over to the side of the highway. For five minutes she sat there, her head against the steering wheel.

Then with a short scream of tires, she raced the Porsche back onto the asphalt. Annie's best friend Georgette, a psychiatrist, had told her once that speed was her way of staying ahead of the past. "Damn straight," Annie had admitted.

She hit 60 miles per hour in 4.3 seconds.

Chapter 2

Speed

For Annie's seventh birthday, Sam bought her niece a balloon ride. For her eighth, Sam arranged a thirty-minute "Sky Ride" with Dwight Kelvin (D. K.) Destin, U.S. Navy, Retired, a middle-aged African-American Vietnam War vet who owned the tiny local airfield in Emerald, built—he said—on land once farmed by his Algonquin ancestors. He took the little girl up in a Pawnee Cropduster that had his insignia black eagle painted on its side. She so loved this lesson, during which for a few thrilling seconds D. K. handed her the steering yoke, that she persuaded him, a wheelchair-bound grouch, to repair the Piper Warrior her father had left in the Pilgrim's Rest barn and to teach her to fly it. As fast as it could go.

Going fast had been a habit with her father. But by flying, she could go even faster. On her first ride in the *King of the Sky*, Annie yelled suddenly and long from joy, a noise no one in Emerald had ever heard the somber child make.

"Feel good?" D. K. Destin asked her. "Want to fly it solo someday?"

She nodded yes, with her solemn blue eyes. "Fast," she repeated.

"The faster the better," he agreed. "That's my philosophy. And I can't even get out of this chair." When a Vietcong MiG had winged his A-6E Intruder attack bomber on a deep-strike mission, D. K. had crashed into the China Sea where he had held his unconscious navigator up out of the waves on a fragment of wreckage for five and a half hours, longer than he would have needed to (according to him) had anybody "given a fuck about us." After rescue, emergency surgery on the carrier saved the navigator but left D. K. unable to walk.

• • •

After a few dozen hours in the air together, the old combat flyer told her that she was, like him, born to fly. He made her kiss the black eagle painted on the fuselage of his Cropduster and although she was embarrassed, she did so to pledge her allegiance to aviation. Two years later D. K. proclaimed that for her sake he was cutting back on beer. He wanted to live long enough to see her an Annapolis graduate and a commissioned pilot. Annie was going to be Lt. D. K. Destin's final mission for the U.S. Navy. "Baby, you gonna wave at eagles. You'll say, "Scuse me, cloud, y'all move on over, here comes the best in the north, south, east, west, and headed for the Milky Way.' And here's what you'll tell the whole fuckin' world: 'I am Annie P. Goode and I am *Goode* to go!'"

It was vaguely evident to Annie, flying high with D. K. above the farms of Emerald, that he was training her to be his victory over a smashed career. After she'd won her first flying competition, he'd made this goal explicit, asking her to take a sacred vow on her gold medal, swearing that someday she would show the U.S. Navy how D. K. Destin, a black man with Occaneechi blood, a man the military had used as a scratch pad, could make her a flyer who was faster than anybody else in America. Annie would be D. K.'s proof that this country's passing him over for the Medal of Honor had been "racist malefaction."

"For a little bitty white girl," he noted with satisfaction, "you are fuckin' good."

"I don't think you're supposed to talk like that," she primly advised him.

"Talk? Don't get hung up on 'talk.' They shoot you out of the sky? Your plane's on fire and you're falling in the shit faster'n a wino off an overpass? You're going down, the China Sea's rising up, and a lot of water's saying, 'Hellowww, baby!' You know what, Annie? You don't give a flying fuck how you're supposed to talk."

As the years in Emerald went by, Annie proved just how fast she was. She proved it on the ground as well as in the air. Her junior year in high school, she won blue ribbons in hundred-yard dashes. More and more ribbons hung from hooks on the walls of her room. She told a classmate who was urging her to join the cheerleading squad, "I don't want to cheer somebody else on. I want somebody else to cheer me on." By her senior year, the Emerald High band was doing just that, playing "Annie P. Goode" at track meets, scored to Chuck Berry's "Johnny B. Goode." As soon as she walked onto the field toward the starting block, they would start playing:

> Go, Annie, go, go, go!
> Annie P. Goode!

D. K. Destin dreaded every one of those track meets. He had nightmares that Annie would trip or that someone would knock into her, that she'd suffer some disabling injury (like his own) that would ruin her chance to be accepted at Annapolis where she would learn to fly jets.

His other nightmare was that her father would return out of the blue and take her away.

But Jack Peregrine never returned and Annie never was injured. In fact, ironically, her success in track was one of the reasons so many colleges, including the Naval Academy, wanted to recruit her.

By the time Annie was twenty-one, she was flying faster and higher than D. K. had ever gone, for by that time she was piloting F-14 Tomcats and then FA-18E/F Super Hornets straight up into clouds at an acceleration fast enough to make her bones shake.

Her white Navy helmet was stenciled "Lt. Annie P. Goode," with D. K.'s logo of a black eagle under it, and her white jacket was decorated with commendation ribbons. The only cadet at the Academy who could fly faster than Annie was the cadet she married. Brad Hopper.

From the start, D. K. didn't like Brad. When Annie announced she was marrying her classmate, D. K. bluntly asked her, "He can go fast but can he go slow? If you want to know if he loves you so, it's in his kiss."

"Don't be gross," Annie told the old flyer.

"Baby, that's the last of your worries," he rightly predicted.

Clark also had his doubts about the marriage. Only her optimistic aunt Sam kept saying, "Brad's the One."

He wasn't.

Now, legally separated from him, Annie lived alone and taught flying, mostly to men, some of them men like Brad Hopper. She taught them to fly combat jets off carriers for Air Wing Three of the U.S. Navy. A few of her students afterwards sent her emails from Key West or Jeddah or Fujairah, telling their news or congratulating her on promotions or commendations. Their emails quoted back to her the blessing with which she'd sent each of them on a first solo flight. It was what D. K. had yelled at her morning after morning: "You're Goode to go!"

• • •

Annie's passion for velocity was a trait she knew she had inherited not from D. K. nor from Clark or Sam, but from Jack Peregrine. "We fly through the air," he had sung to her at bedtime. "Jump, Annie!" And she would fly off the bed into his embrace; he would hold her tightly by her small forearms, swinging her around in a skipping circle until, dizzy, she would sail off, landing back on the bed, scared but laughing. "You're a flyer," he'd say, placing the too-large pink baseball cap on her head like a crown. "You're off to see the gizzards of the wonderful wizard of Nod."

"It's not *Nod,* Dad, it's *Oz!*"

"For the love of Mike, is it? Well, I'm the wizard of Nod, darlin', and I'm going to make you the Queen of the World."

Decades later, as an adult, she found herself humming, "Wonderful wizard of Nod," when she climbed into bed. Long after her father was out of her life, she could still hear his voice singing. He would sing with the radio or the television; when he heard Latin music, he'd pull her into a dance. "Come on, one, two, cha-cha-cha." And they would dance around the motel room and he would promise, "I'm going to leave you a million dollars. You'll be the richest queen in the whole wide world."

The word "leave" always frightened her. "Where are you going?"

"Nowhere."

But, just like a wizard, her father *had* gone away, taking his smile and his stories with him. And so, of all the tales he'd told her, she had come to believe that not one of them was true.

The story of "The Queen of the Sea" was one of his most elaborate tales. He'd added to it for years, working out its details, changing it this way or that as they'd crisscrossed the big country together on long, wide, unending highways.

He told her that a long time ago, caravans of mules, roped together fifty by fifty, lurched over the mountains of Panama, weighed down with silver from the Potosi mines, with Peruvian gold, with emeralds.

When the mules reached the port of Nombre de Dios, a fleet of Spanish galleons with empty hulls was waiting for them. Crews of slaves loaded the ships with treasure and they set sail on the Carrera de las Indias, around the Cabo, their sailors keeping watch for the high bluffs of the Havana Harbor, where they could safely drop anchor before the long voyage to Spain. Many ships never even reached the open Atlantic but sank with their cargo near Cuba. Over the centuries, hundreds of ships sank. Indeed, by the time of Fidel Castro, the Cuban government was estimating that in their territorial waters lay a hundred billion dollars worth of sunken treasure from these ships. They said that all the spoils, collected or not, belonged to the Cuban people. Their researchers were particularly interested in a sunken ship called *La Madre del Salvador*.

Her father said that *La Madre* was a Spanish vessel that in 1549 a sudden storm had blown up against the reefs near Havana. It sank, bilging tons of gold and silver ballast onto the floor of the sea. A nobleman on board, Don Carlos de Tormes, drowned while removing a statue from a small trunk in his cabin, a wood trunk covered in ornate leather and clasped with ornate iron. In the trunk was a gold effigy so precious that Don Carlos had written home about it in a letter still preserved in a museum in Seville. He called it *La Reina Coronada del Mar*, the Queen of the Sea. It was a reliquary, fifteen-inches high, of the Virgin Mary, crusted with gold and jewels that a year previously had belonged to Inca priests. The priests had handed over the temple treasure to a small squadron of Spanish soldiers who had hacked to death randomly selected members of the Inca community and then expressed their perfect willingness to butcher everyone else. Gold seemed to calm the Spanish down.

A skilled goldsmith fashioned the statue of Mary out of the plunder. He dressed her in the style of the Peruvian earth mother Pachamama and beat out a broad golden cape, studding it with little rubies and sapphires and diamonds. He made her a gold crown, capping it with seven large emeralds, sixty carats apiece, each on a gold rod that formed a sunburst. In the Virgin's arms was a small silver baby who wore a crown of silver thorns. On her breast a little silver door opened into her heart cavity. Her heart was a 135-carat star ruby, resting on a tiny box that held, allegedly, a real thorn from Christ's crucifixion crown, with supposedly his real blood on it.

As Annie's father told the story, when *La Madre del Salvador* sank, everyone aboard drowned, including Don Carlos, who died clutching the Queen of the Sea. For centuries the Queen slept in his skeletal arms, floating slowly along the dark coral reefs among rusted anchors and broken olive jars and bits of majolica bowls, all part of the wreckage of more than five hundred other Spanish ships that had spilled their spoils along the silver route. Time rolled on, nudging the statue loose from the proud nobleman's bony hands, until finally its crown snagged on a spar near the Colorados Reef. Then one day, a fisherman, diving to untangle his net from the reef, saw a gleam of gold only ten feet below the surface. Diving deep to the shimmer, he freed *La Reina Coronada del Mar* and took her home.

Jack told Annie how in 1815 this devout fisherman had donated the Queen of the Sea to a monastery in his remote village. Afterwards, for decades, rumors spread in that part of Cuba about a relic recovered from the reefs. But eventually the stories muddled into idle chitchat until finally only a few old people had ever even heard of the statue.

In 1898 a war had started in Cuba called the Spanish-American War. The U.S. Army invaded the island to free people like the fisherman and they bombed the monastery. Annie's father told her how an American armament officer, searching for survivors in that monastery, found in its rubble the jeweled statue of the Virgin Mary and took it home with him to North Carolina. This officer's name was Joseph Peregrine.

Once home, Peregrine rebuilt the house and called it Pilgrim's Rest. In 1900 he changed the name of the whole town from Aquene (its Occaneechi name) to Emerald. Because he was the richest man around, no one objected. Everyone called Captain Peregrine "Boss" and he bossed everyone in his family and in Emerald until somebody killed him. Before his sudden death, Boss had taken all the jewels out of the statue and buried them at Pilgrim's Rest where nobody could find them, until generations later his great-grandson Jack did just that. Or so Annie's father told her.

When a child, riding along the highways, Annie did not understand most of the details of what her father said about *La Reina Coronada del Mar*. But it was a story she liked to hear. It was a story about a mother, even if only a gold one fifteen inches high; a mother who was lost for a long time and then miraculously found. Back then Annie still hoped to find her own mother some day. She'd always thought that she would suddenly pick her mother out of a crowd, maybe by spotting and identifying her with her special neon-blue X-ray sunglasses, although her mother and she had never met, although her father had made up a different, unbelievable story every time she'd asked him who her mother was.

In her first year at Pilgrim's Rest, Annie started having a recurring dream in which she confused the Queen of the Sea with her unknown mother. She had this dream so often that her aunt and uncle began to call it "Annie's dream." Still asleep, she cried out and they hurried to her room and told her it was just a dream. But she knew that and it didn't help.

In this dream, she was flying a little red airplane over a blue ocean. The colors were uncomplicated, like colors in a crayon box. Red, blue, yellow. Water and sky were the same bright crayon-blue so that there was no way to know air from ocean except for a black line between them. Flying beside her was her father, also in a red airplane. Their planes looked like a children's ride at an amusement park.

As Annie's plane floated out of clouds, she saw a small wooden ship, a Spanish ship with square sails, sailing precariously through the ocean. At the prow of this ship stood a young woman, whom Annie knew to be her mother. The woman had red-gold hair. She wore a gold cape like the Queen of the Sea. Her ship was sinking and she was shouting for help.

Annie flew back up to her father's plane, shouting for him to do something. But he sped far ahead until he was only a fleck of red on the blue horizon. She couldn't keep up with him. So she turned back to try to help her mother. But she was not in time. Waves swept over the ship and her mother disappeared beneath the sea.

And that's when Annie woke up.

The first adult to whom Annie told the details of this dream was neither Sam nor Clark but her flying teacher, D. K. Destin. She told D. K. one day when he was maneuvering them in and out of white clouds high above Emerald; the sky looked so much like the sky in her dream that she began talking about it. She told him about the woman on the ship that she couldn't save. She explained about the golden statue of the Queen of the Sea in her father's story and she told him as many details as she could remember.

D. K.'s cornrows shook as he blew away her father's tale of sunken treasure with a loud puff of air. "Sugar Pie, the man was yanking your chain. There's no 'Queen of the Sea.' He was as full of it as a mountain of guano under a pile of cow patties."

"What's guano?" she asked the cranky pilot.

"Shit."

Annie giggled. "Guano. That's a funny word."

"It's real." He took her hand, slapped it at the control panel of the small Cessna. "This is no story. Wham! You're shot down in the China Sea! You're squiggling through a puckered pocket of metal and all of sudden your legs won't work. What the fuck, your legs won't work!"

"Is that what happened to you?"

"Damn right. Your lungs are bustin' in that cold black salty water and no air to breathe. Air's so high up on top of you, you can't even see it. And you know what? Swimming best I could up out of that water, if I'd spotted a little gold statue of the Virgin Mary with million dollar emerald eyes, right there in front of my nose on some fucking coral reef, I wouldn't have stopped for *two seconds* of my dying breath to get that sucker loose. Not two seconds!"

"Amy Johnson wouldn't have stopped for two seconds either."

"Damn right," he agreed. "Amy's in the fuckin' English Channel, poor thing, her plane's down in the fog and all they come back up with was her pocketbook with her goddamn lipstick in it. In real life, you gotta make some choices."

The dead World War II pilot Amy Johnson had recently become Annie's idol. D. K. had told her about the beautiful young British flyer who was the first woman to fly solo from England to Australia and who died at only thirty-eight in World War II while ferrying bombers for the RAF. Annie had Amy's picture on her bedroom wall. D. K. was full of such lore about bygone pilots and their heroic deeds.

"Courage," he told her. "That is the only thing worth guano. All the money in the world's not worth shit." He slapped her hand again on the panel. "What's the only thing?"

"Courage."

"That's right. Give me that toothless smile of yours, Orphan Annie."

She frowned, indignant, tightening her lips over her missing front teeth. "I'm not an orphan, I've got Sam and Clark. I've got parents."

D. K. laughed. "You got too many! You got more than you know what to do with."

She covered her mouth grinning. "You're guano."

"And love's a game of give-and-take, baby. Me and your Uncle Clark. We both loved America, we gave it all we had and the U.S. took it all and look at us now."

"What's wrong with you and Clark?"

"Not a damn thing." The old vet D. K. banked his plane and they headed home.

Chapter 3

Thunder from the Hill

When, at seven years old, Annie first heard her "uncle" Clark Goode calling to her as she hid in the barn beneath the airplane, she had to wipe her eyes on the knees of her jeans in order to see him. A tall, thin man in khakis and plaid shirt stepped through the big doors, closing them against the rain. Crouched on the dark dirt, the child hugged the wheel cover of the Piper single-engine plane, frightened by the sound of the doors and by the lightning that cracked across the sky, as if one of the fairy-tale giants in her father's stories had broken open heaven with a sledgehammer.

The tall man ambled over to the lantern and when he saw her he tapped three reassuring pats on the plane's wing. "Hi there, Annie," he said. He had sandy hair and wore glasses with round tortoise-shell rims. Offering her a pair of little blue plastic sunglasses, he asked, "These yours? I found them in the yard…"

She took the glasses but didn't speak.

"Sam's out there looking for you…Want one?" He held out an unopened can of soda.

Annie, struggling to sound indifferent, quoted her father. "'Sorry, no silver cup.'"

"That's a good one." The man had a slow soft accent that she later learned to identify as Tidewater. "That's from an old movie called *Stagecoach*."

"I know. My dad says it, 'no silver cup.'"

"Your aunt Sam loves movies too, so I watch a lot of them. She's out there driving up and down the road, calling for you, figuring you ran after your dad."

"My dad drove too fast."

He nodded. "Always did…Some storm, huh?" There were loud rattles of noise like giants stomping on the barn roof.

"Is it a hurricane?" She had seen those in movies on TV.

"Nope." The man sat on the ground next to the plane, wiping reddish dirt from his hands, looping his arms around his knees, bending his head so it was in line with hers. "It's hail. Ever seen hail?"

Worried, she shook her head, watching his face. "Maybe it'll get my dad?"

He looked at her, thought about it. "No chance. Jack will be okay. I promise." Tilting his head, he smiled. "Jack's always okay, right? Just when you think he's done for?"

She stared at the man squatting there beside her, wondering how he understood her father so well. As if he'd heard the question, he added, "Your dad and his sister Sam and I sort of grew up together. He was her little brother. Well, still is." He took off his wet glasses, shaking the rain from them, cleaning them carefully on his shirtsleeve. "My name's Clark Goode." He held out his hand but Annie ignored it. "I live here with Sam. Your dad ever mention he had a big sister named Samantha, Samantha Anne?"

"That's my name backwards. Mine's Anne Samantha." She scooted a few inches from behind the wheel cover. "My dad showed me Sam's picture. On their bikes. He said he brought me here before. When I was a baby?"

"I believe he did."

Annie tightened her arms around her jeans, leaning over her knees just as the man was doing, his hands clasped on his long arms. She considered pretending she personally recalled that earlier visit to Pilgrim's Rest but decided to admit, "I don't remember coming here."

"I don't remember when I was a baby either. I bet you'll like Sam."

Annie stared at him glumly.

"She's nice," he said.

There was a loud crack of rumbling noise. Annie slid herself a little nearer the man. "Thunder from the hill," he said calmly and finding a small stick, drew circles with it in the dirt. "So Jack hit the road? Gold prospector but it never pans out." Seeing her confusion, he added, "That's a pun. Pun's when a word means two things at once. Like a pan you find gold in or 'pan out' like something works out or it doesn't."

"I know," she said, although she hadn't heard of puns before.

"Did your dad mention where he was going or when he'd be back?"

She shook her head, dropping it with a sigh to her knees.

They sat together awhile, neither speaking. The hail stopped clattering. The barn grew darker and Annie inched forward again, closer to the man. They were quiet a few minutes longer. Finally she said, "His license plate is MJ87143. I can remember any numbers I see."

"Amazing."

She felt compelled to admit, "I can only remember for a while if it's a lot of numbers."

"Still."

"This airplane has a number." She pointed at the Piper. "NC48563."

"Exactly right."

"My dad said this plane's my birthday present. Probably not true."

The tall man stood up slowly, kicked the wheel. "Sure it's true. Been sitting in the barn a long time waiting for you to get here."

Surprised and pleased by his easy agreement, Annie scooted back to show him her father's dragon tail of letters curled beneath the plane's wing, spelling *King of the Sky*.

He admired the writing with her.

"I bet it's fast," she said.

"Probably. I'm kind of a slow-lane guy myself." He suggested they leave the barn to look for Aunt Sam while there was still some light to see by. "Sam calls her movie store Now Voyager. What's your favorite movie? We could watch one tonight and get some takeout. You like Chinese food?"

Annie's favorite movies were *Top Gun* and *Blazing Saddles* but she wasn't about to tell the stranger that. "Do I have to stay here?"

"You're welcome to. Doc Clark is what my kids call me— I'm a kids' doctor. Or just Clark's fine." Leaning down, he offered Annie his hand again but she still wouldn't take it. "Fair enough," he said. "Come on in when you feel like you want to. I'm not going anywhere. Neither is Sam. And well, Annie, this is a damn dumb thing Jack's done but we'll sort it all out."

She hugged her legs, the small lavender jeans dirty and wet. "My dad's in trouble again."

Clark nodded at her, slow, unruffled. "But let's look on the bright side. He enjoys it."

"Annie! Annie!"

Suddenly the tall tanned woman she'd first seen on the porch came running through the barn doors, her clothes wet through. Holding Annie's pink baseball cap, she crawled under the plane's wing and pulled the child into her arms. Annie struggled backward, startled by the stranger's closeness. But the woman nudged her gently toward her again. "I'm so sorry, sweetheart. I'm your aunt Sam. Everything's going to be okay. I'm so sorry." Slowly she rocked them back and forth together, huddled beneath the plane.

There was something in the warm feel of the woman's neck, in her arms, that was familiar. Her eyes were familiar too, like Annie's father's, green as emeralds, but sadder, with a small furrowing crease of worry between the eyebrows that, in Annie's growing up, was never to go away.

On the first night of Annie's arrival, in the large long hallway of Pilgrim's Rest, Sam helped her unpack her blue suitcase;

it was filled with her clothes, including her favorite dress and her white jacket with gold buttons. Tucked beneath the clothes was $12,000 in hundred-dollar bills, around which was wrapped, with a rubber band, a birth certificate from a hospital in Key West, stating that Anne Samantha Peregrine had been born there on the Fourth of July at 8:42 p.m., that she'd weighed 6 lbs., 3 oz., that Jack Peregrine was her father and Claudette Colbert was her mother. Looking at this certificate, Annie asked Sam to pronounce her mother's name and Sam sounded upset when she did so. "Claudette Colbert."

That first night, while Annie picked sadly at the Chinese takeout food, Sam told her about the time she'd been here before, when her father unexpectedly showed up with her in Emerald; how he brought the plane, the *King of the Sky*, on a rented flatbed truck, its wings dismantled, and parked it in the barn. Annie was only twelve months old then and they stayed at Pilgrim's Rest only three weeks. But during their visit Annie took her first step, running into Sam's arms.

Annie said nothing when she heard this story but she'd been intrigued. Then Sam had brought out a bright yellow birthday cake and put on a video of *The Wizard of Oz*, because Annie, lying, had told her it was her favorite movie, figuring it would be a safer choice than *Top Gun*. When Judy Garland chanted, "There's no place like home, there's no place like home," the child, to impress the two solicitous adults, made a joke—having first rehearsed the remark silently to herself—"Okay, I guess I'm in No Place now."

Sam and Clark laughed, pleasing her despite her grief.

The next morning there was a card on the kitchen table that said, There's No Place Like No Place. Welcome Home. Sam was at the stove, flipping pancakes with a dexterity that couldn't but impress Annie. She even flipped one behind her back and caught it in the pan. "Tennis," she explained. "You play?"

Annie shook her head.

"You want to?"

Annie shrugged.

"I'm going to practice today. You could help me out. I pay fifty cents an hour."

Over breakfast Sam told her niece that Clark and she shared her family house but that they weren't married, they were just friends. She added, "I don't know why people say 'just friends.' It's the hardest thing in the world to be."

Annie stared at her aunt carefully. "Are you two gay?" She was trying to shock her.

Sam said, "I am but Clark's kind of gloomy." She held out the yellow birthday cake. "Double chocolate inside."

"You shouldn't eat cake for breakfast."

Sam cut two pieces. "Of all the things we shouldn't do in America, this is way down the list."

The phone rang and hoping it was her father saying he was coming back for her, Annie held her breath until Sam returned from the hall. "Clark's at the hospital. Says we should come there and have lunch with him. He'll show you around his clinic."

"Is my mother dead?" Annie asked abruptly. "If she is, can I see her grave?"

Sam said she didn't know who Annie's mother was; that, despite her frequent questions, Jack had never told her.

• • •

A few weeks later, Sam came home with a black and white female Shih Tzu puppy, tiny and imperious, whose sale had been advertised on the staff bulletin board of the pediatric clinic. She gave the dog to Annie, claiming it resembled Toto in *The Wizard of Oz*, which it did not. Annie named the Shih Tzu Teddy B, after a stuffed bear of similar size, the loss of which, in some motel on the road with her father, had left her for weeks inconsolable.

Like Annie, Teddy cried through most of her first night at Pilgrim's Rest. After that, the little Shih Tzu pretty much took over the house.

Another present arrived in an express mail truck a week later. It advertised itself as "The World's Biggest & Hardest

Jigsaw Puzzle." Clark, who had ordered it, set the puzzle out on a table by a bay window in a room called "the morning room," although no one knew why it was so described. The jigsaw puzzle was a giant photograph of blue sky, nothing but blue, with—so its box claimed—20,000 tiny, nearly indistinguishable pieces. It was as large as the mahogany top of the fat spiral-legged table onto which Clark poured all its pieces.

Inviting Sam and a resistant Annie to help him assemble the sky, he told them, "We'll get the corners first. Annie, see if you can find a corner."

While she was still wary of these two strangers and did not yet return their smiles, she couldn't resist proving how quickly she could locate in the huge pile of particles of blue cardboard a piece that had a 90-degree angle.

"Great!" Sam exclaimed. "We're on our way."

The little girl wrinkled her mouth in disdain. "This will take years to put together."

Clark smiled. "Let's look on the bright side."

"It probably *will* take years. Decades," promised Sam, her sad eyes for a rare moment as playful as her brother Jack's.

The day the puzzle showed up was also the day that Annie's eventual best friend, Georgette Nickerson, plummeted into her life. Georgette lived next door but had been away at a camp for overweight children—which her mother had forced her to attend.

The plump little black-haired girl had suddenly come loudly skittering into the kitchen of Pilgrim's Rest, flinging herself at Sam and shouting, "I missed you! I hated that camp, they starved us and they threw us in the lake and kicked big orange balls at us. I ate purple Jell-O day and night, night and day." She spun around at Annie. "Who are you?"

Sam introduced her niece, who was overcome not so much with shyness as surprise when the fat little girl flopped down abruptly on the floor beside the Shih Tzu and barked loudly. "Woof woof woof!!" The dog barked back at her, growling. "I don't have a pet. My mom thinks I'd eat it. Is this yours?"

"Yes," Annie said. "Her name is Teddy B."

"My name's Georgia Georgette Nickerson, can you believe it? I make people call me Georgette. Dumb, huh? I was named after a state and after my dad George. That's like naming your child like, you know, Rhode Island Rhodette."

"No it's not."

"My dad had a heart attack and died. My mom says the police are after your dad."

"He's too fast for them," insisted Annie, pushed to his defense.

Over the years, Georgette's fast-rising scale of laughter and Teddy's sharp bark, and the hum of Sam's and Clark's voices at Pilgrim's Rest, softly moving back and forth in the slow Southern dusk, conversation leisurely as a river, became for Annie the sound of safety. After dinner, the four of them would sit together at the mahogany table, with Teddy curled on the cushion of the best chair and Georgette staying until her mother telephoned from next door to demand her return, and they'd talk over their separate days, while idly looking for connecting pieces of the puzzle of the sky. Its frame wasn't hard to assemble; in a month, they had all four corners in place. After that, things slowed down.

Annie's father Jack was, as she predicted, too fast for the police. The state patrol eventually found that he'd sold the red Mustang with license plate MJ87143 to someone in Atlanta who hadn't looked too closely into whether or not he'd really owned it. Sam pestered the police and even hired private investigators to search for her younger brother, but without success.

At first, Annie missed him, and his songs and stories, with an ache that hurt like a bruise. But carefully she taught herself to stop hoping. She taught herself that she was alone in her life and would always be and therefore would rely only on herself.

Of course she wasn't alone. Outside her door waited family and friends. But it was a long time before she heard them there. Months passed before she laughed again as loudly as she had when her father had sung his funny songs. And from her first weeks at Pilgrim's Rest, she wasn't restful. She started having the dream about the woman in her gold cape on a ship in the ocean, the mother she'd never seen, the mother whose real name Sam and Clark could not tell her because they didn't know it. She would wake up from her nightmare as the little ship was sinking and she couldn't save the drowning woman and her father was flying away.

For months, whenever it rained in Emerald so hard the sky went black, Annie could see Jack Peregrine's car racing away from her over the hill.

But finally, as months became years, even rain was just rain.

Chapter 4
Wings

Growing up as a child with Sam and Clark, with her friend Georgette and with her flying teacher D. K. Destin, Annie had to learn new styles, very different from the fabled schemes and exuberant stories of her father. In the town of Emerald, stories were for the most part just boring local gossip, tales of neighbors' daily triumphs and travails. She felt them to be much smaller than the tales—like the saga of Spanish treasure under the sea—that her father had told her. Only D. K.'s stories of the great pilots of old had for her the same kind of magic.

Still, over the years Annie listened to Georgette's jokes and Clark's puns and Sam's way of comparing everything in their lives to the movies and eventually their worlds became hers and her father's romance faded. Georgette and she were soon best friends and all through their Emerald school years spent nearly half their lives companionably in one another's company, despite or because of their differences: Annie, small and neat, practical, athletic, serious; Georgette, funny, dreamy, zaftig. Both ironic about life but ready for life to do big things with them.

And then when Annie was seventeen, on a summer day, ten years after her father had just dropped her off at Pilgrim's Rest, he suddenly returned, calling her name.

Sam's heart almost stopped, she later claimed, when her brother ran noisily crashing out of a cornfield and raced into their barn. In the vegetable garden, where on her knees she'd been tying up tomato plants, she had to use a fence post to pull herself to her feet because her legs went wobbly. Sam called the event, "The day Jack showed up like Cary Grant chased by the crop duster in *North by Northwest*."

By this time, it was too late for Jack Peregrine to lay claim to Annie. For almost eleven years, she'd lived a "normal" life without him. She had just graduated from high school, had broken up with her first serious boyfriend, and had been accepted at Annapolis. Her family was now Sam and Clark, who had long since officially adopted her. Her dog Teddy had grown old and they'd recently acquired a new puppy, an exuberant Maltese named Malpy, for Malpractice, whom Teddy tolerated with a begrudging noblesse oblige.

They made a reasonably content family and on vacations together spent more time studying stars from campsites than learning card tricks in hotel rooms, as she'd done with her father. They hiked and climbed rocks and kayaked, then returned together to a home that stayed put. She ate real food at a real table and went to bed in her own room and had her height and weight measured annually by Clark, who'd inoculated her against everything he could think of. Thanks to D. K. Destin, she had her pilot's license and could do loop-the-loops in the *King of the Sky*. She wore on her flying jacket the Navy wings and handmade black eagle badge that D. K. had given her. She drove the car Sam bought for her on her sixteenth birthday. She went to the same schools in the same town where she'd started in the second grade because she'd tested so well.

"Give your dad credit," Sam urged. "He taught you to read and write."

But Annie gave him credit for nothing and credited nothing he'd ever said to her. The fact that he had endlessly told her she was smart and beautiful was meaningless. He had also told her that her mother was Claudette Colbert and that he'd make her the queen of the world.

On the hot summer afternoon when Jack Peregrine showed

up at Pilgrim's Rest, Annie was next door with Georgette. They were lying on the floor in Georgette's bedroom, listening to Metal Urbain's *Les hommes morts sont dangereux* and watching a muted tape of Goddard's *À bout de souffle* with Jean-Paul Belmondo and Jean Seberg. For a party that night, they planned to retro-dress like Jean Seberg in the movie, with short hair and sunglasses, crisp striped shirts, their collars up, and belted flaring skirts that perfectly fit them. They had been enthusiastic Francophiles all year, tying thin black cashmere sweaters around their necks, pulling filters off Mrs. Nickerson's cigarettes to smoke them, and otherwise preparing themselves to spend a month in France on a language immersion program before they left for their separate colleges. Annie even renamed her friend Gigi (for Georgia Georgette, and because it was like Gigi in the movie musical set in Paris), though the nickname never stuck.

When Sam spotted her brother Jack from the garden, her first thought was Annie. How would Annie feel? She ran into the barn, where she found him "in a state" because the *King of the Sky*, the plane he'd left there seventeen years ago, was missing.

"Are you kidding?" she shouted at him. "You're standing there asking me where your goddamn plane is?!! How about your daughter?"

"Where's Annie?"

"Next door!" Sam pointed angrily to the Nickersons' house.

"She okay?"

"She's fine!"

Jack had an excuse for dropping Annie off a decade earlier and disappearing. He claimed he'd been locked up in prison, and that in prison he'd come to believe that the best thing he could do for Annie was to stay away from her and let her have a normal life.

Frustrated, Sam punched at him, shoving him to the dirt floor. "You are so full of shit, Jack."

"Come on, Sam. Where's the *King of the Sky?*"

"Annie flies that goddamn plane, which you gave her, damn it!"

Jack dusted himself off, grinning. "She does? That's wonderful. She flies a plane? Wow. Really?"

"Really. She's going to Annapolis."

"Really? How'd she learn to fly?"

"D. K. taught her. The plane's at his place. Aren't you going to ask me how I am?"

"How are you?"

"Jill left me. Mom died. Clark lives here."

"I know all that."

Sam pointed again at the Nickerson house. "Go talk to your daughter, she's next door! But let me warn her you're here. You know, this kind of shock is rough on normal people." Sam ran inside the house and telephoned her niece.

Across the yard, grabbing at Georgette, Annie held the phone against her heart. "Oh my God, Sam says my jerk of a dad's in the barn. I don't want to see him, okay!"

"*Oui, Jacques qui?*" Georgette leaned far out the window, her spiked black and purple streaked hair giving her the look of a sooty gargoyle. "*Tu ne sais pas Jacques.* Oh, there he is!"

From Georgette's window the two girls watched as Jack ran toward them through the grass, waving up to his daughter as if it had been ten minutes ago that he'd last seen her, not more than ten years. Even from so far away, she could tell that he was thinner and that his pants and his T-shirt were loose. He came close enough to the Nickerson house for her to see that he held a small dirty cloth sack, like a bag of marbles.

The white puppy Malpy raced around him in a friendly frenzy, yapping so loudly that on Georgette's bed, Teddy lifted her head and growled before returning to sleep—uninterested in either Jack Peregrine or New Wave Cinema.

From the high vantage of Georgette's window Annie could see a blue Corvette at the edge of the cornfield, its nose to the road, the way her father always parked his cars—ready to go. She was furious because tears started down her face. She swiped them away.

Her father stood in the yard below the Nickerson windows, yelling up at her, "Hi, Annie!"

She didn't answer but, with slim tanned arms leaning over the sill, stared out at the fields behind him.

"You look beautiful! Come on down, say hello." He made his arms into wings.

She fought to ignore him.

"I hear you're a flyer. Going to Annapolis. Good for you! Come on, let's go to the airfield, take a ride in the *King*! Hey, look at you. I missed you so much!" Her father started doing a cha-cha dance, an imaginary partner in his arms.

Annie pulled her head back inside the window without replying, noticing as she did so that a brown car was coming toward them up the hill, red dirt blowing in spirals on the road, swirling closer.

"Come on, Annie! I owe you one!" She could hear her father calling her name like a chant.

Georgette was saying, "Go down there and talk to him!"

"No."

Her friend tried tugging at her. "Go talk to him! I don't mean like you're lucky, but, God, my dad's permanently dead. At least yours shows up every ten years. Plus my dad just owned a jewelry store. My mom just sells engagement rings and flexy watchbands. Boring! Your dad's a criminal. Go over there!"

"No," said Annie, staring again out the window, pressed against its frame so she couldn't be seen from the yard. The swirls of dirt on River Hill Road swelled, rolling nearer.

Georgette gestured at a large, not very good oil painting on the wall, a "professional portrait" of her father George, aged twelve in blue blazer and tie, with his sister, aged fourteen, in pink summer dress and pearls. "All I've got's my aunt Ruthie's running off with a married man. Otherwise, the Nickersons were 'a terminal snooze.' You don't even know who your mother is."

"Lucky me."

Annie heard tire noise and then Sam calling, "Jack!"

Both girls squeezed to lean out the window.

Georgette shrieked, "Oh my God!" as a brown state highway patrol car, with spinning lights, came skidding fast through the open gate.

Across the yard, Annie heard Sam shout, "Run!" She watched her father dash to the blue Corvette, which soon leapt forward spraying pebbles. The patrol car slewed around in a circle, almost hitting Aunt Sam as it roared back over the crest of the hill in pursuit of the Corvette.

On the TV screen, Jean-Paul Belmondo happened at that moment in the Á *bout de souffle* subtitles to be saying to Jean Seberg, "*Don't use the brakes!*" Georgette slapped her big creamy hands. "*Merde!* 'Don't use the brakes.' I'd like to live my whole life like that, like your dad just drove out of here! Brakeless."

"With the cops after you?" Annie shrugged, she hoped in a nonchalant Gallic way, but it was in fact hard to breathe. "No thanks."

The two teenagers hurried back to Pilgrim's Rest where a distraught Sam kept saying, "I'm going to kill him!" She could explain little more about Jack's appearance than what they'd seen for themselves. According to Sam, Jack was the same selfish nut he'd always been. She wasn't sure she could endure many more of these startling appearances of his, his flying at her out of nowhere like she was Janet Leigh in a shower.

Sam held up a small red dirty marble, saying that Jack had thrust it into her hand just before running off to his Corvette, and had yelled back at her, "Tell Annie happy birthday! Tell her to hang onto that baseball cap!" Then he'd disappeared.

"What else is new?" said Annie. "What baseball cap?"

"Oh, you know," Sam said.

"I have no idea."

Sam sat down, catching her breath. "That little pink hat you had on when you came here. I kept it."

"You keep everything."

"You never know," Sam admitted. "Look how Jack wanted the *King of the Sky* back after all these years."

Annie returned the dirty red marble to Sam with contempt. "Trust me, Sam, he'll forget about the *King* by tomorrow."

Chapter 5

Since You Went Away

The highway patrolman in pursuit of Jack blew a tire at 101 miles per hour on the interstate ramp and flipped his car—although miraculously he walked away from the accident. The Emerald County sheriff, a friend of Sam's, came to Pilgrim's Rest with the news. He'd learned from D. K. Destin that Jack had raced into Destin Airworks in the blue Corvette and was attempting to break open the cockpit door of the *King of the Sky* with a lug wrench when D. K., in his wheelchair, knocked the wrench out of his hand with a lead pipe. D. K. thought he might have broken Jack's wrist. Jack had wanted to take the plane and D. K. told him that the *King* wasn't his, plus its carburetor was on the fritz and up on a rack anyhow. Then they'd heard a siren and Jack ran to the Corvette and drove off. "I'll be back," he'd yelled.

Both D. K. and the sheriff had known Jack from his childhood; neither of them believed anything he said.

The sheriff told Sam that, two weeks earlier, in Savannah, her brother had been arrested for swindling a retired couple; he'd taken their certified check for ten thousand dollars as a deposit on a historic landmark home located on (the aptly named) Bull Street. He'd offered to sell this couple the 1880 mansion cheaply ($1.6 million) because he was dying. On vacation from the West Coast, knowing nothing of Savannah, they'd believed him.

Caught and thrown in a holding cell, Jack faked epilepsy and was rushed to the hospital. In an orderly's outfit he escaped from the ER unit. Hot-wiring a Corvette in the staff parking lot, he headed for some reason home to Emerald.

The sheriff warned Sam, Clark, and Annie that if Jack did get back in touch with them and they failed to notify the authorities, they would be subject to criminal charges.

In an effort at French cynicism, Annie asked, "Is there a reward and can a relative collect?"

"Annie, we'll split it." The sheriff admitted he was still burned because, a long time ago, he had paid twenty-five dollars to join Jack's motorcycle gang, a club handicapped by its failure to secure even a single motorcycle to ride around on for more than one evening's illicit joyride. "Let him go," the sheriff warned the teenager.

"No problem." Annie, congratulating herself on having cut her father dead, expressed the hope never to see him again.

Later that evening, Sam lamented her failure to do something to help Jack. Clark mildly noted that Jack appeared to be more in need of a criminal lawyer than Sam's devotion. "You're like a blind mole bumping along the sides of a black hole. By black hole, I mean for example, your old girlfriend Jill dumping you after seven years. I mean your brother Jack leaving you to deal with your mother."

Sam agreed that love was blind. "Give me a break, Clark. You're always saying, 'Look on the bright side.' Well, if you love somebody, well, maybe you can't see where you're going and maybe there's no light ahead, but that doesn't mean you don't keep going."

Clark ran the stems of his glasses back and forth in his hair. "Sam, doesn't it worry you that you sound like the government's old policy in Vietnam?"

"I'm making love, not war. And I plan to keep going."

"Well, I'm out of here," said Annie, determined not to let her father's sudden intrusion upset her. "The only place I'm going is Paris." As she walked through the morning room, she paused automatically at the huge jigsaw puzzle of the blue sky that still sat, unfinished, on the mahogany table. The puzzle was more than half-filled now, connected from its edges toward the hole still in its middle. Studying the scattered blue bits of cardboard, she slid two of them together.

Sam came up beside her, the old Shih Tzu in her arms. "I keep thinking I should throw this stupid puzzle away but I can't bring myself to do it. You know, your dad had a rough time in this house. Think about being locked in a closet, hour after hour, like our father did to Jack. Our father the judge. Boy, was he ever a judge."

The front door bell rang its old three-note melody. It was D. K. Destin with his wife Dina, of Dina Destin's Barbecue. She was there to confess that this morning a highway patrolman had been in the diner showing people an APB photo of Jack Peregrine, asking if anyone knew where his family lived. Dina gave this state trooper directions to Pilgrim's Rest, thereby leading them to Jack. She apologized. She'd thought Jack was a million miles away.

"You got that right, baby," D. K. told his wife. "That's where Jack's gone now. 'And don't you come back no more.'"

They all had nachos and margaritas in the kitchen. From Annie's bedroom, where she was packing her suitcase for France, she could hear them loudly laughing. It baffled her that "grown-ups" could find anything so funny about life.

Late that night Jack telephoned Sam from the road.

"Hold onto my leather jacket," he said. "I'll call you tomorrow, tell you where to send it."

Sam told him to come back right now and turn himself in or leave them alone. "Jack, since you went away, I've gotten older. I can't take much more of this send-things-and-save-things and you tearing out of the cornfield like *North by Northwest*."

He laughed. "Love ya, Sam. Gotta go."

But of course, as Annie predicted when Sam recounted this conversation, Jack didn't call them the next day, although his sister waited near the phone. He didn't call the day after that, or for month after month, or as far as Annie knew, ever.

Sam kept Jack's old brown leather flight jacket that he'd flung off in the hot summer barn. It was unnecessary to instruct her to hold onto things. Her habit was not to throw even the useless away. While she never talked about the past, she did keep its relics, amassing memories in boxes. She was impervious to facetious warnings that the attic floor of Pilgrim's Rest was going to collapse under the weight of what Clark called her great conscious collective. The past needed saving. Clark should understand that. All the biographies he read, all the time he spent cleaning the old pieces of blue glass bottles they'd dug up gardening. Without the past, she told him, our lives would be as thin and shallow as the news.

So, that day, Sam had gone to the attic and squeezed between stacked boxes (one of all her old girlfriend's exercise videotapes) and found the baseball cap with the word ANNIE spelled in bright-colored glass beads, packed with some other childhood clothes of her niece's, like the green velvet dress, the small cowgirl boots, the neon-blue sunglasses.

As she studied Annie's cap, Sam noticed something written in pen on the inside band—a faded almost indecipherable sequence of numbers and letters. They made no sense to her but she put the cap back in the suitcase and added her brother's flight jacket to it.

• • •

The morning after Jack's escape in the Corvette, Sam scrubbed dirt from the red stone that he'd told her to give Annie as a birthday gift. The stone looked like a ruby. Sam asked Georgette's mother, Kim Nickerson, who'd inherited the local jewelry store from her deceased husband George, to examine the stone. Kim (called that by Georgette since the seventh grade, with a familiarity that Annie found both alien and enviable) said that it *was* a ruby. It was a good ruby, worth at least a thousand dollars. Georgette's mother, a mercenary enthusiast, was sure this ruby proved that Jack's old story was true: There were precious gems buried at Pilgrim's Rest, whose recovery might well be "finders keepers."

The town of Emerald had long dined out on Peregrine fortune and misfortune, gossip of how Peregrines used their wealth to build a mansion on a hill and in general felt so superior that most of the town privately rejoiced when personal tragedy struck them and all their money was swept away in some crash or other, leaving them nothing but their name to feel smug about—and eventually not even that. The town assumed the Peregrines' money came from financial savagery—tobacco trading, bank foreclosures, and the like. But occasionally there floated to the surface old tales of untold wealth in buried precious stones, rumors passed along for generations.

In their spare time, from grade school to high school, Jack and his neighbor George Nickerson shoveled through hundreds of square feet of hard clay looking for buried emeralds and rubies. They never found a thing except the foundations of a swimming pool that Jack and Sam's father had long ago filled in.

"There was never anything in that ground but ground," George was often in his later years to complain to Kim.

But maybe, just maybe, Kim now whispered at the counter of Emerald Jewelers, holding her magnifying glass to the unpolished ruby, maybe George had been wrong and Jack's teenage story had been true after all.

Beside Sam, Annie leaned on the counter. She turned to Georgette. "*Je ne crois rien.*" Both the high school graduates raised their eyebrows in a practiced way.

"*Ton pere et la verité sont l'etrangers, et ma mère Kim est tristement une femme très folle.*" replied Georgette.

"*Bien sur, Gigi, et mon pere est un tas du merde.*" Annie and her friend laughed.

"You girls are going to have the best time in Paris," gushed Kim, having no idea what they were saying. "And then you're both going to fall in love and have wonderful lives."

They did have the best time in Paris. Annie even kissed a taxi driver on a dare from Georgette. She did it because

Claudette Colbert had fallen in love with a Parisian taxi driver played by Don Ameche in the old movie *Midnight*, which she'd seen several times. Because her birth certificate said Claudette Colbert was her mother, she'd seen all the actress's films.

Unlike Don Ameche, this cabbie charged the American girls full fare.

• • •

While Annie was in Paris, D. K.'s wife Dina suddenly died in a fall. He made Sam swear not to tell Annie until she returned. Sam promised but then told her anyhow, knowing she would want to be at the funeral of her beloved teacher's wife. Sam even paid for Annie and Georgette to fly home on the Concorde and she was right to think the fact that Annie had flown at twice the speed of sound across the ocean would give pleasure to the grieving young pilot.

Chapter 6
Always

When they returned a month later from France, Annie and Georgette discovered that Georgette's mother had begun spending her weekends in the local library, researching Annie's family and the possibility that long ago Boss Peregrine had buried treasure at Pilgrim's Rest. Moreover, she'd bought a metal detector to search, with Sam's permission, for emerald rings and ruby necklaces in the yard. So far, she hadn't found anything but metal jar lids and belt buckles. She blamed her failure on the Peregrines themselves, just as she blamed her husband George's death of a massive heart attack at Emerald Jewelers on the Peregrines, because Sam and Jack's crazy mother had broken the store window with a hammer and that's when George's heart attack had happened.

Listening to all the town gossip about the Peregrines, Kim Nickerson had come to believe that the more information she had about Annie's dead ancestors, the more likely the dead were to give up their buried treasure to her. It eventually became, as Georgette said, an *idée fixe*. So whenever "the girls" returned home from college for the holidays, she would bribe them to go with her to view the locations of the Peregrines' long downfall. Both girls found these tours tedious; year after year Georgette's mother repeated the same anecdotes, in narrative log-jams that monotonously meandered through irrelevant details to some point or other that she usually forgot.

While Georgette loved her mother, she'd never really liked her. The two of them were always, as Georgette explained to Annie after completing her first psychology course, profoundly incompatible, a fact that Kim could never admit because she couldn't grasp it. Georgette said this was because her mother, while not bright, had been a pretty child, a pretty teenager, and a pretty young woman, and as prettiness had been her only gift, naturally she overvalued it. According to Georgette, in the past her mother had taken secret pleasure in her daughter's gawky plumpness, loving to dress them in similar outfits—like tangerine stripes—in which Kim looked crisp and her child Georgette looked like the giant Garfield the Cat balloon in the Macy's Thanksgiving parade. Kim was so lacking in, and oblivious to, her daughter's very different gifts that she failed to notice that Georgette was very smart, with a *belle laide je ne sais quoi* that someday would dazzle somebody or other.

Annie certainly had no desire to drive around town with Mrs. Nickerson on her college breaks, hearing about dead Peregrines, but because she loved Georgette (and was vaguely interested in the family history), she kept going.

They saw the boardinghouse where Peregrine females were "taken in like laundry" during "the War of the Confederacy."

They traced the footings of the Aquene River landing where Boss Peregrine's grandfather burnt to a crisp in a steamboat explosion.

They walked through the courthouse lobby where Boss's father was driven so mad by his son's death at Gettysburg that he shot two Yankees occupying the town and got himself hanged.

They located the exact spot on River Street where Boss, stabbed in the back of the neck, "dropped down dead as a dead dog," in front of his own bank, and the spot in St. Mark's cemetery where his Negro mistress leaped into his grave—to the mortification of his widow.

Georgette's mother lured "the girls" with dainty pimento cheese sandwiches to listen to her tell them how Jack and Sam's father, the judge, "lost it all due to alcohol, down to his self-respect and lower than that." How Grandee, Sam and Jack's mother, had gone so crazy that the sheriff was forced to subdue her on Main Street in her bare feet, because she was breaking store windows with a hammer and then dancing on the bloody glass.

Over deviled eggs, Kim told them how Jack remained a bad influence on George until Kim straightened him out and married him and gave birth to Georgette.

She told them how Jack was jilted by George's sister Ruthie and left town.

How Sam started kissing a woman in public and then openly lived with her till the woman ran off.

How the judge drove off River Road at a high curve "on a fateful night" and drowned in his car in the fast Aquene rapids below, his body not recovered for weeks, and how Grandee was unable to grasp the fact that he was dead and kept asking for years where her husband was.

Kim said she knew the whole story: Sam had called the police at midnight to say that the judge was missing. Emerald police had gone looking and found his tire marks in the muddy ruts of River Road, gouged over the side. It took them three weeks to dredge the car from the water below and by then the judge's body was "no more recognizable than the side of a cow in a meat locker."

Some people said it was odd that Judge Peregrine had driven off to Raleigh in the worst rainstorm in a decade; they started rumors of suicide but the rumors didn't go anywhere. Judge Peregrine's funeral service at St. Mark's was the biggest that Emerald had enjoyed since the funeral of his grandfather, the Boss.

The funeral was when Annie's father had robbed his dead father, stolen his sister's car, and left town for good. "I was the one who saw him go," Kim boasted. "'He's got your car!' I yelled at Sam. But would she do a thing about it?"

The answer was presumably no.

After the reception, Jack and Sam's mother retired to her bedroom, locked the door behind her, and stayed there for a year, overcome, the town assumed, by grief. Sam told the cleaning lady, who "did the house" once a week, that she was never to bother Grandee, that Sam would clean her room herself. But the cleaning lady later told Kim that she'd once seen the judge's widow crouched on her brass bed, eating a live mouse, her lips smeared shining red. Grandee would still be loose in Emerald, a certifiable madwoman, if she hadn't stabbed Sam with scissors and the sheriff hadn't talked Sam into signing her mother into a home.

In fact, said Kim, not to mince words, over the centuries the whole Peregrine family had gone bat-shit crazy.

Annie had no reason to doubt the truth of these sad stories; she knew far less about her family than Georgette's mother did; in fact she knew only what Mrs. Nickerson told her. And, given these sagas of dementia and sudden death, of lost wealth and lost love, of a house filled with such sorrow, she could easily understand why her father had called Pilgrim's Rest a pit of snakes, a cage of tigers, and had told his young daughter that he'd never go back there; why Aunt Sam—although insisting that her own childhood at Pilgrim's Rest had been "just fine"—had such sad eyes and why she declined to talk about any family but the one she and Clark and Annie had made for themselves.

Chapter 7

The Smiling Lieutenant

Racing the storm home to Pilgrim's Rest in her convertible Porsche, Annie outdrove the memories that had unexpectedly jumped out at her because of Miami Detective Daniel Hart's phone call.

Thunder rolled across the tobacco fields and a fat drop of rain splashed her knuckles as she downshifted to turn onto the gravel road that wound to the top of River Hill Road. Speeding up the drive, she parked efficiently in the open barn.

Above the porch of Pilgrim's Rest a banner flapped loudly from the overhang, its letters spelling *Happy Birthday Annie. 26!!!*

Aunt Sam, tall and nutmeg-tan, ran onto the porch. The storm blew the door from her hand, slapping it against the house. Sam's cropped hair was prematurely white now, but she still played tennis every day and she still looked trim in her shorts and purple T-shirt with the logo of her movie rental store Now Voyager across it. She was waving a FedEx envelope. Annie had the irrational feeling that her aunt was gesturing "Back up," as if she were trying to warn her to turn around.

Clark's Volvo drove slowly into view behind her. He backed into the barn beside the Porsche and emerged carrying the two large plant cones. "You win," he called. "You beat me."

Malpy ran into the yard from the side of the house and raced in circles around Annie. Wind blew back the Maltese's white fur from his face.

Sam, running toward them, stopped suddenly. Then she shouted, "Phone," turned around, and hurried back inside the house.

"Gonna let loose!" Clark yelled. As if to prove his point, rain poured suddenly down; a twisting gust yanked his hat off and spun it like a top across the yard. Dropping the cones, the long-legged doctor loped after it. Up on the porch steps, he shook his legs to unstick his rain-soaked khaki trousers. Behind him, his little white dog shook his short wet legs too.

"Hi Malpy." Annie kissed the Maltese. "Teddy still bossing you around?"

Clark said, "Bosses everybody." The Shih Tzu (who'd been chosen for Annie because they were the longest-lived of dogs) was now nearly twenty, blind, arthritic, self-important as ever; these days, Clark said, she never left the velvet poof in her pagoda except to reassert her supremacy over Malpy.

Annie stood with her uncle on the porch, looking out at the rain. On the horizon a black mass of clouds tinged with an eerie green twisted and swirled off to the east, like an old satin cloak dragged across the sky.

Clark rubbed water off his sandy hair. "Actually I got here only two minutes after you did. Just goes to show."

"I had to pull off the road for a phone call. A weird cop from Miami, looking for Dad. I told him I had no idea."

Clark nodded thoughtfully. "Why'd he call you?"

She shrugged. "Exactly."

"You bring your cat?"

She told him that her friend Trevor was taking care of Amy Johnson back in Chesapeake Cove.

"That's good." Clark wiped his glasses on his shirt. "I just don't see why you never ask that fellow down to meet us. Plenty of room at Pilgrim's Rest." Trevor, her condominium neighbor, was a single man her age.

"He wouldn't take the time. Workaholic."

Clark shrugged excessively and pointed at her.

"Don't start," she warned. She pointed at the house next

door. "But Georgette would like Trevor." Annie had been trying to fix up Georgette since high school.

Georgette now lived alone with a Siamese cat named Pitti Sing; her mother Kim had moved recently to a golf community in Southern Pines. Clark shook his head at his neighbor's house. "You want to talk workaholic? Georgette's at the hospital fourteen hours a day; at night, she watches television or she comes over here, watches movies with Sam and me. I want her to fall in love."

Annie touched his face. "You want everybody to fall in love."

"I tried it myself a couple of times. I enjoyed it." Clark stepped back as wind blew the rain in on them. "It's let loose. Told you." He stretched his hand out into the downpour as if to test it. "My grandma used to say they would get rain so big one drop could drown a cat. So when I was little, whenever it rained, I hid our cat in a dresser drawer—"

Annie had heard this story before. "—and your cat had her first litter right on top of your blue crewneck. That's why you went into pediatrics."

"It's sure why I never wore that blue crewneck again. So, go on in and happy birthday." Gesturing at her Navy uniform, Clark held up the forefinger that meant a pun was coming. "You hear about the red ship that collided with the blue ship and all the sailors were marooned?"

"Top ten worst," she said. She ranked most of his puns in the "top ten worst."

He pushed on his glasses, bent to examine the service ribbons on her white jacket. "So, is that for sure, you're getting divorced next week?"

She shrugged. "The lawyer swears."

Clark nodded. "Good."

She nodded back. "Yep." They'd been able to talk to each other with nods since the day they'd met long ago in the Pilgrim's Rest barn.

"About love?" he added. "Next time, go for the package. Looks, brains, job. Don't settle." He hugged her. "Or on the other hand, settle and be happy."

"Got it, Clark." She smiled at him, his favorite smile.

"You're not planning on taking Brad back, are you? Don't even think that."

She raised her eyebrow at her uncle. "Aren't you always telling me I move too fast?"

"That's sure what I told you when you married Brad."

Annie changed the subject. "Want to hear some good news? I can't wait to tell D. K. He'll love this." She said she had been chosen to test pilot a new short-takeoff vertical-landing carrier jet they were testing for Navy purchase. An F-35. The Lightning II.

"Lightning II, that's great. Sounds easygoing."

"I think I can get it over 1200 miles per hour. That'll be a speed record. So it's July 14, five in the morning. Another pilot will do the same test."

"How do you feel about this?"

"Don't mind competing. Don't like losing. There're a couple of guys faster than I am. At flight school, Brad could always kick it over that extra point-whatever. But who knows, this could be my time."

Clark patted her cheek softly. "I'm mystified as to why anybody would *want* to set a speed record at five in the morning; five in the evening either." He rubbed her back. "But, hey, you like that dark blue world."

"I do." She looked at the roiling clouds. "I do like it up there."

Aunt Sam stepped out to join them on the porch. She stared at her niece. "That was the phone. What's wrong with you? Were you crying?"

"A little while ago. But I'm fine." Annie looked carefully at her aunt; the vertical lines between Sam's eyebrows were frowning more than usual. "What's wrong with *you?*"

Sam squeezed Clark's hands. "What's the matter with Annie, Clark?"

"Nothing. Her divorce isn't final yet."

Sam reached out to her niece. "A FedEx just came for you, from Jack."

Annie stepped away. "From Dad? I just got a weird phone call from Miami about Dad."

Sam pointed back inside at the hallway. "This FedEx came just a little while ago with some balloons. Was the phone call from Miami a man named Rafael Rook?"

Annie shook her head. "Rafael Rook? No, it was from the Miami police. A Sgt. Daniel Hart. He's looking for Dad. For 'fraud.'"

Clark said he wasn't surprised. "The police were always looking for Jack for fraud. But balloons? That's a first."

"Happy Birthday to me," Annie said flatly. "I'm twenty-six. I haven't heard a word in a decade. Now it's a FedEx card and balloons. Sweet."

"So, who's Rafael Rook?" Clark asked Sam.

"A good friend of Jack's. He wanted to talk to Annie."

The porch door slapped again, loudly, flung against the house by the strong wind. Clark pulled it shut. "Sam and Georgette have been working on your party for a week. But we better cancel. This could be the big one. A real twister."

"That's what you always say." Annie pulled her aunt closer. "Okay, Sam, what's the problem? Something's wrong with you, and it's not my birthday party getting rained out. What's this about?"

Frowning, Sam put her hands on Annie's shoulders. "It's Jack."

"What's he done now?"

"He wants you to come to St. Louis right away, Annie. He's dying."

Chapter 8

The Man from Yesterday

The storm had darkened the sky and in the hall Annie had to turn on a light. Carefully she read the small grubby wrinkled sheet of writing paper that was all there was in the FedEx envelope. Its letterhead showed a gold sun either rising or setting on a gold horizon line. Below the sun was an address: Golden Days Center for Active Living on Ficus Avenue in Miami, Florida. The penciled handwriting slanting up across the note was unsteady and smeared.

> Annie,
>
> Meet me in St. Louis where we stayed before. Fly the *King*. Crucial. Sam says she kept my flight jacket. I need it. Did you hang onto your pink cap? Bring it. I hear you're brilliant and beautiful. Always were. If something happens to me, remember, Queen, King, Sam. I love you. Come fast.
>
> Dad (Jack Peregrine)
> PS Lindbergh

Nothing else was written under PS. Instead, pinned to the paper by the minuscule hook of a fuzzy dry fishing fly was a small key. A key to what, she had no idea, although it looked like a file cabinet or maybe a lawnmower key.

For a long time, Annie stood there in the hall of the house, turning the letter in her hands, caught between rage and distress. A dozen helium *Happy Birthday!* balloons floated on the ceiling.

Wet through, Clark and Sam returned from the yard, where they'd done what they could to protect their gardens from the storm—stake the hollyhocks, secure the cone protectors over the roses, wrap the peonies and shrubs and borders. Malpy shook rain at Teddy, who growled at him.

Sam, running a towel through her short hair, watched Annie.

Her niece held out the FedEx. "And this was it?"

Sam dried her arms. "No...Well, yesterday Jack calls and tells me he's dying and to give you this FedEx that was coming today...I guess I must have told him you always come home on your birthday."

"Good God, Sam, how much do you talk to Dad? According to this Sergeant Hart, he had my goddamn new cell-phone number written on the back of a photo." Annie jerked loose her white Navy shirt.

"Sit down, you're upset," Sam told her.

"I sure am."

Sam looked defensive. "I don't talk to him much. Not all that much. Lately twice a month, he calls."

"Twice a month?"

"Lately. He just asks me how you are, then he hangs up." Sam took Jack's letter from her niece, studied it. "But yesterday, out of the blue, he calls, says how he's really sick, asks me if you still fly the *King of the Sky*. Then today this FedEx comes. He says he's dying, but well, you know Jack."

"Not very well." Annie shrugged.

"All I can hope is," sighed Sam, "he's lying. He usually is. That's all I can hope."

"What's the fraud they're after him for?" asked Clark, returning downstairs in dry shorts and T-shirt.

"False pretenses," said Annie. "Ha-ha."

"And a Miami detective called you about it?"

She summarized her conversation with the pleasant-voiced Detective Hart about the gold relic, the Queen of the Sea.

Sam gave a sympathetic squeeze to her niece's arm. "Cuba thinks Jack's got something that's real?"

"Stupid Cuba," Clark muttered. "Sam, you ought to change out of those wet clothes."

Sam hushed him. "Don't be a doctor. The other thing is— this guy's been calling all afternoon—"

"Sergeant Hart?" asked Annie.

"No. Rafael Rook. A weird-talking guy. He's in Miami too. He says Jack's really 'going fast.'"

Annie raised her eyebrow in a way she'd copied from old Claudette Colbert movies. "Jack was always going fast. With Jack, it was always the back of that leather flight jacket you were looking at. Dumps me for nearly twenty years and now a FedEx message he's dying, lend him my plane, and rush him his flight jacket to St. Louis? I don't think so." She unbuttoned her shirt, fanning herself. "I'm going to go put on some shorts. First it's pouring rain, now the air's dead. I'll hurry."

"Everything will be okay," said Clark, shaking his head, watching Annie race up the stairs two at a time. "No hurry."

• • •

When Annie thought of her father, it was always scenes of perpetual motion and precipitate change. A measureless highway of mildewed motels.

It was not until she was flying jets for the Navy that memories of those road trips rushed out of the past at her as if they'd been waiting in the sky. The scenes were underscored with fragments of old songs.

"Meet Me in St. Lou-ee, Lou-ee," he'd sung to her when they'd gone to that city once and had almost gotten killed in a motel there.

"Happy, Happy Birthday, Baby," he'd sung in a white and gold hotel suite, marching in from the bathroom, carrying a cake with five sparkling candles, with a crowd of strangers in loud-colored clothes around her bed, laughing so loudly so close to her that she'd burst into tears.

"La Bamba" he'd sung in the shiny plastic booth of a Taco Bell while carefully cutting a burrito into small pieces. "This is all we've got for supper, Captain Kid, we're busted. If money mattered, we'd need to 'go back and get a shitload of dimes.'" She'd laughed with him at the reference to *Blazing Saddles*. That time they'd driven all night and then had slept in the red Mustang at a rest stop with the doors locked and with a can of Mace nearby. "Just spray it in their face," he told her.

"Whose face?"

"Anybody that gets in this car."

When she asked him why they were always speeding down the road, he made his arms into wings and glided around her in the parking lot. "Because we're Peregrines! The peregrine falcon is the fastest bird in the world, Annie. It can do a 45-degree dive at 217 miles per hour! Imagine that. Lindbergh in the *Spirit of St. Louis* could only go 117 miles per hour. So that little Peregrine bird is going 100 miles per hour faster than *Lindbergh!*" Years later, to her amazement, she was to discover that this fact about the diving speed of a peregrine hawk was one of the few true things he'd told her.

When she'd asked her father to identify the shadowy men from whom they were running so fast, and who'd occasionally almost caught them, he'd exasperatingly offer her cartoon names, like "Snidely Whiplash" or "The Penguin" or "The Man from Yesterday" or "The Man from U.N.C.L.E."

Whenever she wanted to know who her mother was, he made up some romantic story: Her mother was a circus acrobat, her mother had the highest IQ ever recorded in her hometown, her mother was the heir in exile to the throne of some small country whose name he would change from one nonsense word to another.

Even as a child she'd noticed inconsistencies. He was a compulsive liar, in fact a professional one. The only constant in his remarks about her mother was the claim that this woman had always said how much she loved Annie and how wonderful she thought Annie was. But the truth was hard to avoid: It did not appear that her mother had wanted a daughter in her life, however wonderful she might have thought her. And when Annie asked why her mother had left them, the answer was always that she'd thought her child would be better off with her father. Even at five and six, Annie found this assumption, if true, culpably naïve on her mother's part.

Whenever she asked Jack Peregrine about his own work (fathers on television had jobs), he told her that he "lived a Life of Art." By five, she had decided that what he called "a Life of Art" was in fact a life of crime. With her small solemn face she had watched him with a skepticism that time only increased. He was always on the phone, sometimes in a language she didn't understand—he said it was Shangri-lang—always meeting strangers in peculiar places, sending cryptic messages, getting envelopes in return. Packages got left on his car seat or atop a restaurant table or even inside a trashcan in a city park once. Envelopes often had cash in them.

Just before they'd driven suddenly to Emerald that last time together, she'd sneaked a look at an unstamped mailer that had been slipped under their motel room door; inside it she'd found an Irish passport with a picture of her father but with a different name. Folded in the passport was a street map of Havana, Cuba.

Aunt Sam and Uncle Clark didn't contradict her when she'd told them her father was a criminal but Sam could or would give her no details other than that in the year of Annie's birth a card had arrived from Jack, postmarked Key West, with the entirely surprising news that he was raising an infant daughter on his own and that the two were "doing fine." A year after that, he'd shown up with this baby (Annie) and his single-engine airplane. The two of them, father and daughter, stayed at Pilgrim's Rest slightly less than a month, during which time Annie learned to walk. He then took Annie away and left the *King of the Sky* behind.

Afterwards, Sam heard nothing for six years. Then out of the blue he called to ask if he could drop Annie off "temporarily." Two days later, he arrived with the child asleep in his red Mustang convertible, stayed only long enough to beg Sam for help because he was "in big trouble." He didn't explain what kind of trouble, or where the girl's mother was, or *who* her mother was, or how he could bear to leave his daughter behind on her seventh birthday, after he'd kept her with him for so many years on the road. He asked his sister to hide Annie if anyone came to the house in the following weeks asking for him, and to say that she hadn't seen him in years. Then he kissed her good-bye and told her, "Annie's a great kid. I'll be back."

But of course he wasn't.

In Annie's early years at Pilgrim's Rest, she asked Sam to tell her stories about her father's youth. Sam told her tales of his escapades back when their next-door neighbor George was his buddy and the two boys were always "in trouble." Stories of how they sold off family heirlooms at a Raleigh flea market and used the money to take the bus to California (the Phoenix police returned them); how they spent months on end digging in the yard for buried rubies and emeralds that they never found. But Sam told only childhood stories. She said that by the time Jack reached his teens, she was in college with her own troubles and knew little of her brother's adolescence, except that when George's sister Ruthie ran off with an older married man it had broken Jack's heart.

Mostly Sam defended him. She denied Kim's claim that he had robbed his dead father on the day of the man's funeral, leaving Sam behind to deal with their crazy mother. She assured Annie that he'd always had a good, loving heart.

Pressed to explain why, if Jack's heart was so good, he had dropped his only child off like an unwanted pet at the pound, Sam would fall back on assurances that he had loved his daughter "more than he could say."

"Obviously," the girl agreed as soon as she'd mastered the ironical eyebrow she had learned from Claudette Colbert.

"Let it go," advised Sam.

In large part Annie did. But one day, in her teens, out jogging alone, she was running slowly along the path that wound through the old cemetery of St. Mark's Church, where all the Peregrines were buried, and she came across a story her father had never told her. Studying the family grave markings there, she noticed a little marker with small curved wings, sunk in grass and obscured beneath the big purple blossoms of a rhododendron. Crawling under that bush's branches, she rubbed at the moss and lichen obscuring the name on the grave. When she finally was able to decipher the carved letters, the sight knocked the breath out of her and she slithered quickly backwards, as if she'd been bitten. The small stone said:

JOHN INGERSOLL PEREGRINE

1946–1948

TAKEN FROM ME

John Ingersoll Peregrine was her father's name.

Out of breath after racing across town to her aunt's store, she asked Sam to explain why her father had a grave that said he'd died. Sam, her brow furrowed, handed Annie a glass of water, her remedy for all ills, then explained that the name John Ingersoll Peregrine was the name of Sam and Jack's older brother, whom they'd never met because he'd died at two years old, before they were born. She said that their mother Grandee had chosen to give the dead boy's name, John Ingersoll Peregrine, to the baby Jack. It might seem odd but it must have been Sam's mother's way of coping with the loss of her first son. The child who'd died so young had been called "Johnny," whereas Annie's father had always been called "Jack." Sam was sure that Jack, wherever he was, was alive and doing fine and that Annie shouldn't worry about him.

Annie ran next door where Georgette's mother told her that, yes, there had been a baby Peregrine but she hadn't been able to find out much about it. She clamped her hands over her eyes, her ears, her mouth in a hyperbolic pantomime.

Annie returned to Sam with Kim Nickerson's report. Why was the gravestone at St. Mark's so hidden? Why had the town been reluctant to talk about John Ingersoll Peregrine?

Sam's teeth bit her mouth, then she sighed, then she said that it wasn't a happy subject. Johnny had died in an accident. Her mother had been pregnant with Sam at the time.

"What kind of accident?"

Sam rubbed her eyes. "In a pool we used to have."

"A pool? Where?"

"Just in the yard. Where the herb garden is now."

"The pool that's gone?"

But at that moment a shopper interrupted them, bustling into Now Voyager hoping for a just-released movie; Annie learned no further details about her long dead toddler uncle Johnny. That evening her aunt had brushed the questions aside, claiming she was late to a hospital board meeting. A teenager with her own life, Annie wasn't much intrigued by a long dead relative she'd never met. She let the subject drop. In fact, in general she lost interest in asking Sam about Kim's Peregrine stories. It was best to keep on the move anyhow, stay out of reverse, stay out of the past. The past was a deep pool covered by grass, like the grave marker of John Ingersoll Peregrine.

Chapter 9

Remember the Day

The storm rumbled across the fields that rolled down from Pilgrim's Rest. Clark pulled off his glasses to examine the tiny brown and red object that Annie had unhooked from her father's letter. "It's a dry fly. Royal Coachman." He showed her the key. "And this looks like, I don't know, maybe a powerboat key. Maybe Jack's planning on a sort of reconciliation father-daughter fly-fishing trip before he passes away, if he's passing away, which I'm having trouble believing. He's only forty-eight."

Annie studied the FedEx envelope. "Why would he be in Miami, in a place called Golden Days for Active Living?"

Sam rubbed her white hair. "I'm older than Jack, and I'm way too young for one of those places."

"You play tennis," Clark reminded her. "Jack played the horses."

"You don't die at forty-eight from playing the horses." Tightening her brow, Sam felt the stationery's logo. "Cheap. Golden Days. He told me he was calling from a hospital."

Annie shrugged. "Why's he saying, 'Meet me in St. Louis,' if he's in Miami? If he's dying, why's he hopping around the country?"

Clark rubbed her back. "Travel was always Jack's strong suit."

Annie opened the porch door to look up at the greenish-black swirls of fast-moving clouds. "That's one way to put it."

What did she remember of that last trip her father and she had taken to St. Louis? She could recall only how long the bridge had looked, reaching over the Mississippi River, how high the Archway had curved above the city, how the arch was sometimes gold, sometimes silver in the sky.

She suddenly remembered the television screen in a motel room in St. Louis, on which Egyptian clouds were gusting around in *The Ten Commandments* as Moses parted the Red Sea. She'd been watching that movie. Her father had been trying, unsuccessfully, to reach somebody on the phone. She'd been hiding under his arm, upset with Moses for closing the Red Sea over the Pharaoh's horses. Terrifyingly, there was a banging on their door, a raspy voice calling out, "Pizza." Her father threw her into a closet so fast he hurt her arms. Peeking out, she saw a big man in a windbreaker kicking at the door, snapping the chain and falling into the room. The man shoved her father back into the desk chair, tipping it. "Nice to meet you, Jack."

Her dad said, "You've got the wrong guy. Swear to God."

The man showed him a black pistol under his belt. "Be nice. Your little girl, where is she?"

"Not here."

But Annie ran from the closet, hurling herself at this man, knocking him off-balance. Quickly her father crashed the man's head down onto the glass coffee table, cracking the glass. The man fell to his knees as abruptly as the Israelites had done when Moses parted the sea in *The Ten Commandments*. He rolled off the table and dropped unconscious onto the rug.

Grabbing their suitcases, Annie's father hurried her through the motel parking lot. When they passed a cream-colored BMW with a Florida license plate, Annie said that just this morning she'd noticed the same car, with the same plate numbers, in the truck stop where they'd had breakfast in Memphis. Her father said, "Good girl," and he used the gun to smash the BMW's headlights.

Two hours later, they stopped at a service station and he bought her candy bars, so many that they fell out of his arms all over the seat, like a shelf had collapsed on a candy rack.

"Who was that man back there?" she asked him.

"The Crocodile," he said, nodding, breathing carefully. "Tick tock tick tock." The Crocodile who'd chased after Captain Hook was one of her father's favorite names for their pursuers. "That was a little scary, wasn't it? You did great, Annie. You did. A-plus. You saved us." He pressed her small hands against his puffed-out cheeks, making a funny splattery noise as he pushed in on her fingers. Although she was still frightened, the noise made her laugh. She poked her fingers in his cheeks hard.

He asked, "Do you love me, darlin'?"

"No."

"Oh for the love of Mike." Reaching across the seat, he hugged her to him, close against the steering wheel. "Nothing bad's ever going to happen to you," he promised, pointing through the windshield at the white crescent of the moon tilted among the stars. "The moon is my witness," he vowed. "The moon's smiling because you're so beautiful."

"Be quiet," she told him sternly. "I don't want to go back to that motel."

"Me either. Don't like their room service." He kissed the top of her head.

"Where are we going now?" she asked.

But he just sat there, his arms folded over the steering wheel.

His failure to move scared her. "Go," she told him.

"Okay." He nodded, turning the ignition. "Let's go home."

His proposal surprised her because she hadn't ever formulated what home might be, other than this speeding car, and out its windows the blur of land and towns flying by them on the sides of the highways. "Where?" she asked. "Where I went when I was a baby?" For he'd told her often about the trip to his childhood town, Emerald, about his leaving the plane the *King of the Sky* at Pilgrim's Rest with his sister, although Annie had no memories of her own by which to judge his stories.

"That's right. Emerald City, darlin'."

"You said Pilgrim's Rest was a pit of snakes."

"Oh no no. It's the best place in the world."

With the old familiar surge of speed, he headed up the ramp onto the interstate. She read a sign for 55 East. After driving a while, he told her, "Snuggle down. I'm the Wizard of Nod and we need to take your ruby shoes to bed."

She held out her legs, braced the cowboy boots with their green lariats against the dashboard. "I'm not sleepy."

"Sure you are." He tapped a cigarette from his pack.

"How do you know?"

"Because you're the queen of the world and queens need to rest." He slipped the pink baseball cap onto her head like a crown.

The next day he left her in the yard at Pilgrim's Rest.

• • •

Out on the Pilgrim's Rest porch, Annie's twenty-sixth birth-day banner, hand-painted by Sam, tore loose from the overhang as the storm swirled overhead. A few of the Mylar birthday bal-loons had floated from the hall into the morning room where Annie, in her Navy shorts and T-shirt, stood in the bay window beside the old library table. The giant jigsaw puzzle of the sky was filled in now, except for a circle of about six inches diameter right in the middle of the flat blue rectangle. She idly searched among the pieces. Near the bay window, a branch fell from the oak tree.

Clark held out the fishing fly when he walked into the room. "I checked. It's definitely a Royal Coachman fly. Meaning what? Why can't Jack ever just say things?"

"Who knows?" Sliding the little key out of her pocket, she put it with the fishing fly back in the envelope. Lights blinked on in the window across the lawn. "Looks like Georgette's home. I'm going over."

"She'll just analyze you." Georgette, now a resident in psy-chiatry at Emerald Hospital, did therapy on her neighbors. "You wouldn't believe her theories about me."

"Clark, I heard her theories about you ten years ago." Annie turned back to the jigsaw puzzle, fitting together two of the pieces.

He watched her. "Sam just doesn't want to finish this damn thing. It'd be easy but then she wouldn't have it here on the table taking up space and collecting dust."

As he spoke, Sam came into the room. "Guess what, Clark? Life takes up space and collects dust. How's that?" She reached over, tugging at her niece's dark-gold tangled hair. "D. K. can get you to a Raleigh flight in the morning. You can fly to St. Louis and find Jack and bring him home. I'll fix up his old room for him."

Exasperated, Annie gestured at the world outside. "Find him where? How do I know where we stayed in St. Louis? I was seven years old!"

Her uncle was listening to the wind. "No flight's leaving RDU tonight, that's for sure. This will turn into a twister, I kid you not."

Sam took the balloons back into the hall. "This is not turning into a twister, Clark; you always think it's a twister. But I admit it's getting ugly. I canceled the birthday party. I called my list and Georgette is calling hers. What we'll do with two-dozen spicy tuna rolls, I don't know." She held up a small blue Samsonite suitcase. "Found this in the attic."

Annie took the bag, surprised by how familiar it looked. "Good God, I came here with this."

Sam had found it behind boxes of big out-of-fashion Christmas lights. "I was pretty sure I'd packed Jack's leather jacket in here, when he left it behind. Remember that day? When he showed up like *North by Northwest,* right before you and Georgette went to Paris?"

Annie raised her eyebrow. "The last time any of us ever saw Jack? Strangely enough I do remember that day."

Sam said, "Give him a break. He could be dying."

"Or not." Clark shrugged.

When they opened the blue Samsonite, the past jumped out. The old brown leather flying jacket her father had often worn lay on top of her pair of small lavender jeans. Her pink hat with shiny multi-colored glass beads was folded inside the green velvet dress that she remembered as once having been her favorite.

Sam held up a pair of child's plastic neon-blue sunglasses.

Annie took them, looked through their lenses. "Dad said they had X-ray vision. I wanted sunglasses because he always wore them."

Sam recalled that Jack had always admired great sunglasses. He'd always commented when women wore sunglasses in the movies. Simone Signoret in *Les Diaboliques*, Anouk Aimée in *La Dolce Vita*, Jeanne Moreau in *Jules et Jim*, Audrey Hepburn—

"Sam, we get the idea." Clark looked at the bright blue plastic glasses. "I remember these."

Sam vigorously shook the brown leather jacket. A small automatic pistol fell out of a pocket and onto the floor. "Jesus Christ! That's been there the whole time."

Clark picked up the gun. "Jack was an idiot." He removed the clip.

Annie studied the black automatic; it was probably the gun her father had taken from the intruder in the St. Louis motel that night. The man he'd called The Crocodile. Was the place they'd been that night the St. Louis motel where he wanted her to meet him now? What was its name? A neon sign…the image wouldn't come.

She felt in the jacket's zipped pockets and in one of them she found an extremely large emerald on a thin chain.

Clark said, "Well, Annie, looks like your dad packed a rod and wore women's jewelry."

Sam told him to stop. "It's no time to joke."

Clark shrugged. "Tell me when."

Sam took the emerald to the light. "Jesus Christ!" she said again.

Annie felt carefully around the lining of the jacket; then picking up a letter opener from the table, she ripped apart its frayed silk. Long expired credit cards, drivers' licenses, passports, all with her father's photo but with different names, fell out onto the hall carpet. Hundred-dollar bills fell out too, fifteen of them, loose.

"Looks real." Clark felt the money.

Annie shuffled through a stack of business cards, all different.

Under a lamp's light, Sam examined the green rectangular gem. "There's no way this *isn't* an emerald." She showed the stone to Annie and Clark. "You think Kim's theory could have been true? Somehow Jack dug up a bunch of precious stones in the yard?"

Annie sneered. No, it wasn't true, no truer than her father's endless promises to make her a queen.

Clark noted with a wry noise that it was no wonder Jack wanted his jacket back, but why had he waited so long to get in touch?

Feeling carefully inside the jacket's lining, Annie found a folded sheet of notepaper from a Hotel Dorado in South Beach, Miami, Florida. On it was written 678STNX211. She made a derisive noise that was an unconscious imitation of Clark's. "Dad wants whatever these numbers are to. It's like a computer password, or bank account, or something. He was always writing numbers down; he could never remember them."

Sam turned the pink baseball cap around, inside out, examining it. She pointed at the faded ink scribble inside the small hatband. "Hang on. I remember seeing something written in here too. Look."

Annie examined the pale ink marks in the light: 362484070N. She was still studying the scribbled sequence when her cell phone rang.

She was surprised by the jolt she felt, like a scramble out of sleep, like a plane in a graveyard spiral, disoriented. The thought raced through her that someone on the phone was going to tell her that her father was dead.

But a familiar voice jumped in and out of static. "Babe? That you, A? A? Can you hear me?"

"Brad?…Brad?"

"Yeah, babe. Happy birthday." It was her almost ex-husband Brad Hopper, who phoned her every few weeks, ostensibly to settle specifics about their divorce but actually to urge her to call it off.

"Brad. Can we talk later? You're breaking up and I'm busy now."

"You're always busy, A." He started quickly singing, "Happy birthday to you…"

"Brad—"

"Happy birthday to you, happy birthday to you…Guess what you're getting as a present? Me. I'm on my way to Emerald."

Chapter 10

No Time for Love

Outside the wind shrieked and there was more static in the connection. "You hear me, A?" He had always called her "A," as if his saying "Annie" would waste her time. "So, what are you so busy with? Busy-ness, that was one of our problems."

"'Our problems,' not my problem?" She muttered, "You must be in therapy."

Brad laughed just a little too long to mean it. "Hey, that's your buddy Georgette's thing, not mine. What happened to your party tonight?"

"How'd you even know about it?"

"Georgette."

Annie glared out the window in the direction of the Nickerson house, where more lights were now coming on. "Brad, I wish you'd stop calling Georgette or you'd marry *her* or something."

"No, you don't," her almost-ex said with his oddly rapid Georgia accent. "You want you and me to get back together and that's why, deep down, A, you don't want a divorce."

"Really?" She gave him her well-known raised eyebrow, knowing that although he couldn't see it, he could sense it.

"Really," he agreed. "That's why the paperwork's taking so long."

She sighed. "The paperwork's taking so long because your lawyer won't return my lawyer's phone calls."

He chuckled conspiratorially. "You bet."

Annie began pacing the hallway. "The final papers are at your lawyer's, Brad. You sign them."

"I'm never home." He laughed again. "I just sold a jet in Charleston and I'm headed your way." Brad, retired from the Navy and now in the Reserves, was the figurehead of Hopper Jets, the highly successful Atlanta-based private aircraft company that had been founded by his grandfather and was actually run by his mother and his twin sister Brandy. "Anyhow, Georgette just told me Sam called your party off because of the weather. It's not so bad."

Annie glared out the window, where she saw Clark out in the yard, bent over by the wind, tying the barn doors shut. The wind blew the tall man's yellow slicker sideways like a big flag of surrender. "You're crazy, Brad. It's very bad here. Georgette told you it wasn't bad?"

"Yeah, well, you know she'd love to see me." Brad, whose mother had persuaded him that he was the apple of the world's eye, had always theorized that Georgette had a crush on him; he'd felt sorry for her as a result. "Sam sent me an invite to your party, so I wasn't like crashing or anything."

Annie glared at her aunt. "Sam sent you an invite?"

"She's my bud."

"Apparently everybody is."

"So weather's really bad there?"

She pushed away the balloons. "Major storm. Stay where you are, Brad." Watching Sam, who was rereading the letter Jack had sent, she added, "I may be leaving town anyhow. I just found out my dad is dying."

Brad was surprised. "No way!"

"He wants me to bring him the *King of the Sky* to St. Louis tonight. I'm thinking I should go because if he *is* dying, maybe he could tell me something about my mom."

"Your mom? You don't have a mom."

"Everybody's got a mom. I'd like to know who mine is." Sam looked over at her. Annie, checking her watch, made a face at the phone. "Brad, even your mom's better than none at all."

"Ah, A, come on." Brad hated for Annie to make cracks about his mother. It was an old argument.

"Fine. Bye. I've got to go deal."

"Go deal. It's bizarro, babe. But I'm sorry your dad's sick. See, I'm nice about him."

Annie couldn't stop herself. "I'm nice about your dad."

"My dad's dead." He sighed.

"I was nice about him when he wasn't dead. Later, Brad."

"Okay, later, A."

She hung up with a decisiveness that she knew reminded him of his mother, Spring Hopper, the real estate mogul. Annie had always understood that Brad feared and admired the cut-to-the-chase take on life that she shared with "Mama Spring," who hated her (and vice versa). Brad had kept photos of the two women in his wallet, separated by a divider. The one of Annie was one that she disliked, from the local newspaper, titled "Emerald's Young Top Gun," a picture of her in her Navy flight suit, arms folded, with her helmet stenciled "Lt. Annie P. Goode" with the black eagle, standing in a starry sky with a vacuous grin as if she'd just successfully straightened out the Milky Way. In the photo her fake smile (she had to admit) looked rather like Mama Spring's.

Sam had hung this same photo of Annie, proudly enlarged, on a big posterboard headlined, "My Niece Lt. Anne Samantha Peregrine Goode!!!" The board sat in the window of Sam's movie store so that everybody in town could keep up with Annie, whether they wanted to or not. Annie found the window display embarrassing and asked Sam to remove it. Sam refused. "Love means never being sure you won't be totally mortified by the people who love you."

"No fooling," Annie replied.

She had separated from Brad immediately after walking into their bedroom and finding him having sex with their squad leader's wife. She told him then that she was never again going to make herself so vulnerable. "It's over, Brad. You need to know that."

"I don't know it, A. I don't want to know it."

Clark, who'd never thought Brad a particularly wise choice, had tried not to say I told you so. But after the separation, when Brad began begging her to come back, her uncle warned her, "Take some time to find your bearings, Annie. I married my second wife too fast, when I was still mourning my first. Result: Divorce."

She raised her Claudette Colbert eyebrow at him. "The only thing I didn't do fast enough with Brad was leave him."

Annie and Brad had met at Annapolis on the first day of their first year. By the time they graduated—Brad by the skin of his perfect teeth, and despite (or in his view, because of) his strategic use of uppers under stress—they'd been engaged for two years. He had set out from the beginning to win Annie's affection because she was pretty and Southern and, like his mother, so competent that she could run his life without troubling him about it.

In the beginning she resisted Brad's flirtation. But the first time that they flew a jet together, she fell in love. In the air, he was exciting, intense, the fastest cadet at the Academy. On paper, he was perfect too: good-looking, star athlete, only son of wealthy parents who doted on him. But in the end—at least this was Georgette's theory—Annie fell in love with Brad because the more she pushed him away, the more he resisted going. It was the opposite of her begging her father not to leave.

With the highest academic grades in their class, she'd been given her choice of assignments on "Selection Day." She'd chosen the Special Weapons School in San Diego, where, after initial training in Pensacola, she would train to fly new Navy jets. Brad, a top-ranked cadet Naval Aviator (holder of a speed record), had also been offered a billet in San Diego. The day they heard their assignments, they lay on his bed in his boyhood room in a wealthy Atlanta suburb, where taped to the ceiling was a poster of a blonde spilling out of a bikini that he'd put up back in the tenth grade. That the poster hadn't been removed should have been, Annie later mused to Georgette, a clue.

After they finished their pilot training, before they were to ship off together to the Persian Gulf on the USS *Enterprise*, Annie and Brad suddenly announced a wedding date. They called their families and gave them only three weeks notice to come to California for the ceremony, which was to be a quiet, almost stealthy one, since their base commander had told them (presciently as it proved) that so quick a marriage would be a dumb-ass idea.

Worried but sounding cheerful, Sam and Clark flew with Georgette and D. K. Destin from North Carolina, bringing all the way across the country the little Maltese terrier Malpy and the old Shih Tzu Teddy.

The service was held in an ugly desert town west of the San Diego base. Georgette was Annie's maid of honor and D. K. Destin, in his wheelchair, gave her away with Sam, Clark, and the two dogs (Malpy wearing a plaid bow tie, Teddy a plaid hair bow). That three such adults and two dogs should perform this ceremonial function much distressed Brad's formidable mother, who told her daughter Brandy that she felt strongly that "a *g.d.* freak zoo is no substitute for a father of the bride."

All through the wedding rehearsal, Annie and her new mother-in-law watched each other like gunslingers in the street.

The South Carolinian Mrs. Hopper, who referred to herself in the third person as "Mama Spring," fired a shot: Where the *g.d.h.* was Annie's *g.d.* father? If Brad's father, Daddy Alton, could make it all the way from Atlanta on oxygen with emphysema, surely Daddy Jack, father of the bride, could have gotten his *b-u-t-t* to San Diego as well?

Annie returned fire in a barrage of sarcasm: the family she wanted here *was* here. Daddy Jack was irrelevant and had either fled the country or had his *b-u-t-t* locked up in a federal penitentiary.

Mama Spring volleyed back with a sardonic smile. Couldn't the father of the bride have gotten a special family leave of absence from prison in order to come give his little girl away, so Annie could have enjoyed what any normal girl craved, a church and a lace veil and a satin train and a *g.d.* maid of honor in something coordinated, instead of having a size-eighteen sleazepot (Georgette Nickerson) at the rehearsal dinner announcing she planned to wear a black bustier with pink satin elbow-length gloves tomorrow? After all, Annie was marrying the most eligible young bachelor in all Atlanta, a large city where the active Junior League was practically draped in black, a whole city where every good mother at every good club had wanted Brad to marry *her* daughter, instead of marrying somebody nobody knew, and without a spit of notice either! But Annie didn't even seem to realize her good fortune! Why, when Mama Spring had first come out, her picture was in every paper in the state.

"Luckily the same thing didn't happen to me," muttered Annie's aunt Sam as she sat down at the hotel bar's piano and began to play "Take My Breath Away" from the *Top Gun* soundtrack.

Brad's invalid father Daddy Alton took a puff of the oxygen attached to the back of his wheelchair as Mama Spring sank onto a barstool in tears. He ordered two White Russians and drank them both while Brad's twin sister Brandy was comforting her mother.

Later, alone with "the bride's party," Sam was taking requests at the piano (she played by ear and only needed to hear someone hum a melody in order to reproduce it). She played "I Heard It Through the Grapevine" for D. K., then "Only the Lonely" for Clark, then confessed to both that Brad's behavior was scaring her. The young man appeared to be on the verge of a fit. Had the others noticed how he kept scratching at his scalp, how his knees kept bouncing up and down and his foot twitching as if some irascible puppet master was jerking on his strings? "What's that boy's problem?"

D. K. Destin pressed big brown fingers together into a pinch, held them to each nostril. "Brad's on a sleigh ride in the snow. Our baby's marrying a junkie."

"No, she isn't," Sam insisted, her face a wrinkle of worry. "That's not possible."

"Anything's possible," Clark admitted. "Lot of Huey pilots in 'Nam were cokeheads. Who could blame them?"

"Not me," said D. K. "I wish I'd had a little snort, anything to pass the time all those hours I was hanging onto two feet of scrap metal in the Commie China Sea waiting for a God-Almighty U.S. Navy 'copter to show up. Stress can get to you."

Sam frowned. "What stress is Brad under?" He had not been shot out of a jet plane and crashed into the ocean; all he was doing was getting married.

"Easy for you to say," Clark told her.

She wondered, "Are we going to make it through tonight and tomorrow?"

Clark and D. K. together told her, "No."

"Oh God," sighed Sam. "You think Brad's not the One?" Since Annie's adolescence, her three surrogate parents had devoted considerable speculation to who would be the right man for their adopted child. Whenever she brought home a new boyfriend, Sam would ask, "Is he the One?"

"He's not the One," sadly agreed Clark and D. K. on the eve of her wedding to Brad Hopper.

Chapter 11

The High and the Mighty

It was not only in retrospect that Annie's wedding was a failure. No one much enjoyed it even at the time, certainly not Annie, too busy to notice that it wasn't an auspicious occasion, although she marched so briskly into the justice of the peace's office in her Navy uniform and recited her vows so quickly, like a pledge of allegiance, it was as if she suspected she would change her mind if she slowed down. Brad's mumbled response to the solemn questions could scarcely be heard and he had trouble keeping his eyes open during the chaplain's (admittedly unsolicited) homily on Jesus wanting everybody—except presumably Himself—to have a lot of Christian children. In general the groom was looking, to his dispassionate sister Brandy, "totally wasted," and his bride "totally hyper."

Brad's best man, Lt. Commander Steve Wirsh, had driven out from the base with his wife Melody. After the rehearsal Melody paddled up and down the hotel pool in a hot pink thong and a black sports bra, attracting attention, including Brad's. Wirsh, mistaking Clark and Sam for Annie's parents, chastised them for allowing their blind dog to bite Melody on the thumb. He was taken aback when Clark cheerfully offered to have Teddy put to sleep immediately.

"Oh my God, oh my God, don't do that! We didn't mean that." Melody tried to kiss Teddy, who growled at her.

After the ceremony, at Hôm Qua, the local Vietnamese restaurant that D. K. had chosen for his wedding gift dinner party,
young Wirsh gave a speech about America's imperial destiny that
Sam could only endure by eating an entire steamed sea bass.

Annie overheard Mama Spring Hopper lamenting to Brandy
that the whole bridal party was "nothing but a parade at the *g.d.*
Mardi Gras!" with Sam a make-no-mistake-about-it pervert, and
who ever heard of a purple satin tuxedo? With Clark, Annie's
uncle, who wasn't even her uncle but just a man who lived with a
Lesbian, never saying two words a bat could hear through a mega-
phone. With the maid of honor, Georgette Something, looking
like Madonna half way through a Kahlúa and chocolates binge—
Madonna the rock star not the Virgin Mary—shouting out wedding
toasts that would have been worse had they not been incoherent;
so drunk she had fallen flat on her face, unable to catch the bride's
bouquet, despite the bride's having tossed it straight at her.

Plus those two horrible dogs had run off with Mama Spring's
purse and torn it to shreds.

And to top it all off, that big crippled black man with dirty
cornrows, wearing black pajamas and sitting in a wheelchair with
Move the F Over! on the back of it, that man had told Daddy
Alton that Daddy had only himself to blame for even being in
a wheelchair, whereas the black man claimed he had gotten his
disability by being shot out of a plane for his country. The whole
thing had so upset Daddy (admittedly not a veteran, except of
thirty years of two packs a day) that he'd ordered three mai tais in
a row from a waitress talking Asian gibberish and had made a fool
of himself by singing "Strawberry Fields Forever" with that awful
Sam playing it on the piano. In Mama Spring's view, and Brandy
could take it to the bank, the bride's entire wedding party was
like one horrible preview of what Liberals would do to America
if given a chance. It assuredly wasn't the kind of wedding party
anyone would want to paste in a book of Treasured Memories.

At this point, Annie had heard enough. Thrusting her
champagne glass at Georgette (who drank it), she tapped Brad's
mother on the shoulder. "A parade? How about my bridal party,"

she said with her icy smile, "is a paradigmatic symbol of progressive democracy?" When that produced a blank stare from Mrs. Hopper, Annie jabbed her with a finger. "I'll rephrase. Drop the g.d. subject of my wedding right now, you racist bitch."

Mrs. Hopper wailed, "Daddy Alton!" and sobbed convulsive tears. The tears brought Brad running, followed by Daddy Alton as fast as he could get there, drunk, with his oxygen tanks weighing down his wheelchair.

Brad's mother cried that Annie's remark had "devastated" her; she was no racist; she made turkey sandwiches for the homeless and served them herself in her church community room.

Brad asked both bride and mother to apologize, "just to smooth things over this little bump."

Mother and bride stared at him ominously, their eyes warning: "You think this is a 'little' bumpy? Stand back."

At 1 a.m., Georgette (unaccustomed to heavy drinking) succumbed to alcohol poisoning, throwing up on Mama Spring after spinning both D. K. and Daddy Alton around in circles in their wheelchairs to an MTV number on the television above the bar. She'd been working hard to get a little dancing going—the Vietnamese restaurant was not really made for dancing—an excuse that did not make Brad's mother feel any better about being vomited on.

In the women's bathroom, where Annie was trying to wash off her maid of honor's face and hair, Georgette kept insisting that Brad had put the make on her two summers ago when he'd run into her at the Atlanta airport.

"You wish," retorted the disbelieving Annie. "Georgette, keep your damn head down." She bent her friend over the sink.

Georgette threw up again and passed out.

She wasn't the only one. Daddy Alton, who'd had too many mai tais for his oxygen to handle, sang "The High and the Mighty" with Sam and then accused his wife of sleeping with their yardman, a Georgia Tech senior, and then he too passed out. Mama Spring screamed, "He's dead! Is there is a doctor in this godforsaken dump?!"

The owner of Hôm Qua Restaurant stepped out of the shadows and raised his hand. Clark acknowledged the man with a wave, then leaned over and pulled up Daddy Alton's eyelids. "He's fine."

At 2 a.m., D. K. Destin grabbed Brad by the hair and threatened to kill him if he ever hurt Annie.

Mama Spring threatened to kill D. K. if he threatened to kill her son.

"Let's all say good morning," Clark proposed. "Then nobody will have to kill anybody." Turning, he bowed to the physician-restaurateur, who stood patiently by the door with his car keys in his hand. "*Cám o'n rat nhieu. Ban that tot. Tam Biet.*"

The owner bowed. "*Vinh biet.*"

Clark laughed.

Annie told Sam, "This is the worst wedding I've ever been to. And it had to be mine." She burst into tears.

"Come on, everybody," Clark said. "Let's look on the bright side."

"Oh shut up, Clark," Sam said, hugging Annie who was hugging Teddy. Malpy barked. "What did that Vietnamese man say that was so funny?"

"I said good night for now and he replied, 'Good-bye forever.' Sort of how they felt in Vietnam in general."

• • •

A month later, Annie and Brad were deployed to the Gulf, where their air wing distinguished itself in Operation Desert Fox, a strike campaign against Iraqi forces in Kuwait. Annie and Brad flew FA-18F Super Hornets off the aircraft carrier *Enterprise* in four separate successful bombing raids, for which they each received a minor medal. Both enjoyed what they were doing.

During the two-year tenure of the young couple's marriage, Mrs. Hopper never ("thank you, g.d. Jesus") laid eyes on Sam and Clark, Georgette and D. K. again, nor on Jack Peregrine once. But she continued to ask Annie with a careful innocence about "the father of the bride" whenever they spoke, which was too often for Annie.

Nevertheless, as Sam remarked to Clark and Georgette when, a few months after the wedding, they sat at Pilgrim's Rest, looking through the wedding photos, it was as if Brad's mother could never recover from Jack's absence, as if she had always imagined him some rumpled grumpy Spencer Tracy, who should have been grousing in his armchair about losing the teen-aged Elizabeth Taylor to a younger man and having to pay for it, whereas Annie's father had failed even to show up, proving himself, Sam had to admit, no Spencer Tracy.

Clark passed around a snapshot of Mrs. Hopper taken at that tempestuous banquet in the Vietnamese restaurant. He noted dryly that Mama Spring was no Spring Mama either. Indeed, she might be more accurately called "Mama Late Summer. Or even Mama Nearly Autumn." Nevertheless, Mama Spring had been dressed for Annie and Brad's wedding as if she'd expected to pick up Keanu Reeves at a salsa bar later that night.

Georgette added—in the wry voice that Sam and Clark had always appreciated far more than her own mother ever had—maybe Mama Spring had been dressed up for that Georgia Tech senior Daddy Alton had accused her of sleeping with. Maybe that undergraduate had been waiting for her next door at the Marriott. Maybe Georgette had slept with him too. She put her hands over her eyes. "Oh God, don't make me remember that night. I think I did sleep with a friend of Brad's that night. It was the worst night of my life."

"You don't know that yet," Clark pointed out.

Sam sighed. "You think Annie will be happy with Brad?"

"No," promptly answered Clark.

"It's so easy to be negative."

As it turned out, negativity was the better bet.

• • •

After their tour in Kuwait, Annie and Brad returned to the San Diego base where Lt. Commander Wirsh's wife Melody had time on her hands and decided to spend it having sex with her husband's best friend. Annie caught them at it and left him. The news came as no surprise to her family in Emerald.

Georgette, now a psychiatry intern at Chapel Hill, explained it all.

Annie had married Brad because she'd wanted to best Mrs. Hopper.

Annie had married Brad because he had none of her father's quicksilver tempo, which she'd taken to mean that he would be like Clark, steadfast and trustworthy.

Annie had married Brad because he'd outflown her in three speed test competitions.

Interrupting this analysis, Annie asked her friend, "How about, I married Brad because I made a stupid mistake?"

"That too," agreed Georgette.

When Annie phoned Mrs. Hopper to congratulate her on the separation—"You win"—Brad's mother pretended not to know what she meant and offered sincere hopes that the young couple would reconcile someday because a marriage between a man and a woman was a sacred sacrament—

"Oh, shut the fuck up." Annie slapped her phone shut.

Over the next few months, Brad confessed eagerly to anyone who would listen that "maybe" he'd done wrong by getting caught sleeping with his buddy Steve Wirsh's wife.

He phoned Georgette to ask her to tell Annie he could do better.

"You can't do better until you stop being scared of Annie because you're scared of your mother."

"Think so?" Brad loved to hear theories about himself, although he never assimilated them.

"Afraid" seemed at first an odd adjective for Georgette to apply to such a daredevil as Brad. After all, he would fly a plane in the worst weather with a kind of reckless glee. But interior weather did frighten him. Annie could scare him with a scream. "I don't want to talk about it," was his white flag.

The night Annie had flown home to California after a flight test at Ali Al Saleem and had found him naked in their bedroom on top of Melody Wirsh, he'd retreated without a struggle. "Aw, shit, this sucks," was all he could think of to say. Annie could think of a lot of things but said none of them. She knew that if she opened her mouth, she would not be able to stop weeping.

On the night she left him, the wildness of her hair (a long unruly tangle) so exasperated her that when she saw herself in the mirror at the motel to which she'd driven in an exhausted rage of tears, she'd cut off her curls to her scalp and thrown the hair in the wastebasket along with her wedding ring.

"I hate him," she told the mirror.

The Navy agreed to transfer her to Annapolis, far from the California desert where Brad and she had danced in jets together, and to give her an assignment teaching at the Academy. She cried from time to time as she drove across the country in the Porsche. On the seat beside her, the gray Persian cat Amy Johnson ignored these emotional displays and licked a paw.

• • •

In Annie's condominium in Chesapeake Cove, on the top floor of a building called Harbor Lights, there was only room for herself and her cat. A few weeks after she settled there, she saw a young man, pleasant-looking in Brooks Brothers khakis, in the hall with a white dog, a West Highland terrier. The next night, the young man rang her apartment bell to ask if she were okay, explaining that he'd heard crying coming through her door. He pointed at his dog, who was furiously wagging his tail and tugging against the leash to leap on her. "My Westie, Elliot Ness. I'm Trevor Smithwall, 7C."

Annie apologized, promising with her appealing smile that she would try to keep her sobbing down after eleven. When the Westie spotted the cat, he broke free, chasing Amy Johnson into the living room where he got himself clawed on the nose. Carefully Annie lured the dog from under a chair and handed him to her neighbor. "Would you keep holding him," Trevor asked, "while I go get his eye drops?"

"I can do that," she agreed. "I'm Annie Goode; I'm at the naval base."

"Figured." Trevor pointed at her white uniform, then at his ID, which was hanging from his blazer pocket. "FBI."

"Figured."

Over that first hard year for Annie, Trevor became a good friend. One night they even made a feint at sex but quit before they got there, accepting that they weren't attracted to each other. Relieved, they began to see one another almost daily, sometimes for dinner, when they would talk over problems at work, how both wanted to move faster up the ladders of their careers, how both worried about falling off the ladders, or being pushed.

Annie was not much of a consumer (preferring to build a retirement fund for the rainy day that would inevitably come) but the few things she did buy were of the best quality, like her entertainment system. Trevor preferred to spend his money on fine wines and restaurants. So there were many occasions, late at night, when he would knock on Annie's door, holding out a bottle of Montrachet and a DVD and they'd sit together watching a classic film on Annie's large state-of-the-art flat-screen. Or they would play poker. Annie almost always won. She'd played poker since she was four years old. They both looked forward to their evenings although they told each other they should be out dating instead.

"This is awful," Annie told Georgette on the phone after one of her evenings with Trevor. "I could end up like Sam and Clark."

"Well, you could end up like Sam *or* Clark but unless you were really schizophrenic—"

"You know what I mean. Why is it only in chick flicks that good friends fall in love? In real life, we keep falling in love with people like Trevor's ex-girlfriend—"

"You're in love with Trevor's ex-girlfriend?"

"People like Brad! People that, if we were totally honest, we didn't even really like!"

Georgette argued that there was something sort of appealing about Brad, so Annie should forgive herself for making such a stupid mistake.

"I'll forgive myself the day I sign our divorce papers."

"And when will that day be, Annie?"

"Why do you keep asking me? Because you want to marry him? Remember when you threw up at my wedding?"

"Obviously you do," grumbled Georgette.

"Well, you were onto something when you puked. You had the right idea."

Georgette agreed that she often did.

• • •

At Pilgrim's Rest, Annie idly tapped her birthday balloons while waiting for Georgette's voice mail. "Call me," she said. "My dad's dying."

She glanced at the storm clouds through the hall window when her cell phone rang. "Georgette?"

But it was Brad again. "A? I'm a little delayed here in Charleston; air traffic gets so freaked. I'll be there in a couple of hours. Got you a great present."

"Brad, don't give me a present. I'm divorcing you."

"For better for worse."

"You should have spelled out how 'for worse' would be me seeing you screwing Melody Wirsh."

"That's gross."

To Annie's relief, she found this remark so bizarre that she laughed.

Brad sighed at her unfairness in referring to that ancient "misunderstanding."

"What?"

"I'll make it up to you, A. I'm on my way."

"Don't bother—" But he'd hung up.

"Maybe," said Annie aloud, "Brad ought to try slowing down."

Standing silently in the hallway, eating a saucy chicken wing, Clark nodded at her. "Good. Now you're getting nowhere."

Chapter 12

Make Me a Star

Only two weeks after leaving Brad, Annie was teaching her first squadron of Navy pilots how to land fighter jets on the decks of pitching aircraft carriers so that the tailhooks would stop their planes from rolling into the sea. She knew she was good at her job. But she worried she was a failure at love. As she lamented to Georgette, she had a fatal weakness for loving men who couldn't stay true to her. "If it's fatal, get over it," advised her friend, sitting beside her on the porch at Pilgrim's Rest. "Here, I'll write you a prescription."

Annie studied the script. "This is for sunblock."

"Right. You need to get out more. Get on a ship and go to South America."

Annie said that she got on a ship every morning.

Georgette grabbed Annie's knee to stop her from pushing the swing faster. "A cruise ship. You need a relaxing cruise ship. I'm thinking like what's her face? In that movie Sam loves?"

"Bette Davis, *Now, Voyager?*"

"Yeah. You need more facials and salsa contests and less landing Super Hornets on an aircraft carrier. Not that life-and-death's not a blast too."

Annie decided to see a therapist. She found the wrong one in Annapolis. Her analysis lasted only one session, which the therapist spent accusing her of trying to overthrow male authority.

"You make me sound like the French Revolution," she retorted. The therapist kept tossing chocolate-coated coffee beans in his mouth as he suggested that anger at her husband was actually fear of the phallus. Annie said no, it was actually anger at her husband. He suggested that she appeared to be sitting on great reserves of anger; it seemed likely that her father, her "uncle," or her Lesbian aunt, or some combination, had abused her and she'd completely repressed the knowledge. Annie said that such a supposition was unchallengeable but bogus. Her father's only abuse had been leaving her alone. Sam and Clark's only abuse had been their rarely doing the same.

As she strode out of the therapist's office, Annie said she wouldn't be back. One hundred and forty dollars an hour was too much to pay to watch somebody eat candy.

"I do it for the caffeine," he said.

"It's too much to pay to watch someone eat a pound of caffeine."

But alone later with Amy Johnson, in her neat, spare apartment, Annie found herself so upset that she called Georgette at one in the morning. "Be my friend and my therapist both? We could do it officially on the phone. I'll pay you by the hour."

"At one in the morning? Not on your salary."

"This fat jerk said I had a fear of men."

Georgette laughed. Men, she said, were the least of Annie's fears. What scared Annie was losing rank, not being in charge.

Annie asked: But had she left Brad to forestall his leaving her?

"Possibly." Georgette thought it just as likely that Annie had left Brad because she'd found him in their bed banging the Implant Slut with the ridiculous name of Melody.

"Good answer," said Annie.

"A good answer is the answer you want," Georgette said. "Am I going to confuse friendship with therapy and tell my best friend she has repressed her pathological dread of abandonment by leaving her husband but not divorcing him, which frees her from the threat of intimacy with another man? That a reaction formation to male irresponsibility has produced in her a pattern of obsessive-compulsive over-achievement within a sexist patriarchal hierarchy like the U.S. Navy where she is addicted to a steady supply of high grades, top prizes, and speed records? So, yes, she does want to overcome and supersede men. But she also wants to overcome and supersede women. She is an equal opportunity superseder. *And* she has a serious eating disorder. Am I going to say any of that, even when she wakes me up at one in the morning? How many best friends have I got?"

Annie asked, "What serious eating disorder?"

Georgette made a spluttering *phht phht* noise. "You say the collapse of your marriage was devastating and yet you never huddled in a fetal position for days, or went on a binge of sex with strangers, or faced the look on the checkout woman's face when you rolled six gallons of ripple ice cream onto the conveyer belt. Did you? Did you ever gain, or for that matter lose, a fucking pound?"

Annie assured her friend that she was a mess and she *was* getting a divorce.

"You haven't even formally filed. Why is this divorce so *slow and messy* when you're so fast and in charge?"

"Okay, Georgette, are we going to talk 'messy'? You've still got boxes of unsent Christmas cards on your dining room table and it's March!"

"Aha, this is why friends can't do therapy on friends. My patients haven't seen my table, much less my closet."

"*You* haven't seen your closet yourself, not in years. You couldn't."

"You can trash my closet all you want and you still won't be divorced."

Annie assured Georgette that the latest delay on the final proceedings (she was legally separated, don't forget) had to do only with lawyers stalling to pad their bills; she would be finished with her marriage to Brad by the end of next week. "By Bastille Day, Gigi, *je serais a liberté*." She then changed the subject. "I want you to meet my neighbor Trevor. For his last vacation, he went on a dig to Baalbek."

"What does Trevor think about how long your divorce is taking?"

"Nothing. Nothing!"

"What's the matter with him?"

Nevertheless, the next morning, a bleak March weekend, Annie, off-duty, drove all the way from Annapolis to Emerald in order to keep on arguing with Georgette about why she wasn't divorced yet.

As soon as Sam had seen her niece driving up River Hill Road in her gray convertible, she'd telephoned Brad, whom she knew to be in Atlanta, visiting his mother. He flew straight to Emerald the next day to try to "smooth things over" with his estranged wife.

Annie refused to see him, although she did hide with her old dog Teddy at the top of the stairs, listening in on her husband's lament to his aunt-in-law. Sam spotted Annie crouched there on the second-floor landing, head pressed between the rails, just as she'd done when she was a child, with the black-and-white little Shih Tzu on her lap. Her eyes were squeezed shut in the same way too, and seeing the young woman, Sam's heart ached for the child.

There'd been a time, a few years after Annie's arrival in Emerald, when Sam and she had stood in the yard on a crisp starry night, watching Clark set up her new telescope. They'd found Venus luminous in the low southwestern evening sky. "The Queen of Love," Sam had said. "Don't bother asking Venus about anything but love because she doesn't care about anything else."

"Annie can make any kind of wish on any kind of star she wants," Clark assured the child. "Doesn't have to be Venus."

Annie tightly scrunched an eye shut and peered with the other into the telescope at the resplendent black-mirrored sky. "Is that Venus that's so bright?"

Clark looked. "Yep. That's her."

Still staring into the lens, Annie said, "I wish you both would never die."

On either side, they took her hands. "We plan," said Clark, "to put it off as long as possible. Tell you what, I'll quit smoking."

Sam added, "I plan to clean out the attic and the basement before I die."

Annie laughed. "That'll *never* happen."

They laughed together and looked up at the stars.

Thinking of that starry night, Sam lied to Brad, although under orders not to reveal her grown niece's presence in the house, and claimed Annie had gone off with Georgette and wasn't coming back until Sam called her.

The handsome naval officer choked up, telling Sam that for some reason Annie thought he didn't respect her. Whereas, deep down in his heart, even though everybody always said that he himself was the best pilot they'd ever met, deep down he believed Annie was the best, male or female, ever seen in the sky. "I mean, I've got the big T and that'll just always kick ass in the end, but truth is, she's Number One. And you tell her I said so."

"What the hell is the big T?"

Brad hit himself in the abdomen. "You know. Testosterone."

With an elaborate thoughtfulness, Sam considered this idea. "Ah...but otherwise, Annie's got at least a tiny little bit of a future in flying?"

"I don't know why y'all have to be so sarcastic. She's the best. I mean, before she went nuts about our problem. Probably not doing so good now. When she stresses, well, you know..."

Sam swung an imaginary tennis racket overhead as if she were going to serve Brad's head to the other end of the hall. "Well, it's true, having her marriage blow up in her face did stress her out a little bit."

Brad said he had no idea how their lives could have gone so fatally wrong so fast. "I wish you could help me smooth this over. Why can't she just move on?"

"I'll give you a hint," growled Sam, the invisible racket swinging back and forth. "Naked married woman under naked married man, not married to each other. Man would be you, you dumb big T dickhead!"

Brad yanked at his thick black hair. "I sure see where she gets this aspect of her personality." He rapidly cracked his knuckles in an elaborate tattoo. Couldn't Sam look at it from Brad's point of view? He was always getting shot out of the water by Annie's smart bombs and it was no vacation. "Sam, with her, it's twelve o'clock high every day of our lives." And while he'd be the last to deny that, given his wedding vows, he'd been out of line with Melody, he felt Annie should admit that she was partly to blame for his "slipup": she had a Terminator temper and she'd been so busy trying to prove she was the number-one pilot in the Navy that she hadn't made enough time for their marriage; otherwise she would have known that Melody didn't mean a thing to him. Annie was a "mental capacity natural" so she didn't understand how hard Brad had to work to stay ahead of the game. He'd had a tough time on some exams he'd taken just before Annie'd caught him with Melody. Plus he really suspected Melody had given him sex pills without his knowing it. He was strictly off all substances now but he had to admit he'd gotten a little high that night after hearing he'd flunked the one exam he thought he'd passed. Melody came over to the bungalow to borrow some olive oil and then she'd started to rub it on—

"Jesus Christ, just be quiet!" Sam exclaimed, hearing a floorboard creak above her. "It wasn't a 'slipup'! It's not something to 'smooth over.' You are so full of shit, I could, I could—" At a loss, Annie's aunt, still almost as athletically trim as Brad himself, swung the imaginary tennis racket down onto his skull while with her other hand she landed a hard jab in the pilot's washboard abdomen. They stared at each other, both surprised. Then straightening up, Brad grinned. "I see where she gets her temper too...Nice left."

"Thanks." Sam took a long breath. "All right, forget about Annie then. Get divorced. Aren't you a Republican? Why don't *you* move on?"

"I'll never get over Annie."

"Why not?"

His face furrowed. Finally he gave up thought. "I don't know what to do without her."

Sam couldn't help but respond. "Oh, Brad." Frowning unhappily, she walked him to the door. "Okay, gut it up. Quit the pills—"

"I'm off those uppers. If Annie told you—"

"She didn't tell me anything. Say you're sorry, mean it, try to win her back."

Brad shook his head. "No-go. I asked her to take me back. Know what she said? 'How dumb are you?'"

"Well, you are dumb," Sam conceded. "But brains aren't everything. Like I used to tell Annie myself, 'Maybe I'm not as smart as you—'"

"Wow, Sam, I used to say the same thing." He hugged her like a comrade.

"'But, Annie, you can still learn a lot from me,' that's what I used to tell her. So, try again."

"No-go." The young lieutenant added with the world-weariness of youth, "Life's a bitch."

"Honey, you don't know the half of it," Sam predicted.

He stepped out the door onto the porch then slipped back inside. "I'm not a Republican. I don't even believe in politics."

She shook her head at him. "Jesus Christ, what does that mean? You can't not believe in politics. It's not like the tooth fairy, Brad...You want me to give Annie a message?"

"Yes." He nodded mournfully. "'Don't hate me.'"

Sam hugged him. "She's just mad."

"How long you think it'll last?"

She rubbed his arms briskly with strong tanned hands. "Oh, twenty, thirty years, max. I love you, you jerk. No cause why I should, love's funny that way...Hang on." She ran up the stairs, whispering into the hall. "Annie, Brad's leaving! Annie?" Sam looked for her niece, but her bedroom was empty. As Annie's father Jack had done as a boy, she had climbed out the window, run across the roof and swung down the old wisteria vine that twisted around the back porch corner post. She was sitting by the thick root of the old vine, her head in her arms.

If Brad had known Annie better he might have looked near that wisteria. But he didn't know her well at all. He drove next door to see if she were with Georgette and if not, to get Georgette's advice. Not finding the young psychiatrist at home, he called her at the hospital and poured his best wheedle into his voice. "My heart's about broken. I flew all the way here and Annie won't see me. I'm staying at the Omni; meet me for a drink? I need help and all the roads are leading back to you, Georgia."

With a sigh, Georgette declined. He was the only person who made her like her full name, Georgia Georgette. He knew it and was always singing "Georgia on My Mind" whenever he saw her. He was a very good-looking man. "You know what, Brad? I see you, I see a box of Dove bars in the freezer. I know they're bad for me but I eat them anyhow and all of a sudden, they're gone and I feel sick."

"Come on, Georgia. Just one old sweet song!"

"You cheated on my best friend."

"Yeah. I know. And she's totally right to be mad. But she won't even see me and I flew all this way…I'm not a rocket scientist. I need help figuring out what to do. Come on. I need some company and you're the absolute best."

Georgette sighed.

He said, softly sad, "Omni in half an hour? Room 1405. Really nice suite; I'll get room service."

"Brad, if you were the last man in my entire life who was going to ask me to come have a drink with him at his hotel—and, frankly, you very well might be—I would say no. Why? Because if I was on the *Titanic*, Annie would get me into a lifeboat."

"Well, hey, give me a break. I can't help it if I'm not 'Women and Children.'"

"What?"

"And let me tell you, Annie was no piece of cake. It was always twelve o'clock high with her." He had liked the sound of that phrase when he'd said it earlier to Sam.

Georgette hung up the phone. Brad figured he'd lost the connection.

• • •

It didn't take a rocket scientist to notice that disloyalty made Annie angry. Her absent mother, her capricious father, her unfaithful husband, all had produced a young woman determined to bring down the gavel on Life until Life behaved in a dependable way. Annie was faithful. It was the gift she gave and that she wanted to receive. Georgette's loyalty, Sam and Clark's loyalty sat safe at the core of her and she loved them for it. The Navy's dependability was one reason she had chosen the Navy. Its discipline was reliable. She wanted not only to defend her country but also to help keep it in order, the way she kept her closet in order—her shoes side by side on the shoe rack, her tailored uniforms, blue and white, evenly spaced, her slender white T-shirts and jeans ironed and in a row.

As a student at Annapolis, she'd beaten back inconsistency and fought against limits, including those of her own muscle and bone. She'd endured instructors who'd bullied her and classmates who'd harassed her. She had worked hard every waking minute of her four years at Annapolis. She'd graduated fit and trim and first in her class. The only clues to what it had cost her were the pale purple circles under her blue eyes and the pinched nerve in her neck.

When Annie received her commission, she made a pledge that she would never let the Navy down; in return, the Navy would never forsake her. After all, despite D. K. Destin's complaints that the Navy had abandoned him, the truth was, they had shown up for him in the rescue helicopter, hadn't they? And each time she'd landed on the deck of an aircraft carrier, the tailhook had grabbed the wire and the jet stopped. She believed that if she should by chance end up clinging to the wing of a plane in the middle of the ocean, they'd send a helicopter for her just as they had for D. K. She believed the Navy would be like Sam and

Clark and Georgette. Reliable. Unlike Brad, unlike her father, she could count on the Navy. She trusted that she was someone who could be counted on. If she were asked to help, she would help; if she were asked to rescue…

Annie picked up her phone and called Georgette again, this time reaching her. "I just made up my mind. I'm going to fly the *King of the Sky* to St. Louis tonight and give it to my father."

"What?"

"He needs it. I can't bitch about his not coming through for me and then not come through for him. He's dying and he needs help."

Georgette took a loud breath. "Well, this emotional break-through of yours couldn't come at a worse time."

"What does that mean?"

"Have you looked out the window, Annie? My satellite dish just blew by your porch. Clark's twister may be headed to Emerald. Sit still, I'm coming over."

Chapter 13

Twelve O'Clock High

Pummeled by rain, Georgette hurried into Pilgrim's Rest. The wind was blowing so hard that Clark had to help her close the door. He draped her soaked raincoat on the newel post.

"Clark, you may finally be right about the weather. It could be a twister coming." Georgette pointed out the window. "I saw old Mr. Neubruck's gas grill fly through my yard. He'll blame me."

"Check out the Weather Channel. It's a bad twister, fifty miles from here." Clark pointed overhead. "I predicted this."

"For like fifteen years."

"Well," he said, "Annie's up in her room."

"Please tell me she's developed a sense of humor because she just said she'd decided to fly the *King of the Sky* to St. Louis tonight to give it to her dad!"

"I know. Stop her." Clark explained what had happened.

Georgette mulled it over. "She's got to think Jack will help her find her mother."

"She's crazy."

"That's a loose diagnosis, Clark." She added that Brad had just called her, with the remarkable hypothesis that Annie would take him back if he flew from Charleston to Emerald in this storm and proposed to her.

"He's crazy too."

"Clark, stick to pediatric orthopedics. You can't just keep saying Annie's crazy, Brad's crazy."

"They are. You need to stop encouraging Brad. He already gets enough of that from Sam. Let's not have him keep fighting this divorce."

Georgette sighed, still single. "At least Annie got married so she could get divorced. I'm a doctor. It used to be that people wanted to marry doctors." She pulled off her rubber rain hat and shook out her spiky black hair.

Clark said, "Those were women who wanted to marry male doctors. Like me. I've had two different women propose to me in the last five years."

"Right, and did you marry either of them? Would you like my analysis of why you're divorced and living with a Lesbian, Dr. Goode?"

The tall thin man laughed. He'd known Georgette since her early childhood, had encouraged her medical school aspirations, and now saw her daily at Emerald Hospital. "I've heard your analysis, dozens of times. You see, here's your problem, Georgette. You're in psychiatry and men don't want a wife who's going to analyze them for free."

The young woman snorted. "'Free.' Oh. So 'free' is my problem? If I ever have another date, I'll charge him."

"There you go. Go talk to Annie."

Pulling a small damp box wrapped in birthday paper from her raincoat, she fluffed up the ribbon. "This is for her birthday."

Clark warned her with his raised forefinger. "You shrink-wrap it?"

"Please, only new puns."

"That's hard at my age. Go on. She's up there, hanging from her door doing chin-ups or something till D. K. gets her plane ready. She doesn't have the body weight to hold that Piper down in thirty-mile-an-hour winds."

"Lucky her."

Clark called after Georgette as she headed up the stairs, "Tell her she can't fly to St. Louis! She won't listen to Sam and me. We're old."

She turned back and did a sixties dance step. "I'm bookin', man. Don't sweat it. I'm hip, I'm cool—"

"Fine. Mock the elderly."

Georgette ran up the stairs to the second floor, where she found Annie in her bedroom, finishing a set of abdominal crunches. She sat on the bed to watch her. "So, your birthday party's cancelled. Frankly, the old gang was relieved. You only see them once a year and they feel like you've, you know, left them behind."

Annie's left elbow briskly tapped her right knee. "Behind how?"

Georgette fluffed pillows. "Well, to keep up with you, they have to study Sam's big window display at Now Voyager. For them, life is a little more landlocked: complaining about husbands, kids, jobs. By the way, Jennifer had another boy."

Annie's right elbow tapped her left knee. "How can so many kids we went to high school with have kids now?"

Georgette pointed at the retro chrome clock on the wall, spinning her finger in a circle. "Well, frankly, it's not like at our age we'd be Burmese child brides. The bio bell *is* tolling."

"We've got a whole decade." Finishing another set of sit-ups, Annie touched both elbows to both knees. "I'm shooting for pregnant at thirty-five."

"If you want to make thirty-five, you might rethink taking this solo trip in a superannuated single-engine airplane tonight." Flying the *King of the Sky* to St. Louis through a tornado was, in a phrase Georgette said she had used only this morning to a detox patient who'd tried to jump off the hospital roof, "not a good travel plan."

The plump young woman tossed the wrapped gift onto the rug beside Annie, whose legs were now doing scissors, stretched in air over her head. "Here, will you open this? I've got to get back. Pitti Sing's freaking out."

"Hang on. Three more…"

Sliding off the bed, Georgette ripped open the wrapping paper herself. Inside was a tiny set of handsome miniature screwdrivers and pliers and wrenches, in a red leather case with Annie's initials in gold, APG. "You know, for the girl who thinks she can fix everything."

"Except her life," smiled Annie, leaning over to kiss her friend's head. "Perfect present." She saw the little scar on Georgette's knee, from the accident when they were eleven years old, and felt a twinge of the old guilt. She had taken Georgette for a ride on Sam's silver Honda 125 (without Sam's permission) and had skidded off a turn on River Hill Road, crashing into the underbrush below. Georgette still felt faintly queasy whenever she even saw a motorcycle. Annie's broken collarbone had healed far sooner than her regret about endangering her friend.

Georgette pointed out the window at the rain. "And by the way, Brad was planning to surprise you by braving the storm and showing up tonight to propose."

"What?"

"Not that you're divorced. But he'll never get out of Charleston, even in a Hopper jet. I better go. My mother's going to call any minute to see if I'm dead." Thunder cracked loudly and the lights went off and on. "Listen, don't dig me out if the house falls in on me; let archeologists discover my skeleton in a thousand years and say, 'God, she had great bones!'"

They walked together downstairs, in unison the way they'd done as children.

"Annie, about your dad? Maybe he's dying, but at least you hadn't seen him for decades."

"That's a comfort, Gigi."

At the door Clark handed Georgette her raincoat. "If Jack's dying, it'll be the first time."

Sam joined them in the hall. "Stop talking about it. Clark, you'd better go tape the windows. Georgette, stay here tonight." Sam suggested they all watch a movie to get through the storm. "*Les Diaboliques*. Clouzot. I've got a great print."

But Georgette moved to the door. "Isn't that a movie about Lesbians that really aren't Lesbians? I love you, Sam, but not that much. I like new movies."

Sam said she liked old movies because she herself was old.

"Right. Old enough to be my mother," agreed Georgette. "And as you know, I've always wished you were."

"Only because I spoiled you."

"Thank God."

Sam noted that she had only told Georgette the same things she'd told Annie—that she was smart and strong and could do anything she wanted to do. That she was beautiful and lovable and someday she'd find the right someone to love her as she deserved.

Georgette let Sam help her into her raincoat. "You introduced me to high heels and Häagen-Dazs espresso ice cream. When Kim sided with Mr. Neubruck after he'd called the police on us about blasting out our Nirvana tape all night, you told Kim, 'You were young once too.' I'll never forget that. Not that Kim ever was young."

"Honey, your dad told me one night your mom sank a 30-foot putt at the golf course at midnight in her bra and panties."

"Sam, you made that up."

"Call me when you get home," Sam urged. "I don't like your being alone over there."

"Neither do I."

"You'll find the One, Georgette."

"That would be nice, just somebody to open jars."

Sam shrugged. "You'll find him. And he's going to love you like nobody's loved you."

Georgette, laughing, asked Annie, "Why does Sam always sound like some awful soundtrack song?"

"Clark and I blame it on Jill."

"Her old girlfriend?"

"Yeah, she ran off to Belize and can't defend herself."

Sam handed Georgette her yellow rain hat. "I'm serious. The two of you should drive up to Annapolis after the holiday. Georgette should meet this condo neighbor of yours, Trevor Smithwall. He's an FBI analyst, Georgette, and an archeology buff. Isn't that right, Annie? They're made for each other."

"Ignore her, Georgette." Annie left for the kitchen, to help Clark tape the windows.

Sam tied the hat straps under her neighbor's chin. "I'm serious, honey. Trevor sounds like a nice guy."

"Sam, you think *Brad's* a nice guy. Even I wouldn't go that far."

"But this guy Trevor could be your type."

Georgette buttoned her raincoat. "He's my type if he's got a combined total of at least three arms and legs and he weighs less than four times his IQ. Can he spell his last name? Has he been convicted of any capital crimes—I don't mean just charged, but actually convicted?"

"Stay here." Sam ran to the kitchen and returned with a big plastic bag of spicy tuna rolls and half the birthday cake, none of which Georgette wanted, but all of which she took.

Sam opened the door. "Run. It's raining."

"Oh really?"

"Call me when you get home!"

"Sam, I live next door!"

"Call me, Georgette! And if this gets worse—"

"I know! Go to the basement."

Sam found Clark alone in the morning room, attaching big Xs of masking tape to the bay windows. She hugged her arms around her Now Voyager T-shirt. "Where's Annie?"

"Still taping kitchen windows. So you hear Brad's going to fly here? I guess he's ready for life at twelve o'clock high again." Brad's repeated use of the phrase about Annie's stress had become a family joke.

The sound of the swing on the porch banging against a window startled them. Sam ran outside to tie it to a corner post. Thunder booms rattled the house and all the lights flicked suddenly off and on.

In the darkness the telephone rang. Carrying her plate of sashimi, Annie hurried in from the kitchen to answer it, assuming it would be Brad again. Sam, Clark, and the dog Malpy squeezed around her in a circle.

It was a strange man with a soft, faintly accented voice. He asked for Annie Peregrine.

"This is Annie Goode. Who is this? Is this the Miami police?"

"Miami police? Those *pingitas*!" the man exclaimed. "No! This is Rafael Rook. Your papa asked me to call you. 'Rescue or else the day is lost,' as the Swan of Avon would put it, and in fact did. Shakespeare. Annie, your papa gravely needs your help."

Lightning forked over the sky. Another branch from the oak tree crashed into the yard. She had trouble hearing the soft-spoken man.

"I'm sorry. Why did you say you're calling?"

"I'm a friend of your papa's from Miami. Pretty much his one and only in these sorrowful times."

Rafael Rook had an odd husky young voice, like rustling straw, with a curious style, as if he'd learned to talk from old paperbacks piled into book bins and sold for a quarter. He told Annie that he was calling her from a South Beach Sam's Club in order to urge her to hurry to St. Louis at the dying wish of her dying father, who was dying.

"From what?" she asked.

"He asked me specifically not to discuss it. A man like that! The key to happiness, Annie, is an education. I am Cubano. Well, I think of myself so. I left Havana young and fell into bad company. I never had the good fortune of college. But your father? Definitely, absolutely an education."

"I bet." Not noticing, she dipped her white tuna into too much wasabi and teared up when she swallowed it.

Rook said, "Jack tells me he taught you to do fractions at four years old."

Annie admitted that this was in fact true. Her father had taught her to read and write, add and subtract, ask questions. Maybe that was why, she sarcastically allowed, she was interested in the question of whether or not he really was dying.

"Nothing's certain, you agree?" Rook sounded as if he wanted to discuss the matter. "But brief candles, quintessence of dust, no way around it. Still, should Jack go to that undiscovered country alone? You, his only child, you're all he's got." Rook paused. "And myself, if you'll permit me, I have the honor to be his friend. Some in Miami may even tell you, who's Jack Peregrine? Who cares if he's dying or not? I reply, is this what life comes to, a man who lost thirty thousand dollars at Hialeah in an afternoon, smiled, what a smile, and drove to Palm Beach and picked up the tab for the whole table at the finest restaurant, a la carte? Where are those friends now that ate Jack's chateaubriand? Not at his side."

"You're in Miami?" Annie set down the plate of sashimi. "Is my dad in St. Louis?"

But the bizarre Latino caller could not be deterred from his philosophizing. "What does Jack's fate tell you about the human race?—"

She interrupted. "Mr. Rook, if you and my father are such close friends, tell me something he's said to you about my mother. Does she live there in Miami with him?"

He was clearly taken aback. "Your mother? Jack's a bachelor."

Sam kept plucking at Annie's sleeve, whispering, "Jack could be making it up. He could do handwritings, voices, anything."

But whoever this stranger was, he wasn't her father. Even after all these years apart, Annie was sure she would recognize her father's bright metallic voice. Rook's timbre rustled like leaves blown across a yard. "You're sure you're a close friend?"

He puffed dismay. "Close? What could be closer than lying side by side in a prison cell in son-of-a-bitch Cuba?"

His response wasn't the one she'd expected. "Cuba? My dad was in prison in Cuba? When?"

Rook said, "To me it feels like yesterday. One year, twelve long months, in that cell. Jack gave me the will to survive. Otherwise? I would have slit my throat on a rusty can lid, if I'd had a can, which I didn't. I would have woven a noose of my own rotted trouser legs. They took away even time. No watches. But the worst was a bastard threw my guitar to the floor and just slowly stepped on it for the cruel pleasure."

She asked if he were a musician.

"Ah...Here's a question: Is what we are, what we might have been? Or is what we are, what with such sorrow, we have become?" He paused as if expecting her to offer an answer. When she didn't, he added, "'I have a reasonable good ear in music.' To my mother's grief I chased rumba down many excessively scummy streets. I could tell you—"

"Don't. Mr. Rook! Mr. Rook—"

"In Miami my cousin found me a job with a dance band. Sad to say, many years later I returned to Havana, with your papa, and that's when the bastards got us." Over Annie's attempts to interrupt, Rafael described how, for twelve months in a small slimy lightless cell, her father had recited Shakespeare from memory every night until dawn. "Oh, the poems and songs. He could just pull out a little verse every night from his head and it would be enough to keep me from misery. Compared to him, that Spider Woman Kiss, that was just silly movies. But this was Shakespeare. Thing of beauty, your papa. I can never repay him...What a heartbreak. And yet death comes to us all if we're mortal, which they say historically we are—"

Annie took advantage of the young man's necessary intake of breath. "Just stop there, okay! If my dad's dying, why did he leave Miami and rush off to St. Louis?"

That sudden decision, Rook confessed, remained a mystery. In fact, Jack had left Golden Days entirely against Rook's advice.

"What about his doctors? Isn't Golden Days a hospital?" Annie paced, yanking the phone cord free of the leaping Malpy.

"Golden Days? It's a petty creep down a dusty hall. I had a connection there and we slipped him in but I would not recommend it. Now he very much needs you to meet him in St. Louis with the *King of the Sky*. There are people who...do not wish him well."

Annie didn't doubt it. "What does Dad want, the big emerald?"

"Big emerald?" The Cuban sounded greedy. "You found a big emerald?"

"Or the password in his jacket? Do you know what this password's to?"

A little too eagerly, he asked her to tell him what the password was.

She declined to do so. "Rook, what the hell are you and my father up to? Why does he need a plane? Can he even fly a plane? Frankly, I never thought he could."

Rook claimed that Jack could do anything. Conversely, Jack and he were up to nothing. "I would basically like to offer him a helping hand at this juncture, because of my great debt to him; that's the simple truth, Annie, no insinuation that truth is simple."

Annie sat down in the chair that Clark carried over to her. "'Juncture,' meaning he's definitely dying?"

"What's definite? But when a man's about to slip off a mortal coil, Annie—I feel I can call you Annie, because he talks about you all the time—a man goes to the core. So, if you want my advice, if it's a password of Jack's, it will have something to do with you, he is so proud of your accomplishments—"

The remark took her aback. Never before had she considered that, despite their long separation, her father might talk about her, and apparently with pride. She was surprised that he would even know of any accomplishments of hers. Sam must have told him. "Have you heard of my aunt Sam?"

The man said yes, "absolutely, of course. His sister Sam sends him news about your goings on. Impressive, number one in your class. In the end, Annie, you cannot take it or leave it with *familia*. This is what—you agree?—gives us our humanity."

Although reluctantly moved to hear that her father had boasted about her, and although already planning to fly to St. Louis, she took a caustic tone. Even if he were dying, she asked, why should she deliver a plane to St. Louis to a man who'd thrown her away when she was seven years old?

Rook coughed as he mumbled, pardon him, but if he had been blessed with Annie's brains, and if *his* padre were dying—which he wasn't alive *to* die, because he had already died, young and much too fast, of this bastard cancer. And *his father's* father,

Simon Rook, had died even younger, in fact a horrible death off
the coast of Cuba, thanks to the lying *cabrones* in the CIA.

Annie jumped to her feet, pacing. Sam rescued the plate as
she flung out her arm. "Twenty years ago my 'padre' unloaded me
on his sister and waltzed off into the ozone! So you'll excuse me if
I don't get worked up over Jack Peregrine's 'dying' wish. So fuck
you!" Her outburst surprised her.

Rook's rejoinder was also unexpected. He shouted loudly:
"*Excuse me,* that is absolutely, definitely a lie! You have
insulted me!"

But then she heard a pounding noise, grunts, and shrieks and
realized he wasn't talking to her anymore but to someone in his
vicinity. Where had he said he was? South Beach? A store?

Finally he blurted out in a choked way that a vicious old lady
was trying to wrestle out of his hand his mobile phone, claiming
it was hers.

Annie heard more thumps and shouts. Then Rook was yelling, "I believe we still have a tiny ember in Florida of what once
upon a time we called Liberty. Do not accuse me of committing
a crime! Why would I steal your cheap cell phone? It's pink!"

Annie could hear a woman's voice shouting something
about how this man had stolen her purse out of her shopping cart
and that he was a foreigner who thought he could get away with
robbing her because she was old, whereas people like him had no
right even to be in Florida.

Rook shouted back, "Pardon me, my great-grandfather Isaiah
Rook was a rabbi in Miami! My mother's brother was up to his
waist in the Everglades for Alpha 66 and my grandfather Simon
Rook was personally recruited for a little something called Oper-
ation 40 by names you'd toss your cookies at if you heard them!
That is what the fuck I'm doing in Florida!"

"What's going on? What's wrong with Jack?" whispered Sam,
tugging at Annie's sleeve.

Annie shouted into the phone. "Listen to me, Rook!"

The Cuban was panting. "Good-bye! The same to you!...Not
you, Annie. That old lady, she's gone, *gracias a Dios!* I apologize...

Ah, let me take slow breaths. As the Great Buddha said, '*La manera no está en el cielo. La manera está en el corazón.*'"

Annie ignored a sarcastic impulse to inquire into Buddha's ability to speak Spanish and instead asked Rook to tell her exactly what was wrong with her father's health.

Rook caught his breath loudly, like a balloon losing air, slowly calming himself. "He's dying."

"Dying from what?"

"Slings and arrows. Life. Pretty much."

"Was it an accident?"

He coughed. "Accident? Annie, I'll tell you my personal theory. When you're born, in my opinion, they send you down here with everything worked out ahead of time, like, you know, a fixed race or a stacked deck of cards or a book they wrote the end of first. It could be your astronomical stars, your karma or, I don't know, a lot of people are into this personal feng shui— From cancer, I'm sorry to tell you."

Annie caught at the reality of the word. "Cancer? What kind?"

"Terminal."

"Cancer?" cried Sam.

Clark whispered, "Get the name of Jack's doctor. I could phone, see what's going on."

But the Cuban suddenly shouted again, "You called the cops on me, lady? You called the cops? Annie, I gotta go!"

"Call back," she demanded. "I don't know where in St. Louis he is!"

"Good bye!"

"Don't hang up!"

There was a loud crackle in the phone.

Annie turned to her aunt. "Rook hung up."

"Call him back." Sam grabbed Annie's arm.

Annie dialed the incoming number, but voice mail announced, "This is Evelyn Whitestone's phone. Please leave me a message." Then the line went dead.

Chapter 14

The Palm Beach Story

Sam said, "I told you he was weird, that Rafael Rook."

Picking up the sashimi, Annie absently ate it whole. "He said he was in prison with Dad in Cuba."

"Your poor dad. He would have hated that."

"Anybody would have hated it." Annie turned to Clark. "So he says Dad's dying of cancer."

"What kind?"

"He didn't say." Annie sat down on the bottom stair. "I remember one time when Dad told some suckers he was dying of cancer because he wanted to sell them this fake land and I flipped out because I believed he was dying and he told me it wasn't true, it was just a trick, he was fine."

Clark rubbed her back. "I'm sure he *is* fine." He noted that they should all remember how Jack had pulled the same "I'm dying, buy my house cheap" trick in Savannah and had been arrested for it. "Dying's not in his personality."

Abruptly all the lights went out and they heard the porch door tearing loose. In the dark Malpy raced around the room barking wildly, begging to be picked up.

"Clark, I hope you and the Weather Channel are happy at last!" shouted Sam, upset by more than the weather. "Now it *is* a damn tornado."

The screen door shattered loudly as it blew off the porch.

Clark called out through the darkness. "Get the dogs. Go to the basement!"

Grabbing up Teddy and Malpy, they felt their way down the steep steps to the old Pilgrim's Rest cellar, where Sam had collected all the broken objects, old toys, cracked leftovers of past generations that she couldn't squeeze up into the attic. Here in the cool stone space, Peregrines had hidden for over a hundred years from bad weather and other calamities, like Yankee invaders and teenaged parties with amplified music.

Between the furnace and three of Annie's bicycles, illuminated in the beam of Sam's large flashlight, they stood together, listening to the cracks of snapping trees overhead. Sam used her light to see her cell phone to call Georgette, who told her, "Thanks. I'm in my basement, sitting on a moldy beanbag."

"Call me back every ten minutes."

Malpy whimpered but Teddy fell quickly to sleep.

After a while, Sam started her imitation of Katherine Hepburn. "'Nature, Mr. Allnut, is what we are put in this world to rise above.'"

Because niece and uncle had lived for years with a woman who owned a movie store and who responded to life crises almost exclusively by quoting classic films, the inimitable Hepburn voice, even badly mimicked, was somehow as soothing as a lullaby.

"*African Queen*," Annie said.

Howling wind tore a whole tree loose with a terrible noise; it crashed near the house. "Oh God," moaned Sam. "This is scary."

Clark began: "'Fasten your seatbelts.'"

Annie finished. "'It's going to be a bumpy night.'"

"You two are making fun of me, aren't you?" Sam shined the flashlight in their faces.

Annie and Clark told her yes, they were, and made her laugh. On they went, thinking of more quotes for Sam, soothing her with the murmur of memory; it was what they had done for decades, watching old movies on the couch together, eating with chopsticks from their Chinese takeout boxes.

Finally Sam told them to stop. "It's like getting your hair brushed too long. First it's a pleasure, then it gets on your nerves."

Silence fell. After a long pause, Clark asked, "Know why the poor man became a baker?"

Annie answered, "Because he kneaded the dough."

"Guess I already told you that one. How about the butcher that backed into his meat grinder and got a little behind in his work?"

Sam muttered, "Please. Top ten worst." She phoned Georgette, whose line was busy or dead.

Gradually the noise of the storm subsided. Malpy stopped squeaking. Clark pushed open the cellar doors and they looked out. Rain was falling but the wind had eased. Pilgrim's Rest had survived another storm.

Back in the front hall, Sam lit the half-dozen kerosene lanterns she kept for such an emergency, just as she kept extra water in jugs and extra gasoline in cans, extra salt for the driveway, first aid kits, antidotes. She telephoned Georgette next door again and reached her. "I told you to call me in ten minutes! Have you got candles?"

Georgette said she had found the five-dozen candles Sam had given her during last winter's predicted power outage. "I was on the phone with my mother. I told her I was alone hiding in the basement in the middle of a twister and she said she'd gotten a birdie on the eighth hole."

Sam sighed. "Tell me something you don't know."

"Okay. Annie's not up in that plane. Is she?"

"Ask her." Sam handed Annie the phone. Clark and she carried the lanterns around to check the house.

Annie told Georgette that she definitely planned on going to St. Louis. "The storm's pretty much over."

"It is? Look out the windows."

"I have to find my dad."

"Wouldn't you have done it by now? I mean, almost twenty years? It's a big house, but it's not that big."

"Don't be funny. This so-called friend of his, Rafael Rook, called and says he's got terminal cancer."

"But somehow you don't believe it." Georgette sighed. "Take it from me. They do die. George is in an urn next to his Rotary awards. On the other hand, Kim's in a golfing retirement center shooting birdies. Count your blessings? Okay, I'm going to bed. I wanted to watch the History Channel. It was the excavation of Pompeii. I don't know why a petrified dog should be so fascinating."

Annie's shoulders relaxed; it soothed her to talk to Georgette. "I'll keep you posted. I've got to settle this so I can get back to Maryland for my test flight."

"Yeah, well, it's always some world record or other with you. Sam wants me to drive back to Maryland with you to meet your condo buddy Trevor."

"Why don't Sam and Clark worry about getting themselves dates and leave us alone? *Salut, cherie.*"

"Love you. I strenuously advise you not to fly to St. Louis tonight but when did you ever listen to me?"

Annie raised an eyebrow. "When you told me marrying Brad was a good idea."

"Don't ever listen to me." Georgette shrugged her soft shoulders. "I'm a sucker for muscles. I'd like to swing through a jungle like Lucy, from one Homo erectus biceps to another. I'd teach them all to talk and they'd all grunt that they loved me. *A bientot.*"

• • •

As she packed, Annie called Trevor at Chesapeake Cove. Their agreement was a long-standing one: she took care of his West Highland terrier whenever he went on vacation; he took care of her cat whenever she had to leave home. Now she asked if he could watch Amy Johnson if she had to be away longer than she'd originally thought?

He could. He asked if they'd escaped the tornado. The news had said it was close.

"Very close. But we're fine. Georgette's upset because she can't get the History Channel."

"I don't blame her."

"She's my oldest friend and she's never met you."

"Define oldest," Trevor said.

"You've seen her picture in my living room. She's a doctor, she's single, and she spent last summer on an archeological dig in Sicily."

Trevor said, "What's wrong with her?"

"Nothing. What's wrong with you? *You're* single."

"True."

"I need another favor."

"Date your friend?"

"No. Help me find my father. He sent me a letter he's dying. A FedEx! He's in St. Louis. But I'm not sure where. The Miami police are after him. He's an ex-con; there should be a criminal record. Can you find out what he's been up to?"

Trevor said he'd always wondered why Annie hadn't asked him to do this for her before. Here she was with a criminal father who'd disappeared; here she was with a friend who worked with criminal databases at the FBI. Seemed like a match. He was happy to check into Jack Peregrine.

When Annie was carrying Teddy to her pagoda bed, the lights came back on. The old dog's cloudy blind eyes, blue as glass, seemed to be looking right at her. "What do you think, Teddy?" she asked the Shih Tzu. "What should I do? If I were Claudette, I'd get on a train and I'd meet a millionaire but then I'd remarry my husband."

The dog licked the air, as if to test out this option from *The Palm Beach Story*. Then she shook her head.

"Right. I don't want to remarry Brad." Annie took Teddy with her to the black baby grand piano on which long ago Sam had played duets with Georgette's aunt Ruthie. The old yellowed sheet music was still in the bench. She found a pastel copy of "Lara's Theme" from *Dr. Zhivago*. "Ruthie Nickerson" was written elaborately on the cover, and in the same blue ink "con amore."

Photographs crowded together on the piano's closed lid. As a child, Annie had grown accustomed to freezing with a grin half-a-dozen times a day, while Sam recorded her life with a camera of one sort or another: Annie at Brownie camp, on the track team, on her way to an Emerald High dance, Annie the naval cadet, Annie putting wedding cake to Brad's lips, Annie stretching, eating, napping, Annie just holding up her hands in surrender to the lens. When she'd protested at being subjected to daily photography, Clark had asked her to indulge her aunt: all these pictures were Sam's proofs of a happiness she hadn't expected. They were like red votive candles lit in a church, pledges of gratitude.

On the piano there were a few framed snapshots of the young Sam and Jack as well. And there was an old photo in a bright '70s frame of five teenagers seated on the Pilgrim's Rest porch. All were tan and wore shorts and T-shirts, their arms hung over one another's shoulders, all laughing, knocking into each other: Sam, Clark, Jack, Georgette's father George Nickerson, and a pretty girl who was leaning out at an angle from the porch rail to crook her elbow around Clark's neck. Annie had been told that this was George's sister Ruthie, who'd run off with a married man. In the picture Ruthie appeared to be very attractive but it was hard to see her face because of the huge sunglasses she wore.

There was also a solo picture of Clark, thin and squinting into a Vietnamese sunset. Beside it was a wedding photo of Clark and his first wife, Tuyet, who'd died shortly after he'd brought her home to America, of a rare kind of cancer. Nearby was a framed newspaper photo of Sam leaping to hit a tennis ball ("Peregrine Takes Title" said the small headline) and stuck in the corner of the frame, as if to emphasize the contrast, was a snapshot of Sam at sixteen, unhappy in a prom dress, in front of the Pilgrim's Rest Christmas tree, with a valiant chin, standing between her intoxicated father the judge and her sedated mother Grandee of the Savannah Worths, all three of them with smiles that would, Clark said, "scare the Munsters."

Scrambling to get down from Annie's arms, Teddy knocked off a small black-and-white picture at the piano's far edge. As the old Shi Tzu trotted indignantly onto her velvet poof and sighed a long sigh settling there, Annie picked up the photo. It was a picture she didn't remember, of her dad and her, from their days on the road, shortly before he'd left her in Emerald. She had always divided her past between those blurred years of travel and the start of her "real life" when she had come to live at Pilgrim's Rest. It was a jolt to see the old life—a professional snapshot taken in an elegant beachside restaurant—here in the Pilgrim's Rest living room.

More startling, the picture was the same as the one that the Miami detective Sergeant Daniel Hart had described seeing in her father's room. One of the photos must be a copy of the other. In the restaurant banquette, she was snuggled next to the sandy-haired, open-armed Jack Peregrine. His gleaming suit and slender tie made more luminous his deep-tanned smiling face and his trim blonde mustache. Annie was wearing her favorite dress, the green velvet, and her cowboy boots. Her head rested against the crisp white of her father's shirt; above her head his tan fingers held a cigarette. On the banquette table sat a cake with candles. Other diners filled in the background around them, laughing women, men in thin ties and sleek suits.

Annie took the photo out of its frame. On the back in her father's handwriting was scrawled, "Annie and Jack, The Breakers, Palm Beach." They had been celebrating her seventh birthday a few weeks ahead of the event, for the picture was dated June 1982. So from here they must have driven to St. Louis and then east to Emerald, where on July Fourth he'd given her away to Sam and Clark.

Palm Beach and Miami. The Hotel Dorado on the letterhead of the folded note in Jack's flight jacket was in Miami. The convalescent home Golden Days was in Miami too. The detective Hart and the peculiar Rafael Rook had also both called her from Miami.

Miami. What had her father and she been doing there? Life at The Breakers looked affluent and happy. At what joke of her father's was she laughing? Why had they left Miami and driven suddenly to St. Louis and then just as suddenly come east to Emerald?

There had been earlier birthday celebrations of Annie's that had ended in tears. Her dad had often joked about her crying at her parties. He'd recounted how on her fifth birthday, she'd run out of her hotel bedroom wailing, "Be quiet!" at a drunken, startled crowd of his friends. How, on her third birthday, beside some motel swimming pool in the moonlight, she'd screamed at a friend of her father's to stop swinging a stick at a big piñata hanging from a palm tree. But the man had whacked the Mexican paper donkey anyhow until it broke in two and the other adults had laughed although Annie had kicked at their legs to make them stop.

On that occasion, her father had picked her up, rocking her back and forth, laughing, showing her how the piñata donkey was made to be broken, how it held a broken clay pot of candies and trinkets. She had been inconsolable.

But in this photograph of a celebration of her seventh birthday at The Breakers, Annie's head was tilted with laughter. She studied this child, who wore a small pendant with her velvet dress, recalling that her father had given her that tiny ruby the year before but had then taken it back, "just borrowing it," he'd said. Presumably he'd sold it. The thought occurred to her now that when he'd shown up running through the cornfield into Pilgrim's Rest on that strange hot summer day, when he'd given Sam the raw ruby for Annie's seventeenth birthday, he'd done so in order to make up for the pendant that he'd "borrowed" ten years earlier.

"Happy birthday, have a good life," Annie said aloud to the happy child in the picture. She slid it back into its frame and returned it to the piano.

Looking up, she saw her aunt and uncle in the hall watching her; holding chopsticks; they were eating together from a large platter of spicy tuna rolls. With the now sagging helium multicolored balloons settled around their feet, they looked as if they were standing in a rainbow.

Sam came over and blew out the kerosene lantern on the mantel.

"I told you this was a twister," Clark said, swiping at the smoky air.

"If you tell me one more time, I'm going to clobber you," Sam warned him.

Annie showed them the Palm Beach picture. "I don't remember this being here."

Sam explained that it had come out of Annie's suitcase. "It was in there when you arrived, along with twelve thousand dollars cash and your birth certificate. Wrapped in a velvet dress. A few years ago I came across it and put it in a frame."

Annie said she had a vague memory of those chandeliers in the domed ceiling of The Breakers, the tall beautiful windows and elegant chairs. She thought she could remember the sound of the ocean outside but might be imagining it.

"Your dad lived in Miami off and on," Sam said, studying the picture. "He called me once from The Breakers, maybe a couple of years ago and said he'd just been remembering how the two of you had stayed there on your birthday."

Annie pointed at the photograph. "See this menu on the table? Dad bet a guy a hundred dollars he could show me a page of this menu for fifteen seconds and that then I could repeat it word for word, including the prices…I was scared I would get it wrong." She moved away from the piano. She didn't want to remember how hard she'd tried to impress her father; the pleasure she'd taken in his laughter; how, with big pieces of pastel chalk, she would painstakingly, accurately write down the numbers of cars' license plates on the asphalt of motel parking spaces after the cars had driven off; how she'd correctly identify all the cards in the discard pile of poker games. She'd done it for his praise. "He was grooming me to count cards for him. He always wanted us to go to Vegas. At least I didn't end up working for criminals."

"Really?" Sam picked up her niece's U.S. Navy officer's cap from the couch, flicked the brim skeptically.

"Don't start. Where's that birth certificate that said Claudette Colbert was my mother? Could you find that?"

"I could find the straw from your first milk carton. Probably in the same suitcase as that jacket of your dad's, up there in the attic."

Annie said her real question was why should Jack Peregrine, for whom only the future had ever felt real, now want her to bring him so many pieces of the past?

Clark took off his glasses as if to make sure they were the ones he'd been wearing for years. "My real question is, why are you doing it?"

In the hall, Annie opened the front door and looked up at the black sky. "D. K. won't clear me if it's not safe."

Sam sighed. "Could we remember that D. K. crashed his plane into the China Sea?"

"That was in broad daylight," Clark said. "Look on the bright side."

Chapter 15
The Aviator

Annie phoned D. K. again about the *King of the Sky*, which he still garaged for her at Destin Airworks. He had checked out the plane and needed to do a little more work on the engine. Give him an hour.

She checked through the Pilgrim's Rest kitchen cabinets while she tried to reach Hotel Dorado in Miami. The usual jar of candied papaya pieces that nobody wanted sat on the top shelf. The bag of Snickers bars was hidden where Clark always hid candy from himself, behind the big cobwebby cans of pureed pumpkin that every Thanksgiving Sam planned to make into pies but never did.

No Jack Peregrine was registered at Hotel Dorado.

She called the number on the letterhead for Golden Days. A woman answered in a bright southern voice. "G.D., may I help you?" The woman sounded bizarrely like Annie's ex-mother-in-law Mama Spring Hopper, who had always cursed in abbreviations. But "G.D." proved to be short for Golden Days, an extended-care home. The receptionist conceded cheerfully that most of their patients were "pretty terminal," but declined to provide details about how they'd gotten that way. She did admit that as far as she could tell from her "guest book," they had never had any "residents" named Jack Peregrine, after which she cheerfully clicked off.

Annie arranged dried fruit into geometric patterns on the kitchen table while trying to reach Trevor. When he finally called back, he reported that he'd discovered a few things about her dad: an agent friend had found eleven charges against John Ingersoll Peregrine, with three convictions, a total of twenty-five months served, half-a-dozen aliases. There were three outstanding felony warrants in two states. Also Florida reported an APS for a recent jailbreak. The charges were consistent with Annie's description of her father as a "swindler" and included a variety of white-collar fraud crimes, including forged checks, fake options and securities, counterfeited land deeds, shakedowns, hustles, stings.

She asked if there were anything in the folder about an incarceration in Cuba a year or so ago. Or anything about Cuba's interest in a 16th-century religious artifact known as *La Reina Coronada del Mar* that Jack had allegedly stolen? After a long pause, Trevor said no, he saw nothing about Cuba. "Reina what?"

"*Reina Coronada del Mar.* The Queen of the Sea. A gold statue."

Trevor said such a statue was nowhere mentioned in the files. Curiously, however, the sheet on Jack Peregrine had come to an abrupt end eleven months ago with a sealed indictment. Everything after that was closed.

To Annie it was impossible to believe that her father had reformed. But perhaps he'd gotten so good at his crimes that he was no longer caught, either by the police or by those mysterious men he'd always named for cartoon villains—The Crocodile, Dr. No—those men who'd barged into their lives on the road and threatened them. Like the large man with a gun who'd kicked open the door to their motel room at midnight while they were watching *The Ten Commandments*...She stopped talking midsentence. "Wait! Royal Coach, that's it! Trevor, thank you, thank you!"

He chuckled at her exuberance. "For what?"

"The name of the motel. Dad and I were watching *The Ten Commandments* in the Royal Coach Motel in St. Louis. A man broke in, we got away from him, and we drove straight to

Emerald and Dad dropped me off here at Pilgrim's Rest. So it's the last place we stayed together. Royal Coach Motel. That's where he's gone."

"Sorry. I'm not following you."

She said it didn't matter, she'd explain it all when she returned to Chesapeake Cove. She was heading to St. Louis tonight in her Piper Warrior.

"Why don't I see if I can get a field agent there to check things out for you?"

Annie couldn't explain why she felt that she had to go herself to find her father, but she did.

"Well, good luck." Trevor said to let him know what she found out. "And I'll check into this Cuba thing…So, any message for Amy Johnson? We're headed for bed."

"Tell her I miss her, not that she'll care."

"You never know with cats. People either."

Annie said, "You do know with cats. That's what I like about them."

She ran back to the living room where Clark and Sam were sharing more spicy tuna rolls. "I figured it out. Dad's in the Royal Coach Motel in St. Louis!"

"Ah." Clark nodded slowly. "The fishing fly. Royal Coach-man. What a jerk."

"Dad knocked a man out and took his gun. There was a pink neon coach with four horses on the motel sign near the pool."

Clark mildly wondered why Jack hadn't simply written down the name of the motel in his cryptic note to her. "I repeat. What a jerk."

"Never write things down," Annie explained; it was in the top five of her father's old crime "lessons."

The Royal Coach still had its St. Louis listing. The young man at the desk told her that the motel had been in business in the same location for over thirty years. No one was registered as Jack Peregrine but the clerk, a friendly and bored college fellow, described in detail a late check-in yesterday of a man vaguely fitting her description of her father. The man had returned to the night desk around 1 a.m., borrowed a pair of scissors, and while sitting in the lobby had cut off his very good trousers above the knees. Annie asked the clerk to check the name on the registration.

The man had registered as Clark Goode.

"Fucking wonderful!" Annie took a breath. "I'm sorry. That's not my father's real name. Clark Goode is my uncle's name and he's right here in North Carolina and has been all week."

"Listen," confided the clerk, "nothing surprises me. Last night I had a transvestite pull in driving a 35-foot Gulfstream Yellowstone RV; checked in as Barbra Streisand. But maybe it was Barbra." The clerk added that the man who'd cut off his own trousers had specifically insisted on a particular room in the motel, 115, when he'd arrived—an unusual request, since all the rooms were identical.

That evening the clerk had noticed the man swimming back and forth in the motel pool. Then, hours later, he'd seen him once more, at the pool's edge, this time smoking a thin cigar, lying on his back on the concrete as if he were sunbathing, although it was three in the morning. The man had appeared to be staring up at the stars, not that you could see many.

Annie asked if it were possible to speak with whoever had cleaned Room 115. The intrigued clerk told her to call back in fifteen minutes. She did so and learned then from a Guatemalan maid, whose story the desk clerk translated, that just this morning the maid had seen two men in the parking lot with the person who'd cut off his trouser legs. He'd walked back to his room with these two men, talking nonstop in an agitated way. An hour afterwards, the maid had found bloody towels in the 115 bathroom, where the fan ventilator cover from the ceiling had been removed and was lying on the tile floor of the shower.

• • •

Clark telephoned St. Louis hospitals to see if a Jack Peregrine had been admitted to any of them; he hadn't.

"He hates hospitals," Sam said. "He wouldn't go on his own. What do you mean bloody towels? Like hemorrhaging?"

Annie shook her head. "No no. One of those guys probably knocked him down. Well, I've got a lead now."

"Have some coffee first," said Clark.

Sam sighed more loudly than ever. "I'm having a martini. This is all 'putting me way behind in my drinking.'"

Clark absentmindedly identified the quote. "*Thin Man*. You don't drink."

"That was yesterday."

Outside on the roof it sounded as if a gutter was ripping loose. Malpy wriggled under the couch to hide. Sam and Clark hurried to the porch to check the damage.

Annie was running upstairs to repack when the phone in the hall rang again. She picked it up. No one answered. "Hello... Who is this please? Hello, Peregrine-Goode residence..."

Malpy began barking, feeling Annie tense.

"...Hi there. That you, darlin'?" The voice was her father's. No chance of error. She lowered the receiver but slowly brought it back to her ear.

"...Annie?"

"Yes?"

"Annie? It's Dad. Meet me in St. Louis?" He laughed weakly. "How often you get to say that in life?"

Annie sat down. "Where are you? Are you in a hospital? Were you hemorrhaging?"

He laughed again, as always, easily. "You going to hang up if I wasn't?"

Why, she asked, exasperated, *wasn't* he in the hospital if he were dying? Why was there blood in his motel bathroom? Why had he gone to the Royal Coach motel pretending to be Clark Goode?

Her questions appeared to please him. "I knew you'd figure out Royal Coach. I tried to be careful, in case somebody grabbed Raffy when he was mailing you the key. They got to me anyhow. Bad luck."

"Who got to you? And you *should* go to a hospital; you sound awful."

"If you could just fly the *King* to St. Louis tonight…I'd fly it back to you in Emerald, I promise."

While the unexpected had not been unusual from her father, this request amazed her. "Can you even fly a plane? And if you can, damn it, why don't you just rent one!"

He seemed to have trouble breathing and it took several starts for him to get through a sentence. "There's something in the *King* I need. I can't really talk now. I'll explain when you get here. Did Sam find my jacket?"

Annie squeezed her hand tightly around the phone. "Yes and I ripped open the lining. I'm sure you've replaced all the fake cards by now, so what do you want? The gun, the cash? Some password? Is that a password you wrote in the lining of that old pink cap—"

"You kept that cap. Great. Bring it. I'm leaving you a million dollars, darlin'. Just in case, the key I sent's an extra; the panel's in the *King*'s hold—"

"Shut up! I don't want to hear this bullshit, okay? It's just, it's just *bullshit!*" She said that it enraged her that he was so sure she would drop everything, two decades after he'd dropped her, and fly to St. Louis to give him *her* airplane!

He coughed. "But aren't you coming?"

"Yes, I'm coming! That's not the point. You can't *assume* I'd come!"

"Sure I can. Because you love me. It's even odds I'll be dead by the end of the month anyhow. So, Annie, don't you feel a little bit like, well, making up? Take it from me, you'll only regret the things in life you didn't do."

That he should offer her this "advice" on how to live her life was so preposterous, she couldn't even respond.

"You there, sweetheart?"

"…Your buddy, Rafael Rook, says you're 'going fast.'"

"Raffy told you that?"

"Is it cancer?" she asked.

"What's the difference? Okay, tell me the numbers written in the cap."

Her mouth set stubbornly the way it had as a child. "Why should I?"

He laughed cheerfully if without much volume. It had always infuriated her that life struck him as funny. "Because you've got me at your mercy, Annie. It's 'Add and Subtract' time, like we used to play in the car. You still can remember a bunch of numbers? I never could. It amazed me the way you did it. You could remember anything. Tell me the numbers."

Annie was angrily poking her finger at the ornate family motto carved into the square newel post at the foot of the stairs, where a peregrine falcon held a scroll in its talons on which Gothic letters spelled *Peregrinus sum ego*.

"Yes, I can still remember numbers," she told him.

"Bet you're still a damn good poker player."

"Yes, I am."

He coughed. "Okay. What's your price to tell me those numbers? You could say…" He chuckled. "It's life or death."

"Then you should go to the police."

"Come on, tell me. I'll owe you. There's got to be something you want."

"From you?"

"Think about it." He was quiet.

Annie thought about it.

And then all at once she knew that there was in fact something she wanted and that there was a deal she could make with him. She wanted information that she'd long ago put away hoping for, telling herself the knowledge was in any case useless, impractical, unnecessary. She said, "Okay, there's something I want from you."

"Good."

"If I come to St. Louis, I'll tell you the numbers if, *only if*, you'll tell me how to find my mother. And don't tell me she was Claudette Colbert either. That's what I want. That's the only reason I'm coming. My mother."

"…I don't know where your mother is, or how you could find her. That's the truth." His cough was rattling. "But if you come, I'll tell you everything I know."

Annie took a slow breath. "Okay, you give me enough information so I can find out about her. Her name, is she married, does she have other kids? And when I find out everything you know, *then* I'll tell you the password." She glanced at her watch. "I can get the *King* to Lambert in about five or six hours if I start now. Just don't die before I get there."

Again he chuckled with that old infuriating ease. "For the love of Mike, you grew up one tough lady. I'm trying my best here…My game's a little off."

"Are you calling from your own cell phone?"

He said he was and gave her a number.

"And stop using Clark's name. Where are you?"

He said she should stay away from the Royal Coach too. He'd had a "slight screw up" there. Meet him in the Admirals Club at Lambert–St. Louis International Airport as soon as she could manage. He'd wait for her there, as long as it took. But if something should happen to him, just in case, remember this: King, Queen, Sam.

She interrupted. Did he know the Miami police were trying to arrest him in a fraud investigation? That the FBI was involved?

"That's the least of it, honey. Okay, Admirals Club. Sooner's better than later." Again, he seemed unable to breathe easily.

"How sick are you?"

His laughter sounded tight, as if it hurt. He quoted, "'I am peppered, I warrant, for this world.'"

"You stop it, just stop it!"

"Oh, sweetheart, old times. Happy Birthday, Annie. For the record, you really were born on the Fourth of July. You see *The Aviator*? Great movie. The flying part, I mean. Wave of the future." He hung up.

Annie slowly replaced the receiver. She was still staring at it when Sam and Clark came back inside.

Sam hurried over to her. "What in the world's the matter with you?"

"That was Jack," Annie said.

"What?" Sam sat down.

"He quoted Shakespeare and *The Aviator* and then he hung up on me."

"That was Jack?" Sam bent over, rubbing her arms.

"Daniel Hart calls, Rafael Rook calls, now Dad calls. Is this a set up?"

"How did he sound? Dying?"

Taking slow breaths, Annie walked to the porch, looked out at the still roiled sky. "What does dying sound like? He didn't sound good. He told me to fly to St. Louis and look for him in the Admirals Club."

Sam punched at air with a hard jab. "If I hadn't believed he was really on his deathbed, I never would have given you that FedEx! Why do I fall for him?"

"My question for over a quarter of a century," said Clark.

"Well, Clark's right. You can't fly tonight." Sam peered out the window. "This storm has stalled."

"Okay, that's settled." Clark held up the sushi platter. "Anybody want some more?"

Sam started pushing the two of them toward the kitchen. "Let's forget about Jack. People like Jack don't die." She sighed, unable to persuade herself. "Let's eat supper. Who's for forty pieces of chicken korma? Annie, how about some sushi?"

But Annie was back on the phone to D. K. Destin, asking him if the *King of the Sky*'s engine was fixed, if he could get it fueled fast and ready to fly. She'd be at the airfield as soon as she could get there. Please make sure she was good to go. Because she was flying to St. Louis.

D. K. gave a loud derisive laugh into the phone, like a man gone melodramatically mad in a horror movie. "What do Amy Johnson, Amelia Earhart, Bessie Coleman, and Wiley Post have in common?"

Annie knew what he meant but pretended otherwise. "They were all great pilots."

"And?"

"Their planes crashed."

"And?"

"They died."

"Hello baby."

Chapter 16
So Proudly We Hail

Annie and Clark stood in the kitchen, looking out at the rain. Clark said, "Annie, I wouldn't count on the truth from Jack."

Annie shook her head stubbornly. "Either he'll tell me about my mother or he won't. He'll die or he won't. Either way, it'll be over."

From behind Sam's "Gore 2000" magnet on the refrigerator, Clark took a photograph of Annie at a track meet, sprinting to the finish line, her hair flattened against her face, her face twisted, her smile triumphant. He nodded. "You're going to St. Louis. I accept it but I don't like it." He volunteered to drive Annie the eight hundred miles to Missouri instead.

Annie smiled at her uncle. "Clark, if you drove me, Jack would die of old age before we got there. I'm flying the *King*." She had calculated that the Piper Warrior could make it with one stopover to refuel. She could be at Lambert Airport not long after midnight, Central Time. The real question was, would her father even show up? "I'm thinking I should call that detective in Miami, Sergeant Hart." She started to dial his number from memory on her cell phone.

Sam grabbed the phone, agitated; she shoved it into the pocket of her shorts. "No, please, don't call the police. They'll put Jack in jail. He couldn't stand it. Please!"

A sigh, then Annie relented. "…Okay, okay, I won't call the police."

"Just till we sort things out," Sam pleaded.

Annie took her aunt by the arm and walked with her back and forth in the kitchen, soothing her. "But if he's really ill, shouldn't he be in a hospital? If he's bleeding all over motel bathrooms?"

Sam stopped, pulled away. "You said it was practically nothing!"

Annie backpedaled. "Well, I mean, it's not that serious or he wouldn't be on the phone asking me to lend him an airplane, would he? It's just some little screw up." From long thinking about how to interpret her father, she knew he would always be experiencing "little screw ups." Time after time the calamities were a complete surprise to him, as if they'd only by the remotest chance had anything to do with him at all. It dawned on her now that this was a trait he shared with her soon-to-be ex-husband Brad. She recalled how Brad had looked up at her mystified when she'd caught him on their bed in that "slip up" with Melody Wirsh, as if Melody's presence in the bed was as much of a shock to Brad as to Annie.

Clark held up the huge emerald on its chain. "Where do you suppose Jack got this thing?"

"Not by paying for it at Tiffany's," replied Annie.

Sam examined the emerald again. It was doubtless worth a hundred thousand, she theorized. It was very large and looked to be perfectly formed.

"Great. Maybe he wants to trade it for my mother's name." Annie zipped the stone with the fake business cards and the hundred dollar bills inside her father's flight jacket. "Let's go."

Clark left them to go check on Georgette before he brought the car around to the porch.

Annie repeated the numbers from memory, "362484070N and 678STNX211," and wrote them on a message pad, handing the pad to Sam. "Keep this."

Sam checked the numbers against those on the pink cap. "Perfect. And I can't remember a phone number long enough to call it." They walked together through the hallway. "More and more I just remember what happened ages ago, millions of little things, just flashes, from when I was a kid. When you're young, you don't have time to remember your life. When you're my age…" Sam rubbed at her white hair. "The past starts to push the present aside." She pulled from her shorts pocket the copy of Annie's birth certificate that she'd found in the attic. "Know what I mean?"

"Not really." Annie studied the certificate.

Sam's familiar frown deepened. "Well, like when I was eating the chicken korma, I was remembering squeezing soy sauce out of a plastic packet in a booth at House of Joy. The soy sauce squirted onto my mother's blouse sleeve. A gray silk blouse with two little covered buttons at the cuffs. Grandee was furious at me and hit the back of my hand hard with her fork. She didn't like chopsticks and always used a fork." Sam answered an accusation no one had made. "All right, all right, my mother wasn't a loving person. But she had great style."

Annie patted her hands. "No wonder you eat everything with chopsticks, even French fries." She took Sam back into the living room, pointed out a photo on the piano. In the picture, Sam stood among thousands of placard-waving protesters at the 2000 inauguration in Washington. "You've got the love thing and style too. Look at you. It'll always be 1968, Sam."

"I wish," sighed her aunt. "Check out the gray hair in that crowd. We're practically on walkers. Where are all the young people?"

Annie pointed at a group photo of her first flight-school class at their graduation. "Here we are. In a land called Reality where you know you can't change human nature."

"The world is fixable, Annie. You just need to get the real news so you know what to fix."

Annie straightened the Navy photo. Two of those classmates were dead now. She said, "We'd rather hear the news on comedy shows."

Sam helped Annie slip into Jack's old leather flight jacket, rolling up its sleeves for her. "That's about the only place you can hear the real news these days. Vietnam, we had Cronkite."

Laughing, Annie put on her Navy cap. "Sam, just leave war to pros like me."

"You think you're so cynical. Good lord, you telephone Georgette practically every day. There's no reason to do that but love."

"Sure, and I buy organic. But most of all, I work hard to get promoted and—" Annie smiled, patting her flat abdomen, "—stay in shape."

Sam pushed a curl back off her niece's forehead. "Well, an elliptical trainer won't make your heartstrings zing—"

Annie started melodramatically up the stairs. "Please, I beg you, don't sing some awful love song." Her mockery of Sam's romantic songs was an old joke between them. "Love is not a many-splendored thing. Love does not make the world go round."

Sam called after her, "Yes, it does."

Annie turned back at the landing. "Well, I hope it doesn't mean never having to say you're sorry because I am looking for- ward to a major apology from Jack Peregrine!"

Sam patted the carved peregrine hawk in the newel post as she shouted up the stairs to her niece. "Love means saying you're sorry and hearing 'I'm sorry,' every goddamn day of your life. But oh sweetie, maybe you won't hear it from Jack."

There was no answer. Annie had already gone into her room.

"I'm talking to thin air," Sam muttered.

The tall white-haired woman walked back to the piano and picked up the Navy photograph in which her niece was smiling broadly, saluting her commanding officer, Commander Campbell, as he pinned a Commendation Medal on her. Sam compared the photo to the one of the seven-year-old Annie with Jack, seated in The Breakers restaurant. In both pictures, Annie had the same jubilant smile. "Oh, Anne Samantha, look at you." Sam moved her fingers for a moment against the glass of each picture frame, tapped each small exultant face. "Look at you."

The day that Annie's acceptance to Annapolis had arrived in the mail, Sam had felt the heft of the Academy's packet, thinking that it wouldn't be so heavy if it were a rejection; thinking, as she raced up the stairs to Annie's bedroom, that this news would help her niece, this would fix things. Because Annie had been shut up there all day crying. A boy had thrown her over for another girl, a girl on her track team, the girl from whom Annie had to accept the hand-off baton on the last leg of a 4 x 400 relay race. Only a week ago, the girl had dropped the baton behind the fast-sprinting Annie in the blind hand-off and so they'd lost the race. Annie had been furious at the girl, who'd smiled at her smugly, bafflingly. Then the boy had broken the news. After school, Annie had driven home crying so hard that she'd begun hyperventilating and Sam had finally had to hold a paper bag to her face. She hadn't cried that hard since the day her father had left her at Pilgrim's Rest when she'd hidden in the barn behind the wheel of the Piper Warrior.

Late through the night Sam had sat beside the bed where Annie had finally fallen asleep. She knew how her niece must feel. Sam had cried the same way when her partner Jill had not only left her but had charged her for more than her share of their condo equity.

• • •

Wes Campbell, Annie's commanding officer at the Annapolis base, called her cell phone while she was packing. He was sympathetic. "Lieutenant, it's okay. Family emergency. I see here you're owed three separate weeklong leaves that you never took. Make this one of them."

"I just need to find my dad, sir. I don't need a week."

"Lieutenant, you're taking a one-week leave starting at 0800."

"Yes, sir. I'll be back well in time for my test flight."

Campbell chuckled. "I know that. We're counting on you."

"Yes, sir."

"No hesitation?"

"No, sir."

"Well, good." Commander Campbell liked the young female officer, whom he had personally chosen for the new F-35 Lightning II test flight. He made his joke about how times had changed from his own all-male days at the Academy in the '60s, when cadets still wore glasses and had acne and everyone's haircut was as flat as the runway on an aircraft carrier. He made this joke so often to female cadets, it was like a rite of passage when they first heard it from him.

He asked, "Your dad go by Peregrine or Goode? You gals here at Annapolis have so many names hyphened together, it's hard to know what the hell to call you."

"I don't know what name my father's going by these days, sir," was Annie's reply.

The commander frowned as he hung up; he often didn't catch the tone of this generation's remarks. Was that humor? Just a fact?

• • •

Up in her bedroom, Annie slid her neatly coiled jump rope in her duffel bag, then studied her birth certificate before placing it in her purse. The piece of paper looked real. Had she actually been born in that hospital in Key West, twenty-six years ago on the Fourth of July at 8:42 p.m.? Had she really weighed 6 lbs., 3 oz.? Was it even possible that her mother's name had, quite coincidentally, really been Claudette Colbert? Unlikely.

There was a lull in the storm; rain fell slow and soft. Clark was waiting in his Volvo to drive to the airfield when Annie carried her Navy duffel bag out onto the porch. Malpy raced into the opened car. Clark called to Sam, now kneeling in a flowerbed, moving fallen branches off the plants. "Let's go!" They'd driven off so many times in just this way, year after year.

Sam leaned into the car, upset. "We lost most of the hollyhocks and foxglove but for some reason those hideous orange irises of yours look pretty good."

"Every cloud has a silver lining, as I learned when my cousin died and left me his classic GTO." Clark pointed behind Sam. "Did you lock the front door? Go back and check the door."

"Nobody's going to rob us," Sam said. "A tornado just went through here. People are busy."

"Drug addicts don't mind a little storm. Remember that bur-glar that broke into Georgette's house in the ice storm?"

"That was nothing. She played her barking Doberman tape and he ran off."

"I'm locking the door." Clark loped up onto the porch to lock the front door and then returned to the car.

Annie checked her watch. "You want to drive me to the airfield or not?"

"I do not. Did I ever?" He started slowly forward.

From the backseat, Sam called, "Be careful, Clark. The drive's flooded."

"Wait'll she gets to the sky." Her uncle eased the station wagon out into the gravel road. "This cousin's GTO, which I sold for two hundred bucks—"

Annie took a long breath. "—would be worth a fortune today."

"Would be worth a fortune today."

From the back seat Sam muttered, "I've got an Armageddon feeling. Like Tippi, being driven away from the doomed house at the end of *The Birds*."

Annie turned around and repeated what her father had told her so often as he'd spun her in the air all those years ago. "Don't worry. I'm a flyer."

Clark pointed up at the car roof. "So proudly we hail." Tiny pellets of hail were striking the car.

"Now, there you go," smiled Sam. "We are actually hearing a new pun. You never know what life will bring."

Chapter 17

The Great Waldo Pepper

Shortly after Annie's birth, Jack Peregrine had won in a poker game in Key West, or so he'd told Sam, the old single-engine 1975 Piper Warrior, with engine troubles, that he'd brought to Emerald. In the barn at Pilgrim's Rest he repainted its body. He planned to fix its engine and even burnt a crude landing strip into a long flat meadow behind the barn. But as far as Sam knew, Jack had never flown the little red and yellow Warrior on whose wing he had written, "King of the Sky." Instead the plane waited unused in Emerald until the seven-year-old Annie began sitting in it alone for hours, hoping she could, by her stoicism in the cockpit, compel her father to return. She found an ignition key taped to the underside of the wheel cap, near where on her arrival she had huddled so long crying. She used this key to pretend to start the plane, although the motor was long dead.

One Sunday evening, as Sam, Clark, and she sat on the couch with Teddy, watching the movie *The Great Waldo Pepper*, the quiet little girl suddenly announced that she intended to fly the Piper Warrior herself. It was, after all, her airplane.

For the next two years, Annie spent daily hours in the barn playing at flying the single-engine plane, cleaning it, studying it. Since the birthdays when Sam had given her the ride with Georgette in a tethered balloon and the flying lessons in the Pawnee Cropduster at D. K. Destin's airfield on the outskirts of Emerald ("Private Planes, Sell or Rent, Low Monthly Rates, Rides, Instruction, Groups or Single") the small airport had become her favorite place, and D. K., one of the few African American naval combat pilots in Vietnam, had become for a while the most important person in her life. At every meal she asked in her solemn watchful way for flying lessons with the retired lieutenant. It was the first thing for which she asked her aunt and "uncle," other than information about her missing parents.

Sam tried to assuage Clark's concern about Annie's flying mania. "It's like horses, a phase." But years passed and the phase didn't. On rainy afternoons Annie read every book the school library had on aviation; she talked endlessly with D. K. about the triumphs of women pilots, how Katharine Wright had worked right beside her brothers Wilbur and Orville at Kitty Hawk; how Amelia Earhart had flown solo across the Atlantic in 1932; how Jacqueline Cochran, who had broken the sound barrier as early as 1953, held more speed, altitude, and distance records than any other pilot, male or female, in aviation history, more than 200 of them, including in 1964 a speed record of 1,429 miles per hour in the F-104 Starfighter; how the astronaut Sally Ride had rocketed into space from a launch pad in Florida and the whole country had sung to her, "Ride, Sally, Ride!" How Amy Johnson (Annie's idol because the beautiful British pilot had looked so glamorous and been so daring) had taken the record for flying solo from England to Australia in a secondhand De Havilland Gipsy Moth that her father had helped her to purchase, even though back then girls were not supposed to fly planes.

Annie used her earnings from her weekend job at Now Voyager to pay for subscriptions to aviation magazines, which she scanned each month for stories about women pilots. Sometimes she wrote to these women, asking for their autographs. A retired female air-circus flyer, who'd done nine 360-degree loops in an old Cessna 150 to celebrate her ninetieth birthday, wrote her back, enclosing a poster from her flying circus days. The poster was still on the bedroom wall beside Annie's treasured black and white

signed photograph of Amy Johnson. Near them was a framed commemorative U.S. Post Office sheet that D. K. Destin had given
her of the stamp for Bessie Coleman, the African American pilot
who'd had to make her way from Texas to Paris in 1921 to get a
license from the Fédération Aéronautique Internationale because
they wouldn't give her one in America.

"That's right. Her own country treated Bessie like dog-doo
on its shoe," groused D. K., when handing Annie the framed
stamps. "So Bessie got herself to France! The Froggies let that
girl fly. 'Ma cherie, over here you can fly your derriere off if you
want to!' That's a French word, 'civilization,' don't you forget it.
You don't gotta be a white boy to fly; hell, you don't gotta be able
to walk to be able to fly."

Annie said, "I want to fly to France."

"I bet you will one of these days. But you gotta get from one
end of Emerald County to the other first. Finish that checkpoint
list. Master, on. Radios, on. Mixture, rich."

One gray morning on her sixteenth birthday, Annie piloted
the Piper Warrior solo for the first time. It was scary without D. K.
in the plane next to her, correcting, adjusting, without his tapered
big fingers signaling her as if in an urgent language for the deaf.
She'd felt shaky, first climbing into the plane alone, and she'd
stepped back down onto the wing.

He hurried toward her in his wheelchair. "Get back in there!
Don't you prove me right! I'm a sexist child of my times, girl. So
you show me a girl can do solo. Show me you can do it, Sugar
Pie, because you *can*; you're the best in the west, east, south, and
you know it."

Annie believed him because, scared as she was, she knew
he was right. She climbed back into the plane and he waved
her off.

It was D. K. who had replaced the engine in Jack Peregrine's
Piper Warrior and had driven it out of the Pilgrim's Rest barn
and flown it right up off the unmown field into the air with the
girl, thrilled, beside him. Day after month after year, with the
songs of R&B girl groups like the Shirelles and the Supremes

blasting from a boom box beside them—"Baby, It's You" and "Come See About Me" and his favorite, Betty Everett's "It's in His Kiss"—D. K. made her a flyer. He told her that in the cockpit of a plane, nothing mattered but how good you were.

When Annie's pilot license arrived in the mail, she announced to Clark and Sam that they better sit down to hear her news. She planned to go to Annapolis and wanted their help to get there. She wanted a career in the Navy.

Clark not only sat down, he looked as if it might be hard for him to get back up.

"I guess we can't fight destiny," Sam said.

"It's not destiny, it's Destin," growled Clark. "It's that damn D. K. Destin."

Sam advised him, "Don't blame D. K."

That night on the porch, waiting for Annie to return from a party, they argued some more.

"You know what? I blame you, Sam! You've been behind this from the get-go! Secretly egging her on."

"It wasn't all that secret." Sam smiled, pride in the corners of her mouth. "D. K. says Annie's a natural."

Clark slapped his hand on the porch rail. "He says *he's* a natural too! You want Annie pushing herself up River Hill in a damn wheelchair for the rest of her life?"

"That was in Vietnam. We're not in Vietnam, we're in North Carolina."

"We could be in a lot of places where Annie could get herself killed."

"Why did you say that? I'm already worried. Where is she, why aren't she and Georgette home? It's after eleven."

Clark showed her his watch. "It's ten after eleven. Take it easy." It was in this back and forth way that they calmed each other.

When the catalogue arrived from the Naval Academy (the Navy was the first branch of the armed services willing to train women pilots), it started the worst fight of the family's life together. Clark accused D. K. and Sam of collusion in supporting

Annie's desire to go to Annapolis. "It's all his macho Mach
and fixing up damn Jack Peregrine's damn Piper Warrior. And
it's you, Sam, with your 'women can do anything,' even stupid
things like drop bombs for the U.S. Navy."

"Nobody said I was going to drop any bombs," Annie
shouted. "What is it with you two and bombs?"

"Right," Clark threw open his arms. "I'm sorry, those Tomcats aren't carrying missiles. My mistake." He swung an arm in
outstretched irony, knocked over the salt and pepper shakers on
the table, quickly sprinkled salt over his shoulder. "Have a life,
have children—"

Annie yelled at her uncle. "You don't have children! This is
because I'm a girl! You think a girl can't be a fighter pilot?"

Sam agreed. "You're a Republican and a sexist pig, Clark
Goode."

To their shock, Clark, leaped to his feet, shouting. *"I'm a
Republican and I think a girl ought to have more sense!* And D. K.
should have more sense! And Sam, the Great Liberal, you should
have more sense. But I'm a sexist pig because Annie wants to
go learn how to fire Sidewinder missiles on poor bastards on the
other side of the fuckin' world?"

His outburst, indeed the length of his sentence, left Sam and
Annie slack-jawed and produced an agitated growl even from
Teddy. "Take it easy," Sam advised.

"Excuse me. I was eighteen years old in Nha Trang and my
friend's head was blown off and hit me in the fucking chest. And
I'm a sexist pig? Why do *you* want Annie fighting some idiotic
war for fat rich bald men to make money blowing up other coun-
tries and then make more money selling them reconstruction?"

Sam handed him a baby aspirin from her pocket. "Take this
before you have a heart attack! For God's sake, Clark, it's 1993.
There are no wars anymore! The Navy's a career for Annie, not
an invasion."

"Oh, fine! Then there's no problem!"

Clark slammed out of the house in a temper so uncustomary
for him that the aunt and niece looked at each other stunned.

He didn't come home till late that night and strode past them straight to his room.

But the next morning he was back in the kitchen, slowly making coffee as usual. He raised his mug when they sat down to breakfast. He said, "I guess the problems of three little people don't amount to a hill of beans in this crazy world." He took Annie's hand. "You want to join the Navy?"

The young woman squeezed his hand affectionately. "You joined the Army. You thought it was right to go to Vietnam."

He moved his hands away to his glasses, took them off, put them back on. "I was wrong, Annie. There was nothing right about it. Nothing."

She noticed his hands were old, freckled. "Yes. I want to fly jets. D. K. says I'm really good."

"Of course you are." He kissed her hands, one, then the other, pressing them together. "It's just…" He sighed. "You want to fly, fine. Fly tourists to Heathrow, fly college kids to Cancun."

She pulled away. "I want a chance to do something special and the Navy's my chance. Sam! Tell him it's my life."

Clark folded his napkin. "I know it's your life. That's my point." He left the kitchen.

Sam called an old friend, a state senator, about Annie's applying to Annapolis. The senator arranged a nominating letter. Jack Peregrine's daughter became the flyer that she had always assumed her father had never become himself, just as she'd assumed he'd never swum around Manhattan, or won a Silver Star, or beaten Minnesota Fats at nine-ball, or almost sold her to gangsters for $25,000 dollars, or studied with Einstein—unless he'd misheard Einstein's theory of relativity and thought $E=mc^2$ meant that nothing could ever be true.

• • •

At Destin Airworks on the outskirts of Emerald, Sam, Clark, and D. K. huddled under the overhang. The wind suddenly swung back like a boomerang, bringing rain again, blowing the black eagle banner sideways above the hangar. Annie untied the lines from the wings of the Piper Warrior. The plane was old but—as D. K. said—"If you keep your parts oiled, old can be better than new."

D. K. was much grayer than when he'd first begun to teach his prize pupil; his tight cornrow braids, even his once sable-brown skin, had grayed. And his torso had so fattened from decades of being confined to his wheelchair that he wore nothing but black pajamas all year like, he said, "the fuckin' Viet Cong."

Now that Clark and Sam had seen the latest air traffic weather readout, they were urgently trying to stop Annie from leaving for St. Louis until morning.

"I continue to blame the two of you for this whole thing," Clark told Sam and D. K. "If it wasn't for you two, she wouldn't know how to fly a plane."

Sam said, "Oh shut up, Clark. If it wasn't for the two of us, you'd have her still riding a tricycle."

"That's a real slow way to St. Louis," laughed D. K.

Annie called from under the plane. "Just keep talking among yourselves if it makes you feel any better."

"Fine," sighed Sam. "If you're flying…fly."

Chapter 18

Honor Among Lovers

Lifting himself in his wheelchair to ease his back, the crippled vet said maybe it was just as well that his legs were numb because everything else had started to hurt. "Getting old sure isn't for sissies."

Staring glumly at the weather radar on D. K.'s small screen, Clark mumbled, "Isn't getting old what we want Annie to do?"

D. K. admitted that Annie's insistence on taking her small plane up in this rain, when no commercial planes were flying, was "Mustang but shaky."

"'Mustang' meaning foolish bravado?" asked Clark.

D. K. stroked his grizzled cornrows. "There's a lot of bravado rusted in gook at the bottom of the China Sea. Bad day, you get hosed, you deep-six fifty million bucks worth of A-6E without a cloud in the sky, so what the fuck, who knows?"

Clark looked dubiously at the black whirling clouds. "I hope you do. Exactly how dangerous is it?"

"Don't ask me, Clark. Dina fell down four little steps and she was dead the next morning. I knew this old guy, flew in the 303rd, Hell's Angels, out of England, 364 combat missions by 1945. Not a scratch on him." D. K. shrugged, shoving his wheelchair over to the Piper Warrior and calling under the wing. "You done under there? You check it all again?"

"Done." Annie crawled out from where swirling script still faintly spelled *King of the Sky*. She wiped her hands on an old towel and handed the vet her checklist. Then she took her uncle aside. "Clark, you want to know something, don't ask D. K., ask me."

"You'll just say you can do it."

"'Cause that's the answer. The answer is, I landed a fifty-two-thousand pound Super Hornet fighter jet in force-three winds on the deck of the USS *Eisenhower* when it was rolling in twenty-foot swells. That's the answer."

"Annie's got the stuff," D. K. called over agreeably.

"Excuse me." Clark pointed at the wheelchair. "*You* had the stuff, according to you, D. K."

D. K. winked at his star pupil. "In St. Louis, whatcha wanna bet, they won't be firing rockets at her."

Sam patted Clark's arm ironically. "'We've got that going for us.' But, D. K., is the *King of the Sky* mechanically sound for a long trip?"

Annie made a comic choking noise. "Sam, you're a woman who's owned—just in the twenty years *I've* known you—a Gremlin, a Pinto, and a Yugo, and you're asking about good mechanics? Ha!"

"It is what it is." D. K. spun away in his wheelchair, calling to Sam to help him throw on the runway lights. "Go, Annie P. Goode!" he yelled over his shoulder.

Clark masked his distress by giving Annie a wry hug. "If this is good-bye, can I have your Porsche?"

"No. It goes to Georgette. What do you need a Porsche with a souped-up eight for? You never go over forty." Annie tossed the duffel bag into the plane along with the tote bag of food Sam had packed for her. "You okay, Clark?"

"I baked you a cake. You know how long it takes to squirt icing for 'Happy Birthday, Annie' out of a soggy paper cone? Too long. That's why your cake says 'Happy B'd'y, A.' I figured, know what? She'll think Brad made it."

"You baked a cake for me?"

"I'm freezing it. So come back."

She straightened her uncle's glasses; one stem was taped. "Okay."

He held up the Maltese. "Say goodnight and good luck, Malpy."

Lightning lit the distant sky and thunder echoed along the tin roof of Destin Airworks. Jumping out of Clark's arms, the dog raced off into the darkness.

Sam was wet through by the time she ran back into the hangar. "Annie, I changed my mind. Let's do call the St. Louis cops. You're right. Let the police find Jack! You stay out of it."

Annie retied her shoes. "No, you were right. If we try to bring in the police, he'll either disappear or shut down. If he's got something to tell me about my mother, now's when he'll do it."

Sam frowned. "Remember, you can't believe everything he says."

"Don't warn me. I'm the one who lived with him. I'm the one he almost took twenty-five thousand dollars for."

Sam sighed. "Oh, he just saw that in some old movie." She patted Jack's leather jacket, which Annie was now wearing. "What I mean is, you may not find out what you want about your mother."

Annie kissed Sam's cheek. "Then I won't. Stop worrying."

"When I'm dead, I'll stop worrying." Sam looked out at the rain. "So tell Jack from me: Don't do anything stupid."

"Like die?"

"Like die; don't do anything stupid like that." She tapped Annie's nose and stepped away from her. "Either one of you."

"I promise." Annie climbed up onto the wing.

Lights on the runway glimmered in the hard rain. Clark stepped back to the little television screen to watch the red splotch on the Doppler moving toward them.

While Clark was looking at the weather report, Annie waved at Sam and climbed briskly into the cockpit. Sam watched the propeller turn over, catch, and the little plane head out onto the tarmac.

D. K. Destin's growling voice crackled into Annie's headphones when she reached the end of the ramp. "Tower One to *King of the Sky*. You got that big maple to clear. You see it?"

"Roger."

"You always cut it too close, Annie. And it's bigger'n it used to be. Wind gusting to 22 knots. Go ahead."

"D. K., you don't have a Tower One. You're sitting in a pickup truck and you always say Tower One. Like there's a Tower Two?"

"You crack me up, baby. Go ahead."

She turned the nose of the rattling Warrior into the wind, pushed the throttle forward, squeezed her fingers around the plane's yoke and headed it bucking in protest down the runway. "Don't call me baby, you sexist child of your times. Departing runway 27."

"Wind fifteen…eighteen, nineteen. Too much wind. Roger that? Taxi back? Taxi back. Roger that?"

"Negative. I'm good to go. Thank you. Go ahead." The windsock flapped frenziedly. Annie had a breathtaking sensation—a kick of the heart—that she was making a stupid mistake and couldn't even say why. She peered out across the airfield. There they stood, under the light, Sam and Clark, huddled in the hangar doorway, wet through, waving to her. Above them fluttered D. K.'s huge tattered banner with its hand-stitched black eagle flapping wildly as if fighting hard not to fall from the sky. She waved back at her aunt and uncle, although she knew they could barely see the plane, much less her face inside it.

The radio spluttered. "You listening to me, Annie? Go ahead."

"Roger. Departing VFR westbound. Over."

Why in God's name had she insisted on going to St. Louis in the *King of the Sky*? Even if Rafael Rook (whoever he was) was right that Jack Peregrine was dying and that Annie was his dying wish, why should Jack Peregrine get his dying wish? Clark and Sam, far more deserving, had had many wishes that had never come true. Why should she respond to a request for help, or unearned forgiveness, or whatever he wanted this plane for? Why, against all reason, including her own (she knew far better than Clark and Sam the danger in the sky tonight), had she felt (as undeniably as she felt hunger or cold) that whatever it took so she could have this talk with her father, she would do it? That if it took her flying a rattling thirty-one-year-old Piper Warrior into a storm that had caused the cancellation of all commercial flights, she could fly it. She would just head west-northwest, 290 degrees, and slip around the weather system, and fly herself to St. Louis. She would do it because, as the odd Rafael Rook had predicted, she could not take it or leave it.

D. K.'s voice rumbled. "Wind sixteen. Down to fourteen, ten. Okay, Annie, ain't no mountain high enough. Go!"

Halfway down the runway, she eased slightly off the throttle, pressed her face against the dirty window, her eye on the windsock under the light on the hangar roof.

"Baby, what the fuck you doing? Left rudder, full throttle, full throttle."

"D. K.! Stop mothering me!"

She watched the sock flick backwards, fall, quickly fill again, unfurling full and straight, pointing away. Oddly she suddenly remembered a rainy night, when she'd sat next to her father at the steering wheel of his red Mustang in the predawn quiet of some big city intersection. There was a soft rain so shiny black on the streets that they'd lost their boundaries; buildings shimmered in black pools broken by splashes of traffic. There was a fat man in the backseat of the car. Her father was betting this man that he could drive thirty blocks hitting green lights without ever having to stop for a red one.

In the Warrior now, all these years later, it was as if she could feel her father's leaning over her, rubbing his face softly in her hair and whispering, "Darlin', the readiness is all." The car jumped forward. She could hear her laugh joining his as block after rainy block flew by, green, and green, and green.

Annie went fast to full throttle. Lightning pulsed in the clouds, silhouetting the wall of trees. She let the wind take the plane as if a giant had lifted it in the palm of a hand and moved her over the treetops. With a tip of one bright wing shaking leaves from the tallest maple, she left home behind her.

D. K. Destin's voice crackled in her ears. "Mustang Annie, who do you owe?"

"Baby, it's you…" Annie saw a far-off jet approaching from the southeast. "Hey, you got something coming in. Private jet? Over."

"Fuck, yeah! Hot spot tonight. Nowhere to run, baby, nowhere to hide, go ahead."

"Love you, D. K., over and out."

Chapter 19

Flight

Shortly after the little Warrior soared away, a huge roaring noise suddenly shook the hangar at Destin Airworks and a white jet landed and taxied back to not far from where Sam and Clark were still standing beneath the overhang. The jet's bold insignia *Hopper Inc.* glistened in the big yellow arc light. Brad Hopper leaped out of the cockpit in a crouch, tenting a briefcase over his head against the rain.

He ran up to Sam and Clark, said "Aw, shit!" and cupped his hands to look out at the black sky. "Was that Annie? Did she just fly out of here?"

Clark yelled above the noise of the still-humming jet. "I swear, we really postponed the birthday party. We're not having it without you."

"We told you it was canceled, Brad!" Sam hugged him.

The handsome young man ignored Clark as he hugged Sam back. "Hi, Sam. Was that Annie?"

"Brad! Jesus, I can't believe you're here! She took off five minutes ago. She's flying the *King of the Sky* to St. Louis."

"In this storm?! I figured D. K. wouldn't let her go till morning." From his raincoat pocket Brad pulled out a small velvet jewelry box with a black silk bow. It was as hip as his stylish black jacket and square-toed shoes. "I had everything planned. I was going to propose." He stared at the ring box, perplexed, as if it had tricked him.

"You don't need to propose. You're married to her," Clark reminded him grouchily.

Sam stepped between them. "She needs help. Go to St. Louis, Brad. If you miss her at the airport, try the Royal Coach Motel." She touched his face. "You've got a mustache. That's new."

"Yeah. You like it?" Brad touched his fingers to the trim black mustache.

"It looks good."

Clark rapped her shoulder. "Sam!"

Brad stared at one, then the other, uncertain.

She shoved him. "Go, go on. 'Put your hands up, Chief.'"

Not sure what she meant by the "Chief" remark, Brad nonetheless felt moved to kiss Sam. "Where's that wankhead D. K.?"

Clark pointed to the lights of D. K.'s "office," a trailer nearer the runway. Brad ran off through the rain in that direction.

"You're crazy," Clark told Sam. "Why are you encouraging him? Don't encourage him."

"Oh Clark, she's got to marry somebody. She wants to have a baby."

"Says you. Besides, that's no reason to marry the same somebody twice. How many times does she have to be Mrs. Hopper Two? Or t-o-o? Two times?"

"Funny." Sam found a pack of Destin's unfiltered cigarettes on a shelf crowded with engine parts. She shook one out. "You're probably right."

Clark stared at her. "What the hell are you doing, smoking?! What about your vow to give it up if Jimmy Carter won?"

Sam inhaled with satisfaction. "Yeah, well, the right wing outfoxed me and Jimmy both. Jimmy and Roslyn are taping up Sheetrock in Uganda these days and neocons are running the country."

"Maybe so, but they're only smoking the occasional Cuban cigar, even though of course they despise Cuba as an enemy of the freedom to hang out in Mafia night spots where big shots used to be able to have a little fun."

"You're getting cynical, Clark."

"No, I'm not. I love my country."

"And don't think I don't know you've been sneaking cigarettes for years."

They stood for a while, watching Brad's silhouette gesticu-
late behind the dirty window of D. K.'s small trailer. Finally Sam
asked, "Do you believe Jack was actually in prison in Cuba?"

"It's entirely possible." Clark grabbed at the cigarette but
the athletic Sam spun easily away from him and sucked in a long
drag before grinding it out.

After calling for Malpy, they decided to wait there for the
Maltese to return from whatever exploration he was on. They
stared together into the night, Clark leaning against a doorpost,
Sam leaning on him.

Sam sighed from time to time.

Clark said, "Annie's too smart for Brad."

Sam sighed again. "Smart? Love's not smart. Hey, I'm not
stupid and I opened a joint bank account with a woman who
ran off with my life savings to Belize, and it was her investment
manager at the bank that she ran off with. The bitches."

"Sam, there's no honor among thieves."

"I guess they were really in love."

"Will you stop defending Jill?"

"I want Annie to be happy." Sam looked sadly at car tail-
lights in the dark, hurrying away from her. "That's all I want."

Clark laughed, shaking his head. "Jeez, our generation.
Annie's right. We still believe it all—true love, true grit, New
Deal, huddled masses, anything your heart desires. We still think
if you want something, you can have it."

"'Keep hope alive,' Clark."

"Were you happy? Why should Annie be happy?"

Sam said, "Because in America things are supposed to get
better."

Chapter 20

Wing and a Prayer

The little plane was shaking. Her fingers doing a drumbeat on her instrument panel, Annie cheered as she climbed through the turbulence. To her surprise, a single sharp bark echoed her. She shouted again. There was another unmistakable yelp.

"Malpy?!"

Annie twisted around to see the opened tote bag in the tail of the aircraft. Out of it scooted the Maltese.

"Oh, great! Malpy! How'd you get in here?"

The little dog crawled toward her, flopping from side to side and made it finally into her lap, where he snuggled his head against her stomach, lifting his chin with a whimper. "Okay. Shh shh shh," she told him.

The plane shuddered with a buck and Malpy yipped in a plaintive fret.

"We're fine! Why, Claudette Colbert could do this, right?"

She radioed D. K., asking him to tell Clark and Sam that Malpy was in the plane with her, that she'd set her course for Elizabethtown, Kentucky (her refueling destination) and that she would call air traffic there with her ETA. "So, whose private jet was that?" she asked.

"That was Mr. Brad Hopper Jets, that guy I never liked and told you not to marry? New VLJ Mustang."

"What? Brad?"

"How many husbands you got?"

"None," Annie said. "I don't have any husbands. I'm getting a divorce. Over."

"Roger that." D. K. growled, "Man just slammed into my office, madder'n Charlie at My Lai, 'cause you'd left. He even know you're divorcing him? Over."

"Don't tell him where I'm headed...It's rough up here, D. K. Go ahead."

"You can do it, baby. Feel the wind and ride it. Wing and a prayer. You can do it. Over...Roger that."

"Go ahead...D. K.? I can't hear you. Come in."

"Annie? Come on in, Annie..."

"D. K., go ahead."

All D. K. heard was static.

• • •

Back on the ground at Destin Airworks, Clark put his wet arm around Sam's shivering back. "Malpy must have sneaked in the damn plane again."

"It was the chicken korma. I packed some with the coffee. She'll call us. She'll be fine...Clark, this is where you say, 'She'll be fine.'"

They walked out of the hangar into the rain.

Sam clutched his arm. "I don't even know if I want her to find Jack. Could be he'll just hurt her."

In his slow soft drawl, Clark tried to offer comfort. "If Jack loves anybody, he loves her."

Sam pointed out that terrible things were done out of love and that love was no excuse for them.

"Let's go get that cake out of the freezer," Clark suggested.

Just as they were getting into the Volvo, D. K.'s truck squealed to a stop beside them. "Annie's got your dog with her," he yelled from his window.

"We figured."

D. K. yelled out the window again. "That was her cheatin' husband Hopper in the VLJ."

"We saw him," Clark said.

Sam rose to the young man's defense. "Brad flew up to propose to Annie. He really wants to patch things up."

"Too bad he dropped a nuke on their marriage bed," D. K. shouted.

"He's following her to St. Louis," Sam yelled.

D. K. laughed. "Yeah?"

Clark asked mildly what "Yeah?" meant.

"Means I don't give him any fuckin' fuel till I fix my fuckin' radio. I'm hearing nothing but duck-quack on it. It's going to take 'least two hours, maybe three, for me to fix that radio. Brad can chill."

Sam jumped out of the Volvo to run to D. K.'s truck window. "Here, I forgot. Take this sushi and chicken korma." She handed him a large plastic bag. She turned back to him. "And you and Clark have never been fair to Brad."

"Love don't come easy," D. K. predicted, gunning his motor with his special hand-levers. "You know that, Sammy. Didn't your girlfriend leave you and run off to Cancun?"

"Belize! Jill went to Belize."

"Wherever." He thanked her for the food, popped his clutch, and was gone.

As Clark drove carefully away from the airport, his pager beeped. It took Sam a while to find his cell phone and call the number back.

"My name is Dan Hart," said a pleasant voice. "I'm trying to reach an Anne Peregrine Goode. She's not answering her cell. Is she available? Or a Dr. Clark Goode?"

"Clark's right here. When you call our house, he gets the page."

"Is Annie there?" the man asked.

"No. I'm her aunt. Are you a friend of Annie's?"

"I gotta tell you, I love the way she laughs. She's funny as hell."

"Annie?" Sam was confused. "Funny?"

"Will she be back home soon?"

"Sorry?" Sam was more confused. "You mean, in Maryland?"

"Aren't I reaching you in Emerald, North Carolina?"

Sam said they had just this minute left Annie at Destin Airworks. "She's taking off for St. Louis to see her father."

Hart's attitude changed. "Give me her flight number. Where's Destin Airworks?"

"It's her own plane." Sam caught her breath. "Oh, wait, wait a minute, Hart. Sergeant Hart. You're the Miami police detective!"

"Yeah, I just flew in here. Can you confirm her father's in St. Louis?" His tone was challenging.

Clark whispered at Sam, "What's the matter? What's going on?"

She waved the phone at Clark to be quiet. "Listen, Sergeant Hart. What kind of fraud are you accusing Jack of? Does he have a lawyer? If he doesn't, I want to find one for him."

"You ask a lot of questions, ma'am."

"So do you, Sergeant."

He laughed but cut it off. "If you talk to your niece, have her phone me at Miami Police, Vice and Fraud."

"She knows nothing about any fraud. She's just trying to get Jack medical help. My brother's very ill."

Hart took on an even more official briskness. "Then the best thing his family can do is assist the law in finding him. Have her phone me. Nice to speak to you, Mrs. Goode."

"My brother is not a criminal and my name's Peregrine. Sam Peregrine."

The pleasant voice returned. "Ah, Sam, like Grace Kelly, Tracy Samantha Lord."

"What?"

"*High Society. Philadelphia Story.*"

Sam gripped the phone. "You like old movies?"

"Love 'em."

"Wait a minute. How old are you, Mr. Hart?"

"Twenty-six."

"That's a good age. Don't waste it."

"'Stuff that dreams are made of.'" He hung up.

Sam recounted the conversation. "If I'd known he was a cop, I wouldn't have told him about St. Louis."

"Sam, you'd tell Goldfinger where you kept Agamemnon's mask." Clark dimmed his lights at a fast-approaching car.

"That young man knew his movies," murmured Sam.

The speeding car whooshed past them in the opposite direction, headed toward Destin Airworks so fast that Clark felt the pull of the wind tunnel buffeting the Volvo. The fast-moving car swerved onto the exit ramp to the airfield and slammed to a stop beside Destin's "business office" in front of which sat D. K.'s pickup truck, decorated with caustic bumper stickers about the government and with a big medallion of his trademark black eagle spread across the hood.

A young man jumped out of the car, ran through the rain, and exploded into the office. He was a good-looking young man, tawny-haired, wearing jeans and a blue T-shirt. "Excuse me, sorry to bother you. I'm looking for Lt. Annie Goode," he said with a friendly smile. He began stretching his legs as if they'd been cramped.

D. K. Destin sat perched in his wheelchair, smacking the side of a transmitter radio in the expectation that repeated blows would solve the problem. He yelled at the young man, "Who are you?" as he rolled out from behind the desk.

"My name's Dan Hart." The tawny-haired man spoke affably. "Her aunt just told me she was here at the airfield. Is that her jet there on the runway?"

D. K. shook his cornrows, bemused. "No. It's her husband's. She's divorcing him. Thank the fuck God."

Hart pulled out an old photo of a handsome man seated in an elegant restaurant banquette with a little girl of six or seven. "That's Annie, right?" D. K. took the picture and laughed at it. "I mean I know she's a lot older now."

"Try twenty years," advised D. K. "But that's her. Where'd you get this?"

"It's got her phone number on it. She still got that smile?"

"What's it to you?" asked the grouchy vet in the wheelchair.

"I need to talk to her. Are you the Destin of Destin Air-works?" Hart held out his hand to shake.

"Damn right." D. K. studied the young man for a moment. "What do you want Annie for? 'Cause it's not just to shoot the breeze."

Hart met D. K.'s stare. "I'm with the Miami Police Department. I've got a warrant on Jack Peregrine. I was just told she was flying out of your place to go get him in St. Louis. She may think she's helping her dad. But this is more complicated than she knows and she could get hurt. I mean bad hurt."

D. K. thought this information over and made a snap judgment—as was his nature. "She left fifteen minutes ago. Took off in her Warrior." He pointed out the office door at the runway. "The guy who owns the jet's in the john. Her soon-to-be ex, I hope to Jesus, Brad Hopper." D. K. pointed at the toilet door. "He's going to St. Lou to get her back. He'll make it in half her time and be there waiting for her. She's just trying to get her fuckup of a dad into a hospital, so he can die there, I guess."

Hart asked quickly, "Is there some way you can get me a ride on this guy's jet but not tell him I'm a cop looking for Annie? I swear to God, I'm really trying to help her. Jack Peregrine's got some major-league crooks after him, and he's got the U.S. fucking government after him, which as we all know..."—he gestured at the political stickers on D. K.'s wheelchair—"...makes organized crime look like babies in a playpen."

D. K. stared at the detective a moment. Then abruptly he spun his wheelchair toward the restroom door just as Brad was slamming out of it. The crippled pilot looked at Brad and then at Daniel Hart. He made another of his snap judgments. He growled, "Dan, this is Brad Hopper. That's his jet. Brad, Dan's a friend of mine, local businessman, needs a quick ride to St. Louis. He paid me two-hundred bucks and I'll give it to you." (Dan looked at him alarmed.) "That's all he's got. It's about a woman he's in love with. Ain't it always? Give him a lift and you're cleared for takeoff."

Brad made a derisive noise. "I get it. Your radio's working fine. You just been holding me up so I could give a lift to your lovesick bud here."

D. K. nodded cheerfully. "We're all standing in the shadows of love, Brad, don't you know that?" He wheeled himself backward to his desk and opened a metal cashbox, from which he took two hundred-dollar bills. "Better use Runway Two-Seven. Only one we got."

When Brad took the money, D. K. made sure their fingers didn't touch.

"Thanks for the loan. I'll pay you back," Dan told D. K. after Brad had left the room.

"That guy loves money." The cranky vet had never forgiven Brad for breaking Annie's heart. "I lost my legs and that was nothing compared to losing Dina. My wife. Money don't mean shit and only shits don't know that."

Chapter 21
Imitation of Life

On the slow drive home to Pilgrim's Rest, Clark and Sam talked as they always did, slowly, easily. They talked about Annie's risky flight—it distressed them—and about Brad's reconciliation prospects, which Clark considered nil.

They speculated about what Jack really wanted from Annie, and why he wanted it. Was he trying to cut some deal with the law to reduce a sentence, or with criminals to stop them from beating him to death for unpaid debts? What was he trading— the plane, the emerald?

"That was a very real emerald in his jacket," Sam mused. "That emerald was big enough to be in the Smithsonian."

"Oh, Sam, come on."

"Clark, you don't know your jewelry. Remember the summer Jack showed up like *North by Northwest*, right after Annie graduated, when the highway patrol almost got him, that little ruby he gave me for Annie; it's worth thousands now. You know what? Maybe Kim was never crazy. Maybe there *were* Peregrine jewels buried at Pilgrim's Rest."

Clark snorted his skepticism. "Sam, you'll believe anything. That ruby came out of a bucket at some ruby farm in the Smokies. And if that emerald's real, then Jack stole it. Maybe he stole it from the Smithsonian."

Sam nudged him impatiently. "Just listen. Say Kim

was right and there *was* a stash of precious stones. What if Jack found them? He always said he was going to be a millionaire."

Clark drove slowly, approaching the turnoff for River Hill Road. "You just listen! One, practically all that Peregrine land is gone. You sold it. That land is now sitting under a hundred acres of sweet potatoes and Christmas trees."

"That doesn't mean there're not gems buried in it."

"Two, you'd never find them. A hundred acres of clay and muddy river? You couldn't even find your motorcycle when it flew out from under Annie and crashed down in that gully and she broke her collarbone, so you're not going to find a couple of little rubies and emeralds."

Sam frowned at the memory. "What an awful day. Thank God you were there to get her to the hospital."

Clark carefully turned onto the gravel road at the top of the hill. "This St. Louis thing is not about real emeralds. It's a wild goose chase. Jack's up to some scam, whether he's working with the law or against it, and he needs Annie to pull it off. She'll figure that out and she'll come home."

"I hope so," said Sam sadly, sinking back into her seat. She was quiet for a while, looking out at the black Aquene River hurrying along below them.

Clark reached over for her hand. "I know why you want those Peregrine jewels to be real."

She smiled wanly. "How about, 'It was a toss-up whether I go in for diamonds or sing in the choir. The choir lost'?"

"Don't give me Mae West." He squeezed her hand. "It's about Jack. It's about hoping that if your little brother's after some real jewels, then he isn't dying. Am I right?"

Sam hugged herself. "Possible."

Clark clicked the turn signal before the gates of Pilgrim's Rest, although there was no one else anywhere behind them. "And Jack's not dying. You'll see. It's a big con."

Sam kept running her fingers along the ridge of an old scar of her forearm, "What I remember most is how he was always trying to make me laugh. He'd jump up and down on my bed and make faces. 'Come on, Sam, don't cry, don't cry.'"

Clark nodded. "I know."

She stared out the car window at the flat, empty night. "It took a lot to get Jack down. But that goddamn closet, that's what got to him. Otherwise he could blow off even the tough stuff. Poof, like a dandelion. Dad would take away his allowance, his dinner, Jack would laugh. Dad would lock him in his room, Jack would sneak out the window and crawl along the roof into my room and we'd splice into the TV antenna and watch late night movies together. He would stick his face in front of the screen and act like a hyped-up announcer: 'Get more out of life, go to the movies!'"

Pulling into the driveway to the house, Clark gave Sam's hand another slow pat. "You and your movies."

Sam said she was not to be teased out of her faith that movies showed people how to live their lives with a great score and the boring parts cut out. In movies you could be braver and luckier than in your real life. And better looking. Sam herself, who had watched a movie a day since her adolescence, suspected that without their comfort she might have taken to drink, or worse. Given their Peregrine genes, Sam sighed, Jack and she had really needed Hollywood.

It was true that despite their blessings, the Peregrines had always been a sad family. Most of them were American enough to believe they had a right *not* to be sad, an inalienable right not only to the pursuit of happiness, but to its capture. So, while a few had skidded down the shale of life without digging in their heels, most Peregrines had died scrabbling at every outcropping they passed along the way—a new job, a new marriage, a drink or a sport or a church or a chance—determined to grab the American dream before they landed at the bottom. Wasn't it the national story that failure was the fault of those who failed? That if people only got themselves to the right place at the right time, they could find a fortune in emeralds and rubies? That not believing the dream was not to believe in their country?

So for hundreds of years the Peregrine family had lived unhappily on a hundred-plus acres of rich farm land (their slaves did the farming) that had once been the home of the Algonquin ancestors of D. K. Destin, who was always saying that the Peregrines should give the "native As" their land back.

Sam was the first Peregrine to sell off any of the family land. She sold all but ten acres and used the profits to build Clark's pediatric clinic at Emerald Hospital.

"Best thing I ever did," she always told the town, who found it hard to believe it could be a happy thing to give away over $3 million worth of land to a hospital and to try instead to rent out movies for a living.

But Sam was absolutely sincere. "That land was cursed," she told the town. "And now the curse is lifted."

It was true that war and weather, bad luck and their own dissatisfactions had plagued her family since 1795 when the first Peregrine house washed away in a flood. They'd built another one on the hill above the fast red river that the Algonquins had named Aquene, which meant "Peace"—not that Algonquins had gotten much peace after the first pockmarked Europeans showed up in their yard.

A third Peregrine home rose out of the rubble of the second. Nestled just below the hill's crest, it was a large two-story white frame house with eight chimneys and a wide, columned porch and two copper-roofed wings that had their own small porches in back. This house was named Pilgrim's Rest. But it was never very restful. During the Civil War, Federal troops had commandeered it and the family had been forced to move to a boarding house; a few had even hid in a makeshift tent in the woods and sneaked over at night to steal their own chickens. During Reconstruction, they'd moved back to the house and for the next seventy-five years felt sorry for themselves because they were no longer well-to-do.

They were not well-to-do, that is, until 1899. That's when Joseph Peregrine returned from the Spanish-American War, via the Philippines. He returned a hero. A Spanish rifleman in

Cuba had shot out his right eye and he had the patch and the medal to prove it. Joseph was a flashy man; he renamed the town "Emerald" and wore an emerald ring as large as a marble and was called "Boss" and opened a bank and ran it like he was J. P. Morgan. When he lavishly refurbished the dilapidated Pilgrim's Rest, gilding its cracked molding with gold leaf and replacing its pine with mahogany and marble, rumors started to spread about where he'd gotten all his money. The rumors turned to buried treasure when his wife began displaying at their annual New Year's party rubies the size of quail's eggs on her locally famous bosom. The prevalent theory was that Boss, on his way home from war, had gone prospecting in the Blue Ridge Mountains, that he had squinted over flume lines, sluicing rubies and emeralds out of the dirty water. The town speculated that he had stashed away hundreds of these precious stones somewhere on his property; that whenever he needed money, he sold one of them; that he had so many gems he could never run out; that his neighbors the Nickersons knew all of this for a fact, Mrs. Peregrine having told them that the Boss refused to reveal even to her where he'd hidden the jewels.

When Boss Peregrine died suddenly in front of his own bank—with the one eye, he hadn't noticed a farmer, enraged about a foreclosure, approaching to stab him in the back of the neck—any secret about his treasure died with him. Despite his written wish, Boss's widow didn't bury him with his emerald ring, but wore it herself, along with the ruby necklace, to his funeral. At the service, the St. Mark's minister asked the congregation to meditate on the word "Peregrine," a word carved in the newel post in the marble entryway to Pilgrim's Rest. Above the name was a peregrine hawk, wings wide, with Boss's personal motto in its beak: *Peregrinus sum ego.* The minister said the phrase came from a play by Plautus and meant, "I am a pilgrim," although it also meant, "I am a Peregrine." "Peregrine" was why, the minister mistakenly explained, the house had been named "Pilgrim's Rest." Boss Peregrine was on a journey to heaven, where, if it was God's will, he'd soon be enjoying a pilgrim's rest for all eternity.

Privately, the minister thought Boss Peregrine had no chance at even a stopover in heaven and that he would have done better to buy a new organ for a Christian church than to carve puns in Latin on his grandiose staircase and give his son a silver baby tub with his name engraved on it—a Greek name, Ulysses, the name of that Yankee general who had been elected president of the United States when the people of Emerald hadn't wanted the states to be united at all. The War had happened a long time ago, but not long enough for Rev. Maddocks, who hadn't appreciated Boss's telling him not only to get over the Confederacy but to shake hands with the future by joining the Republican Party. The reverend also blamed Boss for the disruption in the cemetery at the funeral, when a "family Negress" jumped weeping into the open grave, with every appearance of intimate grief, for reasons no one wanted to admit they understood.

Boss's obituary called him "the quintessential American," which was true enough: there was no edge of the earth he wouldn't push his way into—even as far away as Cuba and the Philippines. For him the frontier was always filled with desirable things that somebody else was going to grab first if he didn't get a move on. But wherever Boss's wealth had come from, it hadn't made him happy. Only his mistress had given him any joy—despite which fact it had never occurred to him that he loved her. Nor had his wealth protected him from getting stabbed to death in the street.

So Boss was laid to rest with other dissatisfied Peregrines under a heavy gravestone in the Emerald cemetery where the mistress famously flung herself at the coffin and then into the grave and then moved penniless to "Darktown," where she married a Native American tobacco farmer named Destin.

From his grave, Boss, if he could watch anything, watched his son lose the family bank and his grandson—Sam and Jack's father—lose his two-year-old son in a pool accident and then years later drown himself, so mysteriously that people in Emerald were still talking about it thirty years later.

The Peregrine graves in St. Mark's, ponderous gray granite blocks, begged their occupants to *Rest In Peace*, but, as Sam lamented, her family had never been able to get any grasp on peace at all. Desire kept them stretching for every new thing they'd ever been told they should want. And when it all turned to smoke and wisped through their fingers, desire kept them longing, as Sam's brother Jack longed for emeralds and rubies buried on Peregrine land.

"And why?" Sam wondered aloud to Clark as they got out of his car. What had Jack *really* wanted?

Clark pulled the barn doors shut behind the Volvo. "Maybe he really wanted emeralds and rubies."

Sam said, no, Jack didn't want money. He wanted what was out of reach, *because* it was out of reach. Like he'd wanted Ruthie Nickerson, George's sister, who appeared to have been one of the few people in his life who hadn't loved him back.

"Love's a slow dance," said Clark. "Jack didn't have the patience."

Sam caught his arm, stopped him. "If you're going to say Jill wasn't the real thing because she left me, you'd be wrong. Just because love doesn't last, doesn't mean it isn't real."

"I wasn't going to say anything about Jill. Why do people always think you're talking about them?" Clark's pager beeped. As he waited for his service to connect him to the hospital, he pointed into the dark. "There's a deck chair in our driveway."

Sam looked too. "I think that's Georgette's chair."

"It's been broken for years anyhow." Clark tipped the chair over. "It'll go into that stuffed garage of broken dreams she's got."

"Don't be so cruel. Georgette's just too busy to have a tag sale."

"Sam, is there *anybody* you wouldn't make excuses for?"

"Hey, you should hear me defending you."

Together, they carried the teak deck chair up onto the Nickerson patio.

Afterwards, they climbed their porch steps together and righted the overturned green rockers and sat in them. In a while, Sam said, "So, anyhow, this Miami detective thought we were a couple."

Clark rubbed her knee. "We're not?"

Chapter 22

Bright Eyes

Samantha Peregrine and Clark Goode were certainly not a couple in any ordinary sense, although when Annie spoke to friends about her "aunt and uncle," most of them assumed she meant a married couple. But the two hadn't expected even to be friends, much less to share a home and raise a child.

Both were bachelors, battle-weary after a number of defeats in the wars of love. Both believed the other had suffered more damage in those battles. According to Sam, Clark had never gotten over the early death of Tuyet, whom he'd met and married while a teenager in Vietnam, and that Ileanna, the Chicago radiologist whom he'd hurriedly wed during his bereavement over Tuyet, had sideswiped him. Since his divorce from Ileanna, and despite the earnest efforts of a number of women in Emerald, no one had made a serious claim to become the third Mrs. Goode. It was Sam's contention that Clark had "given up on love."

Meanwhile, according to Clark, Sam had never recovered from the loss of her partner, Jill, whom she'd met on a whitewater-rafting vacation in Arizona, and who'd run off with someone else after living with Sam for seven years. Sam insisted she was still willing to try again, although she claimed vaguely to friends that she'd been about as lucky in love as the Barefoot Contessa. Few in Emerald had any idea what she meant by this analogy, or

that the role in the movie had been played by their fellow Tar
Heel, Ava Gardner.

In her goodbye note, Jill said their biggest problem had been
Sam's mother, Grandee, whom Sam wouldn't institutionalize,
and whom the town wouldn't arrest (even after the widowed
Mrs. Peregrine had smashed out the glass of a whole block of
front windows on River Street, including Nickerson Jewelers).
It was only after Grandee had attacked Sam with a pair of hem-
ming shears (Sam still had the scar on her forearm) that the lat-
ter was persuaded to put her mother in a nursing home.

By then, according to Jill's note, "the damage was done."
Jill left their new condo and Now Voyager, the travel agency
on the floor beneath it that they'd started together. She flew
off to Belize to start a cave-canoeing business with somebody
else. She took their Djuna Barnes first editions and left Sam
the tropical fish. Sam had to buy her out of the condo and the
business; while shocked by the price Jill demanded, she told her
lawyer, "Just do it."

That winter was a tough one. Sam's mother was evicted from
her convalescent home for hitting a nurse with a concrete elf and
Sam had to move her back into Pilgrim's Rest to care for her.
Grandee died of a stroke a year later, a few weeks after biting a
piece out of Sam's shoulder.

Some people in Emerald knew that, between them, Jill and
Mrs. Peregrine had broken Sam's heart, but few felt free to offer
their sympathy since (a) they had never admitted that Sam and
Jill were anything more than business partners who happened to
live together above their travel agency and (b) had never publicly discussed the fact that Sam's mother was insane.

Sam sat alone in her condo night after night thinking that
happiness would always hover outside, like a hummingbird,
never resting.

Then one day her old friend, Clark Goode, returned to
Emerald. He came back to hire someone to run the family's
business, Goode Landscapes, in which he had no real interest.
He was at loose ends since resigning from the Chicago hospital

where he and his ex-wife Ileanna had done their residencies. It seemed to Sam that Clark, withdrawn, listless, had resigned from life itself. She knew the feeling.

Running into him one night at a grocery store, and seeing that he had nothing in his cart but frozen pizzas and a bag of doughnuts, on the spur of the moment she invited him to join her for dinner. Clark looked into Sam's cart, at the packages of shrimp and monkfish, mussels, sausage, and chicken. "I'm making paella," she told him. "It's nuts, cooking for one. Go pick up some bread and stuff for a salad. Not iceberg. Come on over, why not?"

They made the paella together and sat in Sam's condo eating it, watching the old classic comedy *The Wrong Box*.

"I'm laughing! I'm laughing out loud." Clark told her, amazed.

"Me too. I can't believe it," Sam said.

A month went by. Clark didn't leave Emerald. The old friends became better friends. Sam told him that their evenings together were the best part of her life these days.

"Me too," he said.

When her woodstove set fire to her condo and Now Voyager, Clark was the first one there. With a slow look around the blackened living room, he blinked his blue eyes at the smoke. "Still carrying a torch for Jill, huh, Sam?"

She fell into laughter, in a way she hadn't felt all winter.

Clark sat down on a sooty chair. "Maybe you ought not be alone so much."

"Maybe not," she agreed. "I'm moving back to Pilgrim's Rest. I'll rent you one of the wings."

A week later, she took him to the local Chinese restaurant, The House of Joy, for a "serious discussion." Clark was a little worried that she was going to propose a romance.

"You wish!" she told him with such obvious sincerity that the subject was settled. "We're here to talk about what you're going to do next. What's your passion? What can't you live without? Mine's politics and tennis and movies and gardens. And that's just to start. What's yours? Because you've helped me a lot, Clark, and I'd like to help you."

If Sam had many passions, Clark found it difficult at first to come up with any single compelling one. He mentioned his love of reading and baseball. But finally he confessed to a large dream that was yet unformed.

"That's what I want to hear about," Sam told him. "Talk."

And so, evening after evening, they began to imagine the details of an up-to-date pediatric clinic here in Emerald that Clark could run.

A few months after Sam had moved back to Pilgrim's Rest, she brought Clark some news that—as she predicted—took him entirely by surprise. Local buyers had long been approaching her about Peregrine land and she'd just sold them the 118 acres that surrounded the ten-acre site of the house; the land had gone for twenty-six thousand dollars an acre. With the three million, sixty-eight thousand dollar profit, she wanted Clark to help her set up a foundation to build the John Ingersoll Peregrine Pediatric Clinic at Emerald Hospital. She hoped he would stay in Emerald to run that clinic.

Clark was motionless for so long that Sam asked if he were all right. He stood up and nodded. "I'm just fine."

She asked if he wanted time to think her proposal over. He shook his head. "The answer's yes," he said. It was the fastest decision he'd ever made, except in Vietnam or in an operating room, and it was a decision he never regretted.

Over the following year, Clark sold his family's business and his family house. A year after that, the clinic opened in Emerald Hospital.

At Pilgrim's Rest, the two "singles" took up watching classic movies after supper almost every night. Clark had never been the film buff that Sam was, although he'd been named Clark by a Southern mother infatuated with Clark Gable. But under Sam's influence, he became a fan. The famous lines of movies gave them a language that made them feel closer. If Sam wanted a drink, she'd growl in Garbo's voice, "'Give me a whiskey and don't be stingy, baby.'" If Clark was battling a Christmas tree into its stand, he'd snarl like Bogie, "'Nobody gets the best of

Fred C. Dobbs.'" When Sam played on the piano the song Jill had loved most, "Wind Beneath My Wings," Clark shouted, "Don't play it again, Sam!" and Sam yelled back, "'Are you talkin' to *me?*'" They were particularly fond of movies in which incompatible misfits, who'd been given to each other by the accidents of life, became friends, to the good of both.

Clark helped Sam restore Now Voyager and, without even having to change its name, reopen it as the town's first video rental place. Now Voyager was a much greater success in its new incarnation. People so much liked staying home to watch movies that the Paradise, Emerald's only downtown movie theater, went out of business. Next, Sam started a mail-order service for serious rare film collectors. Eventually customers throughout the country were contacting her for help in locating film footage—even the most obscure independent movie, newsreel, preview, director's cut, and studio screen-test. Her promise was, "If they made it, and if anybody, from a projectionist to a grandchild, saved at least one print, I can find it for you." For local customers, she would transfer old Super-8 movies or slides of their children, their weddings, their reunions and graduations and anniversaries, onto first video, then, in later years, DVDs. "Past Perfect," she called this popular service.

Above the store, her restored condo became a small theatre called Sam's Place, where friends and neighbors came to "Play It, Sam," the free double and triple features she showed on rainy weekends. "Bite Night" featured meal movies like *Big Night*, *Babette's Feast*, and *Eat Drink Man Woman*, and at intermission served a fusion buffet. On "Phys Films" night she screened films like *Magnificent Obsession* and *Invasion of the Body Snatchers*, and had Dr. Clark Goode speak (to a chorus of "Louder!") on "Doctors in American Movies." "Phys Films" started the town rumor that Sam and Clark were a couple, secretly in love. (Though why their love should be kept a secret stumped the theorizers.)

Then one day in July the seven-year-old Annie showed up in their yard, abandoned by her father. Within days of the child's arrival, they were sitting together on the couch, watching Shirley

Temple in *Bright Eyes* sing about wanting to be an airplane pilot on the Good Ship Lollipop. Within a week, the imperious puppy Teddy, moving from lap to lap, joined them. The couple became a family.

It was Clark who figured out the recurring dream that was awakening Annie nightly in those early months. He brought home some paints and suggested she draw her dream on the barn wall behind the airplane parked there. It was something he asked his child patients to do, draw their dreams. She painted a picture of a girl in a little red airplane that chased after another red airplane on a straight blue line of horizon. Between the sky and the ocean, she painted a brown ship on which a woman in a yellow cape stood, her arms in air.

After Annie finished her picture and carefully cleaned the colors from the brushes, she reached up and put her hand in Clark's. Clark told Sam that when he felt the life in Annie's small hot hand race up his veins to his heart, he knew it would stay there the rest of his life.

The next morning, Annie asked Sam if Clark was her in-law. Sam explained that he was not an in-law, but he was an in-love. She said that sometimes in the end an in-love could be more counted on than a "real" relative. "You can always count on Clark," Sam told the child.

Annie agreed with a quiet solemn nod. "He's not going anywhere. He promised." She was predisposed to believe that if Jack Peregrine were any example of a "real" relative, she could do without them.

A year later, Sam and Clark officially adopted Annie at the Emerald courthouse. The judge, a married woman with children, questioned Annie carefully about whether she wanted to live at Pilgrim's Rest with Sam and Clark. Annie said she did. "You can always count on them."

As they left the courthouse after the hearing, Annie heard a woman say she'd just been awarded damages because a department store's elevator cable had snapped and plunged her down two floors, breaking her leg. Annie found this notion of legal retribution for suffering so comforting that the following day, forging an excuse from Clark about a doctor's appointment, she left school and found her way back to the courthouse. Judge Susan Patterson answered her office door in Bermuda shorts and with her peppery hair held up by a big paper clamp. When Annie said she'd come to ask a question, Judge Patterson told her to take a seat and ask away. Annie said she wanted to find out how she could sue her father for leaving her.

"That's a tough one," admitted Judge Patterson, nodding. "You could maybe sue him for support. For money."

Annie struggled to sit maturely in the large leather chair. "No." She gave her head a fierce shake. "I don't want money."

"What would you like?" asked Judge Patterson.

The child thought. Finally she sighed. "I don't know."

"I told you it was a tough one. Well, think it over and let me know. It's an interesting question."

Judge Patterson located Sam and sat with Annie in the lobby to wait for her. "You ought to be a judge yourself," she told the child. "The bench could use some more smart women."

For the next year, whenever adults asked Annie what she planned to be, she told them "a judge like my grandpa and Judge Patterson." Some people in Emerald thought this was "precious." Some thought the less Annie knew about her grandpa the better.

Clark warned Annie, with one of his terrible puns, that she was too fast to be a judge. What she wanted was wheels. "Whoa, slow down, you've got the court before the horse. You need a job where you don't sit still."

Years later, when Annie flew her first mission for the Navy, she joked to Clark that he'd been the one first to predict and then to make possible the "dangerous" profession of aviation from which he'd tried to divert her.

"See, Clark, it all balances out." She patted his shoulder. "As long as you and Sam don't go anywhere, I can go 1200 miles per hour."

"So Sam and I just get to hang around here waiting?"

She laughed. "That's what parents do."

• • •

On the Pilgrim's Rest porch, Sam sat with her cell phone on the table beside her rocker, waiting for Annie to call to say she'd made it to St. Louis. Clark was still at the hospital, where he was removing a .22 slug from the thigh of a ten-year-old whose little brother had accidentally shot him with one of the family guns.

Sam couldn't sleep. She told herself to stop worrying about Annie. Annie flew every day in all kinds of weather—much faster than she was flying the *King of the Sky* to St. Louis tonight. In fact it was almost impossible to conceive of the speeds Annie flew. How was it imaginable for anyone to travel at 1000 miles per hour, at 2000? What must that feel like? In a big passenger plane, you had almost no sense of speed at all and yet you were sometimes going as much as 600 miles per hour. But suppose you were moving three times that fast? It must feel…well, impossible to grasp.

Sam looked over at the Nickerson house next door. All the lights were off except the one in Georgette's bedroom. She went back inside. In the hallway her glance caught something glittering. It was the pink baseball cap that Annie had worn here nearly twenty years earlier; the cap Sam had taken out of the suitcase with Jack's flight jacket tonight. Annie had forgotten and left it sitting on the newel post.

The green and red beads spelling ANNIE on the front of the cap drew Sam's attention again. A few of the brass-set round beads sparkled in the chandelier lights as she turned the pink brim. Finding the bone-handled magnifying glass that Clark kept in the hall table drawer because he couldn't see the print on envelopes as well as he once had, she studied the capped round beads, noticing that they'd been painted over with green, blue, and red paint. Where the paint had worn away was where the sparkle was. She scratched more paint off with her fingernail; wherever she removed the paint, a shimmering twinkle of bright color flared in the light.

In the kitchen she scrubbed with a soapy brush on the water-based paint until all thirty-eight beads were clean. There would have been, she counted, forty-two little beads spelling ANNIE, except that five were missing.

She took the pink hat into the living room to hold under a halogen lamp so she could examine the exposed beads in its brighter light.

In her excitement, Sam couldn't stop herself from calling next door. Georgette took a long time to answer her phone.

"Did I wake you up?"

Georgette told Sam that she'd been trying to read herself to sleep with her own upcoming conference paper on sleep disorders but that all she'd done was convince herself that her paper was stupid.

"I know the feeling," Sam commiserated. "When I can't sleep, every wrong I've ever committed slips in through the cracks in the doors and windows like the ghosts in *Poltergeist*."

"Is that supposed to make me feel better?"

"I want you to come over here and look at something."

But Georgette didn't want to get dressed in order to come over to examine Annie's childhood baseball cap. Besides, Georgette's appraisal of the true value of the glass beads on the cap was useless. Although she had grown up working in Nickerson Jewelers, she had never possessed what her mother Kim had called "an eye for the real thing." "So, good night, Sam. I have a feeling those glass beads are just glass beads. You're sounding a little too much like my mom."

But Sam Peregrine had always had a good eye. Good enough to win the state championship in her division in competitive tennis singles for six years running and to make it to the finals last year against opponents half her age. Still good enough to spot an intact 1922 print of Murnau's *Nosferatu* in a tin can at a Paris flea market last autumn. Still good enough to see that the "glass" beads spelling the five letters of Annie's name on the pink baseball cap, the cap that Jack had always oddly insisted that Annie "hang onto," were not glass beads at all: they were precious stones.

Those beads, mounted in bezel-rimmed settings of cheap brass, were in fact, in Sam's opinion, ten rubies, five sapphires, five diamonds, and five emeralds, all of very high quality and each approximately 6.5 millimeters in diameter, or three carats in size.

And here, thought Sam, Clark and Annie had always given her such grief about never throwing anything away.

Chapter 23

Family Honeymoon

Annie was more than an hour west of the small Kentucky airfield where she'd refueled. She was thinking about the odd peacefulness she felt with Sam and Clark at Pilgrim's Rest. From her childhood, there had been the part of Jack Peregrine in her that was relentlessly unsettled, like a craving for salt she couldn't satisfy. But that restlessness eased when she came home to the tall house where she'd lived as a child. At Pilgrim's Rest she could look out over the land and wait for the reddening of the sky and the sound of Clark and Sam's voices as they pushed together in the porch swing at dusk. They were in her memory—though she knew them now to be far more complicated—like the clear figures in an old-fashioned snow globe of America that had somehow survived on this small hill in this small town. Here at Pilgrim's Rest she could wait for the breeze to lift the air, for Teddy's old arthritic sigh, for what in the moment let her feel easy, when her shoulders, her neck, her hands, everything loosened, because she was home.

But she never stayed long. She was her father's daughter and needed to move. Pilgrim's Rest was too fenced in. Her first remembrance of the place was its borders: the white gateposts, the red barn doors, the corners of the blue-sky puzzle, the square picture that she'd painted on the barn wall for Clark. And the vast open world outside the fences pulled her to the horizon.

As an adult it was only in the fast world of the sky that she found the ease she'd once felt at home with Sam and Clark, Georgette and D. K. Maybe, she thought, this trip to St. Louis could somehow help her bridge horizons and borders. Maybe her father would ask for her forgiveness for old injuries she'd almost forgotten; he would tell her how to reach a mother she hadn't much thought about for a long time. And when that happened, Annie's sinews would untighten for good, all the restlessness would still.

Or maybe not.

Who knew what Jack Peregrine would tell her, or whether it would be true? How much could she trust a man who made his living by telling lies? Would he now, even on his deathbed, if he were on his deathbed, tell her the truth about anything?

Annie gave the little white Maltese a pat, awakening him. "It's a good thing I'm going to St. Louis," she said. He looked at her sleepily. "Okay, Malpy, here's where you say, 'You're absolutely right.'" The dog barked in a cooperative manner.

There was a faint, almost imperceptible catch in the Piper's engine before its steady humming resumed. Some pilots might not have noticed but Annie had unusually acute hearing. At medical checkups in Annapolis, she had always scored in the top one percentile on auditory tests, as well as tests of her vision, reflexes, and coordination; it was why she was the pilot so often picked to fly test runs. Georgette teased her: "You've got the brain, you've got the body. We just need to work on the heart a little bit."

"There's nothing wrong with my heart," Annie insisted to her friend.

"Really? Seems to me it hurts."

"My neck hurts, that's all. Pinched nerve."

"Right."

Now Annie moved her neck side to side, hearing the crunch and crackle. At Annapolis she'd had to wear a brace late in her senior year, so painful was the pinch, or alternatively compressed disk, or myofascial trigger points, or displaced vertebrae—the neck specialists all had different diagnoses. Clark thought Annie's problem went all the way back to the motorbike accident. Georgette thought it was psychosomatic.

In the *King*, flying through the black night, Annie rolled her neck, humming, "Don't tell me the lights are shining, any place but there." She rubbed at the knot in her shoulder's muscle. The instrumental panel was so familiar she knew right where to tap it when a light blinked. The red engine-overheat warning light flashed on, then off. Or had it? Was she losing thrust? No, indicators looked fine. "...Lights are shining, any place but there."

• • •

Back in Emerald, Clark returned home from the hospital after removing the bullet from his young patient's leg and assuring the parents that the wound was superficial.

In the kitchen he ate a little more birthday cake. Sam found him there. "You're going to get diabetes," she prophesized, watching Clark cut off a second piece of the cake.

"That's your only hope for justice, isn't it?" His weakness for late-night sweets never put weight on him. "Did Annie call?"

"Not yet." Sam said she had some news: the beads on Annie's pink childhood cap were worth hundreds of thousands of dollars. She couldn't wait to tell her.

"That's ridiculous." Clark carried the baseball cap into the morning room and under a lamp studied the beads of colored glass. He said the odds were a million to one that they were real gems.

"Well, they are," Sam said, leaning over his shoulder. "And Annie will be glad Jack wanted her to have something valuable from him, some kind of inheritance." Her brow tightened. "Especially if he's dying."

Clark looked closely at the beads. "If these beads are real, Jack's getting her mixed up in something criminal."

"It won't be the first time," admitted Sam.

"And dangerous. Don't even bring this up to her."

She sighed. "I care about one thing. Is that terrible? Her happiness. Let them settle this before he goes. All I want is Annie to be happy and get married and have children and bring them here for me to play with."

"That's more than one thing."

"No it's not." She surfed cable movie channels for a late-night classic, settling on *Giant*.

They watched for a while. Clark broke off a taste of the cake for Teddy, who took it back across the hall to her pagoda.

Sam mused, "You remind me of Jordy Benedict. How Jordy rejects Rock Hudson's macho ranch business and becomes a doctor and marries a Mexican nurse."

Clark slowly scraped icing from his cake. "Except my father was no Rock Hudson and he was in the not-so-macho landscape nursery business."

"That's what Rock Hudson did in *All that Heaven Allows*. Maybe your dad was secretly gay."

"As far as I know," Clark said, "My father was not secretly anything. When we cleaned out his drawers and closets after he died, there wasn't a secret in them. Unless you count a box of gold-plated golf tees that had never been used. It was heartbreaking how unsecret he was. And for another thing, I did not marry a Mexican nurse; Ileanna as you know was a radiologist from Argentina." He grabbed the remote, switched it to the Southeastern Doppler "Storm Alert" on the Weather Channel.

For a while, they listened to alarmist predictions for the St Louis area.

"We should have gone with Annie." Clark ambled to the door. "We could have all died together."

He returned with another piece of birthday cake to find Sam on the floor, briskly touching her toes. Finally she stopped, out of breath, and crawled back to the couch. "Is the only point of life to look better when we die?"

Clark said, "You look pretty good for your age."

"What a compliment. I'm not through talking about Annie's search for love."

He scooped off the icing from the cake and ate it. "It seems to be not so much Annie's search for love as it is your search for love for Annie. What are you, her personal love shopper?"

She muted the Weather Channel. "Brad is hanging in there. Maybe she should give him another chance."

"Sam, it's only in old movies that women never stop loving their first husbands. Believe me, Ileanna moved onto a new life before my U-Haul left the driveway. Before the tax year was out, she'd married her accountant."

"You ought to do that. You wouldn't get audited so much."

Clark finished his cake. They sat watching the weather. It wasn't good. Finally he announced that he'd met a radiologist at Emerald Hospital and thought he'd invite her home. Maybe they could cook Jill's sautéed chicken with ginger recipe. "That recipe's the only good thing Jill left you."

"Not true." Sam turned off the television. "She left me those damn tropical fish. I thought those fish were going to live forever. I thought they were going to outlive me."

"They might have, if your mother hadn't poured bleach in their tank. There's always a silver lining."

Sam laughed. "Are you planning to leave me for another radiologist?"

"Nope. It's just you and me, kid. Family honeymoon." He clinked his empty tea mug against her empty wine glass. "Well, you and me and that woman you met on the cruise to Alaska."

"Her name was Rachel as you very well know. And she went back to her partner."

"She did? I'm sorry."

Sam smiled at the lanky man in his loose, frayed khakis; she patted his arm. "This town has had their hearts set on us ever since I had a meltdown at St. Mark's about your dying. And then you didn't even die."

He smiled back at the tanned woman, trim in her golf slacks and polo shirt. "Remember when Georgette and Annie had the wedding for us under the big beech tree, with 'borrowed' rings from Nickerson Jewelers? What were they, nine, ten?"

Sam headed for the kitchen. "You just couldn't get over Ileanna in time."

"In time for what?" Clark followed her. "Like you were waiting? Like you could get over anything. You radicals are so damn conventional."

"What's that supposed to mean?"

"Jill." He put his dishes in the deep Victorian sink. "Jill."

Sam butted him from behind. "There were plenty before Jill and there've been plenty after her too."

Clark laughed as he rinsed plates. "Plenty? Sam, you're starting to believe your own FBI report."

Sam was proud of the FBI file on her. Back when she'd been an active protester, showing up at rallies and marches and vigils, the government had kept a secret dossier on her. She sent away for it under the Freedom of Information Act. To her surprise, she found herself accused of sleeping with radical Lesbians she'd never even met. She told everyone she felt like a disappointment; her real life had been so much less exciting than the Right had pretended. In her real life, she'd been hard-pressed to find any partners at all, much less well-known rabble-rousers like the names in the secret report.

"Your problem," Clark said, wrapping the leftover cake in aluminum foil, "is you pick the wrong people."

"I pick the wrong people?" She folded the dishtowel. "Ileanna got your Chicago house and everything in it! What is it with you and radiology?"

Clark opened the front door to call Malpy in before he remembered that Malpy was on his way to St. Louis with Annie. "I admit, that particular radiologist was a mistake."

The phone in the hall rang. They both reached for it.

But it was only Brad Hopper. He wanted Sam to know that he was landing right now at Lambert–St. Louis in one of the Hopper corporate jets. He had an unexpected passenger with him, someone that D. K. Destin had forced him to take along. A guy named Don somebody, some kind of business-man buddy of D. K.'s. The guy was asleep in the cabin. D. K.

had practically blackmailed Brad into giving this freeloader a lift.

Brad said it had been a rough flight to St Louis, but if Annie's father was dying and had asked for Annie and if she had gone to find him—well, that was a wonderful thing for her to do, considering the negative comments Brad had heard her make about her father. "But you can't help loving your dad. Losing Jack's going to wipe her out."

"Yes, it is," agreed Sam. "But she doesn't know that yet. You've got to help her now, Brad. We need to keep Jack out of jail and get him in a hospital. Be there for her. You want her back? That's the key."

Brad told Sam he had well-placed connections in St. Louis. "I'll see what I can do."

"Find Jack before he gets arrested and get him out of St Louis. If he needs medical help, get it. Otherwise, bring him here if you can. Just don't let him get arrested. We're counting on you."

Brad chuckled the way he always did before conniving to negotiate a trade; even Sam recognized the laugh. "How 'bout this? I help Jack and you stop Annie from signing the divorce papers."

Sam tried to walk away from Clark, but he followed her. "I can't stop the divorce but I can maybe slow it down a little. And don't tell her we had this conversation. Bye." She slapped shut the phone.

Clark shook his head. "I don't believe you."

Sam bit both thumbs. "I wish there were a God and She'd work things out this way."

"You mean sneaky?" Clark opened the door to the kitchen porch. "What are you going to do, hang out at Annie's condo, wait for the mail, and shred her divorce papers before she sees them? Why are you Brad's best friend?"

"She must have loved him." Sam followed Clark outside. "You'll have to gut it up, Clark, and let her go."

He looked at her astonished. "Me? *You* gut it up and give it up. Sam, you're getting desperate and she isn't even thirty!" Clark headed into the backyard. Stars blazed in the summer night as if they'd never been extinguished by the storm. Sam came after him and together they dragged a fallen hickory branch away from the bay window.

She said, "I always believed in 'the One.' But you can wake up, you've been waiting for 'the One,' and your life is gone. *Some Like It Hot?* You think Jack Lemmon thought Joe E. Brown was the One? 'Nobody's perfect.'"

"Sam, listen to me: Joe E. Brown says, 'Nobody's perfect,' and then the movie says, *The End*. Movies end, life goes on. You think Joe E. Brown and Jack Lemmon lived happily ever after?" Clark ambled off toward the Nickerson house.

"We sort of do," she shouted after him.

He turned around, walked back to her. "Sort of…but look at us, a couple of old baby-boomers that thought America was going to give the whole world liberty and a great big free clinic. We thought everybody would just get along and go to good public schools and use good public transportation…"

Sam held up the two-fingered symbol. "Peace, baby. I still believe it."

Clark blew her a kiss with his fingers.

She caught the kiss and brought it to her cheek. "Hey, if I suddenly go straight, Clark, you're the first to know."

"Sure." He gestured at the Nickersons' house. "Just want to grab Georgette's cat."

"Nobody can grab a cat. Leave her alone. She'll get out of the tree when she's ready."

Clark yelled back. "How come you don't take that advice about Annie?"

Sam called across the long black yard. "Tell me Annie's okay."

"Annie's okay. This yard looks so different."

"Yeah, it's got trees lying all over it. I noticed that, Clark. Tell me she'll find the One. I don't care if he's good-looking, homely, rich, poor, dumb, smart, tall, short—"

His voice came through the darkness, steady and slow. "Well, it's better to love a short man than not a tall."

"Oh God. No more puns. Top ten worst."

Chapter 24

The Spirit of St. Louis

At this time, Annie, flying westward through the humid night, was less than fifteen minutes from St. Louis. She was talking aloud to the sleeping dog beside her, remembering numbers. Number games and word games had long been a way to pass the time while flying, a heritage from her father: "A is for Acapulco," they'd played on the road, coming up with a different foreign city for every letter, "B is for Buenos Aires, C is for Calcutta." She had loved to be praised for her quick answers. Now she repeated the "passwords" from the Hotel Dorado notepaper and from the inside band of her pink childhood baseball cap. The more she repeated them, the longer she'd remember: 362484070N. 678STNX211.

She said the two codes together. Each was an alphanumeric; joined, they made a combination of twenty numbers and letters that long ago her father had written down for some reason and now couldn't remember but needed to know.

Nine digits followed by an N, then three numbers, then two letters. N678ST. She repeated it: N678ST. N678ST. Easy. It was an airplane identification code. It had to be.

And NX211. That was also an airplane's ID number. Every plane in the United States had such an ID. It was federal law. The number painted on the side of the *King of the Sky* was, for example, NC48563. (The old designation, NC, she had once mistakenly thought stood for North Carolina.) A solitary "N" meant that the plane was registered in the United States. The N was always followed by alphanumerical characters of varying configurations, normally five of them. So N678ST would identify itself to air traffic as "N, six, seven, eight, Sierra, Tango."

All right, then, one of her father's passwords had to do with the FAA registry of two airplanes, either real or contrived. N678ST and NX211. She just needed to look up those numbers to find out to whom the planes belonged. But there were nine more numbers: Three, six, two, four, eight, four, zero, seven, zero. She broke them into combinations: There was something familiar about the final four numbers. Four, zero, seven, zero.

Her calculation was interrupted by the faint stutter in the engine again. But the gas gauge showed a quarter tank remaining. She checked the mixture but it was fine. All warning panels seemed to be working. Everything looked okay. Annie patted Malpy, who licked at her hand.

She was thinking about a remark made earlier by her father's friend Rafael Rook during his odd phone call from Miami. "If it's a password of Jack's," he'd said, "It will have something to do with you, he is so proud of your accomplishments—"

Four, zero, seven, zero. Annie flipped the numbers around as if she were looking at them in a mirror; something she recalled her father doing—he'd hold up a piece of paper to a mirror in a motel room in order to read it. She remembered how he'd done so once as he'd been smoking one of his long thin cigars. He'd puffed out smoke rings at her and said, like the Caterpillar in *Alice in Wonderland*, "Whooooo aaaarrre yoouuuu?" Afterwards he'd set fire to the piece of paper in an ashtray.

"That's it, Malpy." Annie gave the dog a squeeze. "It's zero, seven, zero, four. It's the Fourth of July." July Fourth, her (at least alleged) birthday. The rest of the numbers in the code were inverted as well. Three, six, two, four, eight. They should be eight four two—8:42, her time of birth—and six, three—6 lbs., 3 oz., her birth weight. She only recognized the numbers because her father had mentioned them on the phone earlier this evening and then she'd checked them against her birth certificate. Had his mentioning her birth been a signal? But to what?

Annie was almost letting herself think that it was sweet of her father to remember her birth weight and the exact time of her birth, sweet that he had kept her birth certificate and then enclosed it with twelve thousand dollars in the blue suitcase he'd left with her in the Pilgrim Rest's yard.

She stopped herself. What was she doing? Her father hadn't remembered *her*. He'd left her there in his sister Sam's front yard and vanished, just as he'd made up the passwords and then had forgotten what they were. Nothing stayed with Jack Peregrine. Nothing held.

Below Annie, the lights of St. Louis sprinkled the far horizon. The name of the city had always given her a good feeling because it was the city that had believed in Lindbergh, whose citizens had come together to raise the money to give him the plane the *Spirit of St. Louis*.

"St. Louis. Malpy, look!"

As Annie reached for her radio mike, abruptly, the propeller noise changed, then the Piper Warrior engine missed, spluttered. The warning lights came on and stayed on, the engine lost thrust and a sudden air pocket dropped the plane down through the pitch-black night.

The frame of the *King* rattled loudly, its wings jerking back and forth at a tilt, spilling Annie's thermos of coffee. Gauges on the instrument panel quivered. The yoke shook in its socket. A small compartment door slapped open and closed. Malpy began to shriek, scrabbling at Annie's arm to be picked up. "Okay, okay," she told the dog. "Just take it easy." She corrected but it was hard to keep the plane flying level again.

"Malpy, we're in trouble."

The exasperated air traffic controller at Lambert–St. Louis International Airport lost his temper when Annie described engine trouble and requested emergency landing priority. What the crap was she doing up there in that single-engine Piper in this weather anyhow? He snarled that it was a madhouse down

here at STL and unless she was in a death spiral, she would just
have to get in line. And whoever the Lt. D. K. Destin was who
had called him with her ETA from Destin Airworks, in bumble-
fuck Emerald, North Carolina, wherever the shit that was, that
man had the foulest mouth ever heard in this control room…
Okay okay, just hang on. Circle. Keep circling.

She went into a holding pattern. To calm Malpy as she
waited for further instructions from the air traffic control
tower, she hummed, "Meet me in St. Louis, Louis, meet me at
the fair…"

A memory of her father softly singing that song floated up
from some long ago highway drive. "We will dance the hoochie
koochie…" What in the world was 'the hoochie koochie'? And
why had he sung that particular song so often? What did St.
Louis mean to him? Why did he want the Piper Warrior brought
there after all these years?

As a child she had been always questioning everything,
uncertain of Jack Peregrine, checking a compass that couldn't
hold true north. But with Sam and Clark, she'd found her bearings. And now, horribly, her father had brought that disorienta-
tion back into her life. Was his asking her to meet him in St.
Louis just one more scam of his? Wasn't it likely that his "I'm
dying" was just the setup of another swindle?

When Trevor had scanned the FBI database for her father's
name, he'd found "John Peregrine" under "Confidence Men."
Jack was an "artist" of con art, that's all. He tricked the gull-
ible and greedy into handing over what money they had for an
impossible means of making more.

Make another circle, the ATC radioed her.

Maybe this was some inheritance scheme of her dad's to get
Pilgrim's Rest away from Sam. Or maybe he needed Annie's help
with a big con that somehow involved an airplane, a con of the
sort that had made up her bedtime stories as a child. She'd heard
dozens: How he planned to pass himself off as the illegitimate
son of the current king of Spain, Juan Carlos I. How he planned
to use her photographic memory to access data (like a human

keystroke logger), in order to work out the biggest wire-transfer bank heist in history. How he planned to seed a gold mine in the mountain wilderness of Colorado or plant a fake Chagall in Boca Raton. How he planned to sell shares in a cure for aging, shares in the future, in possibility. All the stories were versions of the Queen of the Sea. Con art.

Her father had told Annie with reverence that the showman P. T. Barnum had once glued fish tails to monkeys and persuaded the public they were mermaids. That the swindler Count Victor Lustig (who worked the card tables on Atlantic crossings with Nicky Arnstein) had sold the Eiffel Tower to a reputable Parisian scrap iron dealer. That a larcenous midwesterner named Oscar Hartzell had made sane Americans believe they were descended from Sir Francis Drake and that the Drake millions still sitting in the Bank of England could be theirs. Seventy thousand of them had given Hartzell their hard-earned money to fight for their rights. The big con.

Make one circle, the ATC told her.

It was in him, Jack claimed, to pull off the big con. He could sell Mary's milk, Buddha's earrings, and Cleopatra's suicide note. "Your daddy," Jack would say grinning to Annie, tossing her in air, "your daddy understands. You sell people dreams they want to believe in. Remember that, darlin'. Tell people that life is what they dream."

But Annie had developed a different take on life. Life was what you *did*, not what you dreamed. For years she had made up dreams about the mother she'd never met, dreams that were variations on the romances her father had told her. Her mother a sad princess, a dying star, a lonely heiress, a scientist who could save others but not herself. Always in these romances her mother's life was incomplete until Annie walked into it. But her dreams weren't true; deep down she always knew it and by Annapolis she'd given them up. You couldn't dream a hundred push-ups in a field of frozen mud at Annapolis. You couldn't dream a plane off the rolling deck of an aircraft carrier. You had to fly it.

You couldn't dream a safe landing after your engine stopped firing, you had to keep your speed up; you couldn't let your plane slip into a stall.

The gas gauge of the *King of the Sky* plunged to empty. Annie hit its glass cover but it didn't move. She listened to the ATC's instructions for her shortened clearance.

Suddenly a gust almost flipped the plane. She was close to a snap spin and knew she was in real danger. The engine was practically dead. Annie hadn't flown the *King* in a long time. She sped back in time until she could hear D. K.'s voice beside her, talking her through the crisis. "Get the nose down. Listen to me. Not up, down, not up." With the runway lights of the airport closing in, she fought against instinct, forcing the nose of the Piper lower and banking the plane into a glide less than a thousand feet above the concrete of Lambert–St. Louis International Airport.

Chapter 25

Dark Blue World

The air traffic controller was enthusiastically describing an amazing landing to a young VIP executive who'd asked to see him in the Control Tower. "We're a nuthouse here at ATCT, it's Fourth of July, whole corridor's socked in. So in comes some Navy bimbo in a, get this, 1975 Piper single-engine! She blows in, tail of a tornado, circles, her engine's conking out, I mean whacked. We gotta give her emergency clearance. Then this shitass 505 from DFW screws up, swings out on her runway, whap in the Piper's nose. Jesus, this kid, I swear she lifts that damn Piper *over* the 505 on fumes and *still* puts it down like a dragonfly on a fuckin' lily. Another sixty feet, she would have rammed the 202 to London. I'm on the floor popping digitalis like M&Ms. I should retire tomorrow. But how often you gonna see something like that? Welcome to St. Louis."

The dyspeptic air traffic controller shook hands with a tall young man with rich black hair and a trim black mustache, in an expensive black suit. The man tapped him on the chest. "Excuse me, sir. She wouldn't like you calling her a bimbo." He spoke in a Georgia drawl.

"Calling who?"

"The flyer, the naval officer in the Piper Warrior."

"Jesus, you know her?"

"My wife. And I don't think you want to be using that kind of language with a lady."

"Your wife?"

"Lt. Annie Goode. She never used the Hopper." The young man added wistfully, "Not even when she was on Connie Chung."

The controller shook him by the arm. "What are you talking about? Was she on the news? Did she hijack that plane or something?"

"Annie, ha! Annie is totally by the book." The young man introduced himself as Lt. Brad Hopper, U.S. Navy Reserve and president of Hopper Jets, Inc.

"Oh, *you're* Hopper. Hopper Jets; yeah, we got your call you were okay with her coming in at your gate. But the message got screwed up. Anyhow we hauled her Piper over to Terminal E already, because—"

Brad shut him off smoothly. "I wanted to come on in and personally thank you for your cooperation. 'Scuse me, I've got to take this call." He flipped open his cell phone. "Hi there, Sam! Yeah, I'm here. She just landed." He listened for a long while. "Well, hell, you think that's what Annie really wants? Okay, I'm with you, 100 percent, but I can't be getting involved in anything that's not, you know...But I want to help...Listen, I'll make a phone call, I've got friends here. I'll do it right now...I know, I know, I won't say a word to her...What, here?...Damn it!...Okay, tell him to stay right where he is. I'll call you back in ten. Just keep my name out of it."

● ● ●

At the same time, down the corridor, Annie, holding over her shoulder the cloth carrier in which Malpy was squirming, phoned Pilgrim's Rest and spoke to Clark, who was now in bed reading a biography of Thomas Edison.

Annie skipped over the details of her emergency near crash-landing and told him only that she'd arrived safely in St. Louis. The trip had been routine. No problem.

Clark let out a breath. "God knows what you mean by 'routine,' but okay, don't feed Malpy seafood. Remember he's allergic. Don't give him coffee; keeps him awake. I don't know where Sam is. She's been running off every few minutes to talk on her cell phone ever since I got back from the hospital...I'm not sure what she's up to. Maybe she's in love..."

"It's overrated."

Clark said that only the young could be so sure. "By the way, Brad showed up in a jet at Destin's, right when you were taxiing out."

Annie had heard that news. "D. K. radioed me about it. I gotta say, it was nice of Brad to set up parking for me here on the Hopper lot."

"He's only nice for a reason."

She noted that everyone was only nice for a reason.

"Brad came to Emerald to propose to you," Clark warned. "He had an engagement ring in a box with a ribbon. I think Sam's all for it. For a Lesbian, she's obsessed with marriage."

"Brad had a ring? You're kidding?!" But she sounded a little uncertain as she added, "What do I need Brad's ring for? I've already got a real zillion-carat emerald from Jack Peregrine, right?"

Clark made himself chuckle. "Yep, you've got a zillion-carat emerald." He was wondering if she was thinking of going back to Brad. "Hey, maybe Brad's got the same ring he gave you the first time. Didn't you give it back to him when you caught him with Harmony?"

"Melody."

Clark said, "He's headed for St. Louis now."

"No way."

Suddenly Sam burst into Clark's room, flipping on the light, stuffing her cell phone into her bathrobe pocket. "Is that Annie?"

Clark put the phone to his chest. "No, it's Jill calling from Belize; she wants her tropical fish back. Of course, it's Annie. She's at the airport—"

Annie interrupted. "I've got to go. Headed for the Admirals Club. Just hug her and tell her I'm okay."

But Sam pulled the receiver away from Clark. "Annie, all those Peregrine emeralds and rubies are real. Really real. Your dad must have dug them up. They're on your hat."

Clark took the phone away. "Ignore Sam," he advised.

"What's she talking about, emeralds and rubies are real?"

"Just that she loves her brother. Don't get yourself mixed up in something illegal. Good night, sweetheart. Call us. We love you."

"You too. Okay, off to find the Dying Dad."

Sam and Clark talked for a while about how it was a relief that Annie had landed safely in St. Louis, despite the storm. Clark hoped, but doubted, that Jack would be at the Admirals Club waiting for her. "Maybe now we can all get some sleep," he sighed.

Sam was biting her lip so nervously that Clark asked her what her problem was. "Nothing," she said evasively and hurried out of his room.

• • •

At the airport, Annie took a shuttle from the hangar to the main terminal where, glancing up at the dome, she was struck by what she saw. Floating in space above her hung the St. Louis airport's prize possession, Charles Lindbergh's 1934 Ryan Monocoupe D-145 with its sleek black-striped body. There was its registration number: NX211 in bold black letters on its orange under-wing, the ID number Lindbergh had been allowed to transfer to this plane from his earlier craft, the *Spirit of St. Louis*. NX211.

It was the same alphanumerical that made up part of one of her father's passwords. So that was it. NX211. That's why the PS in her father's FedEx said "Lindbergh." Now she had the bulk of the code, which combined her birth certificate information with the ID number of Lindbergh's plane. All she needed was the other plane whose identification number was the last part of the password. She could solve this problem and return to her life.

In her peripheral vision she noticed a man, about her age, leaning against the wall by a news rack, leafing through magazines. He looked up, smiling broadly at her. He was a very handsome man with short dark-gold curled hair, wearing tight jeans, a sky-blue T-shirt, and old brown leather cowboy boots. Flustered, she forced herself to look at him. Neither of them looked away. Then Annie continued through the B/C/D connector and headed toward the Admirals Club.

As she passed by this young man, he waved at her. She waved back, but sarcastically.

The young man was the Miami detective whom D. K. Destin had forced Brad to bring along with him from Emerald, the young man who had persuaded D. K. that he had only Annie's best interests at heart. He had been waiting outside the Admirals Club for Annie's arrival ever since he'd landed at the airport in the Hopper Jet. As he watched Annie hurry away, he flipped open his cell phone and spoke briefly but urgently into it.

• • •

Back in Emerald, D. K. Destin, sitting in his wheelchair in the small messy office of his close-to-bankrupt Airworks, suddenly had an urge to call Sam, despite the late hour. He was a man who always acted on his sudden impulses. "I just got a feeling," the Navy vet told Sam. He described the detective he'd met tonight named Dan Hart—

Sam jumped out of her bed. "Daniel Hart? From Miami?"

"Yeah, him. He was here, looking for Annie. I got Brad to give him a lift in his jet to St. Louis."

Sam muted the DVD of Simone Signoret in *Diabolique*. "Why'd you do that? Sergeant Hart's after Jack. He wants to arrest Jack."

"Yeah, let him. This guy Hart said Annie's in over her head with Jack's crap and I believe him." D. K. shook out his graying cornrows and spun his wheelchair around to look at a knotty-pine wall crowded with photographs. He located a framed clipping from the *News of Emerald Weekly* showing a grinning fourteen-year-old Annie pinning a ribbon on him as he sat in his wheelchair in front of the *King of the Sky*; a blue ribbon she'd just won in the national youth speed race. "Anyhow, why rag on me? You're the one who told him Annie took off for St. Louis."

Sam sighed. "I know. He tricked it out of me."

"Nah, instincts," D. K. insisted. "I got a good feeling from this guy, Sammy. It's like I get a tickling in my legs every now and again and I know who's gonna win the Super Bowl. Hart's a good guy. He's trying to help Annie out of a big mess Jack's trying to get her into. Let the guy do it."

"Brad can do it. That's what I sent Brad to do! Get Jack out of St. Louis before he gets arrested."

D. K. laughed. "You're such a goddamn fairy godmother. Did you send in the Marines too?"

"Are you still in that office, D. K? Go home."

"No thanks." Since the death of his wife, D. K. had hated the sight of his house and almost always slept on the daybed in his trailer at the airfield. "Sammy, love's a bitch."

"Love's a bastard."

"That too," he agreed. "Nothing that's much better though. Beer maybe."

"Cigarettes." Sam sighed. "Hey, listen, when I'm eighty, I'm going to start smoking and drinking again."

"Your mistake was quitting," D. K. told her. "Like love. You gotta keep at it."

Chapter 26

Midnight

Inside the spacious Admirals Club, Annie asked a receptionist if she would page Jack Peregrine. To her surprise, the receptionist gestured at Annie's naval cap and slacks and shirt and said, "Oh, Jack Peregrine. Hang on." She came back with a co-worker, who asked, "Are you Lt. Anne Goode?"

"Yes, I am," said Annie, surprised. "Why?"

They told her that a nice elderly woman had come into the Club just recently and left a birthday card for her, insisting that Annie would be by soon and pleading with them to give it to her. It had no envelope and was a flowery Happy Birthday card. *To My Daughter* it said in raised letters on the front. There was a scribbled unsigned message inside under a terrible poem about a little bud of a girl blossoming into a beautiful woman. The message said:

Annie. Wrong to get you involved.
Stay out of this. Go home. Love you.

She squeezed the birthday card into a tight ball, shoved it into the pocket of her father's old flight jacket. "Goddamn him."

"Pardon? Are you okay?" the older of the receptionists asked her. "The woman said to give you the card."

Annie asked, "What woman? Who left it? What did she look like? Did she give a name?"

"No, no name. Just an elderly woman," replied the receptionist defensively. "She said that someone had asked her to drop off this card, that you were in the military. We thought it was strange but she said she was running for a plane and she left." Both receptionists went back to helping other customers.

Annie looked everywhere in the Admirals Club, even waited for a man to come out of the bathroom and asked him if anyone else was in there. No sign of her father. Not much of a surprise. Her cell phone rang. She didn't recognize the number. With foreboding she answered it. She almost wasn't shocked to hear Jack's voice. "Annie, you okay? Where are you?" He sounded out of breath.

"The Admirals Club in St. Louis, damn it! Where are you?"

"You made it! Sam gave me your cell number but it wasn't answering. Where's the *King*?"

"Terminal E. Are you back at the Royal Coach?"

"Annie, listen." He gathered more breath. "Tell me the password. Tell me the password! I've got a pencil. Go."

She was pacing so intensely that the Admirals Club receptionists stopped what they were doing to stare at her. "No, you give me my mother's name. That's the deal. Give me her name."

Between short breaths he said, "Geraldine Jeffers…The cops are all over this place. If I try to get to the *King*, they'll grab me."

Memory clicked. "Geraldine Jeffers was in *Palm Beach Story*. Claudette Colbert played her! Fuck you, Dad."

"Calm down. Just walk out, go back to the *King*. There's a panel in its tail. Use the key I gave you. There's a courier case in the panel. Take it to Raffy. You understand? Go to the Dorado in Miami. Raffy will meet you there. He'll find you. Help me out, Annie. And don't talk to anybody unless you have to. If you have to, say I never showed at the airport, say I blew you off. Don't let them know you're going to Miami."

Her father sounded so close that Annie jerked quickly around to look, as if he might be calling her from a few feet away. But the modern expanse of lobby, granite floor and cherry wood walls, was empty. From the doorway a slender middle-aged woman, wearing flip-flops and a pink sweatshirt with kittens on it, looked in tentatively, then as if she'd made a mistake, closed the door. A small gray-haired Japanese couple in matching blue blazers came in and studied the Departures screen.

"Hang on, Dad." Annie ran out into the terminal gates area and checked up and down the busy connector to see if she could spot her father. She wasn't sure whether she would still recognize him even if she did see him. "Are you here in this airport?" she yelled into the phone. "Goddamn it, answer me!"

The young good-looking man in the blue T-shirt, who was still reading at the news rack, glanced over at her.

Annie turned her back on him and lowered her voice. "Answer me, Dad!"

"…I've got to go. Just be careful, Annie. I don't want you hurt."

She took a fast breath. "A little late for that!"

"We'll hook back up in Miami. Bring the case. And thank Brad. Here I go."

Annie muttered, "'Thank Brad'?"

The phone went dead.

She felt in the pocket of the leather flight jacket. The emerald was there. So was the tiny key. "Use the key," her father had said. "There's a panel. Take the case to Raffy." What case? What panel? She hated this, having her life flipped upside down, like their past on the road, like a plane in a spiral.

The woman in the pink sweatshirt knocked into Annie as she strode out of a Starbucks and headed into the terminal walkway. She was talking on her cell phone, telling someone to hurry because their flight was leaving. Her cheaply dyed hair was pulled back in a ponytail that she kept yanking. "Hey, watch where you're going!" Annie called after her.

The woman turned back and frowned, yelled, "Sorry," hurried on.

Annie set down her travel bag, which barked sharply.

Across the corridor the handsome man in the blue T-shirt laughed.

Frustrated, Annie yelled at him. "What are you laughing at?!"

He smiled and called back, "I see a beautiful woman in the midnight hour, it makes me happy."

"Give me a break." Annie slammed back through the doors into the Admirals Club, but her heart pounded and to her astonishment, she realized that the jolt came from the compliment the strange young man in the blue shirt had paid her.

Trying to shake off the effect of the remark, she hit Incoming on her phone, reaching the number from which her father had just now called her. A gravel-voiced woman answered immediately with the phrase, "Baggage Claim." When Annie asked who she was, she said that she was a security attendant at the St. Louis Airport's East Terminal. Annie advised her to keep a closer eye on her desk phone and hung up.

So her father had been leaving the airport from baggage claim only five minutes ago. Should she run around looking for him in this huge space? Should she call the police on him? Or should she follow his instructions, go to Miami, and assume she would meet him there?

Everything in Annie had been trained to commit to go. But it would take more than a day to fly to the southern tip of Florida in the little Piper Warrior, even if she could find somebody here at STL who could quickly repair or replace its engine. She thought about letting her father, and so her mother, disappear out of her life again. She thought about forgetting this mysterious panel in the *King* with the courier case inside that she was supposed to deliver to this mysterious Raffy Rook. She could find herself a nice motel here at the airport and get some needed sleep. In the morning she could fly home to Emerald one way or the other and have her birthday party at Pilgrim's Rest and in general go back to her life without Jack Peregrine in it.

Walking fast as she hurried to a decision, she found herself on the lower level of the main terminal, where she passed a large five-paneled mural on the wall. The mural was titled, "Black Americans in Flight." Studying the group portrait, she felt disappointed on D. K. Destin's behalf. He would have loved being one of the pilots depicted there. There could have been a picture of D. K. holding his unconscious navigator up out of the China Sea, clinging to the wreckage of their attack bomber's fuselage, waiting for rescue for all those hours. She thought of how D. K. hadn't let his crewmate slip into the sea, how (as Rafael Rook would have said), he had found that he couldn't take it or leave it.

All of a sudden Annie's old childhood nightmare curiously came back to her, her dream of flying the little red plane, her father tilting away to the horizon, the woman on the ship in the ocean waves, arms raised as if calling for help.

Now it was her father who was like the woman on the ship in her dream. It was her father who was calling, "Help me, Annie."

And she couldn't take it or leave it.

● ● ●

Trevor was asleep when Annie phoned him.

Good for her, making it to St. Louis in that storm, he said sleepily. Good for her. Get some rest. Call him in the morning.

"I need your help." She asked Trevor to check one more thing for her tonight. "Please!"

"I'm trying to sleep here."

"Come on," she urged. "Why are you even in bed at this hour? It's a holiday."

"It's almost 1 a.m. You're going to *seriously* owe me," he warned.

"Absolutely. That Burgundy you're always talking about? Romanée-Conti, 1980? It's yours."

"Are you crazy? It's five thousand dollars a bottle."

"That *is* crazy. Forget I offered." All she needed was the Federal Aviation Administration's registration information for an aircraft with the identification number, N678ST. Trevor promised to call her back if she'd keep Elliott Ness for a month while he went on a dig to Turkey.

"Deal."

• • •

Annie took the long MetroLink ride out to the gate at Terminal E, where a Hopper Jets tug had towed the *King of the Sky*. As she rode there, she called the Royal Coach night desk clerk. The same young man was on duty; he admitted cheerfully that her odd inquiries were the only interesting things going on at the motel. The strange customer, whom he'd told her about earlier, the man who'd cut off his pants legs and taken a swim and left the bloody towels, the man named Clark Goode? That man had stiffed the Royal Coach with a fake credit card. Annie gave him her card number to reimburse the motel.

"If he comes back, I'll have to call the cops."

"He won't come back," Annie predicted.

At the Hopper ground transportation desk, she told a female guard that she'd accidentally left a package in her plane. After examining all her paperwork, the guard walked her onto the tarmac and let her reenter the *King*.

Setting Malpy down in the copilot's seat, Annie used her flashlight to search for any panel the key might fit. In the rear of the dark fuselage, near the tail, behind a quilted van pad, she located, to her surprise, a built-in panel that had a keyhole in it. The panel looked rusty at the hinges. After so many years of spending so many hours in the *King*, wasn't it odd that she would never have noticed this panel? But then there had never been a reason for her to crawl to the far inside tip of the tail to examine the fuselage for hidden compartments.

She fit the key into the lock. It turned. But the section of the panel was stuck shut. Annie felt in the flight jacket pockets for her birthday present from Georgette—the little red leather case with the miniature tools in it. She used its screwdriver to pry loose the panel.

The beam of her flashlight illuminated a small rectangular case of shiny stainless steel inside the dark cavity. It was about a foot and a half long, eight inches tall. Between its two handles, it had a central combination lock with four spools of numbers

Backing carefully out into the cockpit, Annie removed the protesting Malpy from his large cloth bag, shoved the courier case deep inside it and then put the dog on top.

With a jump down from the Piper's wing back onto the tarmac, she waved at the guard, calling over, "Found it! Thanks a lot."

Annie was back in the main terminal by the time Trevor called her. N678ST, he said, was the FAA identification number of a 1983 Cessna TU206 Amphibian, with a 1990 affidavit of ownership issued to a Florida Limited Liability Company named La Reina; La Reina had purchased the small seaplane at an auction of aircraft seized by the U.S. government. The two signatories were Clark Goode and Rafael Rook, both of 302 Ficus Avenue, Miami. The plane appeared to rent hangar space in Key West. "How's that for helping you out in a hurry? I had to call in some favors."

"Thank you very much." Annie repeated, "Clark Goode and Rafael Rook."

"Yeah. Rafael Rook's that weird Cuban that called you?"

"Yes, Jack's best friend."

"And Clark's your uncle, sort of."

Annie air-spit indignantly. "Clark? Clark has no idea he's been off buying amphibian planes and getting beaten up in motels. My dad just uses Clark's name. So is this why the FBI's involved? Is this why the government seized the aircraft? Did my dad and Rook really steal a gold statue called *La Reina Coronada del Mar* from Cuba? Trevor, I need you to find out about this Queen of the Sea."

"You've got nothing left to trade."

"I know. You have to do it for friendship."

With a sigh, Trevor asked Annie to repeat details of the phone call she'd received from the Miami detective, Daniel Hart, about the Queen of the Sea. "I'll find out what I can," he promised. He'd also try not to get her father in worse trouble. He'd tell his contacts in Justice that Annie was just a friend trying to locate a long-missing father, that she knew nothing about anything illegal her father might be up to, and that Trevor was just doing her a personal favor.

She pointed out, "Well, it is a personal favor."

"You know the government. Everything's personal. I'm going to bed." Trevor added that Annie's cat was already in bed with his Westie.

"Don't make too much of a one-night stand."

"I thought Brad's one-night stand was why you left him."

Annie gave a sharp laugh. "Didn't I tell you I found out he'd already been sleeping with Melody even before we left for Desert Fox?"

"If you'd known, you could have taken him out in Kuwait. Talk about unfriendly fire." Trevor yawned. "I'll call you in the morning, late in the morning. I'm turning off my phone now."

Back at the Admirals Club counter Annie spoke again with the receptionists. "Any chance you can help find me a seat on a plane to Miami tonight? Any plane."

The older woman turned to her companion. "Come on, she's in the military. Let's see."

But unfortunately, because of delays and cancellations caused by the storm, there proved to be no seats on any commercial flights to Miami, not even for the military, until 10 a.m. tomorrow. "You could try to hitch with one of the private companies," the other receptionist proposed. "You're Navy?"

Annie tapped the insignia on her cap and white collar. "Yes, a lieutenant; I'm a pilot. Combat jets." She pointed at ribbons on her shirt. "Desert Fox."

The women were surprised. "You were in the Gulf War?"

When Annie nodded yes, the older receptionist solemnly crossed her hands on her chest. "I think that's great. My cousin was in Desert Storm."

Annie said, "My aunt says it's all about the oil and the armaments industries." The woman's frown darkened, but then Annie smiled and she smiled back. "My aunt's an old hippie." The younger receptionist smiled too. There was something about Annie's smile, when she did smile, that was irresistible.

Chapter 27

Let's Make It Legal

Even near midnight on the Fourth of July 2001, Lambert–St. Louis International Airport was crowded with still largely cheerful people waiting for flights not yet delayed, with families pushing strollers, men and women lugging golf bags and tennis rackets, college students bent under backpacks, headed for far-off places.

In the terminal connector near the Admirals Club, across from where the handsome man in jeans and boots had gone back to reading his magazine, Annie called home again.

This time Clark answered the phone from his bed. Hearing that Jack had fled the airport after sending Annie to recover a courier case from the fuselage of the *King of the Sky*, Clark admitted, "Nothing about that man surprises me anymore. Come on back home, Annie."

"Let me talk to Sam."

Clark knocked at Sam's door. "It's Annie again." Sam was sitting up in bed with her cell phone in her hand. "What are you up to?"

"Nothing."

After listening to Annie's story of what had happened in the airport, Sam told her, "Watch out for Sergeant Hart."

"Sergeant Hart? In Miami?"

"He may be using you to get to Jack. Don't say anything incriminating to him if he calls you. I'm getting Jack a lawyer.

He shouldn't have to die in jail. I mean, if he's dying, which he isn't. But if he does, bring his body back to Emerald."

Clark took the phone from her. "Sam's up to something furtive here, Annie."

Sam shouted, "No, I'm not. Call us later."

• • •

In the corridor, someone grabbed Annie from behind. She spun around, defensive, assuming it was the good-looking man from the newsstand. Instead, her well-dressed, soon-to-be ex-husband Brad Hopper stood in front of her, grinning. He scooped Annie off her feet. "Hey, get you, blast from the past!"

"God, Brad," she finally was able to say. "What are you doing here?"

"Why, looking all over creation for you." He grinned his best dimpled grin, the one he had used from infancy to cajole women into spoiling him. Even his formidable mother Mama Spring had been unable to resist it, and neither (for a few years) had Annie.

"So much for flying to Emerald, Brad, like you said you were going to." Leaning her head around his, Annie looked up and down the corridor for the man in the blue T-shirt but didn't see him.

Brad set her back on her feet. "I did go to Emerald. You'd taken off for here. Then D. K. blackmailed me into giving some—get this—'business' friend of his a freeload ride; said if I wouldn't do it, he wouldn't give me taxi clearance. D. K. said this guy was trying to hook up with his girlfriend in St. Lou. Whatever."

Not paying much attention, she nodded. Brad kept talking. "They needed another Hopper jet here anyhow, so I figured, hell, I'll fly it myself. Because Annie might need my help." He gave her his sweet look.

"That's a lot of trouble to go to, Brad." She was touched, she admitted. "You've got a mustache. It looks good."

"Thanks. Happy Birthday, A." He clasped her in a hug. "Sam filled me in. Guy from air traffic was gassing on to me about this old Piper Warrior coming in on a *w* and a *p*. So I go, that's Annie! Good job, babe. Rough?"

"Could have been worse. Sam talks too much."

The little white Maltese's head stuck out of the cloth carrier, barking shrilly. Brad jerked his hand back. "Malpy? What's he doing here?"

Annie pulled away, studying Brad's face. "My dad just told me on the phone to 'thank' you. What does that mean? Thank you for what? Has Sam put you up to something with Dad and told you not to tell me?"

Blushing pink, Brad stretched his arms behind his head as if he were starting an exercise. He shrugged in an unconvincing way. "Sam's my bud. She just wants us to get back together."

"Wants you and her to get back together?"

"Come on, don't be sarcastic, A. You and me." Malpy kept barking. Annie shoved the dog back inside his carrier bag as Brad turned truculent. "Sam said your dad was, you know, real sick. So what's wrong with her staying in touch? You hate Jack so much, maybe she never wanted to talk about him."

Annie was taken aback. "Everybody in my life seems to be in touch with each other except me. Why is that?"

He cuffed her chin, a gesture that had always annoyed her. "Here, looks like your shoulder's bothering you." Despite her resistance, he took Malpy's carrier and tucked it under his arm. "Damn, this dog's a porker."

Annie decided not to defend Malpy's weight by going into the details about the courier case hidden beneath him. "So you don't know what my dad meant by thanking you?"

"No idea."

They walked down the corridor toward the food court.

"How's Clark? Haven't seen him in ages," Brad lied.

Annie was distracted by the disappearance of the man in the blue T-shirt. "Same. Good."

"Not my biggest supporter but a great guy." He looked her up and down. "You look awesome. How long's it been since I've seen you?"

"Eight months."

"That long? Amazing." He gave his handsome head a shake.

"Not really, considering we're getting a divorce." Annie knew Brad was lying to her about Sam and her dad, but wasn't sure of what the lie consisted. It certainly wouldn't be the first time. As for her father, presumably he'd done just what he'd said he was going to do—flee the airport for Miami as quickly as possible—so there was no sense in continuing to wait for him here.

She walked with Brad back past the Admirals Club. "I need to fly to Miami," she said. "But there're no seats available."

He replied, "Did you eat dinner?"

"No."

"You need to eat. Then we'll figure out Miami. I know people."

During their marriage the only place Brad hadn't tried to make decisions for her was up in a jet plane. He had always been proud of her skills as a pilot, just as she'd always admired his. His talent for flying was the first thing, after his looks, that she'd liked about him. But when not in the air, they were as awkward together as footless birds.

On the upper level of the main terminal, they found a table at a "bistro" overlooking the rotunda, near where the Lindbergh plane hung from the ceiling. They ordered chef's salads that arrived too quickly to be anything but prepackaged. Annie watched Brad eat his food the way he always had, flinging the chopped lettuce about on his plate with his fork, as if he were desperately searching for something missing. Whatever he found, he loudly tried to stab to death. This tossing and stabbing went on until his bowl was empty. The avidity of his eating had once horrified her but watching him now, what she felt was sadness. For what undefined satisfaction was he so violently looking? Why had he never been able to find peace? Why hadn't she?

Moved to sympathy, she reached for his hand. "Brad, did you ever feel like there was nothing else to want?" Her question confused him; he just stared perplexed at her. She smiled. "I want to apologize. Because I never made you feel peaceful and you never made me feel peaceful and I should have told you sooner it wasn't working and you wouldn't have had to prove it with Melody."

He spoke solicitously. "A, you're just all upset. Because of your dad dying of cancer and all." He shook his head in sympathetic mystification at the odd fact of mortality.

She gave up, turned her neck side to side. "You're right. I'm just all upset."

"It's tough. And it'll be tough on Sam. I'd like her to catch a break."

Annie looked at him carefully. He had the twitching eyes he always had when fearful of being caught out. She said, "You got my dad out of this airport for her, didn't you?"

"Hey, don't be crazy."

Leaning over the table, Annie grabbed the sides of his head and turned him back to her. "He was in the airport; the police had spotted him and were watching the gates and he said he couldn't risk contact with me, even though I just flew here in a fucking tornado. He told me to meet him in Miami." Both Brad's eyelashes were flickering, twice, a pause, twice more. When she was only five, her father had taught her how, playing poker, people can't help giving signals about their hands. Brad had dozens of these "tells," including the eyelash flicker. "So my question for you, Brad?" She paused for a long stare, knowing it would break him. "How are you getting my dad to Miami?"

It took only minutes to trip Brad into admitting that he had helped Sam out ("That's all I did, try to help!") by talking to a friend who had a cargo express company that flew out of Lambert to Miami.

Under the table, his leg bounced up and down. "The way Sam talked, all your dad wants is not to die in a prison cell. Why is that too much to ask?"

Her eyebrow went up. "Sam'll say or do anything for her brother."

Brad didn't see why Sam shouldn't.

His logic stopped her. "Okay. I suppose it's not too much to ask." Annie studied the Ryan Monocoupe that had belonged to Lindbergh. "I don't know if he's really dying."

Brad shrugged sadly. "Daddy Alton was on oxygen one minute and the next minute he was on his way to heaven." Brad horribly sounded exactly like his mother Mama Spring. She wondered if she herself would start saying things Clark or Sam said. Would she start making awful puns and comparing everything in life to an old movie?

Brad was going on about how all he'd ever wanted was to be helpful. How his St. Louis office could bring in a machinist to look at the *King of the Sky*'s engine and see what could be done to get it flying again. How in the morning he could get her on a flight to Miami. Meanwhile, why didn't Annie stay the night in St. Louis? Hopper Jets had a suite right here at the Sheraton. They could both stay. He'd sleep on the couch.

Annie slowly shook her fork at him like a metronome. "Don't try."

He looked earnest. "We're still married."

"We're legally separated. Let's keep it legal."

"Tell me what you want, A, you've got it."

What she wanted was to find her father as soon as she could.

Brad smiled. "You need a private jet."

"You've got plenty of them."

He tapped the embossed logo on his glossy briefcase: Hopper Jets, Inc. "That's right. Doing great. Private jets—it's the way everybody's going. You hear on the news how the attorney general, what's his name—? He's flying private from now on, I heard that on the news tonight. The threat level."

"From what?"

"Everybody's going private. It's the way to go. You should get out of the Navy."

"I love the Navy."

Brad shrugged. "Hey, you ask me, serving your country's just bullshit." He slipped the white Navy cap from her head and looked at the braided brim sadly. "I tell you, Annie. I was so over that 'yes sir, no sir' rulebook, do unto others. I'm about me now. Like you always said, don't count on anybody, don't hope, be first, keep it going, see the goal, get there. You taught me all that."

Annie felt disconcerted to hear her views so brutally summarized. "You make me sound like *Ayn Rand for Dummies.*"

"I'm not kidding. You nailed it. And Hopper Jets's doing great now. The tax breaks we're getting? It's like Fort Knox is your personal shopper. Still, I'm in the Reserves; they could haul me back. Ali Al Saleem, when I got assigned, you remember? Forward Dissemination? Man, I did not want to go."

She gave his hand a rub. "Everybody's scared."

"Oh, I wasn't scared. I was just having too much fun at the base." He grinned. "I'm strictly off the pills. Long time now."

"Good…" They'd always pretended the problem was not a problem.

They talked for a while about jet planes, about the successor to the Boeing FA-18E Super Hornet; about the old superstar, the Blackbird SR-71. Talking the language of planes had been the closest they'd gotten to intimacy. She thought about telling him she had just been chosen to do a test flight of a new F-35 Lightning II.

The waitress was pretty in a hefty, gold-electrolyted way. Brad, as was his habit, began to flirt with her, telling her about his having once met Laura Bush, although he kept referring to the First Lady as Laurel Bush. Annie listened, puzzled that she'd never before registered how loudly Brad spoke, taking up public space as if unaware that anyone else was in it.

Hearing that he was a pilot, the waitress pointed at Lindbergh's Monocoupe D-145's bright orange under-wings, suspended in air. Last night, she said, the cleaning crew had noticed a man in a security uniform, standing atop a hydraulic lift that was raised to the height of that airplane. This man had crawled into its cockpit.

Annie interrupted. "Which man? Who was he?"

"Well, that's the whole point," said the waitress. The cleaning women had assumed the man was airport personnel when he'd ascended on the lift and climbed into the plane. They'd watched him, figuring he was going to dust off the plane or something and then suddenly he'd crawled back out of the plane onto the lift and had started to do a kind of Latin dance to the Muzak, like a mambo or a salsa, right there on the little platform of the hydraulic lift. When he'd lowered himself to the floor, one of the cleaning women had told him that he was a great dancer. He'd put his arm around her and led her around the floor in big waltzing circles. Then he'd kissed all three cleaning women. He'd run away when one pointed out that he wore a baggage crew jumpsuit, which appeared to have nothing to do with maintenance of the Monocoupe. "Wasn't that weird?" the waitress asked Brad and Annie.

"Very," Annie agreed. She did not believe in that much coincidence. While she wasn't sure why her father had been dancing around in air, she knew for certain that he'd been the man doing so. She pressed for further details but the waitress could give her none.

As they waited for the check, Brad pointed out an ad for Hopper Jets on the wall. "Got our hub in Atlanta, plus new offices in Miami, Houston, and Nashville. Fleet of three-fifty. Leather, marble, whole top of the line, A."

"Wonderful."

"Learjet 45s, these new Cessna Citation Mustangs." He leaned toward her. "Quit the Navy. I'd hire you in a nanosecond." He grinned with his old seductiveness. "You could jet a lot of celebrities around. We've flown stars you couldn't even imagine."

"Courtney Love."

"Who? What's so funny?"

Annie shook her head. "You had your picture taken with Courtney Love, but it turned out to be a male impersonator."

Brad stared at her. "I don't remember that."

"Sam's got the picture of you and Courtney in one of her photo albums." She snatched the check from the waitress who was offering it to Brad. "This is on me." She pulled out the roll of hundred dollar bills that she'd found behind the lining of her father's flight jacket.

Brad pushed her hand down. "Annie, Jesus! You don't want to be flashing that kind of wad!" Holding the money beneath the table's edge, he looked at it. "You back to the poker?" Annie had played a lot of cards at Annapolis and had invested all the winnings in IRAs that Brad's divorce lawyer wanted "put on the table" of their settlement. Brad said, "You didn't use to carry so much cash."

She shrugged. "People change."

"I guess. These VIPs we jet around never carry a cent. They are living the sweet life. But I tell you this, doesn't buy happiness."

"I thought you were sure it did." Annie glanced at his hand. He still wore the thin gold band she'd put on his finger at their wedding. It seemed a long time ago.

"No," he insisted, "Money can't buy you love." Brad said he had just sold a jet to a gorgeous country-western superstar who had confided when he'd taken her on a test-flight that her whole life was miserable. "All that gold dust was just sand in her eyes."

"Is that one of her songs?"

"No, I made it up." He added, "Mama Spring likes to meet the big names. I hate to disillusion her with how fucked up they are."

"Your mom sent me a Christmas card." Spring Hopper stenciled her own holiday greetings and had mailed one to Annie, signed "Mama Spring." In her note was the news that Brad was "seriously involved" with the daughter of a friend. "She said you were seriously involved with a friend's daughter."

"Who? No, I'm not." He frowned. "Mama Spring's having trouble. It's angina."

"I'm sorry." The tasteless coffee reminded Annie of all the cups of coffee she had stared into, day after cold winter day, in the first months after she'd left Brad, when she'd awakened at four in the morning and had sat playing solitaire until dawn released her. She pushed aside the coffee and stopped herself from wondering if he had slept with the unhappy country-western star to whom he'd sold a jet. To her surprise, the prospect didn't hurt that much. Wasn't such a revelation in itself worth the whole flight to St. Louis? She no longer wanted to choke Brad. It was a great relief.

He was saying, "Yeah, and my sister Brandy's doing totally okay. Sam told you about her twins?"

No, Sam hadn't mentioned it and the news gave Annie a strange spasm behind her breastbone. Once, shortly after they'd married, she had thought she was pregnant. Brad had been terrified by the prospect.

"Boys," he grinned. "Back in February."

She nodded, forcing cheerfulness into her voice. "Twin boys, wow. Tell Brandy congratulations. Funny, we used to wonder if you and I'd have twins—your grandmother and you being a twin—and here they are. Twins. I told you Brandy would have kids before we did."

He didn't remember that either. It was as if they had traveled through their marriage in separate tunnels under the sea, parallel but invisible and inaudible to one another. He was holding his wallet open to show her a picture of two fat little blond babies in blue knit jumpsuits. "Brandy had a rough time last winter. She woke up Christmas Day and Dylan had left her."

"*Left* her?" Annie was shocked. Her sister-in-law's husband had always seemed too passive to choose a piece of chicken off a platter, much less desert his wife on a major holiday.

"But hey she's got her kids." Brad pointed at the fat babies. "That one's named Bradley for me and that one's Bobby. Cute?"

"Very," she agreed. "Brad, Brandy, Bradley, and Bobby. Now if you ever have twin girls, will they be Babs and Brenda?"

Hurt by her sarcasm, Brad closed the wallet. "Family's why you come home. We shoulda had some kids, babe."

She looked away.

"Not too late."

"Yes it is."

"I'm never going to stop loving you."

She didn't want to argue with him about whether he'd ever loved her at all. She changed the subject. "So your mom's basically okay though?"

He flipped the wallet back open to a photo of Spring Hopper smiling at an oversized check she was holding. "Ever since Daddy Alton died, she can't sit still. Spring Hopper, Inc.'s in the Hundred Million Club now. Just in the last year she's sold seven luxury homes in this new golf community Windermere Rise. She got elected president of the Atlanta Women's Realtors Club."

"Well, Mama Spring always said she loved to close a deal so much she'd sell her own house if she didn't need it to sleep in."

Brad looked puzzled. "She was joking."

Annie doubted it.

"It really worries me about the angina. I sure don't want to lose her." He stared around the corridor nervously as if someone might be going to steal Mrs. Hopper from him right then. "You know how I feel about that lady."

"Yes, I do." Annie noticed that Brad's hands were trembling. And there was a little line of sweat by his ear. "You okay?"

"Just hot in here."

Annie felt his forehead. It did feel hot. "Drink some water."

On the floor beside her, Malpy managed to twist and wriggle out of the opening of his carrier case. Before Annie could grab him, he raced away from the bistro and took off in the crowded terminal. Annie and Brad gave chase but the little Maltese was quickly lost in the mass of passengers.

Brad trotted after him, turning back as if he expected a football pass, calling, "You need a leash for this dog!"

As Annie ran in and out of storefronts, searching for Malpy, she saw that the good-looking stranger in the blue T-shirt was now standing at a nearby ATM machine. He was in the midst of a phone call on his mobile phone that had apparently upset him. Spinning about in a tight circle, he flung his arms into the air.

Suddenly the little white Maltese sprinted toward Annie, turning back to bark at Brad who was in pursuit. Malpy raced at her, leaping into her arms and she gave him a hard shake and stuffed him into the cloth case.

"Get him a leash." Brad stopped, hands on his knees, breathing hard. "Be back." With a wave, he hurried into the nearby men's room entrance. She suspected he'd gone in there to take a pill or sniff a powder.

She waited. The man in the T-shirt finished one phone call and answered another.

Brad was smiling on his return, rubbing his well-shaped head. He surprised her with a question as they walked along. "You think life's ironic?"

"Brad, life's so ironic that after nearly twenty years my dad suddenly sends a FedEx to Emerald saying he wants to see me before he dies. Then he cons me into flying here through a twister, then he blows me off and disappears. Then Sam cons you into flying my dad to Miami. Now here you and I are, chasing Malpy. Yes, I think life's ironic."

Brad's handsome face turned defensive. "I didn't fly Jack anywhere. Personally." He crumpled with sympathy. "I guess he's a little mixed up from being so sick and then getting the crap beat out of him."

Annie said "Ah." She recalled that she'd often said "Ah" when married to Brad; he'd never appreciated the variations she could play on the short syllable. "How do you know he was beaten up? And did Sam tell you *who* beat the crap out of him?"

He shook his head vigorously. "Probably muggers." He couldn't hold her gaze. "Annie, losing your dad's a tough assignment, take it from me. Look, hell with it. I'll fly you to Miami myself, right now."

His sudden decision surprised her. "You will?"

Brad slowly nodded, pleased by his generosity. He'd fly her in the new Cessna VLJ that he'd just brought here from Charleston. He'd enjoy showing her what it could do. They could be at Miami International Airport in a few hours. True, he had been scheduled to spend the Fourth of July with his mother in Atlanta but Mama Spring would understand. Annie and he could have a blast in Miami; catch a Marlins game, scuba, stay at the Biltmore in Coral Gables—

She interrupted the fast burst of talk that was another indication that he was high. "I've flown the Citation Mustang."

He nodded in a rush. "You can fly anything. Anything."

Annie looked closely at his eyes. His pupils were now pinpoints. On their wedding day, he had promised that he was quitting drugs for good. When she'd found out otherwise, he'd allegedly gone cold turkey but six months later he had blamed his infidelity on amphetamines.

She patted his flushed face. "Listen to me, you need to get some sleep. Lend me your jet. I'll fly it to Miami and bring it back Friday." He winced skeptically at her. "Okay, look, I'll make a deal. We'll fly together to Atlanta. But then you go to your mom's. I'll go on to Miami alone. You need to get home and go to bed."

"You're a riot." He patted her hand. "Lend you my jet."

She felt his pulse. It was racing. "Come on, do this for me, Brad, come on."

He stared at her hand on his, then looked her up and down again, head to foot. "You just look great. Life treating you okay, Annie? Well, I don't mean now, with losing your dad..."

"I'm okay."

"Sam says you could marry somebody else on the rebound from me."

"Sam said what?" Annie glanced over at the ATM. The man in the blue T-shirt was no longer standing there. After a search, she spotted him in the crowd by a distant gate, walking away, speaking into his cell phone. "Brad, I'm not getting married again for a long time." The man turned down a corridor and was gone.

Brad grinned at her. "Don't get a divorce and then you won't need to get married again for a long time. Good plan?"

She gave him a rueful smile. "Don't you think I need a break?"

He looked hurt. "What happened wasn't so bad."

"Yes it was." She gave his hand a quick squeeze. "Come on, I'll drop you in Atlanta. Lend me the jet."

Brad brought out the ring box from the pocket of his Italian suit jacket, showing her the diamond. "Marry me again?"

It was a much larger diamond than the first one he'd given her, which she'd liked and had, in fact, missed looking at after she'd returned it. Annie wore very little, and very good, jewelry—a small string of pearls, a plain gold bracelet. This new diamond setting was the sort of thing she didn't want, and amazingly enough she was beginning to feel absolutely sure that she didn't want Brad either. He had come to win her back, was even really helping her, but it was over. She shook her head slowly. "I'm sorry. No."

"Okay," he grinned. "But can we have sex?"

It made her laugh, as he'd hoped. "No. No sex either. Keep on being the good guy here."

He gave an elaborate pretense of thought. "Okay, last offer. Will you slow up on this crazy divorce? Just one month. You wait one little month and you can fly my plane to Miami tonight."

"Come on, that's blackmail!" Their whole marriage had been negotiated this way, like clauses in contracts drawn up by hard-boiled lawyers.

"Yep, it's blackmail." Brad held out his hand.

She thought about it. "If you get off in Atlanta."

He grinned. "I copilot."

"As far as Atlanta." She held out her hand.

"No divorce for a month?"

She sighed, then nodded.

His glance flickered sideways to two young laughing stewardesses hurrying in tight skirts down the corridor.

Breaking the Sound Barrier

As CEO of Hopper Jets, Brad was persuasive when he assured the air traffic controller that, despite Lieutenant Goode's earlier daredevil landing of the Piper Warrior, she was a serious, decorated military flight instructor with the proper license and endorsements; she was one of the best pilots male or female ever seen in the sky, a flyer ranked second at the Naval Academy and second at Fighter Weapons School at San Diego only to Brad himself. All Brad wanted was quick clearance from ATC. If the air traffic controller couldn't trust the U.S. Navy...

"Why is it, A, I can talk anybody into anything except you and my mama?"

Annie pushed Malpy down inside the cloth carrier atop the courier case. "Because we know you better than anybody else."

"You think?"

"I think. And take your hand off my butt."

"Just trying to help."

Annie shook off Brad's hand as they climbed into the cockpit of Hopper Jets' newest acquisition, the Cessna Mustang jet.

They waited for clearance on the taxi runway where Brad talked to her through their headsets. It had always been her favorite way of hearing his voice. "They're phasing out the Super Hornet?"

"Looking into the F-35," she said.

"I hear it's got problems."

"Everything's got problems." She adjusted her helmet.

Ten minutes later, they were first for takeoff. "You good to go?" she asked him.

He wriggled in the copilot's seat. "All yours, babe. Take this thing to the max. You break the sound barrier, it makes the earth tremble."

Annie smiled. It was a joke of theirs, from the past when they'd thought they'd have a future.

At 12:53 a.m., July 5, sprays of rocket bursts and roman candles exploded above as the VLJ started its tight loop.

The logistical nightmare caused by all the backed-up planes had shortened the temper of the surly traffic controller. But now as he watched the super-light Hopper jet corkscrew straight up into the night, headed for the stars, he turned to face his overworked staff and grinned at them widely. To grin widely was not something this man ever did. "You see that?" He shouted at them, "That woman's a goddamn flyer! God bless America!" They stared shocked at their boss until he yelled at them to get back to work.

By chance, as Annie flew to the southeast of the airport, the last clusters of red white and blue fireworks burst into air, illuminating the silver chrome of the St. Louis Archway. The Cessna Mustang seemed to go right through the fireworks. Then it tilted in a falconlike glide and headed toward Atlanta, Georgia.

"Does it get much better than this?" Brad was not really asking a question and Annie did not give him an answer.

She tipped a wing of the jet at the parabola of the arch over the Mississippi River, in tribute to the city whose merchants had purchased an airplane for Charles Lindbergh. Lindbergh would christen it the *Spirit of St. Louis* and honor it years later by transferring its ID to the Monocoupe D-145 that was now hanging from the ceiling in the St. Louis airport—high off the floor but not high enough to stop her father from taking something (she had no idea what)—out of its cockpit.

• • •

The Hopper jet was very fast and the flight was not a very long one. When they landed in Atlanta, Brad climbed onto the wing and then leaned in to kiss her good-bye. "You find Jack, tell him, well, good luck. You don't want to let your daddy die in jail."

"No, I guess I don't," she agreed.

Brad looked better, his eyes no longer darting. "Maybe Jack let you down when you were little, but give him a chance. Could be he's just trying to make it up."

"Could be…"

"I'm all for a second chance."

She rubbed his cheek, touched the mustache. "I know you are. Third, fourth, fifth chance." She smiled at him. "Thanks for the loan."

"You owe me a month of marriage." He acknowledged her raised eyebrow. "Name only. But we're not signing any papers for thirty days."

She nodded. "After that we're getting a divorce."

"No, we're not." Brad patted her gloved hand. "You take care of yourself, A. Happy Birthday. You're looking great."

She gestured at his muscular body, fashionable clothes. "You too."

He socked himself in the stomach. "I keep at it. Wow, our first year at Annapolis? That bastard Johnson shoving our faces down in the slush with his boot? Remember that? 'Give me another hundred!' And it's sleeting ice? Those were hard times."

She nodded. "Yes." But those weren't the hard times she remembered. "Take it easy."

"Always do." He brought out the ring box again but before he could open his hand to show her, she closed her fingers over his.

"It's a very nice ring," she said. "I'm grateful." She moved his hand back down to his side, smoothed out his lapel. "But no."

Brad put the box back in his pocket. "You're not going to find anybody better, A."

"Probably not."

"In a month, I'll ask you again."

She turned back, looked seriously at him. "Why? Why would you? We weren't happy."

He frowned as if thinking through their life together. "I was pretty happy. And let's face it, babe, you weren't ever happy. I mean, before it was my fault, you weren't happy either."

The truth of what he said took her aback. She'd always blamed him for her unhappiness as she'd blamed the boyfriends before him, or the stress of school, or her father or…She nodded at him. "You're absolutely right, Brad."

He looked puzzled. "Don't be sarcastic."

"I'm not being sarcastic. It's true." She cradled her helmet. "It was great, flying with you again. I'll take care of your jet."

He gave her a thumbs-up. "I know you will."

She had decided against telling him this news but now she offered it in gratitude. "I'm taking the Lockheed JSF X-35 up later this month."

His eyes widened. "Pax River?"

She was surprised. "You know about these tests?"

He shrugged. "You hear things."

Excitement slipped into her voice. "Brad, the landing's totally vertical. I mean zero. You can drop it on a dime. There're two of us testing for the Navy in a couple of weeks."

He swung his headset from its strap. "Who's the other one?"

"Don't know. But I'll get higher faster."

He grinned. "Than anybody but me."

It was true. She'd never clocked as fast a speed as Brad Hopper had.

"Dropping the X-35 on a ship…" He said it as if it were ice cream on his tongue. "Love it. Well, if you can't do it, babe, just call me."

"I can do it. Bye."

"Remember, thirty days."

Brad leaned into the cockpit to kiss her. She turned her

head so his lips, a thin hard hot line, pressed against her ear. Handsome as ever, he jumped down to the tarmac and waved good-bye. Tightening the strap on her helmet, she watched him turn under a floodlight and grin. His grin had always both attracted and infuriated her. She knew, looking at that grin, that there was no doubt in his mind about her. He was sure that she would never divorce him.

But she would.

She recalled that she'd never liked the way Brad jabbed his tongue into her ear. While his lovemaking was efficient and generally effective, his kisses had never done for her what the old songs Sam played on the piano had claimed for romance; they had never given her the sort of chills run up and down your spine, take your breath away feeling of love songs. With Brad it had not been an unchained melody, rope the moon romance. She laughed at herself. So? Life's not a movie, love's not a song. Hadn't her father taught her that love didn't last?

On the road as a child with her father she would lie on a towel beside a motel pool while he named the stars for her. One night he told her how, millions of light-years from the Milky Way, hundreds of new stars were igniting. Among them was this quartet of galaxies. The galaxies were uncontrollably drawn toward each other, just as if they were falling in love, just the way he had fallen in love with Annie's mother before Annie was born.

He said the stars were on fire because of their love for each other. It had all happened millions of years ago, and millions of years ago he had loved Annie, even before she was born, eons before she'd floated down to Earth, a tiny perfect piece of an exploding star. He'd been waiting for Annie a million years before he'd been born himself.

Long after their starry nights on the road, when he'd talked about the galaxies falling in love, Annie was studying astronomy at Annapolis. She had learned then that there'd even been a little truth in her father's story of the play of gravitational draw. In the southern constellation Phoenix,

160 million light-years from Earth, four galaxies that made up Robert's Quartet crowded together into space, pulled there by a kind of attraction. And drawn together there, stars in Robert's Quartet did burst into flames.

Stars did fly toward each other, irresistibly, as if they were falling in love. And millions of years later, lovers on Earth drew together and fell in love, watching the stars fall.

Annie flew through the night of stars, wanting like everyone else to be loved forever. She headed the Hopper jet to latitude 25°47'35" N, longitude 80°17'36" W, Miami, Florida.

● ● ●

At this moment, in a small bare Golden Days hospital room in South Beach, Rafael Rook sat beside the bed of a slender man who smoked a cigarette. Raffy spoke quietly. "It seems by no means an inevitability, Jack, all things considered, from all points of view, and with your past relationship not so good, that your daughter Annie will be arriving here in Miami to help you through your present troubles."

The slender man in the bed raised the cigarette to his lips with bandaged fingers. "She's on her way," he said. "As sure as the sun."

"Ah," smiled Raffy. "The great Swan tells us, 'the rain it raineth every day.'"

"She's coming."

part two

South

Chapter 29

It's a Wonderful World

After the muggy hues of Emerald, North Carolina, Miami had almost blinded her. Miami was in Technicolor. Annie felt as if she'd awakened in a tropical cartoon of hot pink birds and purple flowers, set to salsa music. What's more, she felt rested, although the rest had been imposed on her.

It was July 6. She hadn't found her father. She hadn't reached Daniel Hart. Rafael Rook had set up two meetings that he'd skipped and another one for today to which he was now hours late. She was waiting for him at the Hotel Dorado.

The hotel stood proudly among other rainbow-painted buildings along the oceanfront in South Beach. Its curved windows, neon flutes, and wavy roof made it the prettiest in the line of boxy Deco buildings on the shore. It looked like the sort of place Jack Peregrine would enjoy staying in.

From the chilly air of the silvery lobby, with its steel S-shaped bar and blue velvet stools, Annie moved back outside to the deckchairs beside its turquoise pool. There she again studied the message she'd been handed by a desk clerk hours ago; it claimed that Rafael Rook would be coming to see her here (presumably to pick up the courier case) at one this afternoon. She squinted at her watch. It was after three.

With her hair hidden inside her black Navy baseball cap, in her fresh, ironed white T-shirt and black shorts, Annie and the little white dog Malpy seemed to be the only black-and-white objects in the vivid landscape. In the long open avenue of sand across the street, a yellow lifeguard station stood under an orange striped umbrella. Beyond the beach, sun glittered on blue ocean. Even wearing sunglasses, she found it hard to see in the afternoon light. It was hard to hear, too, above the squawking macaws and the boisterous merengue music booming out of the honking cars that cruised in a caravan up and down Ocean Drive more slowly than pedestrians weaving in and out of their way.

Her father had told her to go to the Dorado to meet Rook. As he'd also written to her on Dorado stationery and it was on a Dorado notepad that he'd long ago scribbled his mysterious password, the hotel seemed a key, somehow at the heart of whatever this big con/sting/dying-wish of his was. And while there were no records of his having ever registered here, some of the older staff—a waitress, bell captain, concierge—had recognized him from a police photo that Annie's friend Trevor had emailed her. The concierge remembered her father's cufflinks, the waitress his tips, and the bell captain recalled that while Jack never seemed to have any luggage, he'd nonetheless been always immaculately dressed. These people had no idea what his actual occupation, or his real name, was.

On arrival, after a few hours sleep, Annie had begun her search, helped by Trevor's useful access to FBI information. There appeared to be no Peregrine in any phone listing of Dade County Directory Assistance, or on any driver's license or police record or in any hospital or any morgue.

She drove to the Golden Days "rest home," entering glass doors etched "Center for Active Living" only to be stopped at the lobby desk by a Miss Napp (as she identified herself), who stretched out her hand—lavender manicured fingernails—as if she were going to sing "Stop in the Name of Love." Miss Napp said visiting hours had not begun; moreover, they had no patient named Jack Peregrine, nor any patient with any of the aliases Annie read off her father's fake business cards. Under persistent questioning, the receptionist's tight, made-up face grew increasingly hostile: only visitors who could give the right name of the patients they wanted to see would be allowed in to see those patients. It was hard to argue with such a rule; nevertheless Annie refused to leave. Finally Miss Napp called security. Two men who looked as if they'd been taking steroids walked Annie to the door and stood in front of it with their arms crossed (as much as they could cross their arms), until she drove away in her rental car.

Back at the hotel, after further unsuccessful phone calls to the Miami Vice Sergeant Daniel Hart, who remained "away from his desk," she kept herself busy on her laptop; she answered her emails, went over her divorce papers from the lawyer, paid her bills, prepared for her fall class at Annapolis, and edited a lecture she would deliver in November at the International Organization of Licensed Women Pilots. She ironed her dress uniform.

Finally she bought a bathing suit and took a swim in the hotel pool, where a peculiar sense of peace came suddenly over her, an acceptance that there was nothing more she could do until she could do something. It was a strange unsettling sensation.

After her swim, with Malpy on her lap, Annie fell asleep on a blue deck chair by the pool. At some point she was half-awakened by what indistinctly felt like a shadow moving across her cheek, leaning over her, shading a coppery sun. Then the shadow moved away. She sat up startled, looking around, but there was no one near the pool. It must have been a dream. She fell back asleep.

Her cell phone sang shrilly on the table.

The caller was Sergeant Hart, finally returning her messages. While he had the same pleasant baritone as in their previous talk days earlier, he had taken on a curiously inquisitorial tone. "This is Daniel Hart, MPD. Do you have Jack Peregrine with you here in Miami?"

Confused, Annie rubbed her face to awaken. No, she confessed, she hadn't yet located her father; that's why she'd kept calling Hart, hoping he could help her.

He replied brusquely, "Withhold his whereabouts again, I'll bring you in as an accessory."

Baffled, she sat up. "What?"

Hart sounded bizarrely annoyed. "You should have told me you were headed to St. Louis as soon as you heard from him. You flew there to help him avoid arrest. Aiding and abetting an escaped suspect is a felony."

"Hey, just a minute here—"

"I'm on my way to the Dorado now. I'm sorry you picked it. My ex loves that bar so much it makes me sick even to set foot in it."

Annie swung her legs over the chair side. "What the hell are you talking about? What's that got to do with me?"

"Sit tight. Don't make me arrest you."

"Are you nuts?" Indignation lifted Annie to her feet and sent Malpy tumbling. The little dog trotted to the pool and lay down, staring at his reflection in the water.

Hart added, "And stay away from Rafael Rook."

Annie paced along the pool edge. "How do you know Rafael Rook?"

"You always answer a question with a question, Annie?"

Once again she was taken aback by his use of her name. "What are you, spying on me? What's it to you if I see Rafael Rook?"

Hart told her that her "Cuban muchacho" had "a rap sheet thick as the Miami Yellow Pages," that Rook and her father were notorious in the city for all the cons they'd pulled off together in the last ten years. If she persisted in "hooking up with them"—

She exploded. "Goddamn it, I'm not committing crimes with Jack Peregrine. He's my father—"

"Ma Barker had sons."

"This is insane! He said he was dying of cancer. I'm just trying to find him before it happens!"

Hart turned abruptly affable. "I'll be there in fifteen minutes."

He was not.

For another thirty minutes, Annie paced the Dorado lobby. After a while, she returned to the large tiled swimming pool and paced beside it. Daniel Hart never arrived. The cell phone number he'd given her still didn't answer; his office at the Miami Police Department kept putting her on hold.

A tan waiter with bleached hair, who'd been staring at her legs as he hurried past, almost ran into her. She grabbed at his tray of martinis and stopped the blue glasses from tipping.

"Good reflexes," he told her.

She asked him if he knew where she could go rollerblading.

He gestured up the boardwalk, adding in an expansive outburst, "You're getting a burn. Sun's a bitch." He pointed at her legs.

• • •

On rented red rollerblades, gleaming with sunscreen, running shoes tied around her neck, Annie skimmed along the boardwalk of Ocean Drive, eating slices of an orange, dodging in and out of batches of beach-walkers. She felt her breathing slow as she sped along.

The therapist she'd seen only once had accused her of an addiction to exercise. Perhaps it had seemed that way to a man who could sit in a chair all day, ingesting chocolate-coated coffee beans. But Annie had been raised by a tennis player, her aunt Sam, and by—in his youth—a long-distance runner, her uncle Clark, and from the age of seven on, from sleepy dawns in lap pools to cold nights on track fields, her days had been busy with sports. In sports, as in the Navy, there were rules, and there were prizes; both the restrictions and rewards were ways of keeping life in order. She liked it that in a track event, there were no limits except those of her body's willingness to refuse defeat. Although smaller than her teammates, Annie had graduated from Emerald High School with four varsity letters. "There's nothing a woman can't do," her aunt had promised her, and Annie had believed it and had proved it on track fields and diving boards, in the muddy sleet at Annapolis, in the sky.

All right, she told herself as she skated along Miami streets, so what if the peculiar Rafael Rook hadn't shown up and neither had this equally bizarre detective, Daniel Hart? So what if her father remained the receding mirage he had always been? So what if she had no name for her mother but the one on a birth certificate that was obviously a joke, since it was impossible that her mother was Claudette Colbert, who'd been in her seventies when Annie was born? Hadn't Claudette Colbert done all right as a role model?

When a child, of course, Annie hadn't recognized the famous name of the dead movie star and so had believed when she'd first seen her birth certificate that Claudette Colbert really was her mother's name. Aunt Sam, the film lover, had tried to break the news to her gently and had eventually introduced her to the actress by playing her a tape of It Happened One Night.

From the moment Annie watched Claudette Colbert dive off her father's yacht in the beginning of that film, then hop on a night bus in Miami and wisecrack her way north with Clark Gable—the man for whom Clark Goode had been named—she had liked the small unflappable woman with her chic French bangs, throaty voice, and civilized laughter, with her new moon of an eyebrow raised at the folly of men.

She had asked Aunt Sam for more Claudette Colbert movies and had watched them all, loving the way there were so many airplane pilots in the films; how nothing ever fazed the woman, not Mohawks, not Japanese prison camps, not Nero, not running an egg farm with Fred MacMurray or racing around Paris with Don Ameche in his taxi, not even a whole trainload of drunken quail hunters on their bacchanalian way to Palm Beach.

Annie had replayed Claudette Colbert's movies until she'd memorized them, pausing the tapes to study the actress's gestures. The star gave the child something with which to fill in the otherwise empty concept called "my mother."

Not that she looked for someone to do the day-to-day job. Sam did fine. But she was naturally curious about the original and as there were no other candidates but the star's name on the certificate, it was to the star that she turned. Jack had told her so many contradictory stories that it was clear he couldn't remember what absurdity he'd previously made up about the woman who'd borne Annie. So why not take Claudette Colbert as a maternal ideal?

By her teen years, Annie's enthusiasm for Claudette Colbert faded. The star became just a French joke she shared with Georgette. "*Comme ma mère, Claudette, toujours dit,*" she would say to her friend. She hadn't thought much about her "real mother" for years now. Oddly enough, it was her father's out-of-the-blue demand for help that had brought that unknown woman back into view.

Weaving quickly through traffic, Annie urged herself to take a wry Claudette look at the last few days. So what if—as seemed quite possible—this lunatic misadventure did not provide her with her real mother's real name? Be fair, what had been lost from her life that had been there yesterday morning? She'd missed a birthday party, that's all, and she had never really liked her birthday parties anyhow, not after the one when her father had carried her around a roomful of adult strangers who had laughed too loudly too close to her face and had smelled of alcohol.

So what? Her family, her friends, would all still be there in Emerald when she returned from Miami. Meanwhile, wasn't it a revelation that she could spend three whole hours with Brad Hopper, whom she was divorcing, without crying her eyes out or wanting to murder him? Wasn't it in fact pleasant that here she was in Miami skating along beside the white beach and blue sea? As Clark joked when she fell off her bike once, "Try again. Life goes on. Don't you believe in re-cycling?"

Maybe when this was over, she could just sit in Emerald for a while, visiting with Sam and Clark, with D. K., with Georgette and other friends she hadn't seen for ages. She could take the time to let life go on.

Pulling down her Navy cap, Annie ducked her head and doubled her speed. As she skated into a neighborhood of shady streets, she found herself on a familiar block; pastel stucco houses with tall skinny palms and wide twisted banyans lined a curving flat avenue. When her cell phone sang at her, she sat on the curb to answer it. She heard a female voice she didn't recognize.

"Is this Lt. Anne Goode?"

"This is Annie Goode, yes? Who is this please?"

The woman had a low smoky voice. "You're Jack Peregrine's daughter? In Emerald, North Carolina?"

Annie was so surprised she answered the question. "Yes, but I'm in Miami now. Who is this?"

"Don't let Jack drag you into something that can get you both in real trouble." The call abruptly ended.

"What the hell?" Annie said aloud. On her cell phone the incoming call was listed as "Private." Who had it been? Some enemy of her father's, or some friend? Someone who wanted to steal the courier case, or to whom the case actually belonged? Was it the same person who had arranged to have Jack Peregrine beaten bloody in the Royal Coach Motel? If so, why warn Annie? She would ask Trevor if there were some way to discover the number for a "Private" incoming call.

Looking across the intersection, she recognized the low pink stucco building with its logo in frosted glass—a sun on a horizon line. She'd unknowingly made her way back to "Golden Days," the extended care facility for "active living," where earlier Miss Napp had called security on her.

Suddenly she heard a car braking and then the violent screech of skidding tires. She spun around in time to see a pedestrian walk right into the path of a slow-moving large white sedan. The car's front fender hit the man and he rolled off the hood like a doll made of rags. His cloth knapsack flew into the air. He lay motionless in the gutter.

Out of the big car scooted a tan elderly woman, whose hair and slacks and sleeveless nylon sweater were as pink as her Oldsmobile was white. With a groan the woman bent down to her victim. Quickly, Annie skated across the street and knelt beside the prostrate man. "Don't move him," Annie said to the woman.

"I didn't! Is he dead?"

"I don't think so." There was no blood on the man and Annie could feel him breathing. Then his eyelid fluttered and one large rather sweet black eye blinked at her.

The woman grabbed her arm. "He's dead."

Gently Annie lifted the victim's eyelid with her fingers; a round black eye stared curiously back at her. She turned to the terrified driver. "He's not dead."

The prostrate victim was a slender disheveled Hispanic man, not much older than Annie herself, with long rich black hair, come loose from his ponytail, standing out from his head as if he'd suffered an electrical shock. He had an attractive face with beautiful large soft dark eyes and gently curved full lips. He wore dirty bright-colored clothes that neither matched nor fit—the chino pants were too tight and the short-sleeved rayon shirt (with three fuchsia flamingos across its front) was too big.

The old woman kept shaking Annie's arm. "What's the matter with him?"

"He's fine," Annie told her. "Are you all right?"

The woman gave her a look of scorn. "He doesn't look 'fine.'"

"Fine? Fine?" whispered the man, still not moving. "There is no conclusive evidence that I'm fine." He added in his soft Hispanic accent. "Things are broken."

"What things?" Annie asked. "Leg, arm?"

"I think both," he replied.

"Can you move them?"

"Can? Should? Categorically different. Something's conclusively broken. But do not," he turned to the older woman, "let us have any acrimony." He tried to move and moaned. "We could avoid the hospital, a pleasure for everyone." Pain spasmed through him loosely. "Three hundred dollars? I am not a greedy man. A trip to a Rite-Aid, a few braces, something for the pain."

"Aha!" The elderly driver gasped, reaching on the curb for a big blue-beaded pocketbook. "I'm calling the police!" She poured the contents to the pavement, found a large cell phone in the pile. "I know you! You pulled this same stunt on my friend Louise right here at Golden Days. Four hundred and fifty dollars, she paid you." The woman punched in 911.

"Hang up," the man said, groaning. He grabbed the phone. "We don't need the police." He began lifting one arm, then the other, one leg, then the other; his limbs seemed to move without his volition, like a puppet whose strings were tugged. "I'm feeling much better."

The old woman looked earnestly at Annie. "I don't use this phone when I drive. I watch the road. I'm Mrs. Joyce Weimar. I swear before God, he walked right in front of me like a sleepwalker. I was thinking, is he blind? But where's his dog? Here's my license, Mrs. Joyce Weimar, just renewed. He's a crook."

Annie nodded at Mrs. Weimar reassuringly. She told the victim, "She's right, you walked right in front of her car."

"I am wounded she impugns my integrity."

There was something very familiar to Annie about this man's soft husky voice and polysyllabic speech. "I'm sorry, do I know you?"

The slender man stared at her; an intense look brightened in his immense eyes. He sat straight up in the middle of the street.

Mrs. Weimar squeezed his shoulder. "Just in case, sit still!"

"Lady, really, it was an accident. I don't want you to worry. Here, help me." He reached for Annie. His legs were rubbery, his head wobbled, his pants had ripped open and were sliding down his hips, but he made it to his feet while the two women held him up. He kept staring with a peculiar expression at Annie. Then, pressing his heart above the flamingos painted on his shirt, he turned to the white-haired Mrs. Weimar. "This was not an accident."

"You just said it was!"

He gestured gracefully with his hand, pointing at Annie. "I mean her. She is not an accident. She is, if you ask me, a personalized version, say an allegorical, of fate. I am only His sparrow. His eye is upon the big, we might call it, picture."

The man's remarks were making Mrs. Weimar uneasy. "You've had a concussion," she theorized.

"I am taking a lesson from this experience," the slender man told the two women. "Call it what you will—your sign, your karma, or, if you're like my mother, Christ our Savior, night and day. But in my opinion, as well as that of the Bard, who nailed it with perfection well before our time, destiny definitely shapes our ends."

"Oh my God," said Annie. "Rafael Rook?"

Chapter 30
The Wiser Sex

"Truth is indisputably stranger." The slender man shook his head so enthusiastically that his hair, glossy black and long, flew out of the string of leather that held it.

"He's delirious," Mrs. Weimar said. "Does he make any sense to you?"

"A little," Annie told her.

Rook held out the woman's purse as she refilled it. "Mrs. Weimar, just now the hand of Fate gripped your steering wheel and gave it a twist. In consequence of which, I find myself on Ficus Avenue together with this young woman with whom I had an appointment, not in Samarra, which is a great book and overdue at the library." He hiked up his torn chinos and tried to bow to Annie; the effort obviously drilled a shaft of pain into his scalp for he clutched at his head with both hands.

"Lie down!" insisted Mrs. Weimar.

The man pursed his full lips as if he were going to kiss her. "Mrs. Weimar, this is Lt. Annie Peregrine Goode."

Annie skidded backwards on her skates in order to look him over. "You *are* Rafael Rook?"

He bowed politely. "Rafael Ramirez Rook, expatriated from the unhappy island of Cuba. On my mother's side, the Ramirezes of Havana, silversmiths to the finest families for two hundred years. And as my padre would say, neither Hook

nor Crook, but Rook, plain Rook, from Miami, four genera-
tions, two Orthodox, two Reformed. My grandpapa believed in
America and America left him floating in the surf. Bay of Pigs.
So-called."

"You are the man named Rook who telephoned me in
North Carolina?"

"With all respect." He bowed again. "Call me Raffy."

She skated in a circle around to face him. "Where's my
father? I know he left St. Louis and came to Miami. I know the
police are after him and somebody beat him up."

"What's going on with you two?" Mrs. Weimar shoved
between them. "Are you in on this thing together? Are you going
to rob me?"

Annie pointed at her cap. "I'm a naval officer."

"Anybody can wear a hat!" The woman shook the Cuban by
the shoulders. "He's a con man."

Backing away, Raffy held up his hands. "Annie, I apologize.
I honestly expected your papa to enjoy a reunion with you in St.
Louis. It meant everything to him."

"Sure. Well I was in St. Louis and instead of a reunion, he
ran off from the cops and told me to bring something here to you
in Miami."

Raffy's face took on a crafty look. "Did you?"

Annie's temper flared. "'Did I?' I flew him the *King of the Sky*
practically through a goddamn twister to St. Louis. I had to beg
a man I'm divorcing to lend me his jet to fly here. A man my dad
had just conned into flying *him* to Miami!"

"Jack could always get places."

"Believe me he *better* die. Where is he?"

"You don't make any more sense than he does." Mrs. Weimar
backed away. "Who's dying?"

Raffy gently brought the elderly woman to Annie. "This
is the daughter of a friend who is unfortunately…" He pointed
behind him at the Golden Days facility. "In here."

"My dad's in Golden Days!?" Annie looked at the stucco
building. "I came here this morning. They told me he *wasn't*."

Raffy explained that Jack Peregrine had been admitted under an alias and that security was tight at the extended care facility because they'd recently received so much bad publicity from local television exposés.

Mrs. Weimar took a cigarette out of a pink leather case. "I'll say! After you eat a meal in this place, you'll go to McDonald's and feel like the Four Seasons." She turned to face the building and gave it the finger. "But you're not in Golden Days to eat, you're in there to die." With a long flaring match from a box in her purse, she lit her slim cigarette.

The slender Cuban jumped away from her. "You could set your hair on fire with a match that big. What are you, the Statue of Liberty?"

The old woman puffed contemplatively. "I need to rest. I feel dizzy." She sat gingerly down on the curb. Raffy sat beside her, tenderly brushing aside a Palmetto bug. "You all right?"

"*You* should ask?" She smoked for a moment.

"My grandpapa loved the Statue of Liberty," he told her.

Nearby, Annie removed her skates and put on the running shoes that she had tied around her neck.

Mrs. Weimar smoked some more. "Coming into the harbor, this is from Russia, my mama saw the Statue of Liberty from her uncle's shoulders. Talk about tired and poor, they'd had it!"

Rook nodded. "But it all worked out?"

"Her great-great nephew? Three first-rate delis, two in Manhattan, one in Queens. So her whole life, last Sunday of the month, she takes the Staten Island ferry to pay respects to the Statue of Liberty. They got to be friends."

"That's a beautiful story. That's America." Rook took her hand. "Feel better?"

She slapped his arm. "Watch it. I'll tell you one piece of news, Joyce Weimar will drop dead in the street before they'll dump her in a place like this—" She pointed at Golden Days. "Which is what I told Louise Mischoff. I said, 'Your son Herb is a shit.' *A chazer bleibt a chaser.* But Herb wanted her money, so he put her in here and he took it."

Rook nodded sympathetically. *"Gelt gait tzu gelt."*

"Ah, you're a rabbi." She pinched off the cigarette ash, returned the butt to her leather case, and slowly rose to her feet. "You two work out your own problems, I'm late to water ballet."

Holding up his pants, Raffy ran after her. "Mrs. Weimar, give me your phone number. I'll call you for dinner, maybe a movie. Or we could go dancing. There's a nice clean place in Little Havana. I used to play guitar there. Very nice."

She pushed suspiciously past him. "Not on your life."

He followed, bowing with a smile when she turned. "Forgive me, Joyce, for offering advice to the wiser sex. But the quality of mercy is not strained through a sieve but more or less dumped on our heads like a bucket of heavenly rain. I paraphrase the Bard."

She thought a moment then gave Raffy's nose a twist. "Don't pee on my back and tell me it's rain. Still, I see why Louise fell for you. You're cute."

Mrs. Weimar drove off at 10 miles per hour in her large white Oldsmobile.

Raffy shuffled back to Annie. "That didn't work out," he said mournfully.

"I thought you said you were a musician. Why are you flopping off cars and swindling old women?"

His sigh was itself a melody. "Maybe music's the food of love, but it was never, in my particular case, so much the food of food. Then I met your papa."

"Could you make this brief?"

"Brevity—"

"In fact, don't even talk." She pointed at Golden Days. "Just get me in there if that's where my dad is."

The Cuban, brushing off his clothes, claimed that to get her access to a patient's floor, he would have to make clandestine arrangements with a friend who worked a later shift. There were complications.

She was not surprised. "What's my dad even doing back there? I thought he left."

Raffy glanced all over the sky evasively. Early in the morning, he'd returned home—and he pointed to a modest stucco duplex down the block—to find Jack Peregrine lying on the curb, more or less dead. At first Raffy thought they'd finished him off, but when he put his ear to Jack's mouth, he could hear him cursing. So he'd rushed him into Golden Days, because it was only half a block from his house and because a nice nurse on staff was a close friend. Chamayra had helped them twice now by faking the paperwork and giving Jack a bed where he could hide out. Still, it was tricky for her to sneak people up to the floor where she'd put him. She might do it for Raffy. It would depend…

"Don't blackmail me, Rook. I'll go straight to the police. Who beat him up?"

Jack's friend could only speculate. "He had more than a few enemies. Don't we all?"

"No, we don't," said Annie. "Not that kind. And you're sure he's dying?"

"Terminal, he said."

Annie scoffed. "He was telling suckers he was terminal ten years ago when he was selling them prime real estate in Savannah, Georgia. 'I have to sell my house, I'm dying, you can have it for a song.'" She moved closer. "Why didn't you ever show up at the hotel?"

"I was collared by that s.o.b. Hart! You didn't get my messages?" Raffy swore that he'd been headed into the Dorado lobby today when he'd been suddenly set upon by Sgt. Daniel Hart of the lying Miami police. The violent young detective had dragged him off in a squad car to his office and grilled him about crimes he'd accused him of committing with Jack Peregrine. Raffy could only suppose that Hart was there at the Dorado because of Annie.

Annie agreed it was likely.

"Oh, muy bueno! Gracias!"

Furious, she yanked him over beside her. "Don't you dare get sarcastic with me. You're out of your league. Understand?"

He nodded, eyes wide. "Sí."

"I still haven't talked to Hart, gracias to you, Mr. Rook. He claims my father has a sixteenth-century relic that belongs to Cuba. Does he?"

The slender man shrugged. "I hope so. There are Cubans who would smile and smile, as the great Shakespeare tells us, to see eels in Jack's ribs, if you follow me. 'Full fathom five.'"

She glared. "Do you and my father own an Cessna Amphibian with the ID 'N678ST'?"

Again he looked skyward. He appeared to find no more answers there now than earlier. "There is a plane in which we have an interest, whose ID I don't recall. But 'own' is perhaps not the word. Fees may be in arrears."

"I bet. Talk to me about this gold relic."

He shook his head emphatically. "I hope it's the object you've brought me? Is it?"

She said, "I brought a case."

He looked puzzled. "A case of what?"

"No, a metal courier case." She said she had found it behind a panel in the fuselage of the *King of the Sky*. "Were you planning to fly with him someplace in the *King* to deliver this case?"

Jack, sighed Raffy, was now unfortunately in no position to fly anywhere and he, Raffy, couldn't fly a kite much less a Piper Warrior. Carefully smoothing a long thin cigarillo and placing it, unlit, in his mouth, the Cuban added quietly, "Where is this case?"

"Why should I give it to you?"

His large eyes narrowed. "Because I'll get you in to see Jack, without the cops, who frankly have got a fixation to put your papa away for, well, the rest of his life, pretty much." He crossed nicely shaped brown slender hands over his shirt. "I swear to you on the honor of the Ramirez family. On the souls of my mother, alive in Havana, and my father dead before his time, and my grandpapa, killed by the son-of-a-bitch CIA, I swear I'll take you to Jack!" He kissed a tiny cross on a thin gold chain around his neck. "I'm not necessarily a believer"—he showed her the cross—"but interested in all possibilities."

Annie paced a circle around him. "What's inside Dad's courier case? It was locked."

"You don't know?"

She grimaced sarcastically. "What is it, a million dollars in cash?"

His eyes dilated but he scrunched his thin shoulders up toward his ponytail. "Honestly and truthfully you need to ask Jack." Scooting sideways, he collected his small knapsack from the curb.

Annie's frustration heated her like a rash. "Fine! I've also got a large emerald of his. Very large."

The large brown eyes took on a glitter. "With you?"

She shook her head. "Back at the hotel. In the room safe. The courier case is back there too."

Puffing nervously on his cigarillo, the Cuban walked away from her. With a smoothly languid movement, he opened his knapsack and slipped his hand inside it. "I want the emerald and I want the case."

"Well, you can't have either."

In a sudden move, Rook pulled out a large silver revolver, so long in its barrel that Annie laughed. "Where did you get that thing?"

"My *bisabuelo*, grandpapa, Simon left it to me, if you want to know." With the gun, he gestured at her ominously, smiling his sad sweet smile. "God's truth, I've got nothing to lose. Go with the flow, Annie. We're going to your hotel room and you'll give me your papa's property. To quote the Buddha, I think it was, you can't step in the same river twice. But life has taught me that you can, more or less, by watching where you go, avoid slipping on the dog-doo of our human condition and breaking your neck. Could I use your phone to call a cab?"

Chapter 31

Without Reservations

Within ten minutes of Rook's call, a battered taxi appeared in an outburst of black smoke and backfires. A young man drove it, whom Rook introduced as his "cousin" Julio. In exchange for sixty dollars in cash, borrowed from Annie, this young man drove them to the Dorado and allowed Rook to remove a guitar in a black cardboard case from the trunk of his cab.

"And you still owe me a hundred," the driver growled at Rook as he let them off at the hotel entrance, with a blast of funky rock from his radio and smoke from his muffler, both of which incensed a buff couple in a blue Jaguar XKE Roadster who had to wait behind the old cab for the parking valet.

Annie thought about karate-chopping the Cuban and taking the long revolver that he kept nudging at her from inside his knapsack. He was having trouble managing it with his guitar case anyhow. But she decided that doing so would only slow down her getting into her father's room at Golden Days without involving the police. It was obvious that just as Rook couldn't fly a kite, much less a plane, so he couldn't kill a cockroach, much less a naval officer.

They walked together through the Hotel Dorado lobby and took the elevator up to her hotel room. There she felt to the back of the safe for the large emerald. She tossed it at him by its thin gold chain. It fell to the floor and Malpy bit Rook hard on the hand when he bent over to retrieve it.

"My hand!" he cried. It was bleeding. "I play guitar with that hand!"

Annie shrugged. "So why don't you shoot the dog, you're such a killer?"

The musician snatched a cloth napkin from an uncollected lunch tray to wrap around his wound. "I'm not necessarily going to kill you."

"No kidding?"

She noticed a blink of messages on the room's phone. "Excuse me." Indecisively he shook the gun to stop her but it was evident he had no instinct for violence.

The first message was from Rook himself, left hours earlier, urging her to *"say nothing more!"* to Sgt. Daniel Hart of Miami Vice.

The other message was from that same Sergeant Hart, apologizing gruffly. He'd been dealing with Rook, then gotten called in by his division chief and, thanks to Annie, reamed out. He'd be in touch. Sit still.

She slammed down the desk phone. "Why is it my fault he got reamed out by his chief?"

"With cops, it's always blame somebody else," the young Cuban growled. "I'm taking that emerald now."

"Fine by me." She handed it to him.

Raffy studied the jewel appreciatively. "So give me the case."

"Sure," she said. "The combination lock on the handle is four numbers. I don't know what they are. There's also a long password my dad needs. Maybe two passwords. I'll give you those for free." She said them very quickly, knowing he couldn't possibly remember them. "362484070N and 678STNX211. Maybe it's a bank account, maybe it's a computer code."

Rook squeezed his eyes tight, puzzled but intrigued. "You didn't make those numbers up?" She shook her head. "He said you could remember numbers like that! I wish I could remember Shakespeare that way. I can only keep a line or two in my head, not like your papa; till his illness, he could do whole scenes. Write those numbers down for me."

"Nope." Annie opened a jar of expensive peanuts from the minibar, offered him some. Malpy crawled out from under the bed to beg to be fed. "Do you know what the passwords are for?"

With an elongated shrug, Raffy tried both to claim and deny knowledge. "We need to talk to Jack. Let me use your phone."

Maybe, thought Annie, her father hadn't confided everything to Rafael Rook. Maybe the Cuban was not a partner but just a flopper, a street musician who made his living by rolling off the front fenders of slow moving cars, then pretending that he'd been struck down by drivers like Joyce Weimar, whom he would trick into paying him not to call the police. Annie knew about floppers; her father had said they were low down in the ranks of his profession of swindles and frauds. Floppers threw themselves in front of the cars of senior citizens who were terrified of losing their licenses and were thereby encouraged to "settle" with the scam artists right then and there to cover their minor injuries: A few hundred in cash should do it, the flopper would say, and the frightened drivers would pay off in order not to risk getting charged with some troublesome misdemeanor. It was the bottom-feeding floor of con work, her dad had said; it was "Slots Life" rather than high stakes.

Rook was helping himself to cashews as if he hadn't eaten all day as he tried to reach his friend Chamayra at Golden Days; finally he left her a cryptic message to call back ASAP, telling her mysteriously that 'the Coach's daughter' had a big present.

Annie studied him for a while. "You ever get hurt flopping?"

He admitted that once he'd broken his arm falling under a Land Rover. But usually it all worked out. He only flopped on women drivers, many of whom "to tell the truth, carry a quantity of cash Santo Trafficante wouldn't be ashamed of. Mostly I look to see if they're Jewish, because they're the ones with my attitude, which is, you never can tell when and where outrageous fortune is going to sling a sea of arrows at your head. My papa's papa, Simon Rook? His papa was Rabbi Rook from Amsterdam who was stung to death by wasps in Naples, Florida. Who could predict that? Grandpapa Simon was always looking for doom to strike him in an instant. And it did."

"This was the man at the Bay of Pigs?"

"Yes." Sadly, Raffy kissed his gold cross. "Face-down in wet sand. A teenager he went to Mexico—I think it was gunrunning, but the family never said—and he met those bastards Ché and Fidel there and went off with them to fight Batista. My grandpapa fell for revolution absolutely without reservations. He fought all the way into Havana. Then he fell in love with my *abuela* because she ran from the sidewalk and kissed him when he marched with the rebels into the city." Raffy slid a much-worn photo of two women from his wallet; he pointed not at the slim middle-aged woman with glossy black hair and beautiful eyes but at an old little bent woman in a black scarf and a black dress, leaning on an orthopedic cane, letting the younger woman embrace her but begrudgingly. She did not at all resemble anyone who would push her way out into the street to kiss a strange soldier in a triumphal parade.

"That's your grandmother?"

"Later in life. That's my mother next to her. So, after Castro takes over, my grandpapa stays in Cuba and gets a big job in the *Departmento America*. The DGI. He marries my grandmama and they move in with her family, Ramirezes, gold- and silversmiths."

She gave him back the old photo. "Simon Rook gave up his U.S. citizenship and became a Communist? So he was actually fighting the Bay of Pigs invasion?"

"Not exactly. Here's the secret, which he never told even his own wife. Simon Rook was CIA from that very first trip to Mexico. His whole family was clueless for years. Then one day he disappeared. Vanished. My papa was young." Annie felt a curious empathy with Rook. He saw her response and nodded at her. "Yes, it hurts a child. But I did the same to my poor mama. Left her and came to America with her brother Mano, the only one with the brains to see that the money had left Havana and moved to Miami."

Raffy finished eating the entire jar of nuts. She suspected he'd had nothing else for lunch and while she didn't mind giving him dinner as well, she didn't want to sit here waiting to do so. "How long before this nurse is going to call?" she asked.

"Chamayra is a true beagle." Raffy opened the minibar and removed a Coca-Cola. He carefully poured the soda into a glass. "Well, Annie, enterprises of great pitch and moment their currents turn awry. My grandpapa Simon left his son, my papa, a letter to be opened after his death that told the whole story. Papa showed the letter to me. My grandpapa admitted it; how the son-of-a-bitch CIA had recruited him. They rewired his head and he became a major player."

She looked skeptical. "A major player?"

"God's truth!" He kissed his cross. "My grandpapa knew Posada and Bosch and Chi Chi Quintero. He knew the guys who worked on Phoenix and Condor. That's right!" Rook lowered his voice as if the room were bugged. "Simon Rook is in the Operation 40 photo with Feliz Rodriquez and Porter Goss but you can't really see him because a waiter's in front of his head. You heard of Brigada 2506?" Annie shook her head no. "You should read about it. Operation Zapata? Well, my grandpapa was one of the guys who sneaked the guns in on the *Barbara* and the *Houston*. But then comes April 17, he's floating in the Bay of Pigs."

Annie said she was sorry to hear it but wasn't sure what any of this had to do with Jewish people carrying lots of cash on their persons.

Raffy drank his Coca-Cola in one long satisfied gurgle. "The point is my grandpapa Simon Rook carried five thousand dollars in a belt beneath his undershirt. For an emergency. I don't know what else you'd want to call the Bay of Pigs. But I guess some bastard stole it off his dead body or it floated out to sea at Puerto Esperanza, one or the other, or maybe the funeral home guy got it because it sure wasn't there when my papa went to see Grandpapa's Simon's body."

Annie's cell phone rang. As she reached for it, Raffy pointed the large revolver at her. "Don't answer that phone unless it's Chamayra."

"Don't point a gun at me!" Losing patience, Annie whacked him on the wrist, hitting the same hand that the little dog had bitten, knocking the gun loose. With a heartbroken groan, Rook writhed on the floor. She leaned over him. "As your pal Shakespeare would say, 'Our remedies oft in ourselves do lie.'" Picking up both his gun and the emerald, she checked his wrist. "It's not broken." She answered her phone.

It was Brad. He wanted her to know Hopper Jets had called him to confirm that the jet she'd "borrowed" had been safely returned. Also that in St. Louis the Hopper machinist was repairing the *King of the Sky*'s engine. Annie could leave the *King* there as long as she liked. Or Brad could arrange to have a Hopper pilot fly it home to Emerald for her.

"Thank you, Brad. I'll take care of it but now I've got to go."

Hang on. He was in Atlanta, enjoying barbeque with Mama Spring and Brandy and her kids, but he couldn't stop thinking about Annie. How about if he flew to Miami tonight?

"Thanks, you're sweet but I'm okay. Don't come. I'll have to call you back."

"What's that noise?" he asked suspiciously. "Somebody's moaning."

"It's a friend of my dad's. I had to take his gun away."

"A, what the hell's going on there? You always told me you didn't care about your dad."

Annie sighed. "Everybody 'cares' about their dads, even if they hate them. Give me a break. You and your mother still spend weekends watching home videos of you in the Swing-o-matic and do you really like her?"

"I love her to death."

"Hmmm. Don't come here but thank you. Bye."

Hanging up on Brad, she knelt down beside the Cuban, who was now squeezing his hand against his chest. "All right, Raffy, I've had it. I'm going to Golden Days right now. Either with you, or with the cops." She showed him the gun. "Use your head. How tough do you think a woman my size has to be to fly combat missions for the U.S. Navy? Tough enough to shoot you in the knee?" She moved the muzzle down the veins of his arm. "How about this same wrist my dog bit? Talk about the day the music stopped."

He stared at her for a moment with his soft dark eyes. "Buchstabe…your dad's checked in as Coach Ronny Buchstabe."

Incredulous, she sat back on the rug. "My dad is calling himself 'Ronny Buchstabe'?"

"You play the hand you're dealt."

Annie pulled the Cuban to his feet by his uninjured arm. "I'm going to change my clothes. If you leave here while I'm in the john, I'm going to make sure the Miami police arrest you. Not to quote the Bard—it's my way or the highway."

He nodded with a bow. "My friend Chamayra comes on duty in half an hour."

"Raffy, 'the readiness is all.'"

"Is that Shakespeare?"

"Sure is."

"You had a good education."

In the bathroom Annie dressed in her white Navy officer's uniform, jacket and slacks. She smoothed the starched collar, tightened the tie. Returning to the bedroom, she took her father's old leather flight jacket from the closet. Raffy sat in a chair leaning over a gleamy guitar, softly plucking the strings, singing in his rustle of a voice.

> Si te contara lo que me hizo esa morena
> Esa mujer que solo me hace suspirar
> Con su cadera

Near him Malpy danced in circles on his back legs as if trying to learn the rumba. Annie stood in the doorway for a while, listening to him play. He was a good guitarist. "That's very pretty," she said when he finished.

He thought she meant the instrument, which he held up proudly. "It's a beauty." The guitar had rosewood sides, a mahogany top, and an ebony fret board. "This guitar," he said with affection, "belonged to my grandmother. My mother's mother. Her family was very traditional. She wanted to play guitar but they wouldn't let her be a professional of course. Such were the times. On her deathbed, she gave the guitar to my cousin Rita. In prison with your papa, a bastard guard smashed my guitar to pieces and so my cousin Rita gave me this one. She said, 'You are the musician. You take it.'" He sighed sadly. "I'm not so good."

"You're not bad at all. And your singing? I liked it."

As Annie put out water for Malpy, Raffy strummed the guitar softly and sang,

> What is love? 'Tis not hereafter.
> Present mirth hath present laughter.
> What's to come is still unsure...

"Shakespeare. I can't remember any more. Just don't have the brain for it."

"It's lovely." She picked up her cell phone and dropped it in her purse, then folded her father's flight jacket over her arm. "Ready."

He sighed, fitting the guitar back into its case. "'The readiness is all.'"

Chapter 32
Ace of Aces

The sun was setting and its glow lit up the lawn of Golden Days where a dozen elderly patients (gold suns embroidered on the pockets of their waffled bathrobes) sat slumped in wheelchairs on the lawn. They looked as if visitors, suddenly remembering more pressing engagements and rushing away, had abandoned them there.

The grass was neon-green; big red and purple flowers grew in bright heaps along curving brick walks. In trees, yellow lemons and fat oranges weighed down the branches, glistening as candy drops.

On a bench beside a turn in the walk, three thin little women sat together, their skin shriveled from their bones, so small that their white-socked feet dangled loosely above the grass. The woman in the middle of this group struggled with a red tangle of knitting in her lap while the other two wound together a big twisted skein of blood-red yarn. Against their chalky hands, the red wool looked like a bouquet of roses they were fighting over. Annie set Malpy down on the grass and he ran over to them.

A black Mercedes smoothly stopped at the curb. Its black-suited driver slid out and leaned against the dark tinted window, staring at them from behind his wraparound sunglasses. He wore a phone earpiece. His large black car had a mournful air but the driver looked too stylish in his linen shirt for the funeral business. Rafael reacted in surprise, as if he knew the man.

A well-built gray-haired man in a gray silk suit slipped out of the back seat of the Mercedes. Raffy had been watching the car carefully. When he saw this man in the gray suit take off his sunglasses, he sucked in his breath loudly.

"What's the matter?" Annie asked the Cuban.

"Nada." But he abruptly grabbed Annie's purse and with it raced off to the side of the Golden Days building, disappearing behind flowering bushes.

The gray-haired man bent down to re-tie his glistening shoe. Then he started up the hospital walk, passing not far from where Annie stood near the old women's bench. He passed close enough for her to see that he had a black mole beside his mouth. Nearby, a male nurse stood smoking on the lawn. The gray-haired man approached the nurse, began asking him questions. Their conversation went on for a while. Finally the nurse nodded, pointing at the top floor of the stucco building.

At that instant a slender woman slid out of the backseat of the Mercedes and ran toward the man. Handsome, she looked to be in her forties. She wore oversized sunglasses and a loose stylish linen jacket over a short skirt; everything about her looked like bright metal—from gold bracelet to bronze-hued shoulder bag to dark-gold hair so brilliant it was like a snaky coil of copper wires. She hurried onto the lawn, sliding her arm under the man's arm and urging him back toward their driver. The driver energetically waved a cell phone and called to him, *"Jefe! Pronto!"*

Across the path, the woman caught Annie's eye and she took off her sunglasses. They stared at each other for an instant; it felt longer to Annie because so many disjointed images flashed at her, like slides too quickly changing. The woman looked familiar, yet Annie didn't know her. She had a jarring flash of the woman with pink sweatshirt and flip-flops outside the lobby of the Admirals Club at the St. Louis airport. But the two women weren't at all alike. Besides, why should a woman she'd seen a day before in the Midwest be here at Golden Days in Miami? Then two other images pushed the present aside. Both were out of place here in Miami. They were Emerald images from long ago. One was a picture on the wall of Georgette's bedroom; one took place in the kitchen at Pilgrim's Rest, where Sam sat crying.

Again, the driver called, *"Jefe!"* and waved his phone. Exasperated, the gray-haired man jerked around, striding back to the car, grabbing the cell phone from the driver. Whatever the caller said to the man, it changed his mind about visiting Golden Days. Angrily, he slid into the rear seat of the Mercedes, gesturing at the woman to join him.

The three elderly patients, scrambling up from their bench, accidentally tangled themselves against the woman as she hurried toward the car. Fighting free, she knocked two of them onto the concrete walk.

Malpy jumped on the woman. She flung him off with a violent gesture. With an ear-piercing squeal, the little dog hid in the azaleas.

Annie helped the two old people struggle to their feet. She called after the woman, who had now reached the Mercedes door. "Excuse me! How about an apology?"

The woman turned, took off her sunglasses again; her deep blue eyes looked blank. She slipped into the car, her coppery hair ablaze in the low slant of sun.

The black sedan sped away.

Annie stood watching until it was out of sight. She couldn't shake the picture of Sam at the kitchen table at Pilgrim's Rest. Annie, in her early teens, entered the room. Seated across from Sam was a woman who looked a little like this woman. Sam was crying. Annie stopped in the doorway, struck by the emotional intensity. Sam and the woman looked up at her. That was all she could remember of the scene. It had been so long ago, so brief and so vague she couldn't even be sure exactly how old she'd been when it had happened.

On the Golden Days lawn, the three patients pressed around her, thanking her. One was bleeding from a scrape on her knee; another was clutching her elbow. Annie retrieved her father's flight jacket. "She knocked you down. I saw the Mercedes' plate number. I could call the police."

The woman with the knitting needles shook them in the direction of the car. "She was a bitch, wasn't she? Total bitch!"

Her friend agreed. "Worse bitch than Ms. Skippings!"

The knitter weakly smoothed the thin white curls of her hair. "That was nice of you," she told Annie. "Who do you have here?"

It took Annie a second. "Oh, you mean staying here? I'm visiting my father."

The knitter squeezed Annie's arm with sharp bony fingers. "That's nice of you." She smiled. "What's his name?"

"Jack Peregrine," said Annie. "No, I'm sorry, I mean, Ronny Buchstabe. My father's Coach Ronny Buchstabe. Do you know him?"

"No. I have a daughter."

Another old woman pushed to the front. "I have two daughters."

The woman with the knitting wasn't interested. "Where's the dog, the white dog?"

"Here he is!" shouted a man sliding toward them by means of a walker. Malpy was trotting beside him, his tail a brisk flag not of surrender but of salutation. He'd suffered no damage to his pride from being flung to the grass; in general, he forgot assaults as soon as they were over. Happily the old people circled him. The little dog began busily showing off his back-leg dancing trick in exchange for everything edible they could scrounge from their hoarded rations—bits of banana and apple, Junior Mints, corn chips.

Out of bougainvillea blossoms at the far corner of the building Annie saw Rafael Rook poking his head, like a swimmer in an Esther Williams production number. By complicated gestures he telegraphed her to join him but to leave Malpy behind.

The old people were glad to keep the Maltese while she went inside. The dog was a bouncy, licking, yapping scrap of life, a distraction from dying, and if Annie had asked them instead, "How would you like to be as young as I am and madly in love?" they could not have assented more heartily.

"His name's Malpractice," she explained. They found this hilarious, having been subjected to so much of it themselves. "Malpy. Don't give him seafood."

Raffy returned her purse to her. "Pardon, pardon," he whispered as he led her behind the Dumpster at the rear of the building. "But discretion is the better part, if you take my meaning."

"Raffy! You can't just run off with my purse!"

"I had to use your phone. A family emergency."

Automatically, she checked inside the small black Coach bag for her wallet. It was there. "You knew that man and woman in the Mercedes."

"Not to speak to."

"Well, that much was obvious since you ran away."

"Happiness eludes them. Certain people could definitely use a little less caffeine, up the dosage on their serotonin, aromatherapy, maybe spend quality time on a nature walk or even a cat, little bird even—"

"You ran to the bushes."

Raffy lowered his voice as if he could be overheard. "With that man, I tell you the truth, the bushes are not a bad plan. I am a naked newborn sitting on a shark's molars in comparison to that man, who is not a nice man, any more than Castro was the Second Coming the way he convinced my Uncle Oswardo he was. That's Feliz Diaz."

Annie shrugged.

"Feliz Diaz. There are many people in Miami, when he says vote they vote; go throw rocks, they go. When he says buy that, they buy that. So on. The ace of aces. I heard in Little Havana, he blew a man's hand off with a Beretta 92FS for misdealing the cards. There was talk of the incident on the street for years."

Annie interrupted him. "Is the woman with him involved with my father?"

Rook gestured uncertainty. "I doubt it."

"I feel like I've seen her before."

Raffy shrugged evasively. "Annie, I swear, I'm a prop, I swell a scene, I'm a man of plastic packing bubbles. All I know is, Jack asked for my help: 'Raffy, send this FedEx to my daughter; make this phone call, pick me up off this curb, and drag me into a hospital.' Nightly I read the 'Swan of Avon,' to whom he introduced me in our prison cell in Cuba, for which I can never sufficiently thank him for I hate ingratitude worse—"

"Please don't start talking Shakespeare."

"The complete works from one volume at Costco. The Poet has a way of putting things nobody could improve on. 'Lady, you are not worth the dust the rude wind blows in your face.' That's what I say to the *puta* that knocked those old ladies down. Could you say better than that? Could I?"

Annie was struggling to connect the face she'd just seen with the memory of Sam's crying at the kitchen table. Then abruptly it came to her—the family portrait on Georgette's bedroom wall of Georgette's father and his sister. She said, "I think that woman was my neighbor's aunt, from my home town. I think she's a woman named Ruthie Nickerson. Do you know that name? Ruth Nickerson?"

Raffy looked puzzled. "Why would she be your neighbor's aunt? She belongs to Diaz." Raffy looked furtively at his watch. "We've got to go."

He pulled her around behind the Dumpster, past a pile of garbage bags and up some stairs to the Golden Days rear landing, the door of which he propped open with his sneaker.

"Why can't we walk in the damn front door?" she asked him. "Shhhh."

A pretty Latina woman in a nurse's uniform suddenly appeared in the doorway, her finger to her lips.

"Chamayra!" Raffy embraced her with unexpected fervor. She pushed him away, her finger again pressed urgently against her lips. Then without a backward glance she walked ahead of them.

They hurried along a maze of concrete corridors and up staircases that took them to the third floor, which seemed to be the ward for patients near the end of their lives, whether they knew it or not, and most seemed not to. There was no one this elderly or this ill in Annie's life and until this moment she had never found herself inside such a ward. On the landing she had to squeeze by a wraith of an old woman with blue veins and wild white hair, who beat her head against the dinner tray on her wheelchair and whimpered that she wanted her mother. When Annie, picking up a fallen plastic cup, said hello, the old woman grabbed and kissed her hand.

They passed an old man with huge purple feet leaning on a walker and talking furiously to a mirror. He told the mirror that his son had stolen his shoes so that he couldn't get back to the office.

Finally Chamayra signaled to Raffy that they should wait in the corridor, that she'd return for them.

Annie looked into rooms in which the old were staring without interest at car chases on outmoded televisions hung from concrete ceilings. When she said hello, some smiled gratefully; some stared blankly through her. She wondered if Sam had put her mother, Grandee, in a rest home like this and if so, how had someone as loving as Sam borne doing so?

Beside her, Raffy sighed. "Youth's a stuff." He pointed at a room where two men sat slumped, patient, on the sides of their beds. "Nobody believes that this sad destination could possibly be our own. But it's as true as dirt."

Shifting her father's jacket, Annie turned around to the Cuban. And for the first time she looked deeply into his eyes, which were warm and, oddly, it occurred to her, not unwise. "Occasionally, Raffy, you make sense."

His high-boned face rounded with pleasure. "Gracias. I do have some personal thoughts on our human history, but the Bard provides a more concise and poetical summation." He blinked as if to block out knowledge. "I don't know, should I laugh or cry, because frankly, Annie, what a world, what an awful world. 'Robes and furr'd gowns hide all.'" He tugged at his ponytail with both hands. "Lear found that fact out in stormy weather. If you look around you, and most don't, the world breaks your heart…" He glanced at her shyly. "Chamayra says I talk too much." With his small graceful fingers, he made a time-out signal, then slit his throat, zipped his lips, lowered an invisible bag over his head and tied an invisible string tightly around his neck and hanged himself.

They laughed together quietly.

"Shhhh!" Chamayra appeared on the staircase and motioned for them to follow her.

Midway down a hall of closed doors, Chamayra stopped at a room where a card identified the patient within as "Coach Ronny Buchstabe." With a tap on the door, she told Annie, "Good luck," then gave her hips a shake at Raffy and walked in an efficiently provocative way down the hall, vanishing around a corner.

"See you tonight," he called after her.

Her head reemerged and she put her finger to her lips.

"Sorry," Raffy called.

Annie's hand touched the door. "My dad's in here?"

"Now, Annie, don't let it show, all right? About the cancer. He doesn't want to talk about it." With a careful look both to left and right, the Cuban pulled her in through the door and quickly shut it behind them.

With its blinds closed and lights out, the bare frugal room was in shadows and very still. Motionless on the utilitarian bed, tilted up at an angle, lay a thin man, with his wrist attached to an IV drip and an oxygen feed clipped to his nose. The palms of his hands were bandaged.

Leading Annie to the bedside, Raffy leaned over and whispered to the prone figure, "Jack? You awake, Jack? I got her. Here she is."

Slowly the head turned, the eyes opened and looked at Annie. Years, decades, flung away and memory rushed in. She had known those facetious green gold-specked eyes from the beginning of her life.

"Annie..."

"...Dad?"

Chapter 33
Skylark

Jack Peregrine's face was bruised, his cheek and lip swollen and cut, his color flat white. His breath was so shallow it was slow to fill the next words. "…Raffy, look, what a beautiful woman…"

"Absolutely," agreed the young Cuban as he moved away from them to stand near the window, out of which he kept nervously looking.

Jack Peregrine raised himself with effort. His taped palms had the look of someone about to pull on boxing gloves. "Beautiful. You're just gorgeous."

Annie stepped aside so the slanted light didn't strike her. She tried for irony but couldn't keep sorrow from her voice. "So, Coach Ronny, what's wrong with you? Are you ill or did somebody beat you up?"

He made an effort at a grin. "Like the Ringo Kid said, 'There are some things a man just can't run away from.'" Slowly he wriggled his fingers. "A man can try but some times he's just not fast enough."

"What happened to your hands?"

He held them out to her. "You should see the rest of me. Raffy saved the day."

The Cuban returned to the bedside to corroborate. "He was lying there, blood everywhere, and I leaned down and he whispered, 'Raffy!'"

"I thought I was *yelling*, 'Raffy!' If he hadn't dragged me off the sidewalk and gotten me in here to Chamayra, I'd be dead."

"Inevitable," Raffy agreed.

"Or worse," her father said. "I'd be in jail. Somebody across the street had watched these guys kicking me to the curb and called 911. We saw the squad car arrive."

"We were hiding right out there by the dumpster, waiting for Chamayra to let us in before the bastards came back or your poor dad bled to death. The cops looked around but they didn't see us." Raffy kissed his cross then returned to the window where he banged his back ferociously against the wall. "Those bastard *s.o.b. pingitas!* They would chainsaw the fingers off Elton John."

Her father gestured at his friend's bandage. "What happened to *your* hand?"

"Her dog bit me," Raffy explained. "It's okay. I can still play. She's got your metal case, Jack. And she's got the emerald. And she knows the codes."

Jack smiled. "Good girl." He nodded at the Cuban who excused himself; he'd keep watch by the door.

Annie arched her Colbert eyebrow at her father. "Even *s.o.b.*s have reasons for what they do...So, did 'these guys' have any particular reason to kill you?"

Jack smiled. "Ah, you were a skeptic before you could walk and you're still a skeptic."

She shook her head at him. "This isn't skeptical; it's a real question: Wouldn't sitting in jail be preferable to being kicked to death?"

He shrugged, a frail version of his old nonchalant style. "For some people it's heights, for some it's rats, for me it's jail. Sorry I skipped out on you in St. Louis but I couldn't take the chance."

"Hey." She mimicked his shrug. "Nothing new."

He moved in the bed as if adjusting to pain. "Thanks for bringing the *King*. Sorry I couldn't fly with you."

She told him the plane was now in the Hopper lot at the St. Louis airport. The engine had died on her while she was landing.

He murmured so quietly she had to bend over his pillow to hear him. "Thanks for trying."

"You're welcome. Thanks for the card at the Admirals Club. A little soupy." She pulled the crumpled flowery To My Daughter birthday card from the flight jacket.

He shook his head, looking baffled. "I didn't leave this at the Admirals Club." He read it aloud. "'Annie. Wrong to get you involved. Stay out of this. Go home. Love you.' I didn't write this. Who told you I did?"

"The receptionists at the Admirals Club. Well, they said an old woman brought it in and told them someone had asked her to leave it at the Admirals Club for me."

He looked concerned. "An old woman?"

Annie let out a breath. "Don't try. You know you wrote it. Who else?" She put the card in her purse.

Frowning, he insisted, "Does it sound like me?"

"How would I know?" She tossed his jacket on the bed. "Here's your jacket. So is it mainly criminals who're after you or mainly the Miami police or the St. Louis police or what?"

He sounded preoccupied, his thoughts still on the birthday card. "People get in a rut; they keep doing what they're paid to do. Could be anything; happens to be me they're after."

She told him she'd just gotten an anonymous call from a woman, a warning to keep away from him.

He looked even more worried. "What do you mean? What did she say?"

"She asked me if I was Annie Goode from Emerald, and when I said I was in Miami, she said, 'Don't let Jack drag you into something that can get you both in real trouble.' Meanwhile, what is everybody doing with my new cell phone number anyhow? Where did you get it—Sam?"

"Yes," he said. "Sam."

"Well, please stop passing it around. Who is she, this woman that called?"

He kept shaking his head softly against the pillow. "No idea. What did she sound like?"

Annie thought a moment. "…Like cigarettes in a black and white movie."

"Ah," he said. Then he shook his head.

The hospital room had nothing personal in it. She opened its closet but there was nothing inside, no clothes, no suitcase. Walking to the foot of his bed, she told him, "Talk. Here I am. What do you want?"

He grinned wanly at her. "So you found the courier case?"

Yes, she'd found the courier case in the panel in the rear of the *King of the Sky*; it was back at the hotel. What was in it?

He said matter-of-factly, "A sixteenth-century statue of the Virgin Mary."

Her eyebrow lifted. "Sure."

"Remember, I used to tell you about her. *La Reina Coronada del Mar?*"

"Sure." She gestured in Raffy's direction. "I guess that's why you and Raffy bought that Cessna Amphibian plane for your company La Reina. So you could go visit the Queen in Cuba. By the way, that Cessna's registration number, N678ST, is part of your password."

Jack gave her the smile that as a little girl she had worked so hard to earn; the reason she would try to get all the numbers right, win the prize, the A-plus. "How'd you find that out?"

"A friend in the FBI." She studied him a while. "Can you really even fly a plane?"

"I love to fly." Quietly he quoted, "'To a skylark, the earth is scornful.' Have I got that right?" He pressed his fingers at his temple. "Terrible when you can't remember the poetry you loved. Remember when we used to—"

She interrupted him, holding up a warning hand. "Where's your Cessna now?"

"In Key West, parked in a lot at the Key West airport." He rubbed at his bandages. "On hold."

"Repossessed?"

"Sort of. You know Key West?"

Annie had both trained and taught at Naval Air Station Key West on Boca Chica. She'd even led a practice mission to "bomb" the Marquesas "Patricia" Target, a hulking shipwreck just west of that base. Was that what he wanted, she asked, for her to fly the Cessna somewhere for him?

"Exactly right," he told her.

Raffy inserted himself into the conversation, lifting his thin shoulders to Annie in supplication. "We need help. Even if Jack had his hands, which he does not, there is unfortunately now a new problem. The police are watching the Cessna like foxes."

She looked at her father's bandaged palms; it was true that piloting wouldn't be easy with those injuries. Moreover, his face looked blanched, his lips thinned by pain. Was it the beating he'd suffered or had she been wrong to doubt that he was dying of cancer? "Is there a doctor I can talk to here?"

"The best time's in the morning." He gestured at his bruised face and made an effort at the old lovely grin. "A mess, huh? I had some…" He rubbed his forearms against the sides of his head. "Some treatments."

"What kind of treatments?"

Raffy pulled her aside. "He doesn't like to talk about it."

Her father nodded. "Result is, I can't remember things. Isn't that something? I used to be able to recite whole scenes, whole acts."

"*Hamlet*, start to finish more or less," testified Raffy.

Her father reached under his pillow and took out a small envelope. From it he shook out two large rectangular green stones. They looked to be cut like the emerald she'd brought with her. Impatiently he gestured at her and spilled them into her palm. "They go in the Queen of the Sea's crown, okay? Believe me, they were a bitch to recover. But that's what I get for burying bones."

Oddly enough, she immediately knew what he meant. "You hid one of these emeralds in the cockpit of the Lindbergh plane in the airport," she told him. "You hid one in the bathroom at the Royal Coach. You had to go to St. Louis to get both." They were statements, not questions.

He stared at her, slowly smiled the old smile that she didn't consciously remember but that her muscles knew and echoed.

"You were always so damn smart," he said. "I've sold the Queen. I said I was leaving you a million dollars." He laughed. "I am. More."

Raffy glared at his friend, surprised and not entirely pleased. Jack shrugged. It seemed to be a whole conversation, the look between them.

Annie shook her head. "I don't want a million dollars. I don't want anything from you." She dropped the green stones on the bed tray.

Surprisingly the young Cuban took her hand and brought it to his lips. "Wisdom from *Lear*, Annie. Goneril and Regan? Let us grant those two daughters were 100 percent right. Their papa was not an easy man. Lear had serious—" He searched around the room for a word. "Insufficiencies. But in the end, why couldn't Goneril and Regan show him a little kindness? Like Cordelia did. She didn't take his kingdom from him, and frankly your papa shouldn't exactly give away money he doesn't exactly have, but what did it cost Cordelia to be nice? Nothing."

Annie snorted. "Raffy, Cordelia gets strangled to death."

His chocolate-sweet eyes dilated, his mouth fell open. "She does? Her own sisters kill her?"

"By then I think her sisters are already dead themselves."

He looked distressed. "I'm only in Act Four. Cordelia dies?"

"And Lear and the Fool die too. Everybody dies in the end."

"Ah me ah me ah me." Mournfully the slender Cuban slipped through the door into the hall and closed it behind him.

To Annie the moment felt hallucinogenic. Rafael Rook's dissonant musings, her father's presence in her life again, the thrust of their conversation. Everything was too removed from the ordinary to assimilate, too incongruous with the routines that for decades had organized her orderly days. She felt as if she were being asked to converse in an alien language in a foreign place she'd been told she had once visited but of which she had only the most dreamlike recollections.

Walking over to the small smudged hospital window, she looked out, trying to orient herself. It was dusk; long shadows poured over the lawn. Golden Days patients still sat outside in their chairs, most of them sleeping. She turned back to her father. "Coming to see you, I had a strange run-in with a couple out on the lawn there."

"A strange run-in?"

She described her encounter outside. "And here's what's weird. Long time ago I met Georgette Nickerson's aunt Ruth. This woman on the lawn brought Ruth back to me so..." She thought back to how she'd felt. "...so *intensely*. Is there any reason Ruthie Nickerson would show up here to visit you?"

Jack's mouth tightened, but so slightly that if he hadn't given her early lessons in looking for such signs, she wouldn't have seen it. "Who?" he asked.

"Ruthie, from next door in Emerald, George Nickerson's sister, remember him? You may not have heard. George died of a heart attack, long time ago, before I came to Emerald, before you left me at Pilgrim's Rest."

His bandaged fingers moved lightly over the green jewels. "Sam told me George died. She said our mother scared him to death when she hammered his store window." He pulled himself up on the pillows. "George scared easily."

"I wondered if maybe you were...I don't know...involved with Ruthie."

He said "involved" would be an exaggeration. "For a little while I had a crush on her. It wasn't particularly reciprocated."

She persisted. "Could she have been this woman I saw here today?"

He kept frowning. "Ruthie Nickerson?"

"Yes," she repeated impatiently. "Georgette's aunt. Georgette and I are good friends. Best friends."

He stared at her. "That's nice. George would have liked that." It was disconcerting to hear him talk so familiarly about Georgette's father. He asked her when she'd met Ruthie.

"At Pilgrim's Rest. Long time ago. She was visiting Sam one evening. Only that once. The Nickersons didn't keep up with her. I remember Georgette's mother Kim really didn't like her.

But I've seen a painting she's in with Georgette's dad. And photos. This woman today—"

He shook his head firmly. "Ruthie Nickerson? Not possible."

"She just looked so familiar. This woman drove up with a gray-haired man in a Mercedes. It was like they were headed inside here, then all of a sudden they turned around and drove off."

On his elbows, her father pulled himself up even higher and tried to look out the small window. "Who drove off?"

"Raffy knew them. He said the man was Feliz Diaz."

Urgently, Jack called out in a louder voice than she'd heard him use before. "Raffy! Raffy!"

The Cuban quickly slipped back inside the room, sliding the door closed. "Keep your voice down!"

"Diaz was here and you didn't tell me?"

Raffy gently pressed Jack's shoulders back on the pillow. "I took care of it, Jack. I didn't want you to worry. He's gone."

"Gone where?"

Raffy stroked his friend's arm. "It was really clever. I take Annie's phone. I quick call the driver—I know him from the band days, good cornet player—and I tell him to get Diaz on the phone pronto pronto. He does and I tell Diaz it's me and I've got the Queen for him." Raffy nodded proudly. "That's right. I tell Diaz you're hiding out on the Keys but I know where you left the Queen. I tell him I'll sell you out for fifteen grand, cash. I made it a big number. I say I'm at the Hyatt in West Palm and that's where the Queen is and if he brings me the cash tonight at eight, I'll give the statue to him. He bought it 300 percent. He thinks he got a bum steer, whoever told him you were staying at Golden Days. So he drives off and never knows you're here. Pretty smart, huh?"

Annie could see thoughts move in Jack's eyes, looking for angles. He tapped his friend's arm. "Yes, very smart. Until eight o'clock when you won't be at the Hyatt." He wondered aloud who'd told Diaz he was hiding here at Golden Days.

Raffy hunched his shoulders. The birds on his shirt hunched too. "I do not know the answer to that question. But you don't have to worry. I said some rats were spreading the rumor. I said I'd *tried* to make you stay here at Golden Days, but you'd *refused*; I said you'd told me you'd rather die on the side of the road."

Jack made a rueful face. "That much is true. Okay, thanks, Raffy. Very smart."

The Cuban slipped back out through the door.

With a clumsy movement of his bandaged hand, Jack pulled out a small old-fashioned-looking pack of Chesterfields from under the sheet. The effort appeared to exhaust him and he made no attempt to light the cigarette.

She studied him a while. "Why don't you give yourself up and sort this thing out before somebody does kill you. If you've actually got a relic that belongs to Cuba, give it to the police. Get yourself in a good hospital and for God's sake, stop smoking. I can't believe they even still sell those things."

"Oh, darlin', they sell anything somebody wants and somebody wants everything." Her father pressed his bandaged hands together as if they were shackled. "I can't be locked up again, not even overnight. I really can't. So I was, well, damn grateful to Sam and Brad for getting me to Miami. Me and a whole cargo of express smoked salmon."

Ruefully Annie shrugged at this confirmation that Sam and Brad had arranged to fly her father out of St. Louis. "Sam's fond of Brad."

"You're not?" he asked.

Unaware, she rubbed at her unadorned ring finger. "We're getting a divorce."

He looked saddened. "I'm sorry."

She crossed her arms. "You can love somebody who doesn't deserve it."

He smiled. "Who else is there?"

Abruptly she asked him if he'd ever been married to her mother. And by the way, where was her mother?

His cough sounded real. He seemed unable to stop. "Never married, no clue where she is." The sharp relentless coughing doubled him over.

"Is this cancer operable?" She wondered why there was no medical chart attached to the foot of the bed.

"Nope. But stranger things have happened. Than my dying, I mean."

By now Annie had had time to collect herself. Her face was calm, her voice level. "I only came here to find out my mother's name." She moved beside his bedside table, took the emerald on a chain from her pocket, showed it to him and dropped it on the tray beside the other two. "Just the truth."

He looked up at her, rubbed at his nose where the oxygen tube was clipped. "Dangerous thing..." he whispered. "Truth."

"No, it's a little knowledge that's a dangerous thing—" She started to add, "Dad," but the word now stuck between palate and tongue. She said, "Jack," instead.

"Think so?" he asked. "I always thought truth was a lot more equivocal than its reputation...You are just beautiful." With a delicate incredulous shake of his head, he touched one of the gold buttons on her white uniform cuff. "Remember when we bought you that sailor jacket, gold buttons down the front?"

Her mouth tightened against memory but she admitted, "Yes, I loved that jacket."

"Admiral Annie."

She almost laughed, then thought, why should she laugh or cry or feel any of the things she was feeling? Irony took hold of her and sat her down. "I'm not an admiral but I am a naval lieutenant. Well, first I went to elementary school. Your sister Sam raised me. Sam and Clark. You know, after you dropped me off when I was seven and drove away? I went to high school, and after Annapolis, I went to flight school, oh, and I got married to a fellow cadet, your buddy Brad Hopper, and now I'm getting a divorce, but I told you that. Brad holds the fighter test-flight range record for the FA-18E Hornet. I hold the second-place record. Later this month, I've got a chance to set a new record in an experimental jet."

He smiled quietly at her. "A-plus."

"So thanks for giving me the *King of the Sky*. It was the start of something good in my life."

"I'm worn out," he said, an astonishing admission. "Wizard of Nod, huh? Maybe I'll take a nap."

Annie looked around the room for signs of medical apparatus. Surely he'd be in intensive care if he were in imminent danger; he'd be on a heart monitor; he'd be better attended. "I'm taking you out of here. This is bullshit treatment you're getting; your oxygen isn't even on."

Her father turned his head toward the tank by the bed. "It's not?"

"What's your doctor's name?"

He hesitated. Raffy called from the doorway, through the opening of which his head had periodically projected every few minutes. "His doctor is Parker, Dr. Tom Parker. He'll be here at eight in the morning."

Jack just kept smiling. "Let's don't talk about doctors now. Every night, every motel, you'd line up your shoes at the foot of the bed. Tennis shoes, cowboy boots—"

"I don't want to talk about life on the road. I want my mother's name." She backed away from him. "You faked a birth certificate saying Claudette Colbert was my mother. Last night you told me her name was Geraldine Jeffers, a character Claudette Colbert played in *Palm Beach Story*."

His eyes closed. His hands lifted, fell and he changed the subject, the way he always had. "Your aunt Sam…she's great, isn't she?"

Annie said, yes, she was.

"Sam and I used to sneak off to watch movies together. Get more out of life, go to the movies. And believe me, darlin', life with Judge and Mrs. Peregrine? That was definitely a life you wanted to get more out of—"

Drawn back to him, pulling a metal chair toward his bed, she sat down. "So do better than they did. Here's your chance, Dad. There won't be another one. Talk to me about my mother. Tell me about her."

He turned so the slanted light from the half-closed blinds caught his face; his gold mustache was paler; his green eyes, she realized, resembled Sam's and like Sam's were unmistakably filled with affection for her. It was disconcerting.

"Okay, fine, it's no fun but I'll tell you the story." He began, the way he'd always started, "A long time ago..."

"Don't tell me a story. Tell me the truth."

"This is a true story." He gestured to the window, where the last slant of sun streamed in, blinding him until she adjusted the shade so he lay there in shadows. "Your mom and I met in Barbados. We hustled bridge games at the beach resorts. We were good at it. She liked the life there, so we hired on fulltime at this resort: she's bartending, I'm waiting tables. Tips are great, plus introductions to suckers. We're really young, just hanging, still in our late teens."

Annie's heart quickened. Her father's voice had a flat sound that rang true to her. Was this it finally? Her mother not a princess, not a rock star, just a teenager hustling tourists in the Caribbean sun and surf? Had Annie come all this way to stop dreaming?

Chapter 34
Reach for the Sky

From under his pillow, Jack slid a silver cigarette lighter, with the engraved initial C. He tumbled it between his fingers. Given his burns, Annie would have thought the movement would have been painful.

His cough stopped him and he rested, then went on with his story. "Here's the way it was. Your mother is smart, super-smart, and she talks all the time about wanting to go to college. But she's three months pregnant. We discuss abortion but she's torn; it goes against something in her. We worry the thing back and forth, back and forth. Then, one day, she decides to have the baby. Why?"

Annie raised her eyebrow. "Why?"

"Claudette Colbert. We run into Claudette Colbert on Silver Sands Beach."

She laughed. "Come on."

He waved his hand. "I'm serious. We're walking on the beach; Claudette Colbert's having a picnic all by herself, sitting there in a canvas chair with a big striped umbrella, and a little table with champagne and coffee ice cream on it and she's smoking. Chain smoker." He held up the cigarette lighter. "She was a gorgeous woman. She really was."

Disbelieving, Annie frowned. "You met Claudette Colbert on a beach in Barbados?"

"We get into a conversation. We hit it off." Jack showed the silver lighter to Annie. "She gave me this lighter that day. It happened to be my birthday and I said so and right there on the beach she said, 'Here, Jack, happy birthday.'"

Annie thought, It's possible; things like that do happen.

"So she asks if your mother's pregnant and we get into the abortion thing and she encourages us to have the baby. She was very sweet to your mom and me. Your mom was really listening to her advice. I mean, she was Claudette Colbert. Finally Colbert's chauffeur drove up behind the beach and walked down to get her and we helped him pack her up and she gave us a ride back to the resort."

Annie's memories raced through snippets of all the Claudette Colbert films she'd studied so earnestly as a child. It was easy to imagine the star in the setting. "The movie star Claudette Colbert? It Happened One Night, Palm Beach Story, that Claudette?"

"Yes." He dropped the lighter in her hand. "She had a home on the island; she sort of retired there."

Annie studied the beautiful initial C on the slender silver lighter. She had always assumed that her father had chosen the actress's name entirely randomly. But what if the story was real? On the other hand, C could be anybody's initial. "So then what happened?"

He told her that at about this time they'd met a couple from Ohio whom they'd gotten to know by playing bridge with them at the resort. This couple hadn't been able to have a baby. The wife was sweet and desperate; the husband was practical and rich. After weeks of talking it over, Annie's mother, more and more feeling Jack and she weren't ready for marriage, much less a family, finally decided to carry the baby to term and give it to this couple. She believed giving up the baby would be best for all of them, for Jack and her, and most of all best for the baby, who would grow up in a stable, well-to-do home.

The Ohio couple offered Jack a check for twenty-five thousand dollars to "help with the costs" of Annie's birth. Jack took it. He knew it was really a check to purchase Annie but he never said so to the couple, nor did they say so to him. He cashed it and put the cash in their dresser drawer.

Annie winced. "Cheap at the price."

Her father nodded. "Much too cheap."

Annie thought about it. "So that's where that story came from, about how you could have sold me for twenty-five thousand dollars? Sam thought it came from the movies."

"Things do." He reached awkwardly, only the top half of his fingers free of bandages, for a wallet on the bedside tray. From it he took a faded snapshot: it was a delivery room picture of a pink newborn, minutes old, bawling. "I saved this."

Annie looked at herself, an hour old.

"Fourth of July. Anne Samantha Peregrine. I named you for Sam. Two days later, I'm back in the hospital looking at you. I go in the maternity ward and your mom's checked out. Gone."

"Gone?" She repeated the word; it tasted strange in her mouth. Every word he said was like a bitter taste.

"This hospital is real loose on the rules and I tell them it's just a communication glitch between your mom and me. I take you and I run back to the resort, a little one-room tin-roof bungalow we had, and I lie you down on the bed, pillows 'round you so you won't roll off. I notice, your mom's clothes are gone. The twenty-five thousand in cash is gone. No note, nothing. I run all over the island, looking. Finally a guy working at the resort tells me a taxi drove her to the airport." His bandaged hands stroked along the white starched sheet. "Never saw her again."

Shaken, Annie tried to take it in. "My mother gave me up to this couple from Ohio and then she left you without a word?"

His hands lifted, opened. "I spent months going back over it, everything she said, every look. She'd planned it all, how she'd leave. Tell you the truth, Annie, I didn't mean that much to her. And afterwards? I'm sure she figured you were leading a nice normal Ohio life with nice normal parents. Why should she think I'd keep you?" He turned his hands back and forth close to his face, examining them as if the bandages were a surprise.

"Why did you?" Why *hadn't* he given her to the couple who had paid twenty-five thousand dollars for her?

His eyes closed. "Couldn't."

The claim silenced her. She studied him lying there for a while. Finally he opened his eyes again. "Claudette bought you some baby clothes. Those first weeks, sometimes she'd drop in the restaurant; she'd sit in a chair and hold you and talk to you."

Annie thought of the film star in *Since You Went Away*, with her two daughters kneeling beside her chair. How kind she had looked in that film, in all her films. It would have been lovely, really, to grow up as Claudette Colbert's daughter.

Jack finished his story. The couple from Ohio, who'd prepaid for a baby they'd never seen, returned to Barbados as arranged, the night before he was scheduled to give them the three-week-old. Instead, he fled the island, taking Annie with him. He flew to Key West in a friend's plane and hid out there. Another friend in Key West who worked at a hospital did the paperwork so Annie would be born in America instead of Barbados. "In case you wanted to be president." Friends back at the resort sent him news that the Ohio couple had searched the whole island for Jack and the baby but had never gone to the police about their twenty-five thousand dollars. It was, after all, an illegal adoption for which they'd paid.

A year later, in a poker game in Palm Beach, Jack won the single-engine Piper Warrior that he'd renamed the *King of the Sky*. He took the plane and Annie to Emerald. She was a year old and she learned to walk at Pilgrim's Rest.

Annie didn't speak for a long time. Then she walked to the window and tilted her head so she could see the sky. "Sam said that's why it felt like home to me." She looked back at him.

His hands rested on the faded leather of the brown flight jacket. "So that's the truth," he said. "I couldn't let you go." A single tear fell from his pale face to the paler pillow.

Her eyebrow raised. "Don't try that single-tear thing on me. I watched you practice it in motel mirrors."

"Is there a tear?" he asked her, smiling. "Well, why not cry? It hurt like hell to let you go."

For seven years, he said, crisscrossing the country, he had kept Annie beside him, while he'd supported them by a variety of cons and swindles. But finally he had to stop running. A private detective hired by the couple from Ohio almost caught them on two different occasions.

Annie asked, "He was the man at the motel, at the Royal Coach in St. Louis? The guy with the gun? He'd been chasing you for seven years?"

"No...that was years before. You did great that day." But, he said, what had happened at Royal Coach had decided him to take her home to Pilgrim's Rest. Clearly, word was out that threatening her was the way to get to him.

"You mean I was a liability?"

"They knew I loved you." He looked directly at her. "Believe this one thing. I didn't want you in danger. And I was coming back. I always meant to."

"That's two things." Annie waited quietly but his story seemed to be over; his eyes closed again and he breathed quietly. "Well, you didn't come back."

His eyes fluttered but stayed closed. "Kids like an ordinary life. House, dog, school. Was I wrong?"

She looked away. "Just tell me my mother's name."

Pulling himself up, he lit a cigarette with a sort of rakish defiance. "I don't want to tell you her name and I won't," he said finally. The resolution in his voice surprised her. "Whooooo..." He puffed smoke at the ceiling. "Whoooo was she? Who was she to us? She left us. Didn't I do okay by you for a while?" He made a small shrug with his shoulders. "Didn't Sam do okay?"

"Sam did great."

"So who...cares?"

Annie was trying to imagine the teenaged girl who'd given away her baby then fled from a Barbados hospital into a new life. "You're saying my mother was just some nameless girl who had your baby and all of a sudden walked out of your life."

He sighed. "That's it. That's what I'm saying."

Why, she asked, had he named Claudette Colbert on the birth certificate as her mother?

He flicked ash on the bed tray. "I always thought you wouldn't be here if it hadn't been for what Claudette Colbert said on the beach that day to your mom. She said, 'What a beautiful, interesting child you two will have.' That's what she said."

Annie responded with her skeptical look. "I guess I don't believe you ever met Claudette Colbert either."

"Why not?" he challenged. "Movie stars are real people too."

She walked around the small room, sat back down. "And you never heard from my mother?"

Fumbling at the bedside tray, he retrieved an old postcard lying there beside the green gems. The card was a photo of Claudette Colbert on the cover of *Life* magazine, in 1939; she was standing in billowing white pants on a stone balcony in some Mediterranean or Caribbean garden. Her raised arm held a cigarette.

Jack gave Annie the postcard. "This card came to Emerald… Sam sent it on to me, figuring, well, I don't know…" He fell silent again.

Turning the card over, Annie saw a postmark dated New York City. She'd been a student at Annapolis when it was sent.

Jack Peregrine
c/o Pilgrim's Rest
100 River Hill Road
Emerald, N.C.

And it had the right zip code. There was no salutation, no signature, no return address, just a tight scribble:

Claudette died today. Here's to a great lady.
I'm fine. Hope you're ditto. Better this way.
Reach for the sky…

Annie tried to imagine a woman's hand holding the ballpoint pen, forming the letters—the *e*'s in Greek style, the capital letters with loops that lay under whole words like bowls—to write these words. She tried to see the surface (a table, a desk?) on which the woman had proposed that giving up her baby was "better this way." She tried to see the room, the town, the life the woman had lived.

In the hospital room, light unhurriedly dimmed. Her father reached across the shadows and touched her hand. "'Sorry, no silver cup.'"

Annie thought, Yes, he's right. The cup of this story is not silver, not romance, just a sad ordinary tale of a very young woman who'd gotten pregnant and rejected the responsibility. This story was far more likely the truth than her father's old fables about how her mother was the last of a foreign dynasty or how Bob Dylan had written "Lay Lady Lay" for her. Annie moved her fingers over her mouth's twist. "Nope, no silver cup."

"You'll be luckier. You're too beautiful for luck not to happen. You're the queen of the world." He picked up the emerald by its chain, let it swing like a pendulum. A cough wrenched him.

Annie took the chain. She said quietly, "Just stop it, stop lying. There's no Queen of the Sea."

"Oh she's real. *La Reina*'s head-to-foot real." Suddenly energy went through him like a shock. "Come on! Let's play cards. Old time's sake?" He reached to the bedside drawer, pulled out an old deck of cards and dealt them with a quick fluid rhythm onto the thin blanket, face up, twenty-five cards.

She watched the cards fall perfectly as leaves. "Doesn't using your hands hurt your burns?" she asked.

"Painkillers," he told her. "Come on, do it for me?" He moved his hand over the cards. "Please."

She studied the cards for a minute and then nodded. He gathered them back into a pile. "How many hearts *didn't* I deal out?" he asked her.

Eyes closed, she saw the dealt cards lying face up on the sheet. She counted them "...You dealt eight hearts. So five are left. Ace of hearts, jack, nine, eight, and...the two."

He shuffled through the undealt cards, found and showed her the ace, jack, nine, eight, two of hearts. "A-plus," he sighed. "What a waste. You've still got the gift."

She shrugged. "For three or four more years. I'm better than I was at seven and not as good as I was at seventeen. Age can wither us, Jack. And it will."

He shuffled the cards with easy grace, despite the bandages. Tossing a handful in air, he caught one. "Darlin', age is just an... inconvenient obstacle."

She caught a card at his next toss. "Has this been a life, Dad?"

"No, but it's a gift. You've got the king of spades." Without looking, she knew he'd be right. He pointed at the small metal nametag above the pocket of her spotless white Navy jacket. "Lt. Anne Peregrine Goode." He cocked his eyebrow. "So how is Clark Goode?"

Annie touched the tag protectively. "Clark's fine. And if you ever use his name in one of your scams again, you *will* go to jail. Because I'll make sure of it."

Laughing softly, her father tossed the cards again. "I bet you would." He snatched a card from air and held it out with its back to him. "Jack of diamonds," he said.

Chapter 35
Top Gun

Meanwhile, at home at Pilgrim's Rest, thinking of Annie's race to find her father, Clark sat rocking on the porch. Too blind to see him, the old black and white Shih Tzu, Teddy, stood inside, near the screen door. Finally, annoyed by the slow screech of the rocker, she made her way down the hall into the living room. There, looking up from the piano bench, Sam watched Teddy move slowly to the pagoda, unable to keep her curled tail in air, although her gait still had its old hauteur. Sam was playing "Lara's Theme" from *Dr. Zhivago*, which she'd found opened on the music stand. The music lapped like a warm pool onto the porch.

Clark ran his fingers along the beads that made up the letters of Annie's name on the pink baseball cap. Down the hill, stars were coming out, shining in the deep night river like city lights. He was thinking about a conversation he'd once had with D. K. Destin, after they'd gotten news of Annie's sudden separation from Brad. D. K. talked about how during her childhood he'd worried that her feckless father would show up and ruin her life. But a part of Clark wanted Jack to return, for Sam's sake, and because it would be proof to Annie that love came back around.

Aware that in the girl's life, people seemed to vanish, Clark was always trying to comfort her with his predictability. He even deliberately repeated his worst puns, asking over and over, for example, "What's the difference between an ornithologist and a stutterer?" until she could recite the answer before he could give it. "One's a bird watcher, and the other's a word botcher." His bad puns were a sure thing, regular as the stoplight blinking at the crossroads, regular as Emerald farmland that stretched to the four corners of the sky. In the same way, his gestures—tapping the wide-beamed pine floors with his shoe three times—was a means of reminding her he would keep his promise: "I'm not going anywhere."

"Pilgrim's Rest and I, we just sit here," Clark told the child as they rocked with Sam and Teddy on the porch, looking west at a sunset reddening the river. He lit a cigarette with the lighter he carried always in his loose khaki pants.

"One of these days," Sam predicted to Annie, "it'll be your kids running in and out of Pilgrim's Rest and then this house will laugh all the time."

"Houses can't laugh," Annie informed her aunt. Laughter had been her father's gift to her. Laughter was betrayal.

"Sure they can," Clark said.

"Then can houses cry?"

Sam nodded. "This house used to cry. But not since you got here."

"I'll never sell it," Annie vowed to Sam, who had bequeathed her Pilgrim's Rest. "But I don't want you and Clark to die."

"Me either," Clark said, slowly rocking.

Although Annie had in her teens criticized Clark to Sam, had once even called him "a stupid slug" in an argument, she had counted on, even in those angry years, the steadiness of her adopted uncle. In fact, Clark's promise that the world could be relied on, his advice "to look on the bright side," did not come without effort, for privately he believed in flukes and horrors and knew that chaos could only be absorbed, not defeated. Two years in a POW camp as a teenager had shown him the malignity of man and the indifference of nature. Twenty years of performing emergency surgery on children had taught him how thin the shell of life, how easily cracked. It was hard to reassure Sam that nothing like the drowning of her baby brother would happen to Annie, when deep down he worried too. Like Sam, he wanted the equivalent of dunking both of Annie's feet in the River Styx for safety's sake. What could that goddess of a mother of Achilles been thinking, to miss wetting one of her baby's heels?

Clark's concerns about Annie's safety focused on speed and Sam's on water. Sam held up the school bus to lecture the driver on the dangers of hydroplaning. On Annie's first try at a bicycle, she ran beside her on River Hill Road, ready to fling herself between the child and the rocky river below. She showed up with a life jacket for a camp boat trip that was (as Annie hissed at her) only a three-minute ferry ride across the lake.

But with Clark it was always, "Slow down." He'd call it after her as she sped away on the bike, in the car, in the plane.

Clark was right to sense that their fretting oddly comforted Annie. She could count on him, on Sam, not to want to let her go. And slowly that counting-on gave her back an instinct for trust. Each evening, the little girl would wait for the measured three hoots of Clark's horn as he chugged slowly up the hill in his Volvo. Every Friday, she would drag out of the backseat the large brown paper bag of takeout Chinese food, under whose weight she would stagger across the lawn like a small drunk. The takeout never varied. Sitting in the family room, watching movies, Annie, Clark and Sam ate the dishes from the House of Joy cartons, week after week as years went by. First with Teddy, then joined by Malpy, they watched every classic film owned by Now Voyager so often that they knew them by heart. They didn't always like each other's favorites—Clark thought speed movies like *Top Gun* had about as much appeal as a demolition derby—but they took pleasure in watching together. Simultaneously breaking apart their wooden chopsticks, they ate the fried dumplings, shrimp lo mein, and moo shu pork that were always in the bags, just as Clark's suitcase always contained a "good luck" present for Annie on his return from pediatric conferences. He took no chances and bought her talismans of all faiths, amulets as varied as a Celtic cross, a wooden Buddha, a Peruvian bell, and an Abyssinian wishing box. He filled her room with charms and crystals.

From the porch swing in the evenings, Clark would wait for her to appear at the end of her five-mile jog, looking for the orange glow of the reflector vest to come over the crest of River Hill Road and in through the gates to Pilgrim's Rest. Why did she run so fiercely? He'd watch her small sturdy body keeping to its hard-earned pace, her concentration so intent that she rarely even saw him until she'd dropped to the grass beside the steps, bending this way and that to stretch her limbs. What was she running from, or running to? And what could Clark do to help her, but just to be waiting on the porch?

Sometimes his unhurried style so maddened her that she had to leave the room, but by her high school years no one had more confidence in his dependability than Annie did. When she left for Annapolis, she promised her aunt and uncle that, despite her desire to fly jets for the Navy, she would let nothing harm her. She told them that at her graduation she would point her diploma out toward the field of parents, so that Sam and Clark would know that they shared this triumph. They promised to be there.

But a month before her graduation, Clark drove off to pick up the Chinese takeout for Annie's visit home and didn't come back. When by 10 p.m. he still hadn't honked his horn in the yard, Annie and Sam telephoned 911. It was not until midnight that the police chief came to the door about the collision at a downtown intersection. The two of them rushed to Emerald Hospital, where Clark lay unconscious. Doctors there admitted to Sam they had no hope of their colleague's survival.

For years afterwards, Clark heard the stories of how Annie had sat by her uncle's bed through three nights. "You promised me," she'd told him over and over. "We shook hands." There was no sign that he could hear her.

On the first Sunday after the accident, at Clark's church, St. Mark's Episcopal, Sam suddenly walked in, stood in the aisle, and started talking. Her appearance startled the rector into silence.

He'd met her previously only at family funerals. But bygone Peregrines had donated so much money to St. Mark's over the generations that he couldn't bring himself to ask her to leave.

Sam pointed at a stained-glass window (it was dedicated to a Peregrine ancestor, although she didn't notice). "I'm here for Clark Goode," she told the congregation. "I want you all to pray for him. Clark's like a rock in that river outside that window. Mostly you can't rely on men—" There was a restless stirring here by those who feared a feminist lecture of the sort many in Emerald had heard from Sam before. She settled them with raised urgent hands. "As far as counting on men, Clark Goode is Atticus Finch. He's Virgil Tibbs. He's the Pride of the Yankees. He's the man who shot Liberty Valence."

The congregation was puzzled. They were relieved when she added, "We've all heard Clark's terrible puns. They're just awful."

"Awful," the rector said aloud.

Sam burst into tears. "But you know what? The best pun was God's, when he named Clark 'Goode.' And the world can't afford to lose a good man. So I'm just here to tell you folks, pray for him. I don't believe any of this junk. But just in case…" Sam had to stop again, swallowing hard. Reaching blindly for the minister's hand, she sat down in tears, further confusing the town of Emerald, who'd finally accepted that Sam Peregrine was a Lesbian and now were wondering if they'd been wrong and she and Clark were in love after all.

Clark was still unconscious when Annie had to drive back to Annapolis to take her final exams. She told him again as she left his hospital room, "Keep your promise."

Clark kept it. He came out of the coma and survived. It wasn't easy, and during his convalescence he started smoking again.

A month later, Annie was waving her diploma at the Annapolis graduation. Sam pushed Clark forward in his wheel-chair so the graduate could see him hold up his "Annie Peregrine Goode, Top Gun!" sign.

The car wreck left Clark with a steel pin and Sam with

white hair. Otherwise, Pilgrim's Rest was pretty much the same whenever Annie returned to it. Teddy still slept in her pagoda. The top of Annie's oak dresser with its blue-flowered porcelain knobs still was covered with crystals and magic charms. The photograph of the beautiful pilot Amy Johnson was still on the wall with the flying-circus poster. The commemorative stamp sheet of Bessie Coleman still hung next to a picture of a gloriously grinning Amelia Earhart, looking very much like Charles Lindbergh.

Emerald itself didn't change much, except on the outskirts where the malls spread. On River Street, Now Voyager and Nickerson Jewelers still bowed with their bay windows, side by side, leaning out to customers as if planning to snatch them off the sidewalk. And down the block the sweet tang of Dina Destin's Barbecue, run by her nieces, floated onto the street. In St. Mary's spongy green graveyard, the ivy and moss took their time climbing up the tilting stones.

JOHN INGERSOLL PEREGRINE
1946–1948
TAKEN FROM ME

In time the stone markers were joined by other stones with other names and none of them was going anywhere.

On the other hand, thanks to the Navy, Annie had traveled both far and fast, faster than the speed of sound. In her love of speed, she knew, she was more like the father who'd left her than the one who'd taken her in, Clark, who was like the level lighted path of a runway on which she could land, who was like the arresting hook that caught her jet on the aircraft carrier. He was home safe.

• • •

On the Pilgrim's Rest porch, slowly Annie's uncle rocked to his feet. He walked inside, dropping the pink cap on the hall table. In the pagoda, Teddy was snoring. In the kitchen, Sam was listening to the news. He could hear her retorts. "Lies! Tell the truth!" Why the woman kept believing network television would tell the truth, he couldn't imagine. But he loved her stubborn faith.

He predicted that Sam, caught up in her battle with CNN, wouldn't notice him. Often in the old days, he would pass by Sam and Annie on the couch watching television together—sometimes Annie would have her Walkman headphones on as well—and he would speak to them, even wave his arms at them, but they wouldn't or couldn't see him. He'd say, "Ladies, there's a real live human being passing through your field of vision... Okay, last chance. Okay, I'll say good night."

Sometimes they'd notice him and derisively wave. Sometimes they wouldn't even do that. Sometimes he'd blink the overhead lights at them until they told him to stop it. Sometimes he'd just kiss the air loudly and then proceed with his nightly ritual of locking up the house, turning the old iron keylocks in the doors, turning off the lights, turning down the thermostats, and heading upstairs.

Pilgrim's Rest was so familiar that he didn't have to switch on the hall light to make his way to the kitchen. He reminded Sam that they were supposed to meet friends at a local restaurant soon. Sam waved him off, riveted to a news graph showing the recently elected President Bush's abysmal poll numbers for the first week of July. "Five minutes," she promised.

Back in the front hall, he ran his hand softly around the crown of Annie's pink baseball hat. It seemed to him quite improbable that these glass beads were anything other than glass, much less priceless jewels.

After a while he opened the porch door again and looked up at stars as crowded as lights on Sam's Christmas trees.

For years, starting when Annie was seven, together they studied the stars through a telescope. Annie had written Santa Claus asking for this instrument, not believing in Santa Claus but wanting a way to stay in touch with the stars that her father had pointed out to her on the road. Buying a good telescope had been one of many successful Christmas choices made by Sam and Clark, who always avoided mistakes by scrupulously following the child's wish lists. She was thrilled when they set up the telescope in the yard. Together they made a monthly chart of the reliable, recurring pattern of the constellations. It proved a great pleasure to Annie to chart the order of the sky, every star in its predictive place.

Now Clark looked east to west at the sky. She was somewhere up in that black starry space much of the time, in jets faster than sound. He turned to look south where, far less sure than stars, her inconstant father had gone to meet her in Miami, to ask something unfair of her, after decades of neglect.

"It's okay. Everything's going to be okay," Clark told the sky.

Chapter 36

For the Love of Mike

It was almost dark in Golden Days as Annie turned on the bedside light to look at other small snapshots from her father's wallet, pictures that she'd never seen before and could only identify by their dimmed descriptions on the back. In one, she was standing beside the red Mustang in an anonymous Wyoming parking lot, wearing her neon blue sunglasses and her cowboy boots (paled to lime green in the Polaroid) with the lariats up the sides. In another, the same age—about five—she sat atop her blue suitcase, her eyes the same color, but both faded in the old photo. In another she was a baby, outside some Southwestern motel, crawling up yellowed concrete stairs wearing paper diapers. In a fourth picture, she was crying, open-mouthed, in her father's arms as he showed her the broken birthday piñata in the palm tree by a Las Vegas pool. In another, she was dancing wildly beside a portable CD player in a luxury Chicago hotel room. In the final photo he handed her, she was sitting in a little red airplane on a kiddie park merry-go-round near Vidalia, Georgia. The ride looked just like the little planes in her dream.

Also in his wallet was a small copy of the picture taken in the restaurant of The Breakers Hotel on her seventh birthday, the one that Sam had framed on the piano at Pilgrim's Rest. In this copy, a fold had left a crease between the little girl and the tanned smiling man with the cigarette gracefully arced in his raised hand. On the back of the photo her current cell phone number was scrawled in her father's upward slanting style.

"Keep it," he said. "It's a good picture."

"Sam has a copy at home."

"You can never have too many memories of a good thing."

Annie slid the photo back into his wallet.

It was a distinctive portfolio deeply tanned wallet; it looked like the wallet she remembered from her childhood. Jack said, "So there's your life as I know it. And now here you are, a grown woman, a flyer, like your dad."

Standing just inside the door, Raffy held both arms as if they were wings, tilting them. "Annie's definitely a flyer. Absolutely a flyer. Just like you, Jack."

Annie was offended. "Well, I fly for the U.S. Navy. I don't know who he flies for. Or why."

"My mistake," the Cuban shrugged apologetically.

Her father touched her hand again; his fingers felt like snow falling on her. "Tell me about Sam?" he suddenly asked, willing energy into his voice.

"She doesn't want you to do anything stupid like die."

"Tell her I tried my best." It was an effort now to lift his head from the pillow. "How 'bout some water?" He shook a pill from a bottle beside the bed. When she held the glass to his lips, his chilled hand closed softly around hers. She was shaken by their closeness after so many years; a tremble floated down her back. She said, "Sam will never stop loving the people she loves."

"You needed a home. I knew Sam would be a better mother, Clark would be a better father, than the couple who wrote the check for you in Barbados."

His self-congratulation annoyed her—as if Sam and Clark's virtues had justified his abandonment; as if throwing her out in the yard at Pilgrim's Rest had been his plan all along, farsighted childcare.

Had he no remorse about that desertion? Did he regret the chaos of her life with him, before Sam and Clark? She recalled one moment of many such: he had rushed into the shabby motel room where she sat on the bed eating dry frosted cereal for supper, watching a movie on TV. He flung open her suitcase like a magician. "Let's see how fast you can pack it up, baby, we're out of here." And they were in the car within minutes. Speeding down highways, racing into black sky. Had he thought about how she'd felt about that at all?

There was a screeching rattle as a Golden Days food trolley moved past the door. The thick smell of hospital food seeped into the room. Her father frowned; his eyes fighting to stay open. "'Member, Annie, pasta we used to make in the suites? Used the salad spinner for a colander?"

"No," she said. "I remember Jack Lemmon drained spaghetti on a tennis racket in *The Apartment*."

His voice strained to be audible. "Raffy!" Rook stepped back into the room. "She 'members Jack Lemmon's pasta, not mine. Wasn't for me, she couldn't tie her shoelaces. 'Dada.' First word. Dada, April 9. First dance, two-step, Ritz, Boston. First word read? 'Hat.' Then 'cat,' then 'Annie,' then 'dad.' Doesn't remember, for the love of Mike."

A memory came back, corroborative. "Shoelaces." Annie nodded. "That I remember. I sat on the floor between your legs and practiced on your shoes." She looked down at him in the bed, his skin faded tan against the sheet.

He pointed out the hospital window. A pink moon was rising in blue clouds. "There's your travel buddy, the moon. Remember your pal the moon that always came along for the ride?"

Puzzled for a minute, she let memory drift back to her. "...You said the moon checked into every motel with us. We'd look for the moon in the motel swimming pools—" She stopped herself.

He nodded, waiting.

Annie was recalling a night when she'd floated on her back in the pool of a high-rise motel in a flat desert landscape. Her father lay in a deck chair beside the pool edge, looking up at the domed stars. She had paddled her seahorse float to the ladder and told him how the water in the pool was humming in her ears. He'd asked her to listen for the history of the sea in the loud reverberating echo of pool water. Could she hear Phoenicians and Carthaginians and Columbus's ships and the Spanish Armada?

And she'd said, yes, she could hear all of that. But it hadn't been true. She hadn't wanted to disappoint him. The truth was, she'd heard nothing but the noise of the pool.

She admitted that lie to him now, describing the memory. "I didn't hear any of the things you talked about."

"Oh you just heard them differently," he told her in a curiously gentle way.

It was, she considered, a kind thing to say and she wanted to offer something in return. "When my ears stopped up from diving, you would tilt my head and shake it. And it was a really good feeling when my ears unstopped, the water letting go. The water was so warm leaving my ears."

The three of them were silent together a moment. Then Raffy quietly sighed his rustle of sorrow. "I don't have many memories of my papa. It's like somebody took a long thin needle and poked them out of my head. He worked all the time. I liked the Ramirez side of the family better. My uncle Mano played trumpet so I picked him over my father. I feel bad about it." The Cuban slipped out into the hall again, gently closing the door behind him.

Jack murmured something that Annie couldn't hear and as she bent her head toward him to listen, she could feel his mouth touch her forehead. She thought his face would be cold like his hands but his lips were warm. "Don't erase us, Annie. Even though I wasn't a regular kind of dad."

She let her face stay there a moment, near his, the two of them quietly breathing, no one speaking. But then she drew back and retreated into irony. "True, most dads aren't con artists that get arrested all the time and end up in prison."

He sighed, gathered breath to mimic the sarcasm. "Well, for the love of Mike, most daughters don't get to be the queen of the world."

"Sure, I'm the queen of the world and you could sell the Mona Lisa to a blind man and Christ's tears to an atheist." She stood up and picked up a notepad from the table. "Your passwords are 362484070N and 678STNX211. Do you want me to write them down for you?"

His voice was fading. "Amazin'. We won a lot of bets with you doing that numbers trick."

Her mouth tightened. "I did it for you."

"I know."

"I wanted to make you proud."

Slowly he pulled his shoulders higher on the pillow. "Just do one more thing for me? Fly me to Cuba?"

Surprise made her laugh. "What?"

He tried to sit up in the bed. "I figured I could fly myself but…" He held up his taped hands.

The request was so preposterous that she sat down again, shaking her head. "You can't fly to Cuba from the U.S."

"Sure you can." His eyes took on a little of the old glimmer. "I'm serious about *La Reina Coronada del Mar*. The little jewels are in your hat. Most of the big ones are in Cuba."

Annie watched the pink moon float past on baby blue clouds. "The big jewels meaning your stories about the seven emeralds and that huge ruby heart."

He nodded. "That's right. It's a solid gold statue. These emeralds go in the crown." He held up the green gem on the gold chain. "We've got three now. There are four more even larger, and the ruby, in the bank in Cuba—"

Leaping to her feet, Annie slapped the bed cover. "Stop. Stop!" Her shout brought Raffy back through the door. "Do you ever listen to yourself? You're dying and you're still trying to pull off some fraud about a bogus treasure hunt in Cuba! Do you get it that a cop from Miami Vice is going to arrest you and throw you in jail, that he has been hounding me to give you up, threatening to arrest me for harboring you?"

Her father raised himself wincing. "Daniel Hart?"

"Yes! Sgt. Daniel Hart, Miami Police."

Raffy called from the doorway. "He nabbed me at the Dorado."

Jack squeezed the bed sheet with his taped fingers. "Hart's after me because of the Queen."

"Dad, don't insult me. That statue is not real!"

But his face was stubborn, just as Sam had often told her her own face would tighten. "My great-grandfather Boss Peregrine carried the Queen out of Havana and brought her back to North Carolina in a burlap bag."

"I'm not listening to this craziness. And I'm not flying you to Cuba, or anywhere else till I talk to your doctor. Where'd you get this photo?" She slid out the picture of them at The Breakers from his wallet and palmed it while pretending to put it back. "Daniel Hart raided your room and got my cell number off the back of this."

"Doesn't surprise me. He must have put it back. You know what? I like Dan Hart. He won't quit. But tell him from me, I'm not going to jail, not for a day, not for an hour."

Suddenly Raffy waved his arms for them to be quiet. Then he hurried to the bed, grabbed the emeralds off the tray, yanking on Annie's arm. "We gotta go," he whispered. "Right now!"

Footsteps grew louder, passed the doorway, moved toward the other end of the hall. Raffy tugged at her. "We gotta go! We'll come back and see Jack in the morning."

Jack urged her to listen to Raffy, to leave now. He'd make sure his doctor was here at 8 a.m. "Raffy, watch out for her."

The Cuban ran to look out the crack of the door.

She couldn't resist raising her ironic eyebrow at her father. "It's a little late to start taking care of me now, Dad."

He blew a soft kiss with his bandaged hand. "I really was coming back for you." His fingers reached for hers. "Somehow the years got away."

She remembered how he'd left his wristwatch once in a motel room and although he'd loved that watch, thirty miles later he'd refused to turn around to go back for it. Upset that it had taken her so long to notice that he'd forgotten it, she'd been in tears, blaming herself for the loss.

She told him now, "You always cared more about what was ahead than what we'd left behind."

"Did I, darlin'?"

"Don't you know yourself by now?"

He smiled his old silly smile.

Slipping her fingers away from his, she pointed to his bedside monitors. "I guess it wouldn't be so easy for you to run off this time, would it?"

"Nope." He let his hands lift, then softly fall. "You're the flyer now, Annie."

Raffy flung back through the door. "It's Ms. Skippings! Quick!" He grabbed Annie and pushed her out into the hall.

Chapter 37

Flight for Freedom

Raffy hurried Annie to the elevator bank. An attractive tall silvery blonde woman, sharp-edged and too thin, with a tag identifying her as "M. R. Skippings, Chief Hospital Administrator," stepped around the corner and blocked their path. "Stop!" she ordered. She was Annie's age and wore a remarkable platinum and diamond engagement ring that looked like a piece of modern sculpture.

So, Annie thought, this is "Ms. Skippings," the managed-care supervisor of Golden Days who'd been described so unfavorably by the old patients on the lawn. The woman glared suspiciously at Annie's naval officer's uniform and at Raffy with his long hair in a ponytail and his tight chinos and floppy pink flamingo shirt. "Yes? You are?"

"Just leaving," Annie replied politely, which likely would have been the end of it if Raffy hadn't started slamming his fist on the elevator button, yelling, "Run!"

Skippings stiffened, barricading their way. "No visitors on Floor Five. You're here to see...?"

Annie didn't like her tone and turned sarcastic. "Well, certainly not Dr. Parker since he was nowhere to be found."

"Dr. who?"

Annie gestured widely at the empty hallway. "In fact, where are *any* doctors? If my father is ill—"

"What's the patient's name?"

Annie paused. "...Buchstabe, Ronny Buchstabe."

Skippings began flinging through the pages of a folder she carried.

Raffy, grabbing at Annie, pulled her behind him. "We're not here for anybody. We accidentally by mistake went to the wrong floor. ¡Perdón! ¡Perdón!" His finger pushed at the down button. "Come on!"

Skippings' springs, already tightly wound, snapped with a sudden nasty thought. "The *Miami Herald!*" she exclaimed.

Raffy nodded, "Absolutely not. Good-bye."

"I told you people I'd have you arrested for trespassing. We're doing nothing we need to be investigated for!" She poked the slender Cuban in the sternum.

Flaring, Annie stepped between them. "This is a military matter now."

Confusion momentarily unsteadied the tall blonde woman. "Military matter?" Recovering, she thrust herself closer to Annie. "I'm chief administrator at Golden Days."

"Good for you. I like to see women go to the top."

Skippings now poked Annie on the arm. "Show me the visitors' badges they issued in reception."

Annie flicked away the woman's hand. "I'm with the United States Navy. We skipped reception."

Skippings widened her mouth. "Excuse me?"

"Look, there's no need to be such a bitch. We skipped reception. We came up the back steps." Annie looked over at Raffy, who appeared to be praying to the elevator buttons.

Golden Days visitors did not speak this way to M. R. Skippings. (And patients were too intimidated to speak to her at all.) She let out the steam dangerously compressed in her long throat. "Well, then, we have a serious problem."

Annie surveyed her. "Pancreatic cancer, serious problem. Genocide in Rwanda, serious problem. Hunger, land mines— serious problems. Whether or not we stopped by reception? I don't think so."

But in M. R. Skippings's pink-stucco universe it was. "Are you refusing to show me those badges?"

Annie grinned. "Are you really actually saying to me 'show me your badges,' I mean actually really?" The elevator doors opened. Chamayra stepped out of the car. She looked at them horrified but didn't speak and trotted quickly away down the hall. Annie shoved Raffy inside the elevator, jumping in with him. Skippings struggled to wedge open the doors.

Annie smiled at her pleasantly. "'We don't need no badges. I don't have to show you any stinking badges!'" The doors closed. *Treasure of Sierra Madre*," she explained to the wide-eyed Raffy as they descended. "I could feel it coming. That's the correct quote; most people get it wrong."

He appeared not to know what she was talking about. "I need a moment." The slender man slumped rapidly down the elevator wall.

Annie leaned over him. "Are you okay?" He nodded weakly as she pulled him up by his armpits. "Raffy, pay attention. I want my father out of this place tomorrow. Let them arrest him and put him in a real goddamn hospital!"

"We'll do that, first thing tomorrow. You'll see Dr. Parker; we'll make arrangements. Before we go to Cuba."

"We're not going to Cuba."

Raffy took a deep breath as the elevator shuddered to a stop at the basement. "That was great, how you said, 'This is a military matter now.'"

She smiled bitterly. "Well, I'm a con man's daughter."

He led her by backstairs up to the Golden Days lobby. "But what I mean is, you move fast. I guess you gotta, you fly planes."

In the lobby, she glanced at the rumpled man and sighed. "You know how fast Mach 2.4 is?" He admitted that he did not. She said, "Well, you don't drive your car that fast."

"To be honest with you, my car has been temporarily repossessed."

"You and my dad aren't doing too well. Everything's repossessed."

Unhappily he smoothed the flamingos on his shirt. "We had a lot of setbacks lately. Looking for the Queen."

"Sure." She tapped an insignia on her uniform jacket. "Well, Mach 2.4 is what a Navy Tomcat F-14 could do. I trained on one. The Tomcat could go over 1500 miles per hour."

He nodded appreciatively. "That's fast."

"It could climb 30,000 feet a minute. The Super Hornet goes even faster. And you know what? They're replacing it with jets that may be able to go over 2500 miles per hour."

"That's very fast."

Annie walked Raffy quickly past Miss Napp at reception while she was preoccupied with her fingernails. "The old Blackbird SR-71 can fly at 33 miles per minute, that's Mach 3 or three times the speed of sound. It flies faster than a speeding bullet. Plus, there are unmanned jets that can go twice as fast as that."

They hurried toward the front entrance. "Why?" he asked her. "Why?"

Raffy stopped her. "Why do you need to go faster than 1500 miles per hour?"

Before Annie could answer, a tall well-built young man, looking upset, suddenly bolted around the corner at the end of the lobby. She was astonished. It was the same man who had been staring at her from the newspaper rack in the St. Louis airport last night. He still wore the old boots and jeans but now had on a blue linen shirt instead of a blue T-shirt.

Equally surprising, Raffy let out a curse of horror when he saw the man. He squeezed his hands in supplication at Annie. "Help me!" But without waiting for help he bolted to the front doors like a sprinter and slipped quickly through them.

Annie saw the man recognize the Cuban musician as well and start through the lobby toward them. She could tell he hadn't seen her yet. To slow him down, just at the last second when he passed by, she crouched as if to tie her shoe and the man tripped over her back.

His arms were warm as he pulled her up to her feet. Both said they were sorry for the "accident." He recognized her. "Wait a minute!" he growled. "You're Annie Goode. Damn it, you're here with Rook!"

She thought the man must be one of Feliz Diaz's criminal henchmen. That he must have been in St. Louis on Diaz's behalf, chasing her father, that he must have been the man who'd beaten her father up. "Let go of me!" Spinning free, she dropped back to a crouch and pushed him. He lost his balance, tripped backwards and crashed into an empty wheelchair.

Annie raced out the front doors before he could untangle himself.

"Malpy!" She shouted for the Maltese.

On the lawn, the dog was trotting around with a cheap little American flag clamped between his teeth. A candy striper was handing out the flags to patients, presumably for a belated Fourth of July. Malpy effortlessly dodged two overweight security guards who were trying to catch him. The old people fiercely cheered as he dashed through their wheelchairs and leaped into Annie's arms.

Rook, who'd been hiding again in the huge hedge of bougainvilleas, hurried her into her rental car. Across the street a city bus wheezed to a stop; a man using two canes slowly climbed out of it.

Opening his car window while Annie was backing out of the parking place, Raffy craned to look behind him. "Go, go! There's Sergeant Hart!"

Annie glanced amazed at the crippled man who'd been left on the curb by the departing bus. She pointed. "That's Daniel Hart? The man getting off the bus with the canes?"

"No! Him!" Raffy pointed back to the Golden Days lawn. "The man that's chasing us!"

The young man in the blue shirt was running in and out of clusters of old people like a running back through an extremely sluggish defense.

"I thought that man worked for Feliz Diaz! I thought he was after you!"

"He is after me! He's with the *s.o.b.* Miami police! He's Sergeant Hart."

"Rook!" Hart was shouting as he jumped over an azalea bush and raced up the middle of Ficus Avenue in pursuit. "Rook! You're under arrest! Halt!"

Annie looked in the rear view window, astonished. "*That's Daniel Hart?*"

"Go! Go!" Raffy twisted around to yell out the window. "*Cingao!*"

Unable to catch the accelerating car, Hart bent over in the middle of the street, gasping for breath. Still doubled up, he gave Raffy the finger.

The Cuban, leaning far out the window, returned the gesture, shouting back at Hart, "*Son-of-a-bitch Miami police!*"

Annie watched in her rearview window as a white van suddenly drove up beside Hart in the intersection. It jolted to a stop and two men in suit jackets hopped simultaneously out of its side doors. One wore a porkpie hat. Annie stopped her car to watch but a passing SUV blocked what was happening from her view. When the SUV moved on, she could see that Daniel Hart was no longer standing there. The white van was speeding away, leaving the street empty.

Making a quick 180-degree turn over Raffy's protests, she looked for Hart along the side streets but didn't see him or the white van anywhere. She phoned the number in her cell phone for the detective and when he didn't answer, she left him a message: she didn't know what was going on and she really needed to talk to him. She apologized for tripping him in the Golden Days lobby but she'd thought he was a, well, a criminal. She didn't know why he hadn't gotten in touch with her. She would make any reasonable deal that would keep her dad out of jail, including giving her dad up to the police. Call her back as quickly as possible.

Raffy pounded the dashboard. "Why are you turning your papa in to Hart?"

"He needs medical attention! Golden Days is a joke!" She squeezed her fist around the pink flamingos on the Cuban's shirt, pulling him toward her while she drove. "Raffy, we're going to the Dorado. We're going to sit down, sort this whole thing out, and fix it. You, my dad, the Queen of the Sea! Start now with Daniel Hart. Why's he after you?"

The thin young man held up his hands, shrugging dramatically. "Better to be brief than tedious."

Annie forced herself to slow down. "Couldn't agree with you more."

"That *s.o.b.* Hart has a passionate fixation on your papa and me. *Shtup es in toches,*" he called over the seat back as if Hart were still behind them. "For years. I can't say why."

"Oh, yes, you can." She shook him. "You're going to sit still and talk."

"Today's not good. I've got a final today. Extension class. Composition. Education is the key to human happiness."

She gestured at his bandaged wrist. "In your case, I'm the key to human happiness. We're got a problem here; we're going to solve it!" Driving with one hand, she grabbed his rayon shirt with its three fuchsia flamingos. It ripped.

"Oh, gracias, gracias, my favorite shirt! I played 'Chan Chan' with Company Secondo in this shirt on the stage of the Hotel Nacional!"

"I don't give a shit. All I want is my mother's name!"

He stroked the flamingos. "I don't know a thing about your mother! Except, wait a minute, I asked your papa once, when he was boasting about you. He said a name…wait, wait. Kay Denim."

"Denim?"

"No, Denham. Kay Denham."

She hadn't expected a real answer and wasn't sure it was one. "He said my mother's name was Kay Denham? Why should I believe that?"

Raffy made a face. "Why shouldn't you?" His soulful eyes met hers and she decided he knew no more than he was telling her. "But to be honest, Annie, your mother? You should let her go. When I left Cuba, I said to my own mother, I was headed here to Miami with Uncle Mano, I said, 'Come too, Mama! Hop in the boat.' She wouldn't do it. She wouldn't leave her homeland.

I had to give her up. That's life, more or less." Raffy leaned over to pat Annie on the shoulder.

Appalled, she asked if his mother was right there in the water with him when he left in the boat?

"No no! I was speaking in—oh, what is it?—synecdoche." He shook his head. "My mama is still in Havana, still in the family business. Silversmiths to the finest people, not that of course we aren't all equal brothers and sisters at present thanks to that son-of-a-bitch Castro. She lives with my big brother, who's turned her against me. When you fly us to Cuba, I'm bringing my mother a wonderful gift, due entirely to Jack. And then she'll see that I am not nothing."

At a stoplight, she studied his nervous face. "We're just going to talk, Raffy. Don't worry. And I'll even buy you a drink."

He looked sadly out the car window. "Gracias, no. I'm eight months into my recovery. Alcohol was once a personal problem of mine."

"Just goes to show you. Problems get solved."

• • •

Under the big Miami moon, Annie walked her dog around the Hotel Dorado pool gardens. Raffy had to hurry to keep up as they trotted along the bougainvillea-banked path. Back in the lobby, she handed him Malpy. "Okay. Now talk to me about this Cuban bank where my dad says these jewels are."

His story was inevitably a long one, punctuated with quotes, but what she distilled was that there was a secured account at a branch of the Banco Centrale in old Havana near the Plaza des Armas. Jack Peregrine had been renting a bank drawer there for years under a foreign passport. Only Jack or his designated heir would be allowed to open it. Moreover, to do so they would need not only proof of personal identity but knowledge of two passwords. Annie knew those passwords. Annie could fly a small plane. So for both reasons, with Jack incapacitated, they needed Annie to go to the bank for them and it was unfortunately in Havana.

She asked, "And inside this bank drawer?"

The four biggest emeralds from the crown of *La Reina Coronado del Mar*, each one worth hundreds of thousands of dollars. Plus a 135-carat ruby worth many times that much.

Annie scoffed. "And these alleged jewels actually belong to…?"

"Jack," Raffy insisted with conviction. "But getting hold of them?"

They moved to the bar and found a table by a window that looked out to the ocean. Annie neatly set her phone and her Blackberry down beside her.

Raffy looked around carefully. "Jack is sadly, well, and so am I, temporarily *paisan non grata* with a number of people living in Miami and, well, also in Cuba."

"Let me guess. That number of people includes the Miami police, as well as the glitzy couple in the Mercedes outside Golden Days, correct?"

"There's also the PNR. *Policía Nacional Revolucionaria.* Cuban police?" Raffy offered her a placating smile. "Also, the police in some other American cities where…Jack honestly does not like to be closed up in a cell."

"Maybe he shouldn't have gone in for a life of crime."

"It's more a philosophical point of view." Raffy sipped at his soda. "I didn't mind jail so much; it's a quiet place to think things over. 'I have been studying how I may compare this prison where I live unto the world and vice versa.' That was one of the speeches your dad tried to teach me. *Richard the Fifth,* I believe."

Annie nodded. "*Richard the Second.*" She hesitated. "Maybe *Third.*"

She knew Raffy was not exaggerating her father's fear of imprisonment; Sam had told her of his being punished by being locked in a closet. She remembered how he had always left doors of rented rooms wide open whenever he could; he'd kept bathroom doors open as they slept, with the lights on.

"Raffy, have you ever," she asked, "actually seen this so-called 'Queen of the Sea'?"

"No," he admitted. "But I never saw the Empire State Building either. Or for that matter, Jesus the Savior Christ that my mother was always telling my padre to believe in, which he did not, not that he went to synagogue either. How about a mojito for you? All you drink is water."

"Water's good for you. Sit still, I'll be right back."

Leaving Raffy in the bar, she took Malpy upstairs to her room and waited till the maid left after turning down her sheets and putting chocolates on her pillows. The maid had turned on the television. As Annie collected the metal case, she glanced at an old movie channel showing Rosalind Russell in *Flight for Freedom*. Rosalind appeared to be having serious engine trouble as she flew a secret mission over a foggy Pacific.

When Annie returned to the bar, Raffy was there talking to the piano player. He hurried to her when he saw the stainless steel courier case. His large brown eyes widened. "*La Reina?*"

Annie laughed at his excitement. "My dad is a con man. Since you are also a con man, surely you know that the Queen of the Sea does not exist."

Raffy's glowing eyes scanned the gleaming case as she placed it on the bar table. His fingers stretched for the handle.

She slid the case away from him. "Look at yourself! My dad gets everybody all excited about something and then because they're searching for it, they believe it's real! It's a swindle. It's the big con. It's like…like a Florida land deal."

The Cuban smiled, his large dark eyes dreamy. He told her to look out the windows of the Dorado at the glamorous skyscraper skyline of Miami. "What is that out there? It's a Florida land deal…" He pulled from his pocket a worn dirty folded piece of Xeroxed paper and smoothed it out on top of the metal case. On the paper was a drawing of a statue of the Virgin Mary, and handwritten beneath the figure, "*La Reina Coronada del Mar.*" Crabbed scribbles in Spanish covered the margins. Raffy translated them for her.

Como la madre de tierra del Inca, Pachamama, ella usó un amplio cabo. Like the Inca earth mother, Pachamama, she wore a broad cape. *El cabo era oro*. The cape was gold, studded with precious sapphires, emeralds, rubies, and a small quantity of diamonds. *Su corona del oro sostuvo siete esmeraldas rectangulares grandes*. Her gold crown held seven large rectangular emeralds, each one of them on a gold rod sprayed out like a sun burst. On her breast there was a silver door; inside it, a star ruby. *El bebé Jesu* sat in the crook of her arm; Christ was silver and had *ojos azules del zafiro*. Eyes of silver and sapphire.

Raffy returned the frayed drawing reverently to his pocket. He said it was a copy of a page of a letter that the Spanish Hidalgo Don Carlos de Tormes had sent to his wife, a letter in a museum in Seville. It told how Don Carlos would be setting sail from the New World and would bring this statue of the Virgin Mary to the pious Philip II as a token of his gratitude to God (and king) for all the silver and gold he'd dug out of Peruvian land that (for some reason) belonged to Spain.

"But the ship sank. Like so many. A hundred billion dollars lying on the ocean floor." Raffy's glittering eyes fixed on the case. "This is true not just because Castro says so. It is absolutely a fact. The Spanish shipped $100 billion in treasure safely over the ocean but another $100 billion sank in sight of my homeland. Excuse me—" Raffy waved to the piano player who was taking a break. "That's Juan, my cousin on the Ramirez side. Many musicians. He's the one fixed things up with a guy he knows so this guy just went over for me to the Hyatt in West Palm and explained to Feliz Diaz why I wasn't there with the statue. He told Diaz how he'd seen two plain-clothes PNR collar me in the Hyatt parking garage and grab the case I was carrying and hustle me into their car. He told Diaz he heard these two guys saying how they'd already picked up Jack Peregrine in South Beach and they were hi-jacking us both back to Havana and it wouldn't be for a vacation either." Raffy pointed at his thin chest. "I made that story up myself. Diaz believed it."

"Let's hope." Annie said that Raffy appeared to have a lot of relatives and friends.

"It's an island," he said. "Cuba. A beautiful one. Everybody knows their family and neighbors."

She noted that Sergeant Hart had told her that this so-called sunken treasure, *La Reina*, belonged to the Cuban people. Why shouldn't Raffy agree?

Raffy waved expressive fingers at her like an arpeggio. "Even if that *s.o.b.* Hart says it, it's a possible point. And better the people of Cuba should have the money than the Catholic Church, which is after *La Reina* too in a serious manner. In my opinion Jesus was not a capitalist and this *s.o.b.* Miami archdiocese that wants the Queen already owns more Miami real estate than the mob owns, which is saying something." He sighed. "But the Queen is Jack's and mine. And yours. Greed pulls me one way, my country the other."

"Raffy, I don't know what you're talking about. You want to see what's in here?"

"'The rest is silence.'"

She spun the numbered casters on the combination lock above the handle. "There's probably nothing in this case."

He looked nervously around the bar. "Too many people in here."

She arched her Claudette Colbert eyebrow at the slender man. "Too many for what?"

"Let's go out by the pool." With the case under his arm, Raffy held the door for her. "My cousin Juan? His brother is the branch manager of the bank in Havana. Where we need to go. So, as soon as we get to Cuba—" He stopped talking and waited until a couple in bathrobes left their deck chairs and shuffled back inside in their big terry-cloth slippers. There was no one else at the pool.

"Raffy, you and Dad don't seem to be getting the picture. For a long time now, Americans can't fly private planes into Cuba or even go to Cuba."

He gestured for her to take a seat at a poolside table, under a deco light in the shape of a palm tree. "Not true. Your papa and I did it for years. I have family on the coast there. They're a help, being of the philosophy, as Avon's great son would say, 'What's mine is yours, and what is yours is mine.'" He claimed that Annie's

father had often piloted the hydroplane into Cuba at dusk, landing at a place where a relative of Raffy's was the harbormaster,
near Puerto Esperanza in the Archipiélago de los Colorados. Raffy
himself had such a fear of planes that he had stayed in Key West
in charge of "communications" with his relations.

Annie was rattled; these details sounded real to her.

The Cuban leaned over the shiny locked aluminum case,
carefully sliding the numbers on the four lock dials one by one.
He hadn't sufficiently angled the lid to hide the combination
from her.

"2-5-0-6," she read aloud. "Ah, the Brigada."

He glanced over at her, surprised. "So you know the Brigada?
Bahia des Cochinos? Bay of Pigs?"

"Yes, but that's all I know. I know they called it '2506.' I
don't know why it's 2506."

He told her that 2506 was the number of the first training
casualty of the exiles who had gone in with the CIA to invade
Castro's Cuba. They had amplified their numbers by starting
with "2500" rather than "one," so it had actually been the number six invader who had first died at the Bay des Cochinos. He
added, "And the word is 'fish,' not 'pigs,' so it was really the Bay
of Fishes, though *cochinos* is also the word for pigs. Jack let me
pick the numbers for this combination and I picked 2506 for my
grandpapa Simon Rook. He spoke ten languages." He sighed and
tapped the case. "And for what? He washed up on the Cuban
shore, like *La Reina.*"

"Open the case." She placed it exactly between them.

Each of them clicked a sidelock at the same time and the
latches flew up. Inside the case, padded with gray Styrofoam,
wrapped tightly in green velvet strips of cloth, was a rounded
object, cubic at its base, a foot and a half long. Slowly, holding
his breath, Raffy unraveled it. His sigh blew upward, like leaves
rustling high in the air. "*Madre del Dios. Es la Reina!*"

Even in silver moonlight, the Queen of the Sea was gold.
Gold from the tips of her slippers to the points of her crown.
She wore a broad cape that was gleaming with gold and with

the sparkle of the few small rubies and emeralds and sapphires that were still intact in its borders. Most of the casings were, however, empty. Her crown was a spray of gold rods that Raffy gently loosened from her face. The rods spread into a sunburst, each tip capped with a rectangular frame of gold. These larger casings were also empty.

Holding the statue up so its golden surface glowed in the lamplight, Raffy whispered, "*Buena...*"

Impressed, despite herself, Annie nodded. "It looks real."

The eyeless silver baby in the crook of Mary's arm wore a crown too, but a crown of silver thorns. On the mother's breast a little silver door opened into her heart cavity. The cavity, a 3-inch cube, was silver and was empty. "Inside here—" Raffy touched his fingers to the cavity, "was the heart of the Queen. Your papa gave it to me to give to my mother."

"The ruby?"

"More precious. The Thorn." Raffy cradled the Queen in his arms, rocking her softly. "When the Immortal Bard told us, 'All that glitters is not gold,' he couldn't have been more monumentally in complete and absolute error."

Annie held out her hand. "Give me back those emeralds."

Raffy pulled the gems from his pocket. She took one of them. It was, he told her, an emerald of at least forty carats. She held it against one unfilled rectangle at the tip of the gold rods, then she moved it to next, then to the next. The holes were all too large for it, except for the last one, near the statue's right ear. The emerald fit perfectly into the smallest setting on the crown of *La Reina Coronada del Mar*.

"There are more things in heaven and earth, Annie."

She touched the queen's golden smile. "And in the sea too, apparently. At least we're supposed to think so." Annie placed the two other emeralds into the casings that fit them.

The Cuban brushed his hand against the thin gold rods so that they quivered. "It isn't that thinking makes it so but thinking opens your eyes to see what is otherwise in your blind spot." He hunched his thin shoulders. "At least in my opinion."

All the way back up to her room, they argued about what to do next with the Queen. Annie wanted to turn over the statue to Daniel Hart immediately, in exchange for his help in resolving her father's troubles with the police. Raffy wanted to take the relic to show Jack. Exhausted, she finally agreed. They'd go in the morning. She asked Rook to leave so she could get to sleep. With a blush, he declined. With apologies, he couldn't leave the Queen and if she wouldn't give it to him—

"I won't," she agreed.

"Then I must stay." He made a short bow.

"Fine," she told him. "Sleep on my floor then."

"Floor? This is a carpet. This is comfort." He ran his hand in the soft plush. "When I was in the cell in Cuba with your papa? Now that was a floor to sleep on. Hard, cold stone. Like the hearts of policemen."

Raffy lay down propped against the door of her hotel room with Malpy in his arms. Suspicious that he would steal the courier case, she locked it inside her duffel bag and tied the bag under the bed.

They rested a while, but then Raffy complained he was hungry so they returned to the restaurant, where over a late meal, he continued to argue his opinion that Sergeant Hart was absolutely 100 percent not to be relied on, despite his good looks, which had clearly blinded Annie. Without a blink, Hart would throw Jack and Raffy (and Annie) in jail for so long that they'd drown in their cells when global warming flooded Miami. Instead of giving up the Queen, Annie should honor her father's dying wish by going to Havana to collect the gems from the bank where Raffy's second cousin was first assistant manager. Putting those gems back in the Queen's crown would save her father's last days, because if Jack did not quickly pay off his debts to Feliz Diaz, his life was not worth a *zuzu*.

"What debts to Feliz Diaz? Is that why Diaz is looking for my dad?"

"Pretty much. Jack took an advance payment from Diaz on the Queen, sort of. Seven-card-stud."

Annie asked how much he'd lost.

"Considerable," admitted Raffy. "I am not party to the specifics." As for Raffy himself, a single emerald from the crown would be ample reward. The Queen was Jack's discovery and Jack deserved the reward for it. Raffy was only a minor player, a brief shadow, dust.

After they went back up to the hotel room, Annie put the courier case under her pillow, like, she thought, a tooth for the tooth fairy. And she hadn't believed in that either.

She gave Raffy a pillow and a blanket. There was a strange peacefulness for her in his lying there by the door, with Malpy's chin resting on his shoulder. The shadowy room was quiet.

"Raffy?...You've been a good friend to my dad."

But the Cuban was asleep, softly snoring.

Chapter 38

Boom Town

Very early in the morning, at the oval track of the legendary Hialeah Racetrack, Annie and Raffy watched pink long-necked flamingos twist and strut at the pond's edge. The birds were the same lurid color as the flamingos on Raffy's shirt.

There were no races at Hialeah in the heat of July. The birds were the only crowd at this time of year, hundreds of them flying low over the infield, turning the sky a gaudier rose. Raffy explained that he preferred Hialeah in the off-season, without the thundering of remorseless horses galloping away with his money, as had happened all too often in his old drinking days when gambling had also been a personal problem. He no longer believed in chance, only in destiny.

Annie was feeling a little guilty. She had secretly left a message on Daniel Hart's office phone, informing him that she had the so-called *La Reina Coronada del Mar* in her possession and that she was heading to Hialeah Racetrack with Rafael Rook, who was claiming he'd hidden artifacts there belonging to the relic. That at 9 a.m., the two of them would be meeting her father and his alleged doctor at Golden Days. Last offer: She would trade Daniel Hart the Queen for the promise of a deal to get Jack's immunity from prosecution.

As usual, the Miami detective hadn't answered his phone, nor had he called back, nor had he, so far, shown up here at the

track. She kept glancing at the entrance at the clubhouse cha-
teau, hoping he would.

Raffy had brought her to Hialeah to retrieve "the Queen's
heart," which he had buried here, although he seemed to be having trouble remembering exactly where. Late one night he'd "left
his heart at the track." He admitted he might have been close to
delirium tremens at the time.

As he searched the grounds for some landmark to give
him his bearings, she had to admit it was pleasant to be out-
doors in the early morning breeze, walking along the lush
green oval on mazy lanes lined with tropical flowers. No one
was around but a slow-moving groundskeeper who was raking
a gravel path near the track.

Raffy suddenly whispered (not that there was anyone to
overhear them) that it was all coming back to him; he remembered where to dig (two posts from the finish line) and would do
so as soon as the groundskeeper left. He meant "dig" literally, for
he pulled a small trowel from a knapsack. He said he had buried
the "heart" as a way of keeping it safe from "a bunch of 'smiling
damned villains,'" which included the rotten Miami cops. When
Annie saw this treasure, Raffy vowed, she would also see the
kind of man her father was.

"I know the kind of man he is," she said. "He's a crook.
That's a fact."

"Facts have nothing to do with this. Let me tell you a little
more about the man I knew."

"No, don't. Just go use your trowel."

"Not till that groundskeeper leaves; they don't like you to
dig up the track." Raffy pulled Annie down beside him on seats
in the front boxes facing the finish line and offered her a bottle of
water from his knapsack. "You like water? I never did. But now?
It's my honest preference."

Back in the day, Raffy began, he had hung out here at the
track every afternoon; it was his fascination with possibility—
which horse was going to win which race—that had sadly led
to his loss of his girlfriend, his house, and his car. Betting on

the horses proved a worse way to earn a living even than a jazz band.

So, just as it had been Raffy's preordained destiny that any horse on which he'd placed his entire life savings would inevitably finish dead last, despite the fact that the jockey (his cousin's husband) had often sworn the winner was a done deal, when it wasn't, so it had been his destiny to meet Jack Peregrine. "Jack's name was Eddie Fettermann when I met him." The slender man shrugged. "But what's in a name?"

"Apparently not much," agreed Annie. So, what cheap con had her dad been up to in Miami when Raffy had first come across him?

"Cheap?" He waggled his cigarillo at her. "What you need to know about Jack? For a while, Miami had flatlined." He waved a full circle to encompass the city, let his arm plummet. "Morgue-dead. The Mother of God—for my own mother's sake, may She even exist—couldn't resurrect Miami." He raised his arms to the sky. "Your dad shows up one night and the lights come on. I mean, not literally that night but it's a simile. Or litotes?"

She watched the flamingos turn from one direction to the other, like a ballet of indecision. "Okay, Raffy. And this meeting took place how long before the two of you ended up reciting Shakespeare together in a Cuban prison?"

"Years." The thin man tightened his ponytail, raised his bony shoulders. "But in fact, there was a causality." He said the next words as you might whisper a potent and malevolent hex. "Your papa met Feliz Diaz."

Annie shrugged. "So?"

"Diaz! The Jefé, the banker. El Padrino. Your papa somehow ended up owing him, oh, two hundred thousand dollars. Flushes and straights, your papa couldn't resist them."

Annie's heart sank. "My father owes a professional gambler two hundred thousand dollars?" That was the size of her IRA account.

"Two hundred. Maybe three hundred." Raffy shook out water from his bottle as if he were a priest blessing a church. "Diaz is a gambler like the Garcias and José Battle are gamblers. They own the whole *bolita*. Men like that, like Diaz, they have the cash. And your papa, he has no cash, to tell you the truth. You heard of the Corporation? You do not want to owe them."

"Like a Mafia? He owes them two hundred thousand?"

"Maybe three. Your papa is not a crook; he's a performance artist. But anyhow, Diaz heard about the Queen from your papa, and he wants it, and he sets the debt as an advance on what he will pay for the Queen. And he will pay a lot."

Annie got the picture. "All right, all right, Raffy. I'm going to assume, conclude, believe, pretend, *hope*, this Inca statue is real. This criminal wants it. Give it to him and let him cancel the debt and stop sending his goons after Dad. If my father's as ill as he looks, getting punched out in St. Louis and kicked to the curb in Miami isn't so good for him."

Annie's cell phone rang. It was Chamayra at Golden Days, wanting to speak to Raffy. Annie handed him her phone with a wry grimace. "Is there *anybody* who hasn't been given my cell number?"

The news from Chamayra was not good. Thanks to the scene Annie and Raffy had caused yesterday when they'd left Golden Days pursued by the police, Ms. Skippings, the administrator, was on the warpath. Such suspicion had fallen on Chamayra that she couldn't risk their return to the center today at all; tomorrow morning she could manage things maybe, so they had to just sit tight till tomorrow. Meanwhile, Jack, aka Ronny Buchstabe, would be fine, as long as he too kept a low profile and didn't leave his room. In fact, the rest would do him good.

Annie took the news of the imposed delay reasonably well because secretly she planned to send Daniel Hart over to Golden Days today anyhow, as soon as she could reach him, to arrest her father for his own good. In fact, as soon as they left the racetrack, she was going to Miami Police Headquarters to track Hart down. So she was able to tell herself, "Take a breath, just wait." Sipping water, watching the flamingos, she kept an eye on the groundskeeper and let Raffy go on with his stories.

Raffy said that the first time he had seen Jack Peregrine had been at Hialeah, when Jack had given him a long-shot tip with such confidence that he'd put $100 on it and come away with $890; he'd gotten his guitar out of hock, taken his girlfriend out for a fancy dinner, and decided that Jack (or Eddie, as he called him) was "entirely illuminated with magic."

And as if by magic they met again. Jack walked into the Club Tropigala at the Fontainebleau on a night when Raffy was playing guitar with the rumba band there; these were musicians ordinarily out of his league, but the regular guitarist had broken his arm water-skiing and Raffy's father's sister was the band's accountant so he'd gotten the gig.

"I notice your papa as the gentleman I met at Hialeah; he walks right up wearing this creamy linen suit with a creamy rose-bud in his lapel, and he says hello to me, and then he tells us, I mean the Tropigala band, he wants us to play this particular tango. So Omar, Omar Ordonez, our bandleader, plays it. Slow Argentine tango. So at the best table in the place that night is this woman, sitting there between two ex-big-shots from Cuba, friends of Batista, one in the Church and one in crime. Both making money, we could say, from the sins of the flesh, not to mention the heart's sad aspirations. The churchman is Arch-bishop de Uloa."

"The other is Feliz Diaz?"

"Yes." Raffy went on to describe Diaz, with a keen dislike, as a man of political influence in Miami, whose criminal interests were protected by the powerful and paid for by the hopeless who bought the drugs, hookers, and numbers rackets that he sold. "Castro is on my primo shit list, but kicking Diaz out of Havana showed excellent judgment on Castro's part."

"And the woman in the Tropigala that night? The same woman we saw yesterday at Golden Days getting out of the black Mercedes with Diaz?"

"Yes."

Annie asked for her name.

"Helen Clark."

"So my father met Diaz that night? And?"

"Diaz and this woman are sitting with Archbishop de Uloa. She's all tan in a little white dress. It's nothing but you can tell it's a thousand dollars, you know the kind I mean?"

Annie did.

"I'm watching from the bandstand. I see your dad's asking her to dance. She laughs out loud, but she's nervous. Jack introduces himself to Diaz and the archbishop. Edward Fettermann, vice president of this mining corporation." Raffy pinched off the burning tip of his cigarillo and slid the butt into his shirt pocket. "Your dad stares at Helen, almost mad-looking, and holds out his hand, just holds it there. Whole Tropigala freezes, like the Ice Age broke through the windows in big chunks."

Annie asked if her father had already known Helen Clark before.

"I don't think so. Later he told me that's when they met. She stands up and walks onto the dance floor. I'm thinking, the poor guy (your papa), he's going to wash up dead with the morning tide because nobody in Miami moves in on Feliz Diaz. I don't know this tango and I'm trying to fake it, strum and thump, but I'm distracted like everybody else, watching the two of them. At first it's like she was trying to get away but then it was like they'd practiced." Raffy did a slow graceful sequence of tango steps up the aisle beside their seats. "When the number's over, guess what?"

Annie shrugged. "Diaz shot my dad."

"No. Don't make jokes." Raffy clapped his hands. "Diaz claps. Then the big-shot priest claps. Then Diaz holds his hand out to Jack. He says, 'Join us.'"

"My dad," Annie admitted, "could dance."

Raffy nodded. "Across the sky and never look down." Humming a song, he held out his arms and courteously invited Annie into a dance. She thought, why not? She hadn't danced, except rock-music gyrations, for a long time. They moved down the stairs and onto the close-cut grass. The rumba steps came back to her from her childhood.

Each in their separate memories, Raffy sang and they danced at the racetrack. The moment again felt curiously peaceful to her. It was strange that Rafael Rook should feel so familiar.

Finally she stepped away from him and asked, "Did Helen Clark take up with my dad after that night?"

He leaned against a gate and shook his head no. "Honestly I think they hated each other's guts. But your dad and Diaz, they hit it off big. Diaz loves humongous stakes poker, seven-card stud. It's like an addictive obsession with him. Your papa would play those stakes. Jack was the ace of aces with regard to poker. Except, he had some bad runs."

"I'll say: two or three hundred thousand dollars worth." Annie took her bottled water from her purse.

"Unfortunately. But that was later. So I start to see him and Diaz everywhere. Your dad was on a roll, treating large crowds to dinner at the best places. Taking twenty, thirty people, a la carte. Annie, fast forward five, six years, here in Miami we have condos and clubs, night lights, Marlins, Dolphins, SoBe, the Grove, it's a boomtown, an American Riviera."

Her eyebrow went up. "Miami's urban revival is due to my father's doing the tango with a criminal's girlfriend? I don't think so."

Impatiently, the small rumpled man shook his finger at her. "It *felt* like it. Listen to me. That's Jack's gift. To make you feel it. He was an artist," he said, stretching out the word *artist* with his slender arms.

Annie, taken aback by his intensity, sidestepped into sarcasm. "Right, sure, an artist. The 'confidence art.' I've heard the line."

He sighed, frustrated by his inability to make the young woman appreciate her father's talents. "For a while I was his gardener, you know, gardener? Lay the groundwork with a mark? He was the best I ever saw."

Raffy kept trying to paint a picture of Annie's father as a sort of a racketeering Robin Hood, who only swindled the already corrupt; who lived daily life as a performance art of social skill and psychological 'freedom': "He would make bets how long he could live like a king without touching a cent. No bad plastic or bouncing checks either, though nobody could pass a check like your dad. He'd go weeks without a penny. Nicest restaurants in town, crowded, he'd slip in, dine for free, slip out. Never paid a cent. Best hotel, find an empty suite, put on his tux, drift down to the ballrooms, join weddings, bar mitzvahs, sit at their tables, always the life of the party, never saw the people before or since, but enjoyed their hospitality so much they loved him. You think your father did it to save a penny? He did it for *art*. Some days I would just follow him up and down the streets of Miami."

Annie drank from the bottled water. "Sort of like Ratso in *Midnight Cowboy?*"

"I don't follow you, I apologize." Raffy didn't appear to be much of a moviegoer. "I'm trying to say, he was in that league, with Lustig, Mike Romanoff, Serge Rubenstein."

Annie registered the fact that Raffy kept saying of her father, "He *was* an artist." "He *was* in that league"—not *is*, but *was*. She asked him if he was implying that Jack was, in fact, so critically ill that his life was effectively over?

His response was oblique. "Know what he said when I pulled him up from the curb? 'I will be a bridegroom in my death, and run into't as to a lover's bed.' Annie, he always had the right quote. He wants to die with this one last thing of beauty. He wants to leave you a million dollars. On the other hand, I would like a small share."

She scoffed. "In the first place, he doesn't have a million dollars. In the second, I don't want a million dollars."

"Good." The Cuban smiled. "Then give it to me."

At this moment the groundskeeper finally shouldered his rake and made his way to the exit. Raffy watched the man shuffle toward his truck, where he sat for a long while before driving slowly away. "They must pay him by the hour," the Cuban muttered.

He hurried Annie over to a white fence post at the final turn in the track and began pacing out a distance, one foot carefully positioned in front of the other. When he had counted ten feet, he stopped, made a quick right turn and paced some more.

Annie stood, watching him fall to his knees and dig with his trowel. Was Rafael Rook practicing con art, or was he one of her dad's victims?

When she was a child, her father had told her the same stories about "the great con artists" and how their victims were never the pure of heart. One of his favorite "artists" was the fake Count Lustig who had sold the Eiffel Tower to suckers and had also peddled "green grocery machines" that supposedly could turn one-dollar bills into twenties. Hundreds of larcenous innocents had bought these machines from Lustig for as much as forty thousand dollars each; even the sheriff who'd arrested him had bought one.

Annie wondered if Raffy, urgently scooting on his knees over the sod, knew the *end* of these con artists' stories? Count Lustig had died in Alcatraz Prison. The great Ponzi of the infamous Ponzi scheme had later sold his services to Mussolini and degenerated into a seedy bum. The plundering stock manipulator Serge Rubenstein had gotten himself murdered, and Ivan Kreuger, the Match King, who'd put billions of other people's money into his own fake banks, had killed himself, and so had John Sadleir, bringing down the London Stock Exchange with him. They were all failures. The best of the confidence artists had failed in the end, not so much because they'd lost confidence but because they'd kept going until they did fail. To fail was, as Raffy might say, their destiny. Just as failure and not "a thing of beauty" was her father's destiny. It was somehow deep down his desire.

Near the track rail, Raffy was now cutting out a square in the grass. He carefully removed the sod and scooped away the dirt. As if he'd been following her thoughts, he called out, "Jack's gift!" Holding up a package, he ran back to her with it. Wrapped in green velvet like that in which they'd found the Queen of the Sea was a 2-inch by 2-inch ornately engraved old silver box. The box had a pronged setting on its lid that seemed designed for some (large) missing jewel.

He held the box in the palm of his hand, tapped it gently. "Right here sat the big ruby, 135-carat ruby, now in the bank in Havana. *Inside* this box?" He patted the lid as if it were a living thing. "Inside this box is a genuine thorn from the Crown of Thorns of the possible—who knows for sure?—Savior, Jesus Christ. Your father gave this treasure to me, a free gift, in order for me to present it to my mother, when I see her again, after all these years, in Cuba. This is a generous man, to make me such a gift." He held out the box to Annie.

It did indeed look like very old silver, beautifully crafted. She gave it back to him. "Come on, Raffy, you honestly think a piece of Christ's Crown of Thorns is inside this little box?"

Raffy's sigh was like a yawn of relief. "I know there is. I don't want to open it, you understand, because of the atmospheric pressure." He refolded the cloth, slid the little box into his pants pocket.

Annie glanced around the clubhouse area. She checked her cell phone. Daniel Hart either hadn't gotten her message, or he didn't care about her offer. She wasn't sure what she should do with the Queen.

She walked high up into the stands and took a seat, put her feet up on the rail in front of her, stared at the green empty track to think it through. Maybe she should just give the gold (if it were gold) statue to Raffy and wish him and her father good luck in making their own way to Cuba to collect the emeralds and ruby (if they existed). She herself would take a commercial flight back home to North Carolina. That would be the wiser plan, wouldn't it? Just disappear out of her father's life, the way he had disappeared from hers?

Raffy joined her up in the grandstand. They sat side by side and might have been watching an invisible horse race together. In the silence, the Cuban smoothed the flamingos on his shirt as if they had tried to fly away to join the flock of birds that suddenly wheeled into the sky. Quietly he said, "For me, it's my mother. For your father, it's you he wants to make amends to. The Queen is his way of making it up to you. The Thorn is my way."

"Why do you need to make amends to your mother?" She didn't question that her father needed to do so to her.

Raffy confessed that he had been a terrible disappointment to his mother. If only he had stayed with her and his brother in Cuba, or gone back to them, instead of falling under the influence of her no-good brother Mano, who'd introduced him to the high life in Miami, including booze, horses, craps, and show biz—none of which had done a thing for him but break his heart. In Cuba, he might now be an astrophysicist or at least have finished some kind of education, instead of turning into a deadbeat flopper on the grift.

She touched his hand briefly. "Or maybe worse would have happened to you in Havana. You might be dead. You never know."

"The readiness is all," he agreed.

Slowly they made their way back to her rental car in the empty parking lot. Every few feet he stopped to sigh a long soft sad sigh. "But I'm not a physicist and I'm not dead. I'm a spot-the-pigeon, do-the-chisel, *hasta la vista* flopper. That's me, Annie. Except when I worked with Jack. Because with Jack it was never the score, it was the insubstantial pageant."

"Make one of your own."

"I can't."

"Sure you can. I saw you."

He shook his head. Anything but the simplest scam was too stressful for him to bear. For instance, some floppers made extra money working with accomplices who pretended to be doctors and would validate the injuries of the supposed victims, to scare the elderly into higher payoffs. But the risks posed by partners were too anxiety-producing for Raffy to endure.

"I bet you could do a shell game," Annie said to cheer him up.

"Never had the hands." He held his out; they were unsteady.

She opened her car door. "I bet you could do sob stories. 'I've got five kids and my wife's dying' type thing? You'd be good at that."

He shrugged, morosely emptying a discarded bag of potato chips at the feet of a seagull in the parking lot; the bird seemed to know him personally and to dislike him. "To be honest with you,

Annie, the flopper bit you saw me do on Joyce Weimar, that's about all my nerves can take."

He looked pensively at the cloudless blue sky, then into his water bottle, but there was no solace to be found in either place. "So I'm hoping to give my mama the Holy Thorn—that woman loves Jesus so much and He honestly has been a better Son to her than I have, and so has my oldest brother, to hear him tell it, which he will, like twenty-four-hour talk radio." He blew a mournful foggy note on the bottle's mouth. "Not that I'm defending the failure of my life. Maybe for such a success as your-self, it's not so easy to see how someone could...what?...inhabit so much...insignificance. Except, I think, with an education I could have done a little better."

Annie felt oddly urged by some unspecified impulse of human sympathy to kiss Raffy Rook and in an uncharacteristic impulsiveness, she did so. "It's okay. You've educated yourself."

"You think?" he asked softly.

"Yes." She kissed him again. The full warmth of his lips gave her an unexpected, deeply sweet feeling, strangely reminding her of the healing ointments Sam had heated in her hands before rub-bing them on Annie's chest when she was a child, ill with a cold.

It had been some time since Annie's lips had touched some-one else's lips. The pleasure of it surprised her.

Obviously touched, Raffy stepped back, reaching for her hand, kissing it in the same gentle way. "Thank you," he said. "Your heart goes out to me. It's very kind of you."

"I mean it," she said. "You know a lot of things. You've taught yourself."

"Don't think the worst. And don't feel bad. Sometimes these ladies I flop on? These ladies and myself, at Golden Days, we get to be friends. We go to the salad bars, botanical gardens, zoo, IMAX. They get a senior's discount, I play them a song on my guitar. It's a connection. And in this sad fast life, how many do we make time for?" He spoke wistfully into the water bottle, as if he were depositing his confession inside and then quickly screw-ing the cap back on to keep it there.

Not until they were on their way back to the Dorado, and caught in a morning traffic jam caused by a fender bender at a big intersection, did Annie announce her intention of driving right now to the Miami police department headquarters on Second Avenue to find Sergeant Hart. She explained her conviction that the best way to keep both Raffy and her father out of jail was for her to make a deal with the police as quickly as possible. Tell Hart everything. So that's what they were going to do. Right now.

The closeness they'd established at the track vanished. Raffy refused to let her take him to the "son-of-a-bitch cops." Asked to listen to reason, he declined, lapsing into indignant Spanish that she couldn't follow although she was able to interpret the gist from his tone. Finally she blurted out that she'd already left a message with Hart, saying that Raffy and she had found the gold statue called the Queen of the Sea and that they wished to turn it over to the police. If indeed the relic was a relic, it belonged to Cuba.

The slender musician stared at her in horror then abruptly threw open the car door and tumbled out of it into the street. "*Gracias!*" he shouted over his shoulder.

"Raffy! Come back here!"

But he ran across the divider into the rush-hour traffic on Ocean Drive.

"Raffy!"

Dodging honking cars, threading his way to the beach side of the busy four-lane, he soon disappeared into the crowd.

Annie shook her head, watching him go. The car behind her beeped. She leaned over, closed the door. Traffic moved and she moved with it. Oddly enough, she had no doubt she would see him again.

• • •

The desk officer at the Vice Unit of the central Miami Police Department was evasive when Annie persisted in her demands to speak with Sgt. Daniel Hart, whose home number and address were unlisted in the phone directory. Finally he snarled at her, "Try La Loca. It's a bar in Coconut Grove. Dan's there every night."

Night? It was only nine-thirty in the morning. She needed to see Hart sooner than that. The desk officer was sorry, but could do nothing about it.

He connected her with another Vice detective to whom she gave the basic facts about the fraud case that Hart was pursuing, although she did not give him the details of her father's whereabouts or the whereabouts of the statue of the Queen. This detective didn't appear to be much interested but he agreed to pass along her information to Hart. Clearly the capture of Jack Peregrine was not an urgent priority here at MPD, nor was the current location of Sgt. Daniel Hart.

She headed back onto the expressway, making slow progress through the morning's rush-hour traffic. As she drove, she called Golden Days. They had no Dr. Parker on their staff, or at least wouldn't admit to it. When she asked to speak to Coach Ronny Buchstabe, they tried to put her through to their administrator, Ms. Skippings. Annie hung up. She didn't want her dad arrested until she could set up an amnesty arrangement with Hart. Better just to leave him resting at Golden Days. She called Sam in Emerald to fill her in on her latest encounters with her father, including a report of Jack's weak condition in the hospital. She also described the discovery of the gold statue in the courier case and Rook's endless tales of Jack's criminal past. But it was Jack's current health that Sam most wanted information on.

Hearing that he might really be dying of cancer, Sam made a sudden sobbing noise but stopped herself quickly with a sharp laugh.

"I don't know what to think," Annie told her. "Is it true? Is it a con? What do you think?"

The truth was that Sam thought her brother had terminal cancer, but she quickly reassured her niece that "Jack's pulling our leg. But it's a very, very bad joke."

Annie agreed that it wasn't funny. Meanwhile it seemed likely that, even if terminal, Jack's condition wasn't immediately critical;

when she'd seen him yesterday he wasn't even in intensive care. But she would definitely speak with a doctor at Golden Days as soon as possible and would insist that they move her father to a better hospital, even if it meant returning him to prison. As soon as she found the elusive Daniel Hart, she would sort it all out.

"Poor Jack," sighed Sam. "He got mixed up with a bad crowd."

"Right. Poor dad. This Feliz Diaz must have corrupted him."

Sam said, "Listen, if I've heard of Feliz Diaz, he's a kingpin, because you know I never watch that junk TV news and I don't read the right-wing rags."

"Sam, you think *Newsweek* and the *New York Times* are right-wing rags."

"Bought and sold, baby." Sam urged Annie to collect Jack and fly him home on one of Brad's Hopper Jets so that Clark could get him admitted to the hospital in Emerald where Sam could watch over him.

"I can't keep borrowing Brad's jets. I'm divorcing him."

"Are you sure? I just want you to be happy."

"Come on, Sam. Were you happy? Like Clark says, who's happy?"

Sam claimed that she was much happier than she'd used to be. The older she got, the less she cared about crap that made you unhappy, like what anybody else thought of her, and how much money she had, and what she might have, could have, should have done better in the past. Like that double-fault serve in the '83 national first round that had haunted her for ten years. She just wished she could help Annie not waste these years of her youth that Sam herself had wasted.

Annie said, "Sam, don't get philosophical on me. I've heard enough of that from Raffy Rook today."

"Raffy?"

"Rafael Rook. By the way, he told me Dad said my mother's name was Kay Denham. Think that's possible?"

There was a long pause. Then Sam said, "Sweetie, Kay Denham is the name of the character Claudette Colbert played in *I Met Him in Paris*."

"Goddamn him!" Annie made her exit turn so fast her tires squealed. "Why would he even tell Raffy that?"

"Leave well enough alone," suggested Sam.

Annie said that she *had* left well enough alone for decades. It was Jack Peregrine who had hauled her back into his life. "So too bad. No way I'm dropping this, Sam. Bye."

Annie followed the exit back to South Beach and the Hotel Dorado where she answered all her Annapolis emails and sent her uniform in a rush order to be dry-cleaned. Okay, if she had to wait till tomorrow morning, she'd wait. Maybe that was her challenge; she hated waiting and so she was forced to do it. She hated not working and never took vacations. She had so much unused leave that the Navy had told her to use it or lose it. How long had it been since she'd answered to no schedule? Not since she'd started elementary school. All right, today she'd win the war of waiting. Maybe she'd even go shopping. Maybe she'd go to a bookstore and buy a book and sit by the Dorado pool and read it. She could do anything she wanted. That would be the hard part.

• • •

Late that afternoon, Annie was swimming laps at the hotel pool. As she swam, methodical, classic form, she determined that if she had a mother out there anywhere alive, she would somehow get that woman's real name out of her father and would track her down and...why...?

What would she even want from the woman at this point, besides asking her why she had ever left her baby behind with a man like Jack Peregrine? Maybe it was only that. She would ask her that one question.

Annie thought about how her first Navy flight instructor had yelled at her in the cockpit as they'd sat in the jet on the rainy deck of the USS *Enterprise*. "You gotta go, Goode! You women wanna join the Navy, you gotta fly a Tomcat not a pussycat. *Commit to go, damn it!*" And she had forced herself to set aside both his remark and her fear. She had taken a long breath and then shot her jet forward off the deck of that rolling ship in what the instructor had admitted after they'd landed was a goddamn 90 percent perfect takeoff. Afterwards, he'd made her repeat the takeoff to get the other 10 percent right. And Annie had done it again. And again.

If she were asked to claim a single virtue in herself, it would be that she didn't quit. She had never failed to cross a high school track meet finish line, however much it hurt. She had never failed to crawl over the last wall of the Annapolis obstacle course, however bigger, stronger male cadets mocked her. And in a month she would break a record testing a new jet. Or if she failed, she would try again. She wouldn't quit.

Swimming faster, Annie's hand touched the pool's end; she neatly flipped herself and headed back in the other direction in her smooth steady crawl. Lap forty-eight.

Forty-nine.

Fifty.

As she climbed out of the pool, reaching for her towel, her glance caught sight of a woman at the other end of the large long rectangular pool, standing near the diving board. To look at the woman, Annie had to face into the blinding dazzle of the sunset, so all she really could see was a flame of dark-gold hair and the glint from oversized sunglasses and flare from a gold bracelet. Annie toweled water from her face. When she looked again, the woman was gone. The woman she'd seen at Golden Days.

Annie hurried around the pool edge to the diving board. There was a cigarette crushed in the hotel's black ashtray on a table. It was a Chesterfield, a small lipstick smear on the end of the paper. It was warm. Who would smoke unfiltered cigarettes anymore? Except her father and this sun-shadowed woman in his life.

• • •

At the same time, back in Emerald, Sam was instructing the high-school movie fan who worked for her at Now Voyager to "woman the store." Sam retired to the editing room where she was supposed to be transferring old Super-8 films to DVD for a client. But what she actually did was to sit there in the dark, watching a film called "Annie."

Over the years she'd been adding material to this loop, reorganizing its sequence of clips a dozen times. The movie now began with some poorly lit footage that Jack had shot decades ago on that surprise month-long visit to Pilgrim's Rest with his one-year-old daughter. Anne Samantha Peregrine.

The first clip showed Sam running after the baby Annie who crawled at an amazingly fast pace over to the screen door, which she tried to push open with her head. Sam, laughing, opened the door and let her pull herself out onto the porch. In the next, Annie was careening along the hallway in a bright yellow plastic learning walker that Sam had bought her. It had a steering wheel, horn, radio buttons, a headlight, and turn signals. Annie was laughing in delight.

The next clip, shot at the end of the month's visit, showed Sam on her knees in the morning room. She held her arms out to Annie a few feet away, standing unsteadily in little red overalls. Spike-haired, round-faced, irresistibly smiling, she held her arms tight around a table's leg—the table on which, years later, the puzzle of the blue sky would sit. In the silent film, Sam kept calling to Annie to come on, come on, walk to her.

Suddenly letting go of the table, laughing, tipping, staggering in a joyful unbalance, Annie ran fast across that vast space between risk and safety and fell into her aunt's outreached arms.

Alone in the editing room, Sam clicked the "Annie" DVD forward to later footage, shot with a camcorder sixteen years after those first steps of Annie's. This footage had sound. It opened with a long shot of the Emerald High stadium as the school's marching band came onto the field, playing "Johnny B. Goode." Annie had just won the National Youth Speed Race, urging the *King of the Sky* to a speed of which D. K. Destin had not thought it capable. On the football field the band formed the shape of an airplane, while the bandleader stood on a platform beside cheerleaders who sang into a mike:

Her mama told her someday, though you are a girl,
You will be the fastest in the big old world.
Saying Annie P. Goode tonight.
Go Go
Go Annie Go

The camera then zoomed to a closeup shot of Clark, seated right beside Sam. Clowning, he pulled his bright green Emerald High tasseled ski cap down over his head. Then the camera zoomed back to Annie as she walked out onto the field, waving and smiling. She held up the trophy, and shook it at the sky.

In the edit room, Sam paused the film on the teenaged Annie's face. She looked very much like the young woman who had so long ago broken Jack's heart. Or so at least he'd claimed to his sister.

Sam studied the shot of Annie's face until it went off "pause" and the screen turned as blank blue as the puzzle of the sky.

Chapter 39

Tonight Is Ours

That evening, taking the MPD desk officer's advice, Annie drove to the bar named La Loca to look for Daniel Hart. A bartender there told her that Hart was indeed a daily, usually showing up around sunset. She promised to point him out when he arrived.

Half an hour passed. Young people arrived by twos, threes, dozens. Their voices grew quickly louder at the crowded bar. None of them was the Miami detective.

Annie moved to a booth where she ordered a salad and a bottle of flat water. The waiter looked disappointed by her Spartan choices. Above her head hung blue fish netting in which large neon blue plastic martini glasses tangled with starfish. Barbie dolls in bathing suits lay in the net against G.I. Joes and model cars.

She phoned Trevor in Maryland, describing her visit to her father at Golden Days, the strange call from the woman telling her to stay away, her surprise when Rafael Rook and she opened the case in which they'd found something that resembled the gold Queen of the Sea (which was now locked in her hotel room). She gave Trevor Sergeant Hart's phone number and the license plate number of the black Mercedes she'd seen outside Golden Days: Was it in fact the racketeer Feliz Diaz's car? Could Trevor also find out anything about Diaz's girlfriend, Helen Clark?

Trevor grouchily told Annie that he didn't work for her, he worked for the U.S. government.

"Support your troops," she reminded him.

"Go to bed. I'll call you in the morning," he promised. "By morning I mean like ten, eleven o'clock."

"Trevor, you're sleeping your life away."

He laughed. "How can I with you calling me all the time?"

A well-muscled man Annie's age—with expensive beachy clothes—leaned in, took a crayon from a basket, and wrote a big green question mark on the paper tablecloth. "Waiting for a boyfriend?"

She didn't reply. He grinned in what he clearly hoped was a winning way. He had better teeth than anyone could honestly come by; they were as white as a sink. "Tonight is ours, could be. How 'bout I sit down, buy you a drink?"

Glancing up, Annie said, "How 'bout you don't?"

"Large mistake," he told her.

"Chance I have to take." She smiled with an insincerity he couldn't miss.

He picked a tomato slice out of her guacamole salad and sucked it between his teeth in a belligerent reply. Annie grabbed his wrist, compressing nerves with an accuracy that the Navy had taught her. "Don't put your hands in my food," she advised him, her mouth tight. When she flicked his arm away, he cursed her but left.

A short voluptuous Latina woman wearing the requisite La Loca turquoise T-shirt with pedal pushers and stacked-heel sandals, strode through the crowd. As she approached the booth, Annie recognized her as Chamayra, Raffy's helpful friend from Golden Days. She glared at Annie suspiciously. "Are you spying on me?"

Surprised, Annie asked, "Aren't you the nurse at Golden Days?"

"Nurse technician. I fill in here late nights. I already told Raffy I can't do nothing for you two till tomorrow." Placing small strong hands on the table—Annie noticed a snake bracelet and a gimmick ring with a little pink blinking heart—she demanded to know, "You not trying to get Raffy in trouble, are you?"

"No, I'm doing everything I can to help him!"

Chamayra didn't like this answer either. "Why? You know he's seeing me, almost a year now?"

"He's all yours."

"He gave me this." The waitress pulled an ornately worked heavy gold necklace out from under her tight La Loca T-shirt.

"That's a lot of gold." Annie made a whistling sound.

"His mama made it." She slipped the necklace back under her shirt, shook herself so it would fall into place. "I want to help Raffy but your daddy is trouble for him. Me, too, if I lose my chance at Golden Days. I'm subbing."

Annie nodded. "I understand. I just want to keep my father out of prison while I look for some decent health care for him."

Chamayra made a face. "Don't look in this country."

"Listen, have you ever heard of a Sgt. Daniel Hart? Miami Police. I was told he comes in here every night."

Overhearing the question, another waitress, African American, big, good-looking, thrust herself at the booth edge. "You Melissa? 'Cause if you are, you beat it, you hear me?"

Taken aback by the woman's hostility, Annie stood up. "Excuse me?"

"You wasted a nice guy. Just leave the man alone." She leaned sideways to get a better look. "Oh, you're not Melissa. I saw her picture."

Upset, Annie snapped. "Did I say I was Melissa?"

The waitress rocked back and forth. "No, but Danny told me Melissa was a bitch, so I made the mistake." She huffed away.

Sliding back into the booth, Annie said to Chamayra, "Let's start over." Daniel Hart, she explained, was investigating her father. She wanted the detective's help but he kept blowing off appointments he'd made with her. How ill was her father? Shouldn't he be in a good hospital? To her astonishment, Annie found herself tearing up.

Softened, Chamayra turned sympathetic. "Be easy, hey."

"I'm sorry. It's exhaustion, that's all."

Chamayra sat down in the booth, put her arm around Annie. "I lost my mama last summer. She's asleep in her bed, just don't wake up. I grab her arm; it's like a tray of ice. She's dead. I walk out in our backyard and go down on my knees and I'm making weird noises loud as I can. My son runs out and makes me come back in the house, says I'm setting off dogs up and down the block."

Annie blew her nose. "I'm sorry about your mother's death."

"*La muerte.* It comes to us all," sighed the nurse, apparently under the influence of the philosophical Rafael Rook. She stood again, wiping the booth with an automatic efficiency. "Sometimes, face it, life sucks. I got two kids, my ex-husband gets laid off, eighteen years on the same job, you believe that? He can't help with money for the kids no more. Aw yeah, what you gonna do? You want my advice for the world?"

Wary, Annie nonetheless nodded yes.

Thumbs and forefingers together, Chamayra pantomimed positioning a rectangular sign in air. "Hang out the Love sign and do what you can." She flipped the invisible sign upside down. "Hang out the Closed sign when you gotta put your feet up." She took the imaginary sign from its place in the air and tossed it over her shoulder. "Yeah, I know Dan. He's not here now."

"Sergeant Hart?"

"We're open six nights; he's in here six nights. Raffy can't stand him but I think Dan's a good guy. He was good to my little boy."

"Well, I wish he'd answer his phone."

The plump waitress spun her finger beside her head. "Right now Dan's a stress case. His marriage busted up."

Annie asked, "Today?"

"No, no. Two, three years back. Sit still. I'm gonna locate him for you." She took away Annie's soda glass. "I'll bring you a mojito."

Annie said she didn't drink.

"You ain't drank my mojito."

Annie's white Navy jacket was lying on the bench with her Navy hat. Chamayra gestured at them, made a face. "I got a brother joins the Army. I'm like, don't go, Luis. He's like, 'Hey, you know, it's better'n laying asphalt in this neighborhood, and I like get myself popped in some fuckin' Haitian drive-by.' I go, you know what? You're right, it's a living. So what happens? His jeep rolls over and he like loses a leg. Fuckin' Kuwait. I'll be back."

The minty drink was very good. As Annie sipped it, she studied the fake business cards she'd found hidden inside the lining of her father's leather flight jacket. These cards had different typefaces and introduced different men:

Henry Frank
Antiques and Artworks Appraised

Jarvis J. Rochard III
Deputy Under Secretary, Department of the Interior

Edward Fettermann
Vice President
Southern Hemisphere Mining Corporation

Different addresses were inscribed at the bottoms of the cards. There'd even been a card with the name Clark Lewis Goode. None of the cards told the truth. Not one of them said,

Jack Peregrine
Confidence Man

It had been on the backs of cards such as these that her father had long ago written out the words by which he'd taught her to read: Cat. Hat. Annie. Dad.

Now with a crayon, Annie wrote single words on the backs of the fake calling cards. She wrote *con* on one. She wrote *art* on a second. Then on a third card she found herself writing the word *love*—as if she were making a little version of that Love sign the waitress Chamayra had advised the world to hang out.

She studied the three cards, silently playing with them as she waited for Chamayra to bring her back news about where Dan Hart might be.

Con. It meant at odds, opposed to, contra; as in *pro and con.* But to "con" something also meant to study it. Her father had conned his art, was a pro at the con. On the other hand, he was not always enough of a pro, since he was also an ex-con. Annie wryly tore the *con* card in two.

Art. Raffy had claimed her father's cons were works of art, that Jack had enough confidence in that art to save the whole city of Miami. *Confidence.* It meant "with faith." But her father's faith was specifically that he could con others into believing his lies. Even if the lie was his love. Hadn't he conned her that way? Hadn't she believed in the love he'd betrayed by disappearing? She looked a while at the *love* card, then she set her mojito down on it, sliding her glass around until the word blurred.

While *con* meant *against*, in Italian it was the word for *with.* So *con amore* was what Ruthie Nickerson had written on the sheet music of "Lara's Theme" from *Doctor Zhivago* that was in Sam's piano bench at Pilgrim's Rest—"with love." With love to whom? For whom? Jack? Or had some old piano teacher just written that the song should be played passionately?

Annie might as well admit it; like Sam, like Raffy, like who knows else, she had loved the con man Jack Peregrine. But it was from him that she'd learned that love was the biggest con there was; he would make you feel confiding, confidential love, then when you loved him back, you got left in the road in the rain. You were conned by a pro and the art of it was you never saw it coming.

To hear her father tell the story, the only person who'd been able to resist this con-art love of his had been Annie's mother, who'd walked away.

She looked at the unsigned postcard her father had given her, with the *Life* cover photo of Claudette Colbert smoking on the tropical balcony.

Claudette died today. Here's to a great lady.
I'm fine. Hope you're ditto. Better this way.
Reach for the sky…

Taking the flowery birthday card from her purse, she compared their handwritings. As she suspected, they had the same Greek final *e*'s, the same wide capital letters with their curving loops like smoke rings. She had little doubt that her father had written both in a fake hand.

Annie's phone rang although it took her a while to hear it in the noise of La Loca. Georgette was calling from Emerald, where she was in bed reading about the Roman ruins at Baalbek. She just wanted to check in to hear the news from Miami. Annie gave her the highlights, then asked if Georgette knew what had happened to her mysterious aunt Ruthie, the one who'd run off with a married man when she was still a teenager.

Georgette found her friend's interest in this distant past strange, given all that had happened to her in these last few days. Why would she ask about an aunt of Georgette's that no one had seen or heard from in well over a decade? Annie explained how the woman at Golden Days yesterday had reminded her of images of Ruthie in the Nickerson house. Georgette thought it highly unlikely that her aunt Ruthie had flown first to St. Louis, then to Miami, merely to catch a glimpse of Jack Peregrine, particularly if—according to Kim—she had chewed him up and spit him out back when he was a teenager.

"Your mom didn't stay in touch with Ruthie?"

"No way." Georgette's mother Kim had disliked her sister-in-law intensely, consistently calling her a "cold fish," a "ball buster," someone who "could care less about her family," and who had ruined the life of the married man from Emerald with whom she'd "eloped," abandoning him within weeks. (His wife had taken him back and they'd moved away.) By some unexplained means Ruthie had gotten herself admitted to an Ivy League college on a mysterious scholarship. After graduating, she had climbed some unexplained ladder to success. According to Kim, she'd never given her only brother, Georgette's father George, the time of day. In fact, when George had died of a sudden heart attack, all Ruthie had done was send flowers with a message that she was out of the country and unable to attend the funeral. Kim had vowed then never to forgive her and presumably never had.

"How old is Ruthie now?" Annie asked.

Georgette had to compute it: somewhere around forty-three or forty-four or forty-five.

The only time Georgette had ever known Ruthie to come back to Emerald had been when Annie herself had met her, when they'd been in ninth grade.

"I sort of remember that," Annie said.

She let the memory form, enlarge: they'd driven home from school that day with Georgette's mother. Georgette was in tears because she'd been hit in the face with a field hockey stick. Pacing in the Nickerson drive near a rental car was a tense, well-dressed, attractive woman clearly waiting for someone to come home.

With shocking curtness, Kim did not even greet this woman but told her, "There're three cartons in the garage. The other stuff you can box yourself. It's all in the front bedroom upstairs. I'm sure you're too busy to stay for dinner."

Kim hurried inside the house. The woman looked at the teenagers with deep-blue eyes unfathomable to Annie, then calmly introduced herself as Georgette's aunt Ruthie.

Later that night, at home at Pilgrim's Rest, Annie raced downstairs with her algebra notebook; studying for her final exams, she couldn't solve a problem with which Clark would have been useful had he been there. She had little hope that Sam could help her with the math; she expected only sympathy.

Ruthie Nickerson sat at the kitchen table with Sam, drinking wine. The Scrabble game that Annie and Sam had been playing after dinner was still on the table. As Annie entered the room, the stranger was saying something about Clark, how she was sorry he had to stay late at the hospital tonight, how she would like Sam to tell him hello from her. Sam, with a tug at her short nut-brown hair, introduced the woman as Georgette's aunt, visiting next door.

The woman said, "We already met. Hello again, Annie."

Sam took Annie's hand, proudly squeezed it. "Jack's daughter I was telling you about."

The woman raised her glass. "Where is he?"

Annie raised her eyebrow. "My bet is, jail."

Ruthie toasted Annie with the wine. "Good guess, babe. Listen, sorry. Sam said that's your sky puzzle. While she was on the phone, I did a little of it."

Annie shrugged. "It just sits there."

Taking a praline from a candy box labeled "New Orleans," Ruthie bit into it with beautiful white teeth. "So, how do you like life here in Emerald?"

Annie shrugged again. "Okay."

"I hated it." Deftly, the strange woman slid three Scrabble squares onto the board, moving down from a *j* in the word *rajah* to form the word *jack*. "I didn't know Jack had a kid. We lost touch a long time ago." She started spelling *ruth* off the *r* in *rajah*. "The good old bad old days."

Sam moved away the woman's hand, flicking the little wood Scrabble squares across the board. "Come on, Ruthie, stop messing around. No proper names."

Sipping her wine, the coppery-haired woman shrugged. "Hey, *ruth* means sorrow and compassion. *Jack*'s a word too. It means, oh, an apparatus to jack up a price or an automobile; it means jack-o-lantern, jack-in-the-box, lumberjack, blackjack, hijack, jack-of-all-trades, straightjacket, jackrabbit, let's see, jackpot. *Jack* means whatever the jackshit you want it to."

With perverse pleasure, Annie laughed, impressed by all the rapid effortless words, aligning herself with this stranger against the aunt she knew and loved. "*Jack*," she agreed, "means a lot of things."

Ruthie, swallowing the last bite of her praline, reached for Annie's algebra notebook and pencil, glanced at the unsolved problem written there. "What are you looking for?" she asked the teenager. "The roots of that cubic?"

"I don't usually have trouble with this kind of thing," Annie felt she needed to say.

Ruthie wrote something on the margin then handed her back the notebook. "Just a little glitch. One of the solutions is an imaginary number. Try 2i and the others will come. Okay?"

Annie looked at the equation, now solved "…Oh. Right."

Sam folded, unfolded the dishcloth.

The woman leaned over, affectionately rubbing Sam's short hair. "You never let it grow out?" She found a brush in her purse and drew it through her own rich wild hair. "Listen to this, Annie. Sam's mother cut Sam's hair off when she was about your age. Just ran at Sam with the scissors, held her down and cut it off. Right, Sam?"

Annie's heart jumped in horror. "Why did she do that?"

The stranger said mildly, "I think she went crazy after her husband killed her little boy."

"Ruthie, for Christ's sake," Sam muttered.

"Oh he didn't do it on purpose. Accidents happen."

The phone rang and rang. Finally Annie pulled her eyes away from the visitor. "I'll get it in the hall; it's probably Georgette," said Annie. "Nice to meet you."

"You too."

Annie ran out of the kitchen and through the house to the hallway. From the kitchen she could hear Georgette's aunt saying to Sam, "So Jack had a kid. Amazing. Where's her mother?"

Sam's reply was too soft to hear.

"Georgette, I'll call you right back," Annie whispered, hanging up so she could tiptoe back to the doorway of the kitchen, where she was shocked to see Sam in tears, her long tan strong arms stretched out across the table toward Georgette's aunt. Ruthie said to her, "Well, if this woman ever does show up, she'll see who the real mother's been."

Sam cried more. "I wish you could stay a little longer. Clark would be glad to see you."

"Would he? Why?"

The two were silent a moment and then Sam nodded. "That was a miserable summer, wasn't it? We all messed up."

"You can mess up a lot before you're even twenty when you're moving too fast."

They left together by the kitchen door. Annie watched them slowly walking through the back yard, past the old rose garden, past the orchard of plum and peach trees, toward the Nickerson house. She went into the morning room to look at the blue-sky puzzle that had been left practically untouched for years. There was now only a third left to go.

That night Annie had a version of her old dream that she'd had so often when she was younger that it had been called "Annie's dream." She was flying in her small red airplane over the ocean but this time she had all the flying knowledge that she'd learned from D. K. Destin. Down below her she saw the small ship in the tumbling waves. On the ship stood the young woman in a gold cape. The woman raised her arms, calling on Annie to save her before her ship sank under the waves. This time when Annie's dad flew past her in his little red plane, she didn't even bother calling for him to come help. He soared away to the horizon, leaving behind him a trail of curling smoke. She flew as fast as she could to the ship but it was sinking quickly, waves swelling over the bow. Annie awakened in a sob and Sam came hurrying into her room, promising her everything would be all right.

Everything pretty much was. Annie's life was full and immediate. The next day Georgette and she were preoccupied with composing a letter to old Mr. Neubruck next door, who had called the police because of the noise of their latest party, informing him that his refusal to recycle and his massive use of pesticides on his tomatoes were polluting the planet.

Within a week, they were no longer discussing the mysterious Ruthie, who had left in the night with cardboard boxes from the Nickerson house. (Georgette's mother said they contained Ruthie's share of the family plates and silverware but such objects seemed too mundane to interest such a woman.) She never, as far as they knew, returned to Emerald.

Annie never had the dream again and she forgot about Sam's crying in the kitchen. Still, a vague memory persisted of a handsome woman who'd known how to do algebra and who had made Annie laugh by playing with such quickness on the possible meanings of the word Jack.

Now, all these years later, how odd that the memory had fluttered back at her—like approach lights blinking—the day after she'd seen the woman on the lawn of Golden Days. And even more oddly after she'd seen the woman, or someone like her, standing at the hotel pool.

Georgette thought Annie should go to bed. "This is just a series of coincidences that you've gotten fixated on because you're tired. And I've got to go to sleep."

"Why do all my friends keep telling me they need to go to sleep?"

Georgette yawned. "Human. Your friends are human."

"Trevor is in bed by ten o'clock."

"Bring him on," said Georgette.

"Brad went to bed early too. What I need's someone who can't sleep."

Georgette suggested that midnight might be a good time to go out looking for such a night owl. "Didn't you say you were in a bar? Bars are full of insomniacs."

Chapter 40

Midnight

At La Loca, Chamayra finally returned with Sergeant Hart's home address, which proved to be only a few blocks away.

"Danny's phone's dead, so maybe go by the house." The waitress added, "Don't be causing trouble, okay? Raffy's left me a message saying don't talk to nobody about your dad. Where is he?"

"My dad? I hope he's in Golden Days."

"No, where's Raffy? He's suppose to be like here now and, hey, you see him?" She flung out her arms at the crowded room. "So now I'm gonna worry. You go check on Danny. I can't leave. I can't lose my job." The short woman wiped sweat from her gleamy arms and face.

"I'm sorry I'm causing trouble."

Chamayra pointed at the words "La Loca" on her turquoise shirt. "I been doing my nurse training a long time and waiting tables a lot longer. You ask me? Everybody's like in the same crazy boat. Name of the boat? *La Loca.* Everybody's like, you know, sailing off the edge of the world fast as they can get there. So I say, just whoa. Hang out the Love sign." She leaned into the booth and shook the blue fish netting overhead, where the plastic G.I. Joes tangled with the Barbie dolls. "Raffy's totally like got this thing how Dan's gonna bust him big-time. No way."

"No way?" Annie's eyebrow went up. "Isn't Hart *trying* to arrest Raffy? He sure looked like it yesterday at Golden Days when he chased him down Ficus Avenue."

Upset, the waitress slapped her hands on her arms. "You kidding me? You saw him at Golden Days chasing Raffy?"

"Yes, yesterday."

"Yesterday?! Why didn't you tell me? Motherfucker, I got to get your dad out of that place pronto. Those two *pingitas*, Raffy and your dad, gonna get me fired! What is their *problem?*"

"It's a cops and robbers sort of thing with them," suggested Annie.

"Men, they're so stupid. And me, I had to have boys. And you know what they'll grow up to be?" Chamayra hoisted her tray of dirty dishes. "Men."

"Probably."

• • •

Driving along a moonlit street beside the midnight blue of the bay, Annie finally found Hart's small bungalow (its curb number obscured by weeds). The sawed-up trunk of a large magnolia tree lay scattered about the front lawn in raw stacks. Mounds of chippings and sawdust matted the patchy grass and there were six piles of branches arranged in a tall circle as if in the morning the yard would be the setting for some horrific auto-da-fé. On a grass-choked driveway a blue pickup truck was parked with its doors flung open and with a windsurfer in the back. In the garage sat a vintage Thunderbird coupe, blue with a white hardtop and color-match rings on the whitewall tires and porthole windows.

The 1920s Spanish stucco house had its windows and metal screen door thrown wide open. Out of the windows she could hear Otis Redding sadly singing, "I've Been Loving You Too Long (To Stop Now)," as if the house itself were in mourning. The only light was the blue wavering shimmer of a television screen. Chamayra had given her no idea whether

Hart lived here alone or not. No one answered her repeated call through the opened door and finally she walked uninvited into the darkness.

Without the sound on, a baseball game in a half-empty stadium played on a flat screen television at the other end of the room.

"Sergeant Hart? It's Annie Goode. Daniel Hart? Anybody home?" Turning from the small arched foyer into the first room, she tripped over something metallic and sharp that turned out to be a chainsaw. Rubbing her ankle, she felt for a light switch.

A recessed light revealed a living room in disarray. There were half-emptied packing boxes on the bare terra-cotta tile floor. On built-in shelves along the walls, CDs, DVDs, and hardcover books had been stacked among wood angels, clay mermaids, and tin-toy bands.

On the floor lay a large, smashed framed group wedding photograph, glass slivers sticking into it, obscuring the faces.

There was no furniture in the room except for one tanned leather Deco armchair with an ottoman. Beside this chair was a round glass coffee table that also looked Deco.

Lying on the floor, wedged between the chair and the stereo, through which Otis Redding was pleading, "Please don't make me stop now," Annie saw a young well-built male body wearing nothing but pale blue boxer shorts and one white sock. It was the back of a young man who looked to be in perfect physical condition except for the fact that, judging from his contorted torso and stiffened limbs, he was dead. The rest of his clothes (shirt, pants, sports jacket) lay scattered about the otherwise bare floor like little throw rugs. As Annie leaned over his body, she smelt the agave fumes of tequila and saw a half-empty bottle of Cuervo 1800 in his rigid hand.

Then she screamed, as suddenly the man's other arm flung out, hitting her back and knocking her down on top of him. Pressed against his breastbone, Annie could now see that the body was alive, the chest had a heart in it that was beating, although nothing else moved, not a tremble of the dark-bronze curls. As she tried to lift herself away, the arm stiffened rigidly.

Then the body turned over. The thick long eyelashes flickered. It was Daniel Hart. His arms moved tightly, warmly, around her and unexpectedly he kissed her. The kiss took her breath away, soft, strong, unending until she pulled back and elbowed him in the stomach.

Slowly his mouth spasmed, forming the sounds *ooofff* and then *drinnn...*, which Annie took to mean an effort at the word *drink*. Pulling herself up, she made her way along a hallway whose walls had bright-painted wood crèches and skeletons on them, past two bedrooms (one empty, one with nothing in it but a large bright blue wooden bed, its head and foot hand painted with what looked like Mexican saints).

In the colorfully tiled kitchen, someone appeared to have started preparations for some complicated Asian dish, then lost heart and quit. There were grocery bags and wooden cooking utensils everywhere, copper pans stacked by the stove.

Filling a coffee mug with water, she brought it back to the living room. The body hadn't moved. As she lifted Hart's head, his lashes quivered, then his eyes opened, blue as Miami neon, Deco blue, the blue of the sea in Annie's dream. She held up the mug to his lips.

"'Sorry, no silver cup,'" she said as she tilted the water into his mouth.

He spluttered spitting, pushing the mug aside. In a rusted croak, he growled at her, "You don't look like John Wayne."

Annie was taken aback but replied, "You don't look like Claire Trevor either." Sam had mentioned on the phone that this Sergeant Hart had made some comment about his familiarity with old movies. He certainly appeared to know her dad's old quote from *Stagecoach*. It might have made him interesting if he hadn't so obviously been a hopeless drunk, an emotional wreck, and a derelict housekeeper.

She offered him more water, but he shook his head with a groan, twisting his face as he slowly unbent one rigid leg. "Listen, Duke," he grumbled, grabbing the mug and pouring the water on his head, "Water's not a drink."

"Take it or leave it," she told him exasperated. "I need some information from you about my father."

"Get in line." He rubbed the water in his hair over his face and chest. Yanking his jaw from side to side, apparently to see if it still worked, he lurched to his feet with moans that sounded much like the wailing lamentations of Otis Redding, now singing "Mr. Pitiful" in the background.

He stumbled, his hand on Annie's shoulder to steady himself. "Pardon me," he said. He hobbled down the hall into his kitchen, returning with a long-necked bottle of beer. After a long swallow, he stared a while at her immaculate white slacks and T-shirt. "Annie Goode. You look like a paramedic."

"You look like you need one. You shouldn't drink so much."

"You're telling me."

Tugging at his boxer shorts, he walked to his opened front door, glanced out. In horror, he grabbed at the doorway, staggered back to the huge power saw on the hall floor and picked it up. "My fucking magnolia tree! I fucking sawed down my fucking magnolia tree!" Hurrying outside, he stared aghast at a lawn full of leafy branches and fat cut logs.

Picking up his blue linen shirt, Annie followed him from his house to the small yard. "You are definitely Sgt. Daniel Hart of the Miami police?"

He sank down onto the raw tree stump with the saw in his lap. "I was," he said obscurely. Gesturing ruefully at chopped up sections of tree trunk, he added, "This was my dad's house. My dad planted that magnolia tree the day I was born. Twenty-six years old."

Annie raised her Claudette Colbert eyebrow. "Castration anxiety?"

Hart growled. "What, you're a shrink too?"

Smiling despite herself, she took the saw from his lap and set it down beside him. "No, but I've got a friend who's a shrink. She'd say there was some reason you chopped up your dad's big tree and gave yourself alcohol poisoning today. Is it your birthday? That can be depressing. Mine was two days ago."

"I already know that. I spent a year on fuckin' Jack Peregrine's life." He sat morosely on a tree stump and rubbed his temples. "Yeah, sawing up the tree, that could be a kill-Dad thing. Dad was a cop, full time; you dropped a towel on the bathroom floor, you got chucked in the slammer. But I'd say…" He glanced around his yard. "Chopping this magnolia is more about my ex-wife Melissa. We're divorced."

Annie gestured around the yard. "This'll bring her back?"

He glanced up. "You always so sarcastic?"

She shrugged. "Most of the time." A large pink fuchsia lay on the ground, ripped out of its pot; carefully she replanted it.

"Thanks," he acknowledged. "So where do you get off razzing me? You're divorced too."

She sat across from him, balancing on a pile of logs. "Not because I'm sarcastic." The stars were so bright she could see the thin lariat-braided bracelet that clasped his wrist. She smiled at him. "Well, maybe it *was* because I'm sarcastic. But actually I'm not divorced."

He looked disappointed. "You're not?"

Oddly she felt she had to explain. "Not yet…One more week. Didn't you get all my messages?"

"About your upcoming divorce? Nope." He tilted the beer bottle, drank from it.

"You're pretty sarcastic yourself." Impatient, she tossed him his blue shirt. "I meant the six messages I left to tell you I've got the Queen of the Sea, that Inca statue that belongs to Cuba. My dad actually had it. You drop the charges against him and I'll give it to you. It's in my hotel room."

He nodded. "I like the hotel room part of it."

Her blush surprised her. "Don't be funny."

Pulling his arms through the shirtsleeves, he rubbed at his curls. He was, Annie thought, very good-looking and (unlike Brad) he didn't seem to know it.

He said, "I wasn't being funny. I think what's going on between us is more the light-hearted repartee of incompatible people destined for—well, I don't know what we're destined for. We'll have to sit here and find out."

She smiled, grew embarrassed, held out her watch to show him the time. "It's midnight. So if you want to cut this deal, let's do it. I'm sort of in a hurry to get my dad out of that hellhole Golden Days."

"That's for sure." He shook his head. "Don't put me in there. Drink?" He held out the bottle.

"No. In St Louis, in the airport, why didn't you tell me who you were? What kind of game are you playing?"

He stood slowly, groaning loudly, setting the chain saw down on the tree stump. "Okay, you want to get tough? You're subject to criminal charges for aiding and abetting. On Ficus Avenue, you and Rafael Rook deliberately ignored my order to halt. Not to mention you knocked me down on purpose."

She waited but he said nothing more for so long that finally she asked, "What, are you arresting me?"

He seemed to have fallen into a funk. Finally he stretched with a long sigh. "I wish I could arrest you. I've had a lousy couple of days and you've got a lousy attitude." He moved nearer to her, tan even in moonlight, and slowly held up his arms in surrender. "I can't arrest you. Thanks to you they fired me."

"The Miami police fired you?" She saw him registering her unmistakable surprise.

He pointed at her Navy cap. "Yeah, I know. In the Armed Forces, you probably put people up against a wall and shoot them. But usually at MPD, they fire them." He rubbed his bare foot in the grass. "Well, they shoot them sometimes but usually they just fire them."

"I'm sorry," Annie told him. "But I don't see how you're getting fired is 'thanks to' me."

He rubbed the other foot. "You're Jack Peregrine's daughter. Jack Peregrine turned out to be a puddle of quicksand and I stepped in it up to my neck."

His beer bottle tipped and Annie quickly reached out and righted it. His hand closed over hers and they both looked at their joined hands. Then she pulled away to ask, "Should I go to your former partner then? The police didn't seem interested."

Daniel opened his arms to the sky. "Yeah, well, they're interested. They're so interested your dad's not going to jail. He's as free as Oliver North. The Feds," he explained, "shut down the whole investigation. Like that!" His fingers snapped loudly three times. "Maybe more like this…" He snapped again, softly.

"You're telling me the case is closed? There're no charges against my dad?"

Elaborately he nodded. "Not by MPD. They're out. I'm definitely out. I knew your old man had friends but frankly I thought they were more the Rafael Rook variety. Let's go get some food."

Annie didn't move. "If there are no charges against him, why shouldn't I keep the Queen of the Sea?"

"You probably should." He shrugged. "Meanwhile, you want to hear about my day? Lousy. Yesterday wasn't so good either. Yesterday I'm standing in the street watching you and Rook speed off, after I receive some very bad personal news at Golden Days from my ex-wife—"

"What's your ex-wife doing at Golden Days?"

"She runs the place; big mistake since she never liked old people. Melissa Skippings."

Entirely taken aback, Annie laughed. "Wait a minute." She reached for his beer bottle and without thinking, drank from it. "Wait a minute! Your wife, your ex-wife, is the HMO administrator of Golden Days? Melissa is M. R. Skippings? She's platinum blonde and has long legs?"

His mouth twisted wryly. "The legs are really hers."

Annie handed back the beer. "I'm sorry, that woman's a bitch."

"*You're* sorry?" Dan rubbed at his face with both hands. "So I'm there to see Melissa and I spot you and Rook. I'm watching you flee the scene, by the way at excessive speed, then out of nowhere, I'm grabbed and flung in a high-tech van where some seriously edgy agents of our government behave like they're auditioning for a Matt Damon thriller."

Annie interrupted. "I thought those were your friends in that van."

"Friends? They're Feds. They grill me about your dad, they take me over to Second Avenue, drag me in the back way and they're at me all night. Then comes morning, my chief— otherwise known as the Vapor—tells me the case is closed and when I argue that decision, he tells me to back up before I step off a cliff without a health fund. I tell him, 'Fire me, you chickenshit dickhead!' So he did. At 5 p.m., I get handed a box of everything that used to be in my desk, including my dirty gym shorts. Then he shoves a piece of paper at me to sign about how it's a mutual decision."

She thought about this. "Bottom line is, my dad's no longer being investigated by MPD? He's not going back to jail?"

Hart scowled at her. "Will you stop rubbing it in? He *should* go to jail. He owes three years minimum. And that's just in Florida. Even cutting deals like salami, I would have said he'd get fifteen. It's bullshit the way they shut this thing down."

"All I care is, if he's not going to jail."

She noticed Hart's stomach muscles tighten as he snatched back his beer. He said, "Well, then, you should be happy! Me, I don't like looking like a chump."

She stared at him a while then smiled. "I think it's the single white sock with the blue underwear that makes you look like a chump. Lose the sock."

The young man's smile came toward her, kept coming, kept coming, and for all her skilled deflection, finally reached her. She felt her face loosening, felt herself smiling back, although it made no sense that she should do so. They just sat there a while, smiling at each other.

Finally he said, "I hitched a ride to St. Louis in your husband's jet."

"I heard."

"Wow. Carrying on a conversation for two hours with Brad Hopper makes me wonder what the hell you could have been thinking of, marrying him. I mean, the conversation! He gives me details of every single hole of his best golf game at Southern Pines. Yep, I have had a very rough couple of days," he sighed.

"Because of my ex and your ex?"

"Plus your dad." He counted out with raised fingers a sequence of misadventures. "I lose Jack in St. Louis, thanks to you."

"Don't blame me."

Uninterested in accuracy, he continued, "Then I lose my wife."

"What do you mean? Haven't you been divorced for years?"

He started tossing branches into a neat pile. "I lose my job. I mean, sure, I've been suspended plenty of times, but *fired?* This is a first."

She waved her finger at him. "That's not my fault either. And you had no business conning Brad into flying you to St. Louis."

"Brad is a jerk. Well, I married just as stupid as you." Dan made a fist, striking at his breast. "Melissa invites me to her office where she informs me she's just gotten engaged to an asshole financial planner that I introduced her to." He stacked the magnolia branches more and more quickly. "This was when I was dumb enough to let the man who was stealing my wife manage my very small retirement savings that are now even smaller."

Annie started helping him clear the chain-sawed branches. "I'd say Melissa's new fiancé is doing okay, because I got a peek at her engagement ring when she was throwing me out of Golden Days and it is *big*."

"Yeah, I saw it too. Serious bling-bling." He made the shape of a baseball.

"Tacky." Annie found it baffling that Hart had ever married this woman. But then, hadn't Clark and D. K. found it baffling when she'd married Brad? Even Georgette and Sam, both of whom had fallen for Brad, had wondered why she'd chosen him. She neatly added the final branch to the pile "People make mistakes," she conceded. "I mean, like you."

"Like me? How 'bout *Melissa?*" Sitting down with the beer, Hart gave her a rueful look. "This guy she's marrying? He's a pod person; seriously, the kind nobody can tell the difference when the pod takes over. He proposes to Melissa at intermission of Cirque du Soleil in Las Vegas! You hear what I'm saying? And she's such a pod herself, she's boasting about this to me like it was something great he'd done, as opposed to an act of sleazy toe cheese! She thinks *that's* a good proposal? Intermission at Cirque du Soleil?! Jeez!"

Annie heard herself asking Dan what he would consider a better proposal.

Frowning, he reached up as if he could grab an answer out of the stars. "Okay." He rubbed his hands against his bare thighs. "Say you're ice-skating in Central Park, Wollman Rink, and it starts to snow, big soft pretty snow. Say you can waltz her around the rink, dancing while you're skating. Well, you turn and turn and turn together, arms around each other, and then you stop and skate off the ice. You hold your faces up to the snow, you feel the snow on your eyelids and you taste it on your tongues and that's when you propose. Okay?" He leaned over to her.

She nodded with her wry smile. "That's okay."

Frowning, he jumped up, pacing back and forth across his small yard, the unbuttoned shirt flying open behind him. "Okay, how's this? It's raining outside your house, November rain, and you're wrapped in a blanket on a rug in front of your fireplace and you've just finished eating fresh figs with prosciutto di Parma. You've got Dinah Washington singing "Embrace me, my sweet embraceable you—"

"You mean, a CD of Dinah Washington. Because she's dead so she couldn't be—"

"God, you're impossible! Okay, listen." Grabbing a bough of a banyan tree, the only tree left in the yard, he swayed from it, close to her. "All right, here's the one. You're in Peru, you're hiking at fourteen thousand feet, through the clouds, and you hike for days and sleep under the stars and you make your way around that last curve on the high Inca trail and all of a sudden there you are.

At the same instant the two of you see that big Peru sun rising through the clouds, lighting up the high green mountains. And then it comes out of the mist. The lost city of Machu Picchu." He leaned down to Annie's face. "That's when you propose."

Annie looked up at him for a long moment. She knew she either had to acknowledge what was going on between them or she had to pretend it wasn't there. So she glanced away.

"Oh, you chicken," he whispered as he swung on the bough, back from her.

After a silence, she asked if any of these imagined proposals of his had ever been real. Had one been his proposal to Melissa?

Dan said no, that his proposal to Melissa had been at the Dorado bar. Actually his whole relationship to Melissa had been alcohol-related. He'd first met her when he was a rookie cop, part of a bust-up of a fraternity house binge at U of M; he'd pulled her naked out of a hot tub filled with shaving cream.

It was hard to imagine. "Ms. Skippings? She was so hard-assed at Golden Days."

"Yeah, wild's the flip side of oppressive. You didn't know that?" Dan had next seen her at a salsa club in the Grove. They'd started meeting at the Dorado, then spending his days off at her family's condo in West Palm, which her parents only visited from January to March. The next thing he knew he was standing at the altar of a big church in Coral Gables, wearing rented tails and striped trousers.

"Right," scoffed Annie. "You were an innocent bystander."

Hart walked back to his tree stump and sat down on it, rubbing at his hair. "Fair enough. True. The lush life sucked me right in. Like that arcade game when you're paying to make the little crane grab plastic crap in its claws that you don't even want anyhow and dump it into a drawer for you. So we come to a screeching halt and now she sits in her office and tells me she's going to marry Jeffry...Jeffry without an *e*. This is the guy that advised me to buy Lucent at seventy-five."

Annie thought back to how nasty Melissa Skippings had been to her at Golden Days, and then shortly afterwards how furiously the detective had pursued Raffy. Both those things must have happened right after Melissa had given Dan the news that she was marrying someone else, when they'd both been upset. Annie said, "So you hear your ex is getting married and you deal with it by chasing Raffy and me down the street?"

He flexed a fairly perfect bare leg. "And I pull a hamstring. And I get roughed up by the Feds, and I get fired, and I get stupid blotto and chop down my stupid magnolia tree. I told you I'd had a bad couple of days."

She noticed another uprooted fuchsia in the yard and planted it delicately back in its pot. "Well, Sergeant, I can't say I haven't had a day at the beach myself, because I have." He laughed and, again, as in their first phone conversation, it pleased her that he laughed so genuinely at her humor. She said quietly, "My dad seems to be dying—"

Hart groaned. "My dad's already dead or he'd be so pissed about this magnolia tree." He stared out over his small yard. "He died in a high-speed chase. Head-on collision with a utility pole. Long time ago."

"I'm sorry."

Hart shrugged a sad acceptance. "I've got a mom, nice lady, school librarian in Overtown. By the way, your mom's not really Claudette Colbert, is she? I mean, there's a birth certificate at Key West I got pulled, says Claudette Colbert's your mother, but it's a joke, right?"

She agreed that it was an instance of her father's peculiar sense of humor. They were quiet together a while.

He stood, pulled his opened shirt around him. "You want something to eat? I forgot to eat today. Mexican?" He held out his hand to help her up.

Annie looked at the young man then took his hand. "Mexican what? Food, art, architecture, trip?" Why had she said that? She knew what he meant.

"I was thinking food," he said, letting her hand go, slowly. "Art's good too. Architecture's good. I love the music. Furniture."

She flashed on an image of the blue-painted wooden bed inside his house. Again she blushed. "There's a restaurant at the Dorado we could go to. Then I could show you the Queen."

He shook off her suggestion. "I've got bad memories of the Dorado. Melissa loves it there. Let's grab some Mexican at La Loca. But I do want to see the Queen. Is she real?"

Annie shook her head thoughtfully. "I don't know."

"Hang on, I'll change."

She gestured at his disordered yard. "Your clothes or your life?"

He laughed. "Stick around. Maybe both."

Chapter 41

It Happened One Night

Back at La Loca for the second time that night, Annie sat with the Miami detective in another of the blue-netted booths. In a retro jazzy shirt and taupe pleated trousers, Daniel Hart looked like a radical makeover of the man who'd been staggering around in his boxer shorts with his eyes glued shut only half an hour earlier.

"You clean up nice, Sergeant," she admitted.

"Lieutenant, you stay that way. Don't you ever get a speck of dirt on those white clothes?"

"Nope."

He smiled back at her, lifting a small clay pitcher. "Have a margarita with me."

She rested her hand over her empty glass. "Thanks but I don't handle alcohol very well."

"That's just because you don't practice." He poured her half a glass.

By now the Coconut Grove nightspot was all razzle-dazzle, neon hot, crowded noise, and frenetic young people who shouted at each other over thumping salsa and clattering dishes. Some of them kissed seemingly random partners in booths, others gyrated, tightly sweaty on the small dance floor. With a bemused shake of his head, Hart gestured at the dancers. "Desperate search for elusive alliance."

She followed his glance to the writhing couples. "That's one way to put it."

"Hook up, unhook, hook up…Am I getting old?"

She thought he'd said he was twenty-six. She hoped that wasn't old. It was her age.

"That's just years," he said. "My mileage is high. I do a lot of skydiving. It takes a toll."

"Really? You free fall? I've parachuted but never a free fall."

He looked at her for a long moment. "You'd like it. So tell me, why'd your marriage fold?"

Annie had already warned herself not to let her guard down with Dan. She felt like a small plane blown by a strong wind irresistibly toward a wide-open field where he stood. A field where there was no place to hide. She tried to brake, circle back, but instead she heard herself revealing how it had broken her heart when she'd caught Brad having an affair. "His backup excuse was to claim Melody was just a one-night stand. Turned out, their affair had started like a week after we got married."

Dan nodded sympathetically. "You feel like a fool, don't you? Melissa claimed Jeffry was just financially advising her. I guess he could think better naked."

She countered. "I can top that. Brad actually told me his girlfriend had drugged him."

Dan's grin was contagious. "Listen to us, competing about loving people who didn't have the sense to love us back."

In the next half hour, Annie told Dan almost as much about her breakup with Brad Hopper as Georgette knew—from her jealousy over Brad's winning their first flight competition at Annapolis to her crying alone in her Chesapeake condo night after night.

They finished their mole and Dan leaned back comfortably in the corner of the booth, his leg bent, arms around it. "Can we go see your dad's gold statue now?"

"Now?" Feeling out of focus, Annie stared, surprised, at her watch. It was late and she was exhausted; she was in a bar that seemed all too appropriately named "La Loca," since it was not normal for her to be out at night with strangers in bars. If not at work in Annapolis or at home in Emerald, shouldn't she at least be asleep in the Hotel Dorado with Malpy beside her, gathering strength to deal with her father in the morning, and—if need be—to trade Jack Peregrine the Queen of the Sea for her mother's real name? "Tell me you're not kidding, that the charges against my dad are dropped."

"I'm not kidding. But Annie, understand. This isn't a game like it was when you were a kid."

She said, "If you're going to warn me my dad's a real crook, I've known it longer than you have. Oh by the way, he says he admires your persistence."

Dan gave a wry salute. He described how he had spent months gathering proof about a racket of her father's in which eager Miami investors had been sold revenue-producing ten-hectare parcels of a 500,000-acre Brazilian tree plantation named Cortina de Sueños. This plantation didn't exist. The man ostensibly selling shares in the venture, Bruno Salvador, didn't exist either; he was Jack Peregrine. Jack's attention to detail included providing his victims with official letters about their land purchases, seemingly mailed from Brazil, with elaborate bond certificates, deeds, detailed maps, even glowing articles in (fictitious) magazines about the fabulous profits to be made from Cortina de Sueños.

"I had the evidence on Jack. But when the time came, I had no witnesses." Dan wriggled his fingers. "My case fell through like rain on a bad roof. Tossed. Your dad walked. Nobody wanted to testify about what morons they'd been, buying land that was pure sueños."

It didn't surprise her. Dreams are what Jack sold; he'd boasted of it to her.

"Yeah, Jack was always one step ahead of us." Hart closed his fist in air. "You think you've got him"—he opened his hand, blew the emptiness away—"all of a sudden, poof."

"Poof," nodded Annie wryly. "I'd say you just summed up my whole relationship with my father."

Dan slid his finger through the fish netting, spun the wheel on a miniature white Mustang that sat in a blue martini glass. "So tell me why, when I get close to Peregrine this time, when I get close to you, wham, all of a sudden the Feds shut me down? What gives? Jack's palling around here in Miami with men like Feliz Diaz and Archbishop de Uloa. I start to hear his name all over the place, but he's not hanging with the usual con game type associates. These new friends of his are into crime so big they could be the fucking government. Before, he was a sting. Now he's an operation."

She wasn't sure what the detective meant.

"I mean he's not self-employed anymore. Somebody bigger than he is runs this thing." Dan used his thumb to add more salt to his margarita. "Look at it. Your dad's thrown in prison in Cuba, which ought to mean it's the last place he'd want to show his face again. But apparently he keeps managing to slip in and out of Cuba no problemo. In fact, he's flying not just there but all over everywhere. Mostly he's flying to very rich places, Anguilla, Jupiter Island, Caneel Bay. Why? How? Because somebody's running interference for him. Here and in Cuba both." He poured her glass full from the clay pitcher.

"He's flying everywhere? You know this for a fact?" Annie was more interested in the extent of her father's flying than the cause of it. Plus all these places were islands, so maybe he was making amphibious landings. She was bizarrely proud of him.

Dan's cell phone went off. It played Oscar Peterson's "Night Train"; he checked the number but decided not to answer it. "Damn right, he's flying. And who's letting him? I think the interference is tied to Feliz Diaz."

Annie said she'd heard from Rafael Rook that her dad played poker with Diaz.

"This is not just about your dad making powerful pals because he plays high-stakes poker. And it's not just about Diaz wanting to whitewash his image by giving his local church a pretty little gold statue of the Virgin Mary, though why's an archbishop mixed up with your dad too?" He smiled at her. "Maybe we could go to your hotel?"

The annoying fact that she kept blushing made her blush more. "Don't push."

His smile, unlike Brad's, had confidence without smugness. "I'm not pushing. But I do want to see this statue. The night's young."

She glanced at her watch. "The night's tomorrow."

He kept staring at her. "Your ex-husband was an idiot."

Her blush deepened. "Almost ex."

"Almost ex-husband was a complete idiot to let you go." He looked at her without smiling.

The silence went on too long for comfort. "...Do you know why my dad keeps flying to Cuba?"

"No." Dan poured himself more margarita. "Do you?"

Annie repeated that she had known nothing specific about her father's activities since she was seven years old.

He flicked at the blue plastic netting above their heads, so a sand dollar rolled up against a starfish. "He's doing serious people serious favors and like I say, they're not just favors about a Holy Thorn from the Sacred Crown, although I'm sure Diaz and Archbishop de Uloa plan to showcase the 'Thorn' on a church altar."

Annie stared into her empty glass. "My dad's a sting artist. He's got a fake relic and these suckers are buying it from him. I don't know how he faked it because I saw it and it looks damn real, but he's scamming them."

He waited while their waitress set down two complimentary glasses of almendrados. "Want some advice, Annie? Men like Diaz are not suckers. Get your dad out of this thing. Whether he's really got cancer or not, and frankly I don't believe it, there're things he could die from a lot quicker than cancer." The young man nodded earnestly. "Your dad is a talented, upscale grifter, but just a grifter."

Annie sighed. "Sort of curiously naïve?"

"That's exactly what I mean." Reaching into his jacket, he brought out a folded newspaper. "I'll bet you my '57 Thunderbird, and I love that car, he's got no idea what they're using him for. Or how dead he's going to be when they're done with him."

The *Miami Herald* he held out to her showed a large photo of cheerful men clapping at a dedication ceremony. Near them the governor of Florida waved his arm in greeting to an off-camera crowd. Among those standing close to the podium was Feliz Diaz, unmistakably the same man who'd stepped out of the Mercedes in front of Golden Days, the man with whom the handsome woman had driven away. Diaz stood next to a white-haired priest whose scornful disdain for his present surroundings was deeply etched in his face. "That's Archbishop de Uloa," Dan told her. "These guys are all buddies."

"Business buddies or political buddies?" she asked.

"Same thing in Miami, especially when you're talking Cuba." His phone rang again. This time he spoke briefly with someone. After he finished, he said, "My partner told me that Diaz just sent his girlfriend to Cuba."

"Helen Clark?"

He shrugged. "She calls herself that." He oddly added, "Remember William McKinley's platform when he ran for President in 1896?"

Annie had to admit that she did not.

"There were two big mandates the Republicans had that year—'Protect American Business' and 'Free the People of Cuba.' Those mandates were the same thing. Freedom was the freedom to keep Cuban resources for American business. Boom! 1898. 'Remember the Maine!' 1899. United Fruit Company." Dan picked up Annie's Navy jacket, lying beside her on the bench and held it up.

"I don't want to hear you bad-mouthing the Navy," she warned him.

"Tell it to Spain. They'd been in Cuba four hundred years."

Annie said, "You should hear my friend D. K., the guy that taught me to fly. He's part Algonquin and he's always talking about how the Arawaks had been in the Caribbean a lot longer than the Spanish. D. K. always says, 'Instead of waving at

Columbus, they should have torched the boats and blow-darted the crew.'"

"I met D. K. I liked him." Dan drank from his glass of almond liqueur. "I read Spain kept the heart of Columbus in a box in a cathedral in Havana. You know that? They took it home to Madrid after the U.S. Navy sank their fleet in Havana Harbor and Dewey blew them out of the water at Manila Bay. Talk about torching boats!" He saluted her jacket. "So, here we are again in Cuba, your dad stealing their statue. I'm not sure what the agency's up to, getting involved in this but, Annie, trust me, the Feds will toss your dad like chum to sharks. In a heartbeat. Cuba's a…" He laughed. "Red flag."

Annie, who had studied the naval history about which Dan was talking, suggested that if he looked at refueling maps and harbors, he would see why the United States had to take naval control of both the Atlantic and Pacific, which meant getting the Spanish out of both Cuba and the Philippines. "Teddy Roosevelt was already figuring that out as an undergraduate at Harvard."

"A short gallop from Harvard to San Juan Hill?"

Annie told him it hadn't been a gallop; the Rough Riders had been dismounted cavalry. They'd been running up that hill on foot, not riding up it on horses like they did in the famous paintings. And the famous charge hadn't been up San Juan Hill anyhow, but Kettle Hill.

Dan held out his hands to her in mock admiration. "What were you, on College Bowl?"

"I always wanted to be on College Bowl," she smiled.

"For me it was Jeopardy."

She said, "Did you know the teddy bear was named for Teddy Roosevelt? I've got a Shi Tzu named Teddy but she's not the dog I've got with me. That's Malpy; he's in the hotel room."

Dan took out his wallet. "We ought to check on that dog."

How enjoyable, she thought, to talk with this man, despite their apparent political differences. Now that she looked back, she had never had a conversation with Brad throughout their entire marriage that hadn't been limited to the personal. "My point before," she said, not moving from the bench but pouring herself more margarita, "was just that Cuba's a flashpoint for the U.S. Always has been. Like Israel is for the Mideast. And Miami's the key to Cuba." She gestured at the city lights outside the window.

Dan kept waving his credit card at a waitress. "We've sure got the refugees from both, Cuban, Jewish, right here in Miami." He pointed north, south. "Butterfly ballots, recount riots, secret deals, coming coups, that's Miami. People like Diaz who made money in Cuba? They're never going to stop wanting to get it back."

She drank the margarita as if it were water. "The world's a mess."

"It sure is." He pressed his fingers hard into his temples, rubbing at his tawny curls. They were, she thought, beautiful fingers, long and straight, the nails blunt and gleaming. "Check!" he called.

Annie studied the man across from her. It was obvious he had problems. Drinking problems, for example. Ex-wife problems. Job problems. Insubordination appeared to be a pattern. She asked him what official reason the Miami Police Department had given for his dismissal. "Was it because you pursued my father out of your jurisdiction?"

He shrugged. "Sorry, but your dad, who'd even care? Then all of a sudden, our division chief gets that phone call from the Feds. The Vapor's got his nose so far up the Feds' ass, all he sees is a black hole."

Annie winced. "Graphic." She tried to pour more margarita in her glass but the pitcher was empty.

He held out his hands to her. "You ready to go?"

Annie couldn't look away from his extremely blue eyes with their rings of darker, cobalt blue around their azure irises. She nodded.

He suddenly yelled, "Hey, Chamayra! Chamayra, how you doing!"

Annie looked around the bench and saw Raffy's friend. The short curvy waitress squeezed over to their booth. She was now wearing a sequined jean jacket and clutching a huge shoulder bag with a dozen buckles. "Hey, Danny, I didn't know you was back here in the corner. Who you hiding from?" She leaned in, saw Annie. "Ah, okay, okay. You located him."

Annie smiled at her. "Yes, I did. Thank you."

"Hey, no problem." Chamayra rubbed her knuckles into Hart's bicep. "Why you want to cause trouble, Danny? Answer your fuckin' phone."

Sliding out of the booth, he hugged her and asked how her son Alex was doing.

"Doing great. Ninth grade this fall, you believe that? He ask me all the time, how's Sergeant Hart?"

"Tell him fine. Still wearing the bracelet." He spun the braided lariat on his wrist. "Chamayra's kid made me this."

Proudly Chamayra announced, "Him and my boy did this thing together. FSU Role Model Program."

Dan tapped the bracelet. "Tell Alex, keep it cool. Dry ice."

She made her imaginary rectangular sign in air. "Clean is Cool."

Dan took his credit card and bill off to find a waiter. As soon as he moved off, Chamayra sat down beside Annie. "You not getting my Raffy in trouble, are you? Don't talk about him to Danny."

Annie repeated that she wanted Dan Hart to help her negotiate a deal for Raffy and her father.

Chamayra blew out a noisy sigh of exasperation. "It's bad enough Raffy plays guitar. This mess with your dad is driving me loca. Raffy thinks he's like God and every time it's nothing but heartaches and court costs. You know where he probably is?"

Annie said she had no idea.

"Doing some shit for your dad." Chamayra stuck her thumb under the heavy gold necklace she wore as if she were going to yank it off. "Okay, you hear from him? Tell him he don't show up tonight, then he don't be calling me till he got Alzheimer's and don't know my number." She swatted at Dan as he returned to the booth. Her tight chartreuse pedal pushers disappeared into the crowd. "Bye bye."

Dan waved to the retreating waitress. "Tough life, Chamayra's. Her ex? Complete ass wipe. But she's the best."

Annie insisted she would re-pay him for her half of the bill. "You don't even have a job," she pointed out.

"Next time it's on you." He left too big a tip in cash. His hand brushed over hers as he slipped the money under a glass. "You've had a little too much to drink. How about we take a walk on the beach? Fresh air. Moon over Miami?"

She had the odd sensation that unless she held onto the table she'd float to the ceiling and tangle herself in the blue netting among the toys and seahorses. The thought made her laugh. She said it was odd that she was laughing after she'd talked so sadly about the breakup of her marriage. What her father said about con games was true of love; only the cheats get cheated. It wasn't so much that Brad had tricked her; it was that she had worn blinkers. She'd blinkered herself and tripped and fallen. And if there was blame, it was hers as well as Brad's. She'd been too busy, she told Dan, even to know how she felt.

"I knew exactly how I felt," he said. "Like somebody took an axe to my heart."

Here, she thought, was a man who wasn't afraid to feel his feelings. On the other hand, it was amazing he could feel anything, after the amount of tequila that must have gone down his throat. She asked him how he could drink so much. She'd only had a few margaritas and her head was spinning.

"I bet." He admitted that tonight he had way over-gone his limit. "I keep it to two a day most times. But I've got a hollow drum. Rusted too." He hit hard on his breastbone.

"Oh?" She smiled at him. "I thought you said there was a broken heart in there."

He pulled her hand to his chest and pushed it against the muscle beneath his shirt. "You feel that heart? Doesn't it feel broken?" To her wonder, her own heart leaped so intently that she had to take a long breath.

In La Loca, laser lights crisscrossed dancers on the shiny floor; broken blinks of flashing blue and pink flickered across

Annie's and Dan's faces. Their looking at each other was in a peculiar way simultaneously intense and effortless.

Dan's phone was ringing and finally he checked the number. "Hello?...Hello?...I'll be right back," he told her. "Don't go anywhere."

She felt—and it was a new sensation—in no hurry.

After he left, she telephoned Georgette, who was asleep in Emerald and whose heavy book on Roman ruins slid off the bed when she sat up. Annie told her friend that to her surprise she appeared to be falling for a Miami detective she'd recently met.

"How recently?" asked Georgette, turning the light on, feeling for her glasses.

"Like a couple of hours ago," Annie said.

"Is this a joke?"

Annie laughed. "No. I don't sound like myself, do I?"

"Let me put it this way. You sound definitely under the influence of something," Georgette agreed. "What's his name?"

"Dan. Daniel Hart."

"Oh, that guy. The cop that's after you. Is he nice or just good-looking?"

"Both. And he's smart. But he just lost his job because of the case he was on, which involves my dad. I won't get into it now. He wants to come back to my room."

"His name is Dan? Danny and Annie? Cute. Okay, I'm glad you're having fun."

Annie said, "I'm not having fun. I feel like I'm in outer space, kind of floating in the sky."

Georgette assured her that floating in outer space was not necessarily a bad place to be. "Enjoy yourself and call me in the morning. Bye."

Annie asked, "Gigi? Everything okay with you?"

Georgette said that so little interesting ever happened to her, apart from talking to patients who really were crazy as opposed to just feeling sorry for themselves, that the tornado's smashing her patio furniture a couple of nights ago was the big event of the year. "A bientot. Love you."

"Love you too. Bon nuit."

While Annie was waiting for Dan to come back, the muscled fellow with the white teeth who'd tried to pick her up earlier abruptly stuck his face in front of hers again. Drunk, he grinned close to her, moving his tongue back and forth over his teeth like a windshield wiper. "So where's the boyfriend?" Without waiting for a reply, he slid into the booth across from her.

"Right here, beach boy." Dan grabbed the man by his layered Versace T-shirts. "I told you last week to stop coming in here, hitting on women. Go get a life." He flung the drunk out of the booth. Cheese nachos and mugs of beer flew in air. Dan and Annie jumped up after him. The drunk staggered backward then lunged at Dan. The man in the next booth slid out of it and grabbed the drunk. Within seconds, the bar was a moil of shoves, jabs, grunts, and curses as the "beach boy" seized the opportunity to let off steam by randomly hitting bystanders. A woman who turned out to be a cop and Dan's friend came hurrying up to restrain and arrest the drunk.

In the distraction of the fight's aftermath Dan grabbed Annie's hand and ran out of La Loca with her into the summer's night.

From the restaurant they took a short walk to a side street that led down to the edge of the ocean.

Barefoot, they strolled along the curve of an unlit beach to a spot that Dan knew, where the house owners were never home and no one was ever out in the surf at night. All around them the black velvety sky shimmered; the sea was silver with stars.

Dan threw an imaginary lasso at the sky. "'I'm going to reach up and grab stars for her,' You know that line? Clark Gable? *It Happened One Night?*"

At the surf's edge, she called back over her shoulder, "Of course I know that line. Didn't my dad tell me my mother was Claudette Colbert?"

Standing in the cool silver foam of the water's edge, she billowed her shirt, letting the wind blow under it.

"I'll be back before you know it." He suddenly tossed a handful of sand up in the air and as it fell, ran off into the darkness.

Everything in Annie's life now felt so unpredictable that she thought it as likely as not that Daniel Hart would never return. That, like a magician, he'd blinded her with a puff of colored smoke and behind it he would disappear.

Okay, she thought, let him. She pulled the band from her ponytail, shook loose her tangled hair and stared up at a dome of stars whose names she knew by heart. There in the sky, inside a carefully designed solar system, she could chart her way clearly among the constellations, but floating in space, or sitting at the sea's edge down here in the muddle, wasn't she losing her bearings?

Seated in the wet sand, she let the edge of the waves touch her bare feet. Her cell phone vibrated in her pants pocket; the caller ID said "Trevor." She almost answered. But inexplicably she was seized by an impulse. She pulled out the phone and flung it far off into the surf. Just threw it irretrievably away. She had a rush of regret—and the knowledge that her severance wasn't complete, for her Blackberry was in her purse back in Dan's Thunderbird. Still she felt freer and she liked the feeling. Annie took a deep relaxing breath and sat there, still.

All at once a blaze of light bounced behind her. Dan's pick-up truck came splashing along the sand toward where she sat and stopped with its headlights searching the waves. In the truck bed was his blue windsurfer board. Its slack white sail flapped against its mast in the quickening breeze as he dragged it to the surf. "Sailed one of these?"

"Only once."

He stripped off his pants and shirt, gesturing at her to do the same. "Think you could hang on?"

Annie laughed, recalling the shake and stretch of skin as her fighter jet shot off the carrier deck and climbed the sky. "I think I could hang on," she said.

Sitting on the board, they were floating on the black swells of water, then they were standing, their hands together fighting the sail into trim, Dan balanced behind her so close that she could feel his heart against her back, the heart that he'd said was broken but that felt too strong and steady to break. Quickly he was letting her hands guide his on the bar, responding to how well she could feel the wind.

The windsurfer board raced along the waves, a thread on the foam, sewing the sea.

His face in her wet hair, his mouth warm against her ear, their heads turned and they were kissing, kissing as the board rose with the swell of the wave. He pointed far ahead where a star fell gleaming far off in the night sky and spilled down into the sea. She thought she was crying but she couldn't be sure, because how could she tell her own salt tears from the ocean?

• • •

At this moment, six hundred miles north in Emerald, the phone beside Georgette Nickerson's bed once more awakened her. Grouchily sitting up to answer what she assumed was another call from Annie, she knocked her glasses to the floor.

But unexpectedly the caller was Brad Hopper. Apologizing—with an edge of accusation—for phoning Georgette so late, he wondered if she might be able to tell him where her best friend could be. He knew the two of them kept in daily touch, or at least they had done so all during Brad's marriage to Annie. He'd called Pilgrim's Rest but Sam hadn't been able to help him with Annie's whereabouts and he'd figured maybe Georgette could.

Georgette said, "She went to St. Louis. Then she went to Miami."

Brad was aware of that much. In fact Annie had gone to Miami thanks to him, in his jet. He even knew that she was staying at the Dorado in South Beach. The problem was, she hadn't returned to the Dorado tonight and it was awfully late for her to be out, given the circumstances. He'd had the assistant manager check her room but they'd found no one in it but that Maltese dog.

Annoyingly the hotel had said they wouldn't tell him where their guest was, even if they knew where she was, which they didn't. Annie wasn't in the hotel bar or pool because Brad had checked them all. He was standing right here in the Dorado lobby at this very minute.

"You're in the Hotel Dorado?" Georgette climbed all the way out of her bed, turned on her light and found her glasses on the floor.

"I sure am."

To give herself time to think, she fluffed her pillows. "Why did you go to Miami?"

"It's a holiday."

Georgette snapped at him. "Brad, don't get cute."

"Okay, I'm sorry." He was used to women chastising him. "I'm here trying to get Annie to call off our divorce. I already got her to put it off for a month."

"You did?" With her glasses on, Georgette felt surer of herself. "I thought she was signing the final papers in just a few days."

"Come on, Georgette," he chuckled. "You never thought that was really going to happen, did you? I told her, if she postponed, I'd lend her one of our jets to get out of St. Louis. That's how she got to Miami. Things were a mess in St. Louis, you know, with the storm? She could have never gotten here by now except for me."

Privately, Georgette was happily thinking, "Wow, are you going to be sorry you brought Annie to Miami," but out loud she took a judgmental tone. "You blackmailed her?"

Brad was defensive. "I just cut a deal. And she checked the jet in fine, so that's no problem. What's wrong with saving a marriage? Marriage is a sacrament." He paused. "I think. I'm not really a churchgoer anymore."

Now ready with an alibi, Georgette said Annie was spending the night in Palm Beach at a friend's home, a female friend, someone she had met recently in Chesapeake Cove, someone whose name Georgette couldn't recall just now. Annie had phoned her earlier tonight and had mentioned how she was going to stay with this friend and how she'd be back in Miami

early in the morning to talk with her father's doctor at Golden
Days. Annie always did what she said she was going to do, right?
She was undoubtedly asleep right now, with her phone charging
overnight. So Brad should just stop worrying; he should check
into his own room at the Dorado, go to bed, and call Annie in
the morning.

Brad was accustomed to taking women's advice. He decided
to do exactly as Georgette suggested. "Thanks, Georgia. You're a
peach." Brad had long made "Georgia" into a seductive intimacy.
He added, "I don't know what this Atlanta boy would do without
you. Night night."

"Night night."

"Tell Annie to call me if she calls you."

"I'll tell her."

"You're the best. I love you."

Georgette had to remind herself (as she headed down to her
kitchen where the birthday cake Sam had given her probably
hadn't been too damaged by being thrown in the trash bin), she
had definitely to remind herself, that getting involved even in
the most peripheral way with Brad Hopper would be less like
eating a healthy peach and more like eating a gallon of Häagen-
Dazs Triple Chocolate with a Sarah Lee pound cake on the side.
She would regret it.

Georgette wheeled around in the hallway and returned
to bed.

• • •

At the Dorado, on his way to the elevator, Brad was drawn
into the bar by the murmur of women's voices and the chinkle
of a cocktail shaker. He decided to have a nightcap. Gliding
onto a blue bar stool, he fell quickly into a conversation with a
tall silvery blonde who was drinking vodka martinis with a less-
attractive brunette. They both wore low-cut pullovers and very
high heels whose toes looked lethal. Brad offered to buy "the
ladies" another round. The brunette said that unfortunately she

was just leaving and was going to catch hell for getting home so late. She tottered away, dangerously tacking. The blonde, however, accepted the drink offer, explaining immediately to Brad that she'd had a very annoying day. On top of annoying problems at work, there had been an annoying run-in with her ex-husband, and an annoying quarrel with her brand-new fiancé with whom she had planned to celebrate her engagement tonight here at the Dorado, her favorite restaurant.

Brad made a comic and appealing show of searching under the barstools. So, where was her fiancé? He wasn't here, he wasn't there, where was he?

The blonde laughed. Her laugh wasn't a good one and she seemed to know it and shut it off. She said that her fiancé, a financial planner, had been forced to fly out tonight with his boss, all the way to Japan, leaving her to eat dinner here at the Dorado with her friend, who wasn't even really her friend but her future sister-in-law, who'd just left. It was all extremely annoying.

Brad couldn't have been more sympathetic.

• • •

A few miles away, on a starlit beach, Dan and Annie were slow dancing in the surf. From the open door of the blue pickup truck, parked beside them, Etta James sang, accompanied by lush violins.

> At last
> My love has come along.
> My lonely days are over
> And life is like a song…

It was such easy dancing for Annie, for whom pleasure had never come easily. Such slow, easy dancing. Who would have thought you could kiss, be kissed like this, while you danced? Not Annie, not until now.

Overhead, a meteor shower fanned out to the east and west. They watched the faint shooting stars.

She said, "Probably the Southern Delta Aquarids. Really, it's just debris from a comet's tail. Just cosmic debris."

"Aren't we all?" Dan murmured. "I mean humans. Just cosmic debris? But just for a tiny bit of time, don't you think we can be pretty wonderful?"

• • •

At the Dorado bar, Brad Hopper leaned closer to the blonde. Watching them from a dark corner was Rafael Rook, who sipped morosely on a soft drink. The Cuban was very upset. Not about the Queen, which he knew was locked up in Annie's room. And not about Diaz, who seemed to have fallen for the story that the Queen had been hijacked to Havana. He was upset about Jack Peregrine, who had told him not to lose sight of Annie. But this morning stupidly Raffy had panicked, jumping out of her car when she had threatened to go to the MPD. Now he couldn't find her. She wasn't in the hotel and her phone switched him to voice mail. He'd been waiting here at the Dorado for hours, assuming she would come back. But now it was past midnight and where was she? Moreover, waiting for Annie, he'd had to blow off his promise to meet Chamayra at La Loca earlier and he was now too apprehensive to return Chamayra's furious messages. Nobody could get madder faster than Chamayra.

Nothing, however, would have made Raffy leave the Dorado bar. At first sight he recognized the long-legged blonde as Ms. Skippings of Golden Days. And when he heard the man she was falling all over introduce himself as Lt. Brad Hopper, U.S. Navy pilot, Raffy nearly choked. Brad Hopper was the name of Annie's husband (or her ex-husband, he wasn't sure which), but at least Raffy definitely remembered that name, and how many Brad Hoppers who'd been Navy pilots were there likely to be in this world, much less Miami, much less the Dorado Hotel where

Annie was staying, or would be staying if she were here, which she wasn't? Not many.

The Cuban slid to a closer table in order to eavesdrop more easily. He heard Brad mesmerizing Ms. Skippings with gossip about sex-addict superstar celebrities to whom he'd sold private jets. He then bragged to her about his heroics in Desert Fox. He then told her—hard for Raffy even to listen to—how his unhappy marriage had ended with his wife's infidelity.

As Raffy eavesdropped, suddenly he caught a distant glimpse of Annie herself. She was walking past the bar entrance but, fortunately, she was at the far end of the lobby. Her clothes were soaking wet and she was laughing with a young man whose clothes were also wet, although it was not raining. The man had his back to Raffy, but when he reached the elevator bank, he turned around and kissed Annie. Horribly enough, the man was Sgt. Daniel Hart.

To Raffy's great relief, Brad, with his back to the lobby and his eyes wandering down Ms. Skippings's long legs to her stiletto heels, didn't see Annie at all. Nor did he notice Raffy as anything more than a small thin man with a guitar case who was leaving the bar. Raffy positioned himself to block Brad's view of the elevator doors as Annie and the detective moved inside them.

• • •

The elevator ascended and the doors opened on the eleventh floor. Dan and Annie kept kissing. An old bellboy in his seventies was tiredly pushing a full luggage cart along the corridor.

"Honeymooners?" he asked them. They laughed as they helped him maneuver his cart into the elevator. "Don't go to bed mad. It's worked for me and my wife, fifty-two years." The doors closed on him.

• • •

In Emerald, Georgette was leaving another voice mail on Annie's cell phone. "Annie, it's me. What's wrong with your phone? I hope you get this message. Watch out. I don't know what's happening with your divorce but maybe Brad's going for alimony. He's in Miami. He's looking for you. He's checked into the Dorado. I told him you'd gone to see a girlfriend in Palm Beach but that I didn't know her name. It was the only thing I could think of. Whatever you're up to and I think I know, watch yourself! And don't call me till morning. Somebody needs to get some sleep."

• • •

For a long time, the Dorado lobby had been empty of guests, except for a slender young Cuban who sat behind a large fig tree, leaning against the neck of his guitar case.

Raffy was coming to definite deductive conclusions.

Brad Hopper and Melissa Skippings had left the hotel together and he had seen them rubbing against each other as they waited for the valet to bring her SUV.

Daniel Hart had not yet come down in the elevators. From the way they'd been kissing in the lobby, it seemed unlikely that he was up there in Annie's room arresting her. It was three in the morning. Things were getting more complicated than Raffy felt that he could handle alone.

He stole a phone from a man at the bar and used it to try to reach Annie's aunt Sam.

"'How full of briars is this working day world,'" sighed Raffy to himself. "But, on the other hand, 'Journeys end in lovers meeting, every wise man's son doth know.' And the great Shakespeare was a wise man." He listened to the rhythmic rings of the phone as he called Emerald.

part three

East

Chapter 42
The Secret Heart

Sam in her bedroom at Pilgrim's Rest thanked Raffy Rook for calling her. She really appreciated all he was doing, although she didn't necessarily agree that Sergeant Hart was a lying *s.o.b.* who'd pretend to anything, even love, to trick Annie into giving up Jack and his Cuban gold statue, whatever that was. In Sam's view, the best thing Raffy could do would be to pack Jack and Annie both into a car and drive them up to Emerald where she could get her brother some serious medical attention. That was her dream now that Annie and Jack had reconnected. To bring Jack back home.

"'We are such stuff as dreams are made on,' Sam," Raffy told her.

"Oh yes, *The Maltese Falcon*," she replied, to his confusion, for he knew as little about the movies as she knew of Shakespeare. "'I like talking to a man who likes talking.' Good night, Mr. Rook. Take care of Annie and Jack."

"I am honestly making that effort."

"I believe you."

● ● ●

For years, in the middle of the night, Sam had wandered into unused bedrooms on the third floor of Pilgrim's Rest. No one lived in them anymore. The musty smell of long emptiness always washed over her like memory. Her brother Jack's narrow childhood room with its single dormer window had nothing in it anymore of his young exuberance. Instead, the room was crammed wall-to-wall with mismatched pieces of furniture removed from other parts of the house because they were broken or because they had fallen out of fashion—a grandiose gaslight chandelier, a three-legged Chinese Chippendale chair that Jack had broken, a white quilted vanity that had belonged to their mother, the once formidable Eugenia "Grandee" Worth. None of this furniture would ever be used at Pilgrim's Rest again; yet over generations little of it had been discarded, out of some family refusal to admit defeat that was probably indistinguishable in the end, thought Sam, from sloth or despair.

Every summer she took a carload of "stuff" into town and put it out on the sidewalk in front of Now Voyager with a sign: "Free! Take It!!" Dozens of little wicker baskets, a big plastic globe of the earth, an electric fondue pot, a poplar kitchen hutch with a broken drawer and a missing leg. Every summer, people stopped and took all the things away. Yet the next summer Pilgrim's Rest was somehow filled to overflowing.

A year ago, in one of her periodic cleanouts of the house (during which she could never bring herself to discard very much), she had rolled the round top of an old bleached oak table from in front of the closet door (she never put clothes in that closet, which she associated with their father locking up Jack). On the floor inside, she found yellow boxes of Super-8 films that her teenaged brother had shot in his "movie phrase," when he had announced his intent to become a great film director. This passion had gradually faded, like his other passions, replaced by newer enthusiasms. The expensive camera equipment had been put away with the metal detector and the fossil collection and the speed bike, the magician's kit, the telescope.

When Sam had first come across the short films, she'd decided to convert them into a DVD as a present to Annie. But after she'd looked at the originals, she'd never shown the DVD to her niece.

All of the teenaged Jack's silent movies were shots of his next-door neighbor Ruthie Nickerson. Close-ups of Ruthie's eyes, of the angle of her cheek, tangle of her hair; long tracking shots of the quick rhythm of her walk. George Nickerson's seventeen-year-old sister had been fearlessly intimate with the camera in those days, had known that she was beautiful, and in Jack's movies had dared the viewer not to respond, just as in life she had forced everyone around her into an awkward acknowledgment of her effect on them.

One entire ten-minute film was a single shot of Ruthie standing by the dormer window in Jack's room on a summer's afternoon. She wore a long white thin linen shirt, slightly opened to the waist by an easy breeze. She wore nothing but the thin shirt and loose white shorts. Staring into the camera, she smiled a wonderful smile. And when she grew bored with smiling, she turned to look out the window.

Suddenly, in the last moment of the film, the camera jerked away from Ruthie and quickly panned to the doorway. There stood Sam and Jack's mother Grandee, thin, waspish, unstrung, silently raving at the boy with the camera, at the girl by the window. The footage ended in a sudden blackout.

When watching this movie, years after the fact, Sam understood for the first time what had happened just before the family explosion she'd always called "That *Psycho* Night."

Home after her sophomore year at college, Sam returned late one afternoon from playing tennis with her friend Clark Goode. That summer she taught tennis in the morning and practiced three hours a day, determined to keep up her game, for she depended on a sports scholarship for her tuition; her father had declined to pay her way to college (he thought she wasn't smart) and her mother hadn't cared whether she'd gone or not.

It had been a hard summer for Sam. In the spring she had fallen in love with a girl in her dorm, who not only had not loved her back but who had expressed horror upon learning of her feelings. Clark had enlisted in the Army and been sent to Vietnam; now home on leave, he had just announced that, despite his firsthand knowledge of the war's hellish futility, he was heading back to Saigon in a week to begin a second tour of duty.

In that heavy, heated dusk, Sam was staring lethargically out her window when suddenly she heard her mother shrieking from Jack's bedroom. She rushed into the hallway where she was almost knocked over as Ruthie ran past her, down the stairs.

Sam had to pull apart Jack and their mother by force. Jack, shirtless, a long-limbed knobbly teenager, hurled himself down the stairs and out of the house in pursuit of Ruthie.

Hours later, Sam found him stretched out on their front lawn, smoking marijuana and staring at the stars. His thin chest looked moon-white against the dark summer tan of his arms.

Jack told Sam with bitterness that Ruthie had no further use for him. He blamed their "crazy bitch of a mother" for ruining his chance for happiness. Sam tried a number of strategies to console him, from "you'll win Ruthie back" to "time heals all." She finally resorted to jokes about her being even more unhappily in love than he was. At least, cracked Sam, Jack had a girlfriend to lose.

But to her distress, her brother did not respond with his habitual flippancy. Instead he started to cry; something she hadn't seen him do for years. He muttered that without Ruthie he didn't want to live. Pushing Sam off, he vanished into the night. She heard him jumpstart their father's car and drive it away.

Distraught, Sam called Clark, who came over at once. They spent the night driving around Emerald searching unsuccessfully for Jack. A friend of theirs, a rookie cop (who many years later would become Emerald's chief of police), assured Sam that there were no reports of car accidents anywhere in the county and Jack would be fine.

At dawn, Clark dropped her back home. On the Nickerson porch next door, Ruthie sat on the steps, smoking a cigarette. Clark went over to talk to her. Sam was at the Pilgrim's Rest door when she heard a loud crash and a scream. She rushed into the dining room, where she saw Jack smashing their mother's antique chairs onto the top of her antique table. Grandee was beating him on his back with her fists. Then she picked up a three-foot-tall Tiffany vase that had belonged to her Worth father and hit her son across the shoulders with it. Blue and purple glass petals shattered onto the rug. Jack shook off the glass like water in a rainbow. Grandee flung herself on the floor crying.

Sam ran to the living room where her father sat still as death, drinking his tumbler of cognac, pretending none of it was happening.

"Dad, do something."

He looked up and said in his stiff-mouthed way, "Go to bed, Samantha."

She shook him so hard the glass flew from his hand. "Do something before they kill each other!"

He didn't look at her. "There's nothing anyone can do." He picked up the glass from the rug and poured himself more cognac.

Sam left him when she heard the front door slam. Jack was driving off again. She cajoled her mother up the stairs, one by one, by promising that she would repair the Tiffany vase, that it wasn't very damaged at all.

"He made me do it," Grandee whispered. "Why does he make me do things I hate myself for? He does it on purpose."

"No he doesn't," Sam kept repeating. "He loves you. He loves you."

By the time Sam had cleaned up the broken chairs and glassware, it was morning and she had to leave for her summer job at the tennis camp. All day long she was overwhelmed by the sad certainty that whatever "family" the four Peregrines had ever formed together, this summer had ended it forever.

Five days later, Sam sadly drove Clark to the airport to start his long trip to Saigon.

A few weeks after that, Jack's friend George came over to Pilgrim's Rest to tell him that Ruthie had run off with a married man in the night.

The next evening Jack was stopped a hundred miles from home for speeding in a stolen car, which luckily he had not yet driven out of the state of North Carolina, so his father still had connections to get the seventeen-year-old's sentence commuted. Jack had to pay back his fine by clearing two acres of Peregrine underbrush. Over the next month, he worked ten hours a day at the task. His muscles hardened, his skin darkened. Sam's foreboding proved true. Jack did not ever speak again either to his father or to his mother. He worked till nightfall, walked to town, returned to sleep in the barn.

Six months later, Judge Peregrine was dead. During the judge's funeral, Jack stole all the cash he could find in the house, threw his suitcase into his mother's Mercedes coupe, and left Emerald, as he wrote Sam, forever.

But it wasn't forever. Over the next quarter of a century, he came back to Pilgrim's Rest three times—once to bring home the infant Annie and the *King of the Sky*, once when his daughter was seven, and once when he ran out of the cornfield and gave her a ruby for her seventeenth birthday.

• • •

Now it was time, Sam told herself, for her brother to come home again. She took a DVD she'd labeled "Jack's Movie" across the lawn to Georgette's house. It was three in the morning.

Georgette's sleep-swollen eye peeped cautiously through the front-door glass in her hallway. Only last Christmas she'd had her house burglarized by an ex-con drug addict she'd been treating for bipolar disorder; she'd told him at the police station, "As your therapist, I hope you get help. As a homeowner, I hope you get eight to ten. And give me back my Dad's silver Rotary trophy!"

As soon as Georgette saw Sam waiting outside her door, she swung it open and yelled, "Stop ringing that buzzer! How do you know I'm not upstairs having wild sex with six men?"

Sam pushed past. "If you are, it'll have to wait."

Georgette saw a DVD in her neighbor's hand. "I am *not* watching *Diabolique* with you if that's what this is all about. I have to be at the hospital in four hours. There isn't a movie you could name that I'd want to watch."

Sam sat down on the first chair she came to. "Yes, there is."

Locating glasses in the pocket of her pink fluffy bathrobe, Georgette examined the DVD case. "'Jack's Movie.' What does this mean? 'Jack's Movie'? Is this about Annie's dad?"

"Yes." Sam walked back to the front door as if she'd changed her mind about her late-night visit and decided to return home immediately. But then she slowly let the back of her head fall against the doorframe. She looked at the younger woman. "You may want to sit down."

"Is Annie's dad dead?"

"No. Well, as far as I know, no."

"Is this about Annie and the Miami detective?"

"Oh, did you talk to Rafael Rook too? He thinks Annie's spending the night with that detective Daniel Hart."

"How does he know? She called me and talked about floating around with this detective in outer space. She sounded intoxicated. And/or she's in love."

"Already?" Upset, Sam shook her head no, then yes. "Well, I can't think about that now."

Georgette took the older woman by the arm, leading her back into the hall. "Sam, what's the matter with you?"

"Annie may call you about her mother tomorrow. I want you to be prepared." Sam pulled Georgette down beside her on the painted pine bench.

"Prepared for what?"

"I'm pretty sure I know who Annie's mother is." She pressed Georgette's hands in hers. "Your aunt Ruthie is her mother."

Georgette laughed. "You're joking."

"Do I look like I'm joking?"

Georgette looked at her. "No, you don't. Who told you this?"

"Nobody. Nobody tells me a goddamn thing in this family." Sam thrust the DVD at her. "Watch this home movie. If you don't see what I see, we're both crazy."

Georgette stood up, frowning. "Let me process this. You think my aunt Ruthie is Annie's mother because of a movie?"

"Well, tell you the truth I've wondered about it ever since

Ruthie came back here that night, you remember? You and Annie were fourteen, I think. But this is footage Jack shot of Ruthie about a year before Annie was born."

The young psychiatrist held out her hand. "Sam, I want to take back what I said. I guess maybe there *is* a movie you could name that I'll watch at three in the morning."

They went to the Nickerson "family room," still so called, although there was no one in the family living here but Georgette. Together, while the cat Pitti Sing purred for attention, the two women viewed the DVD of the short silent films that Jack had made of the teenaged Ruthie.

Georgette turned off her DVD player. "Well, I'll tell you one thing. Ruthie was hot. It's clear Jack was crazy about her. It's clear your mother Grandee was crazy."

"Don't go there. Talk about Annie."

"I guess you've got a point about Annie. There's a…"

"Family resemblance?"

"Sort of."

"Sort of?" laughed Sam tensely.

"Sort of. Still it's a stretch. Wouldn't somebody have said something?"

"People don't say things."

Georgette snorted. "Get into psychiatry. People say things to *me* for fifty nonstop minutes. You can't stop them from saying things. They keep saying things as I shove them out the door."

Sam rubbed her hand affectionately on the case of the DVD. "You didn't see Jack's face when Ruthie ran off. I always suspected he went after her when he robbed us at Dad's funeral… But I couldn't even think about it then. Dad had…drowned. Mama'd gone even crazier. This is before your time, of course."

"It's a relief to find something that's before my time," admitted Georgette. "So you think Ruthie is Annie's mother? Wow. Ruthie stood right out there in the yard with us that night in the ninth grade. And then she just packed up the Nickerson salad forks and left and never came back."

Sam said that she didn't think Ruthie knew that Annie was

the child she'd given up at birth. Once, pressed, Jack had told Sam that Annie's mother had abandoned him, believing their just-born baby had been adopted. Sam suspected Ruthie had no idea that Jack had kept the child and that the child was Annie.

Georgette wondered, "Why didn't you ever ask Jack about Ruthie's being the mother?"

"I did ask him," Sam sighed. "I asked him the last time I saw him. I asked him on the phone for years. He says the mother was just some girl he'd known in Barbados." Leaping to her feet, Sam paced the hallway, nearly tripped up by Georgette's Siamese cat. "You know what I think? He was always scared he'd lose Annie if Ruthie found out."

Georgette's cat brushed against her legs. "He *did* lose Annie, Sam! Wasn't that always Annie's point? He lost her when he left her here. And Ruthie didn't find out because she didn't want to… Do I call Annie, tell her about Ruthie, is that what you want?"

Sam took a long breath. "No. No. I don't want you to say anything till she gets through this mess with Jack. Please. I just want you to be there if she needs you." Sam picked up the young woman's bathrobe belt, which was hanging tangled at her feet. "You want to trip and fall on this thing?"

"Oh Sam, don't cry." Georgette hugged her.

After Sam left, Georgette rubbed her plump white arms as if she were warming herself. "*Sacre bleu!*" she said to her cat Pitti Sing, who arched softly against her ankles.

Chapter 43

Misleading Lady

Across the lawn at Pilgrim's Rest, Clark Goode was awakened by a knock on his bedroom door. He had drifted off into a dream in which he was teaching his first wife Tuyet and the seven-year-old Annie to fly-fish on Emerald's Aquene River. In the dream, his childhood tormenters the Fanhart brothers had suddenly ambushed him, just as they'd often done on his way home from school many years ago. But in the dream, Clark was an adult, dressed in his operating scrubs and towering over the Fanhart bullies, who were still fat little boys in the third grade. Easily, triumphantly, he chased them away. But when he turned around, both Tuyet and Annie had disappeared.

"Clark?"

He woke fully, expecting a hospital emergency. But Sam was saying, "It's Brad. He just called me about Annie." Sam held the old dog Teddy in her arms.

"What? What's wrong! Where is she?"

"It's okay." Sam shook his foot. "Somewhere in Miami."

"Somewhere? Why is Brad calling you about Annie in the middle of the night?"

Teddy dropped from Sam's arms onto the bed, where she tried to make a pillow comfortable by pawing at it. "Brad's in Miami too. At the Hotel Dorado."

Sitting up, Clark turned on his light. "Just tell me! Is Annie okay?"

"I think she's on a date."

"What?" Clark felt for his glasses. "Brad called to tell you Annie was on a date?"

"No, Georgette told me that. When Brad got to the Dorado, she wasn't in her room. He's trying to find her; he even called Georgette." Sighing, Sam sat down at the foot of Clark's bed.

To wake himself, Clark yanked hard at his hair. "I'm having trouble here. Go back. Brad's in Miami?"

"Yes. Clark, will you catch up? He went there to talk Annie out of the divorce." Sam started folding the coverlet bunched at the bed's end into neat squares.

As Clark checked the old plastic radio alarm clock by his bed, he noticed Sam was still in her slacks and shirt. "Why aren't you in bed?"

"I went over to Georgette's and woke her up."

"Why?"

"To have a serious talk with her about Annie. Because if Annie needs help, she'll call Georgette. She always calls her."

"That's because your line's always busy because you're calling *her*."

"Go ahead and laugh." When Sam had come home, she'd been unable to sleep. Then Brad had called.

"Why isn't Brad asleep? Why are Georgette and I the only people trying to sleep in this group?"

Sam wanted Clark to come down to the kitchen with her for some more of the leftover sushi. "It won't be any good in the morning."

"Neither will I." He yanked the coverlet away to stop her from unfolding, refolding, unfolding it.

"There's no need to be sarcastic, Clark. Also I had a call from Rafael Rook."

"Really? You're just a little magpie, aren't you?"

"This is serious." It seems that Jack had asked Rook to keep an eye on Annie, so Rook had been hanging out at the Dorado, when Brad Hopper had suddenly come into the bar. Then Annie had shown up in the lobby in soaking wet clothes with a man whom she'd taken up to her room. "It was that Miami detective, Daniel Hart. I told you."

Clark felt with his bare feet for his loafers. "Told me what?"

"That Annie was on the edge."

"You didn't tell me that."

"I've told you that for years." But, luckily, Sam noted, Brad had been distracted when Annie had walked past him kissing Sergeant Hart.

"Is 'luckily' really the word we want here?" Clark asked. He felt he had to add that Sam was not making any sense. It was a shame he didn't have any chlorpromazine hydrochloride in his medical bag.

She gave a theatrical laugh. Sense? Did it make any sense that after what Annie had gone through over the past few days—flying in a storm to St. Louis, flying to Miami, seeing her dying father for the first time in a decade—did it make any sense that Annie—in whose closet the hangers, all facing the same way, were 1.5 inches apart, in whose condominium the little kitchen looked as if the entire USS *Enterprise* crew had been in there cleaning it all day—did it make sense that *Annie*—hurrying to find Jack before she had to be back in Annapolis for a test flight!—would take the time off to wander around in wet clothes with a strange man at the wee hours of the morning, and take that strange man up to her hotel room?

Clark yanked his bathrobe from Sam, who was folding it as well. "I thought you said you liked Sergeant Hart."

"Clark, please! I called her. Six times, maybe more. Her phone's off." She punched a soft spot in the pillow for the restless Teddy. "What if she marries him on the spur of the moment? You of all people know how that can work out."

He leaned over the window bench to look at the sky, an indigo blue. "I don't think Elizabeth Taylor spent any more time thinking about marriage than you do."

Sam carefully placed Teddy on the softened pillow then lay down beside her. Finally she said, "I told Georgette about Ruthie."

Surprised, he walked back to the bed. "Told her what about Ruthie?"

Sam squeezed her arms. "I showed her those movies Jack made of Ruthie. Tell me that was okay. I decided that if Jack tells Annie that Ruthie's her mother…"

Clark sat quietly beside her, rubbed her back. "If Jack wouldn't say it to you, he's not going to say it to Annie. Besides, you don't even know if it's true. Jack told you he met Annie's mother in Barbados."

"Oh, Jack'll say anything."

He nodded. "Exactly."

"I think I always suspected it." Sam sighed. "Ruthie takes off, then six months later Jack takes off, then a year later he shows back up with a blue-eyed blonde-haired baby."

"Lots of people have blue eyes and blonde hair."

Sam gave him a look. "You know what, Clark? Movies don't lie." She reached out for the old Shih Tzu, held her against her chest. "It used to hurt my feelings so much when Annie would go on about 'Where's my "real" mother?'"

Clark nodded. They sat together silently a while longer, listening to Teddy's light rasping snore.

Sam said, "I want her to be happy. Fall in love and be happy."

"Not necessarily the same thing." He returned to the window where now the deep blue of the sky was washed with purple.

"Tell me something good," she demanded.

"Annie will fall in love and be happy."

"Clark, don't joke." The dog wriggled away, toppling with a wheeze off the bed.

"Why not? Here's a new one. You heard about the optometrist who fell into a lens grinder?"

"And made a spectacle of himself? That's not a new one. I haven't heard a new one from you in twenty years." Sam rolled from the bed, picked up Teddy and walked with her to the door. "Okay, I'm leaving. Good night. Thanks."

"You're welcome. Sam?" She turned back. "I think you're a great mom."

"Don't change your mind," she said. "I'm fixing up Jack's old room, just in case he wants to come recuperate at home."

Clark smiled at her. "Just in case."

From the pocket of her shorts, Sam's cell phone played a jaunty melody. She answered. "Oh, hi...No, I haven't heard a word."

Worried, Clark asked, "Who is that?"

But Sam was laughing. "Sure, come on over for breakfast," and she slapped the lid shut.

"Was that Georgette?" He looked at the Nickerson house next door where lights were burning.

"No, it was D. K."

"Hey, let's ask Georgette over too. She's awake. We could look up how to play bridge on the Internet."

Sam glanced out the window. "Those are just the lights Georgette always leaves on. Don't bother her. She needs her rest."

He snorted elaborately. "Oh, okay! I was headed right over there to wake her up. But that's good advice, Sam. Not to barge in on somebody while they're sleeping."

Teddy growled with impatience until Sam took her away.

Left alone, Clark lit a cigarette and leaned far out the opened window, turning south, away from the Nickerson house, toward the dark roll of green fields, as if he could see Annie all the way in Miami if he looked hard enough.

But all he saw were stars, making way for dawn.

• • •

Hours later he was awakened by a sweet smell. Down in the kitchen, Sam was flipping flapjacks at the stove griddle.

At the kitchen table, dressed for work but still in her pink fluffy bedroom slippers, Georgette sleepily drank coffee from one of the "Movie Mugs" Sam sold at Now Voyager. This one showed Claudette Colbert in *Misleading Lady*.

"I'll give you this, Sam," said Georgette, studying her mug. "In so far as an '80s girl can look like a '30s star, Ruthie looks a little like Claudette. It's the eyes. What color were their eyes? Isn't that weird? We only have black-and-white photos. D. K., what color were Ruthie's eyes?"

At the back door, D. K. Destin smoked a cigarette, leaning from his wheelchair to puff the smoke outside. "Give me a break, how the hell am I suppose to know what color? White people's color. Green, blue, one of those colors."

Clark walked into the kitchen with a yawn. "So what's happening?"

"Banana pancakes," Sam told him.

The kitchen wall phone rang. Georgette answered it. "Peregrine-Goode residence."

"Hello," said a cheerful male voice. "My name is Trevor Smith-wall, I'm Annie's next-door neighbor. Are you Aunt Sam?"

Georgette made a *phhtt* noise. "Do I sound like a grown woman's aunt? I'm Annie's friend Georgette Nickerson."

"Oh, you're Georgette. I probably know more about you than you can imagine."

Georgette told him that he had no idea how imaginative she could be.

"Who is it?" asked Clark. "Why don't people say who they're talking to?"

When Georgette explained who it was, Sam ran at her. "Ask about Amy Johnson. Did something happen to Annie's cat?"

Trevor passed along his assurances that Annie's cat was fine. No, he was calling to tell Annie's family that the best thing they could do would be to encourage her not to try to solve her father's legal troubles. Trevor would have told her so himself but she had not returned his calls—

"Join the crowd," said Georgette. "So just lay it out, Trev, what's this got to do with you? You're with the FBI."

Trevor admitted that was true.

"I know it's true. That's why I'm asking, what's this got to do with you?"

"Just tell her to stay out of her father's problems and come home. And tell her to call me. Nice to talk to you. Bye."

Georgette relayed Trevor's cryptic advice to the others.

Dropping her spatula in the sink, Sam shut off the gas griddle. "That's it. I'm going to Miami and bring Jack home. I can't stand this stress anymore." She made a quick phone call to the college student who worked summers at Now Voyager and asked her if she could take care of the store for a few days, that Sam had to go to Miami. The request elicited a groggy "No problem," which Sam decided to take at face value.

"What's the fastest way I can fly to Miami?" she asked D. K., who was soaking his cigarette butt under the faucet.

"In a plane," he told her.

"Can't you tell when I'm serious?"

Clark said, "I need to get to the emergency room where things are a little calmer."

• • •

Clark and Georgette drove together to Emerald Hospital. Neither spoke until they reached River Road. Below them, the Aquene River roiled over its banks, fast, muddy red, still floating debris from the storm. "You know *aquene* is the Algonquin word for 'peace'?" Clark finally said.

"Wouldn't it be nice if we got some of that?" sighed Georgette.

As they parked in the staff lot and walked toward the hospital, she suddenly asked, "Okay, what do you think of Sam's theory that Aunt Ruthie is Annie's mother?"

She turned to wait for him to answer her. For a moment, he ambled along with his old briefcase swinging slowly at his side, not speaking. "Clark," she repeated, "What do you think of Sam's theory?"

He took off his round tortoise-shell glasses, rubbed his dark-blue eyes, wiped the glasses on the lab coat he already wore. "I think we ought to tell Sam more often that she's done a great job raising Annie."

He walked to the entrance, where young smokers gathered.

"Y'all should quit," he told them. The smokers stared at him, hostile.

Georgette walked Clark through the busy hospital corridor to Pediatrics. "We could find out. I could take my blood. Ruthie's my aunt."

He nodded. "That's between you and Annie. So, you hear the one about the midget fortuneteller who got arrested but she was so little she slipped through the jail bars and escaped? Well, they put out an all points bulletin on her that said—"

"—Small medium at large," Georgette finished the pun for him.

He made a rueful noise. "I guess I need to get some new puns or some new friends."

Chapter 44

Daughters of Destiny

Bright and early, Annie arrived at Golden Days for her appointment with her father's doctor. Too bright, too early. She had an excruciating headache from last night's margaritas and a queasy stomach that hadn't been helped by all the hot salsa and mole she'd eaten at La Loca. Far more unsettling was her sense that she'd undergone a transformation in her personality. Insofar as she'd ever known herself, Lt. Anne Peregrine Goode did not wake up in bed in a hotel room with a stranger who was hugging her family dog.

But that's where she'd found herself at 7 a.m., in a Miami hotel bed with Malpy and Daniel Hart. She'd managed to free the dog without waking the detective. The prospect of having him prove indifferent or tasteless or stupid or smug or not everything she had felt him to be last night was unbearable to her. Better to slip away and if he never got in touch again, it would be sad, but so be it. Awakening him appeared, however, to be only a remote possibility, since once again he looked to be dead. Despite Malpy's licking his face he did not budge.

Undeterred by physical pain and psychological shock, she'd listened to messages on her hotel phone line—including multiple requests from both Sam and Trevor to call them back or at least to turn her cell phone on, as well as news from Georgette that Brad had checked into the Hotel Dorado and was looking for her. She didn't feel up to talking to Trevor (much less Brad) but she did phone Sam. Sam was driving to the RDU airport. Annie managed to persuade her that she, Annie, was perfectly fine and could take care of Jack and that Sam should return immediately to Emerald and wait for news. "There is no need for *any* of you to come to Miami. Please don't come to Miami. I am handling this! I don't know why people don't realize I can handle things! I flew fuckin' combat missions!"

"Sweetheart, nobody thinks you can't handle things. Are you okay?"

"I'm *fine!* I'm fine."

"Bring Jack home today," Sam said. "I'm going to fix up his room. Tell him his old room will be waiting for him. Tell him I can't wait to see him. Everything's going to be okay."

Annie promised to tell her father all of that as soon as Sam let her hang up the phone so she could go to Golden Days.

It was an accomplishment to take a shower without screaming, to dress, to walk Malpy, to return the dog to the room (Dan made a noise but didn't stir) and then to leave Brad a note at the hotel desk explaining that she was "out dealing with the Dad thing."

Sunglasses and aspirin enabled her to drive to Golden Days by 8:10 a.m. On the lawn of the pink stucco building, the old men and women sat under an already hot sun. In their waffled bathrobes, with their walkers and wheelchairs and tanks of oxygen, they had settled in to wait for lunch. Two of them, recognizing Annie, hurried over to ask her where Malpy was. They were disappointed that she hadn't brought the little dog along to visit.

In the lobby, the receptionist with the fat made-up face raised a manicured hand to stop Annie from heading to the elevator. But this time Annie had a registered name to throw her. "I'm here," she said, "to see my father, Coach Ronny Buchstabe."

To her surprise, Miss Napp's tight features immediately crumpled like an old jack-o-lantern. "Coach Ronny Buchstabe?" Her voice shook. "That's who your daddy was? Coach Ronny?"

"Yes, that's right. Is there some problem?" Annie wondered if her father had been arrested, despite Dan's assurances that the case had been dropped. "And I'd like to speak with Dr. Parker."

"Doctor who?"

"My father's doctor, Dr. Tom Parker."

"I'm not familiar with that name. But your father...You don't know about him?"

"Know what?"

The receptionist looked strangely sympathetic, even stretching out a plump hand to pat Annie's. "No one's told you?"

Alarmed but not wanting to give anything away, Annie pulled her hand back to grip the curved edge of the counter. "I'm sorry, I don't know what you're talking about."

"He passed away. Passed away?" Miss Napp put an interrogatory glide on the news as if that would help. "Your daddy?"

Annie's lips and tongue felt heavy. "Passed away?"

"Coach Buchstabe died in his sleep yesterday. I'm so sorry, honey."

"...Coach Ronny Buchstabe? Room 540?"

The receptionist nodded sadly.

A curious thud at Annie's heart moved her back a step. Miss Napp was saying something more but she couldn't understand it. Words bounced around crazily as bingo balls, refusing to spell anything meaningful. How could her father die overnight?

Waiting for Miss Napp to stop talking, she bent down and retied the laces of her running shoes, remembering her father's claim that if it hadn't been for him, she couldn't have tied her shoelaces, couldn't have brushed her teeth, couldn't have walked, talked, read, written...couldn't have, what? Couldn't have loved? Was that possibly true?

Miss Napp was leaning forward sympathetically. "I guess there's some problem between you and your siblings?"

Hope stung Annie. "My siblings?"

The receptionist's face bobbed. "I know y'all have been expecting this for months and months, still it's always a shock. And why one of your brothers or sisters didn't manage to reach you before now is anybody's guess but theirs I guess. Did you leave town or something?"

Annie looked around as if these unfamiliar brothers and sisters might be standing behind her. "Where are they?"

The receptionist glared at her watch. "Honey, they're getting ready for the family service right this minute. Not the one back in Tallahassee. But your big sister Jackie told me she already had this private family service ready to go for the past week; I mean, knowing it was only a matter of, well, days with your daddy. Jackie made the final plans yesterday and they're already at Rest Eternal."

From a distance, Annie heard herself stupidly repeating, "Jackie made the plans…" She was thinking that, okay, it was remotely possible that her father had another daughter, older than Annie, whom he'd named Jackie, for himself. Yet hadn't he been under twenty-one when Annie herself was born?

Indignation at the precipitous Jackie led Miss Napp to pour Annie a paper cup of water from a pitcher beside her. "She didn't tell you about Rest Eternal? Why, this is just awful! I just don't even believe this!"

Annie drank the water. "You said he had a stroke? But I thought his heart was fine. He was young."

"To the loved ones, any age is young." The receptionist leaned so far forward that her large breasts rested on the countertop.

Annie asked if she could look at her father's room. Miss Napp hesitated a long time, glanced at her computer and her phone and the lobby, then suddenly agreed.

Room 540 was empty, its bed stripped to the mattress. Annie looked inside the metal drawers of the bedside table. There was nothing in them. There was nothing in the closet or the bathroom.

Miss Napp walked her down the hall again, growing confidential. "Miss Buchstabe, you can't imagine the things I've seen here at Golden Days. I could make your hair stand on end. The old do have to make way for the next generation and life is for the living, but there's such a thing as taking time out to be respectful. Well, at G.D., that is *not* the policy and you are just whistling Dixie if you go around believing it is." With that bright-faced admission, Miss Napp wrote out the address of the funeral home on a pad she was carrying and thrust it at Annie with fierce nods. "*All* a father's children are equal in the eyes of death. You need to leave now to make the service on time."

Annie drove to the nearby funeral parlor as quickly as she could. From her Blackberry, she left text messages for Dan Hart, briefly explaining where she was going and why. She stopped at a service station and tried to call Clark in Emerald but he was in the OR and couldn't be reached. She tried to reach Sam, but couldn't reach her either; she was doubtless still on the road back to Emerald and there were pockets without service on that highway. Nor could she leave a message like, "There's a chance Dad's dead."

She called Georgette. The sound of her old friend's voice mail ("Hi there. You've reached the home of Dr. Georgette Nickerson, where I live with two unleashed Doberman pin-schers") was so reassuring that she could feel her chest loosening. "Georgette, it's me. I guess you've left for work. The rest home down here in Miami says my dad died. People claiming to be his other children are having some kind of service for him right now. He was using the name Ronny Buchstabe. I can't reach Clark. I don't want to leave this message for Sam. Don't tell her anything about Dad's dying. I'm going to the funeral."

That she couldn't reach Sam or Clark strangely distressed her. Here she was, twenty-six years old; it had been a long time since she'd lived at home. She didn't even see them that often; might not visit them for months on end, might not think of them for weeks at a time. Yet suddenly their not being accessible to her was a wrench. Stopped at a red light, she watched her hand on the gearshift knob; her fingers looked blue; her chest hurt.

Ten minutes later Annie pulled into the new flat parking lot beside the entrance of Rest Eternal. It was an ugly place.

How awful that her father, who had always had, if not mor-als, certainly taste, should have to leave this world—if in fact he was dead—via such a tacky route as Rest Eternal, a tan concrete cube squeezed between a log-cabin-style restaurant called Good Mornin' and a car lot called Touchdown that advertised itself with a ten-foot-high balloon of a football player kicking a big dollar sign over a goalpost.

A white stretch hearse waited by the curb at the Rest Eternal entrance. Inside the building, in a fake-marble lobby, an electronic wall scroll listed all the upcoming services one after another, as if the dead were stocks or headlines. Annie slipped quietly into the room where the "Coach Ronald Buchstabe Family Memorial" was just beginning.

In this small auditorium there were fifteen people in folding chairs gathered at one end. They sat dutifully listening to lugubrious music that poured like syrup from large speakers. Floral displays had been tidily spaced in front of a saturated blue curtain on a small stage.

The audience did not look like people Annie would have expected her father to have known, much less bred. The idea kept springing up like a punching bag that Miss Napp's report of his death was a mistake. In what were clearly three generations of Buchstabes, Annie could see no resemblance to Jack Peregrine, nor to her aunt Sam, nor to herself. It was not possible that these Buchstabes were his. Huge and flat-featured, six men and women sat clumped together, flanked by even larger teenagers, all of whom—both male and female—had long lank brown hair. Two young women struggled to hold onto big red squirming babies. A teenaged male surreptitiously checked for messages on his cell phone.

When Annie slipped into a seat near the back of the room, the whole group of mourners turned to look at the young slender woman in a white naval uniform. Frowning mulishly, they turned their backs. She was puzzled by their hostility.

After a long restless silence, the blue curtain slowly opened, revealing on an otherwise empty stage a table draped in blue and yellow satin on which sat a small mahogany box with silver handles. A large-boned white-haired woman made her way heavily onto the stage and began to slide in and out of the tune of "God Bless America," accompanied by a sullen female teenager at an electric organ keyboard.

Annie looked around for Rafael Rook, who wasn't in the room, despite his claim to be Jack's best and only friend. She looked around for Dan, who'd spent so much time trying to put Jack behind bars, but she didn't see him either. She stared at the little mahogany box with silver handles. Whoever these alleged brothers and sisters of hers were, they had cremated Coach Ronny Buchstabe in a hurry.

She asked herself, if these remains *were* Jack Peregrine's, was she upset that she'd missed her chance to view them before the cremation? No; better not to think that this little box contained that fast-moving man. Better not to see how such vital noise, speed, laughter, could be shrunk to such a small container of gray ash and chips of bone.

Two of the dough-faced males carried a cardboard photograph up onto the stage and placed it on an easel beside the crematory coffin. The photo was a colorized portrait of a big bald male wearing a blue and yellow sweatshirt with the letters SFU on it. He had a whistle around his thick neck. Annie let out a long audible breath. If this was Coach Ronny, he definitely wasn't her father.

After the woman finished "God Bless America" and left the stage, a younger, even bigger woman, in her sixties, with long straight grayish brown hair and puffy eyes, stomped up and asked everyone to clap for the singer, "Daddy's sister Clara Louise, widow of Francis W. McGreb of McGreb and Son—that's Frank, Jr., there on the third row with his family from Cincinnati— Wholesale Plumbing Parts. Aunt Clara's the oldest here by far and came the longest way by far, all the way from Winner, South Dakota, where she and Daddy were raised to be winners!" Everybody clapped except the widowed Mrs. McGreb, who looked put out at being described as "the oldest by far."

The long-haired woman's black shiny dress sported green flowers fluffed out at her waist like sprigs of parsley on a glazed duck. The flowers quivered as, in a voice as flat as her features, she introduced herself. "You all know me, I'm Daddy and Mama's oldest girl, Jimmy Stump's wife, and Jimmy and I are here from St. Pete's, where he's retired. We're sorry our daughter Barbra couldn't make it but it's the Once a Year Sale today at Barbra on the Beach, downtown Sanibel, fine women's casual wear, and her manager called in with a 103 temperature. I'm here the same as you, to honor Ronny Buchstabe. My daddy. Frankie's daddy. Your granddaddy. Your brother. Your friend. The Coach has left the stadium. He's gone from the fields of this life to the fields of a better. He played his last game and it was a hard one. But death, where is thy victory?"

A sob was stifled in the first row. Jackie acknowledged it by pausing. The crier, a stolid and stiffly dressed gray-haired man, blew into his handkerchief. Beside him, the teenaged boy checked his cell phone again. Signaling with a hostile gesture that he should pocket the phone immediately, Jackie opened a spiral notebook and flung over a page. "We all know Coach Ronny was all-American all the way. He preached what he lived and he lived what he preached—hard work and family values."

As the speaker went on, Annie looked inquiringly around the room. She saw nothing on anyone's face to suggest that Jackie's eulogy was being delivered tongue-in-cheek. People were even in tears. That this woman should attribute hard work and family values to Jack Peregrine would mean (were she actually Jack's namesake) that she was a deadpan joker in a league with the world's greatest comics. And frankly such didn't appear to be the case. There was no doubt. The dead man really *was* a man named Coach Ronny Buchstabe. Her father had lied when he said he'd made up the name. The relief she felt surprised her and she started to slide out of the row of seats when she suddenly felt it would be unfeeling to leave in the middle of someone's funeral. She sat back down.

"Daddy loved his God and his country, he loved his children and his grandchildren and his great-grandchildren, and he loved every boy he ever coached at SFU." Mrs. Stump suddenly strode in her huge high heels over to the colorized photo of the man in the sweatshirt and kissed his bald head. "Daddy," she said, "you were the best thing that ever happened to the defensive line at Georgia Tech and the best coach they ever had at Southeast Florida University."

A few of the women tried to clap but it was difficult because of their squirming babies.

"When you retired," Jackie told the photograph, "SFU should have sent you that Northstar Cadillac you always wanted with a giant-size wreath that said, Thank You in letters of gold." Suddenly she slapped shut her notebook and spoke from her heart, a bitter one. "But they didn't. They never gave Coach Ronny the time of day from the day he retired to the day he died. And I'll never forgive them for that. Never. Frankie's girls, the Daughters of Destiny, will now entertain us in this mournful hour." She shuddered, too indignant to say more, and strode off the dais. Three young fat girls clambered up the steps and sang harmonies in a medley of "Amazing Grace" and "I'm a Ramblin' Wreck from Georgia Tech," their grandfather's undergraduate song.

Midway through their performance, to Annie's shock, Jackie suddenly lurched out of her seat, marched as aggressively up the middle aisle as if she were in her father's line-up at SFU. She clopped right over, grabbed and shook Annie by the arms. "You're the slut Daddy married!"

Annie was stunned into a loud protest. "Stop that! No, I'm not!"

On stage, the fat little girls slid to an end in a blended slur of vowels. "Was blind but now I see...a heck of an engineer."

Jackie lost control. "Believe you me, Paisley or Pammy or whatever your name is, I will fight you in court till the day I die and I swear before Almighty God you will never set one foot in my mama's house!"

Annie had pulled her arms away from the woman's strong grip. "I'm sorry! Jackie, I never met your father. I'm at the wrong funeral."

"Ha. You just happen to know my name and show up here. Nice try." Jackie spit the words at her as two big flat-faced men, calling to her sympathetically—"Come on now, sister"—tugged her back up the aisle and shoved her down in her chair.

The male teenager who'd been forced to shut off his cell phone joined the singers on the stage. Tall and pasty, he swayed back and forth for a while then began in a loud aggrieved tone, "My grandpa was a complete A hole. But like hey okay who isn't?"

Annie heard *hsst, hsst!* behind her. It was Rafael Rook at the rear of the room, dressed in lime-green floppy trousers and a yellow shirt with alligators cheerfully dancing on their hind legs. She glared at him then turned back to the stage.

The teenaged Buchstabe, dirty-haired, acne-faced, and with his huge hands clinched at his sides went on to say that his grandfather should never have bothered coaching at SFU and that in fact no one should bother attending any college anywhere in the miasmic swamp of meaninglessness that was "this total shit ass dog crap, like listen up, the fucked up world you fucked up, you assholes!" There was a gasp from the front row. Jackie lurched forward bellowing, "If Daddy was alive, Martin, he would kick your filthy mouth right off of your filthy head!"

"I'm keeping it real here, Aunt Jackie, so fuck you."

Jackie's brothers pulled her back into her chair.

A hand squeezed Annie's shoulder. She looked around, recognizing the cinnamon-colored fingers. Rafael crouched in the row behind her. "It's Rafael Rook," he whispered unnecessarily. "It's okay, Annie, it's okay, really. Your dad's not in that box. It's Coach Ronny Buchstabe." He sighed. "SFU didn't even send him a lousy wreath. People just have lost all sense of gratitude and I consider it a shame." Annie glared furiously at him. "Really," he repeated. "It's not Jack. A mistake."

She whispered in a rage. "I figured that out! You and my father told me he made up the name Ronny Buchstabe! Golden Days sent me here to his funeral!"

"Miss Napp?"

"Yes!"

"Doesn't have a brain in her head. Poor Chamayra, they just fired her. And she has—I regret to say—possibly as a result, expressed the desire never to see me again in this world, or the next. 'There is no following her in this fierce vein.'"

"Where's my dad?"

"We need to talk about that."

One of the young mothers with a big baby turned around. "Shhh!" she said loudly. The teenaged girl had resumed playing a mournful "Amazing Grace" on the electric organ keyboard.

Rook leaned closer to Annie's ear. "Chamayra let your dad, well, borrow Room 540, I guess because the poor old coach had gone to ICU and then I guess the coach all of a sudden, or maybe it wasn't sudden, died. 'Gilded monuments of time, tomorrow and tomorrow and—'"

"Rafael, please!" Too upset to sit still, Annie slipped into the aisle and started up the exit. The Cuban hurried after her.

"Come back here!" Annie turned to see Buchstabes staring reproachfully at her. Jackie was pointing her out to the family, no doubt as the evil young woman who'd stolen Coach Ronny's affections and was planning to grab his estate from the rightful heirs.

Jackie's brothers grabbed her stout arms. Other Buchstabes grabbed the brothers' arms. Bursting out of the middle of this huddle, Jackie ran screaming at Annie, "I want my mama's sterling coffeepot back! *And* her diamond solitaire! I know you took them!"

The teenaged girl on stage stopped playing the keyboard, the singers stopped harmonizing, just stared with their mouths open. The teenaged boy slapped his hands in air. "Keep it real, Jackie! Fuckin' A!"

With a grunting noise Jackie charged down the middle aisle after Annie, her thick Buchstabe hands reaching out in an angry twitch as if to grab her. She was not nearly fast enough.

Chapter 45
The Lady Lies

The wet Florida heat steamed from the asphalt of the parking lot. Feeling nauseated, Annie borrowed Raffy's cell phone. ("I don't want to know where you got this phone!" she told him.) She reached Georgette, who was between patients. "Georgette, you didn't tell Sam that Dad was dead, did you? It's the guy whose name Dad stole, Coach Buchstabe, that's dead."

Georgette made a *phht phht* laughing noise. "No, I didn't tell Sam anything. Frankly I wondered if you were still drunk."

"Drunk? When was I drunk?"

"*Phht phht!*" repeated the young doctor. "Now you don't make any more sense than the rest of us. I love it. Where's your detective, Sergeant Hart?"

"I left him asleep at the hotel."

"Um hmm. Seriously, Annie, you need to come home. Your friend Trevor called. He said you're not answering his messages. He says to stay out of your father's problems. *Cherie, je m'excuse*, but are you involved with Trevor—I hesitate to say 'too' but…too?"

"Trevor?" Annie snorted, which made her teeth hurt in a way she'd never before experienced. She watched Raffy, who'd run back to Rest Eternal and given his arm to Coach Ronny's elderly sister, Clara Louise, widow of McGreb Wholesale Plumbing. It vaguely occurred to Annie that Raffy might be lifting the old woman's wallet out of her large embroidered purse. "Georgette, please, it's 110 here and that's just the humidity. I'm hung over in a parking lot at a cut-rate funeral home in Miami with a criminal Cuban that I was kissing a few days ago and I've got a headache and last night I went windsurfing and had sex with a cop who wants to arrest me."

"Because of the sex? Was it *while* you were windsurfing? Damn, I'm proud of you."

"Georgette, stop, why do you and Clark always have to be funny?"

"We succeed?"

Annie tried not to laugh; it was painful.

Georgette felt she needed to ask one little thing. "Did your dad tell you who your mother was?"

Annie said, "No. He told me he *wouldn't* tell me."

Georgette sighed loudly. "Okay. Now, at the risk of sounding like a therapist, how do you feel about Daniel Hart?"

"Oh, come on."

"Just blurt it out. The truth. Whatever comes to mind."

Annie looked at the braid on her military jacket cuff, at the asphalt, at the sky, at the cheerful alligators on Rafael Rook's shirt off in the distance as he chatted with Mrs. McGreb. All right, she told Georgette. The truth? The truth was that last night she'd had the best conversation, the most fun, the greatest sex, the easiest time with a man in her adult life. And it terrified her. The truth? Loving and being loved was scarier than landing a jet plane on a rolling ship. But if you did it right, how wonderful. She was unable to stop thinking of Dan Hart even now, in midst of, frankly, chaos.

Georgette was silent a moment. Finally she said, "Chaos is good. For you, it's good." She added, "What about Brad?"

Unconsciously, Annie looked around the parking lot as if Georgette might be going to warn her that Brad was in it somewhere. All she saw was Jackie Stump pulling her elderly aunt away from Raffy and shoving the old woman into the long white limousine. Annie repeated, "What about Brad?"

"Just a second…" Georgette put Annie on hold. "Sorry, apparently I've got a patient naked in the cafeteria. Brad, your husband, who's looking for you all over Miami."

"Why does everyone keep calling Brad my husband?"

"Isn't he?"

Annie just wanted to point out that her life was none of Brad's business.

"Um hmm. So where *is* Brad this morning?"

Annie assumed that he was still asleep at the Dorado.

"Brad and Dan both. Um hmm."

"Georgette, please stop saying *um hmm*."

"That's what psychiatrists say. It takes a lot of training not to say anything more than *um hmm*." Georgette took another call; a patient with agoraphobia was going to be late again because it was so hard for him to leave his house. "Annie, *à bientot*. Please lock yourself in your room and get some rest. For God's sake, you're having sex with a stranger on a windsurfer. Don't cops have partners? Maybe I could fly down tonight and meet him."

It was Annie's impression that Dan had had a partner before he'd gotten fired but she really didn't know that much about him.

Georgette suggested wryly that she shouldn't bother learning at this point. "It's too late to start getting to know somebody after you're already in love with him. Just go with the flow."

Annie gave her puff of disgust. "I'm not in love. You think I'm in love?"

It certainly sounded that way to Georgette.

"You're right," Annie suddenly admitted. "I don't even know him and I want to spend the rest of my life with him."

"That's what I call going with the flow! Okay, I've got to see about this naked patient. But did you happen to find out from your dad if that woman who looked like my aunt Ruthie *was* my aunt Ruthie?"

"No, that was just a stupid idea of mine." Annie explained that she'd learned from Rafael Rook that the woman she'd seen at Golden Days was named Helen Clark and she was the mistress of a Miami racketeer. Thinking she could be Ruthie Nickerson had been a crazy idea. It was just an odd resemblance. "Why, did you find out something else about Ruthie?"

"No, nothing. *A tout a l'heure.*" Georgette felt very guilty for not telling Annie what she'd learned from Sam. But she'd decided she should honor Sam's wish that she wait until Annie herself brought up the subject of Ruthie's being her mother. On the other hand, obviously Jack had told his daughter nothing about Ruthie, because no matter how bad Annie's hangover or how alluring Sgt. Daniel Hart, if she had had any idea that her best friend's aunt might be her mother, she would have mentioned the fact. On the other hand, surely Annie should be able to count on her best friend to tell her what Sam had said. On the other hand…

• • •

In the parking lot, Raffy glided up to Annie. "I apologize," he murmured.

"I could have killed you," she admitted, handing him back the phone. "I just went through thinking my dad was dead and turns out he's fine."

Raffy's dark eyes flickered away from her. "Annie, 'fine' could be a stretch in regards to Jack. I don't know what it is lately about his personal karma, because when I met him, he was A Man Loved by the Gods, but these days…?"

Grabbing his chin, Annie shook it. "Just nod at me. Is Jack still hiding out at Golden Days?"

Rook used his free hand to hitch up his trousers. "No. Annie, here's the thing. He's gone."

She jerked the small man to her so hard he wobbled. "Don't tell me he *is* dead because I don't believe it."

Rook frantically waved his hands. "Ms. Skippings found out Jack was there and that's when she fired Chamayra."

"Skippings threw my dad out?"

"In a sense. He left in her car."

"Chamayra's car?"

"Ms. Skippings's. Could you quit that for a second?" Annie let go of him; she felt awful.

He caught her as she stumbled, off-balance. "You look green."

"It's the heat. I think I'm going to throw up."

Hurrying her across the parking lot into the log cabin restaurant, Good Mornin', he rushed to a restroom on whose door was painted a picture of Betty Grable in a bathing suit.

Ten minutes later, he led Annie gently to a rustic pine table beside a window that squinted grimily at Rest Eternal. "Drink this tomato juice. Take these." He held out aspirin. "You've been through a lot."

"More than you know," muttered Annie as she swallowed the pills. Something in his look made her blush and she added, "At least I was hoping it was more than you know."

"You and Daniel Hart, who could predict it? 'Clubs could not part them.'" He confessed that last night he had seen her, soaking wet, arm in arm with Hart, going up into the hotel elevator and not coming down. He had seen this from the Dorado bar where he'd been waiting for her, while keeping a watch over Brad Hopper, who was also in the bar.

Annie dropped her head into her hands. "Brad was in the bar? Great."

The slender man nudged the coffee cup at her. "Forgive my bluntness. If you're worried that your husband saw you kissing Sergeant Hart, he missed it completely."

Annie looked out at him through her fingers. "We're getting divorced."

"In my opinion, all things considered, a wise plan." Raffy tapped pepper into his tomato juice.

The coffee, which Annie tried to drink, was both too hot and too weak. "I can't think about that now. Where did Dad go?"

"Poor Jack." He spoke with sympathy. "'There is a tide in the affairs of men' and your papa took it. When the bastard Miami police showed up at Golden Days with—my best guess from their shoes—FBI agents, Jack stole an SUV from the parking lot. Which—it must be admitted—turned out to be Ms. Skippings's Lexus."

"He stole Skippings's car?" She laughed but quickly stopped because of the pain when her scalp moved. "So, where'd he go?"

Surprisingly, Raffy seized her hands. "Annie, I heard on the radio coming here—but, as we know, there's no reason to believe the press." After a pause, he hurried ahead. "They found her Lexus in the bay. But there could be many explanations—"

She pulled her hands away.

Raffy dropped his eyes to his coffee, shaking the mug as if he were reading his fortune in it. "The car went off the causeway, through the crossrail, and they found it on the bottom of the bay. They sent out divers."

Sun splintering through the dirty window blinded her. "Was he in the car?"

The Cuban vigorously shook his head. "No, no, no, no, no. And its windows were open. But his jacket was caught in the front seat, with his wallet in it. His driver's license. Jack Peregrine, West Palm Beach."

Slowly, Annie thought about this. "A driver's license in his real name?"

Raffy sucked wistfully at his coffee. "The cops think he tried to swim to the surface but didn't make it. It's not easy water."

She thought further, motionless.

Raffy gently reminded her that her father wasn't at all well. "Prison wasn't for such a man. Take it from me. He would rather be dead."

Annie sat up firmly. "He's alive. It's a con. He planted the coat and wallet. He sank the car as a decoy."

Raffy searched her eyes. "You think so? I mean, I know you hope it but do you think it?"

She nodded. "I think it."

The Cuban raised his eyes for a long moment as if his imprisoned past were painted in the ceiling and he wanted to study it. "Late at night in our cell, Jack used to tell me stories of the great stings. Like Ponzi. 'A con's a work of art,' he'd say. 'If it's not,' he'd say, 'you might as well stick a .45 in a man's back and steal his wallet.'" Raffy's thin shoulders lifted his yellow rayon shirt in an apologetic shrug. "In regards to which, your papa did steal Miss Napp's wallet…Well, he took her whole purse. Which Miss Napp claims had three hundred dollars in it, but that's a *shvindel*, in my humble opinion."

Annie asked him why, if her father was so *successful* a con artist, was he so hard-pressed for cash that he had to steal the purse of the receptionist in a cheap convalescent center and flee in another woman's car? Why did he live so constantly in danger of the thing he said he hated most—imprisonment?

The small man pointed both forefingers at her like pistols. "I never said Jack was 'successful.' Because there were times when to be honest I didn't think he was necessarily thinking things through. What I said was, and this is as true as truth," Raffy brought the two pistols together and kissed the tips, "he was pretty gorgeous…I mean, artistically speaking."

For a while they sat in the noisy restaurant, both thinking about Jack Peregrine. It had never occurred to her before—the way things don't occur to children about their parents—that her father had style but he didn't really have brains. She laughed at the realization. In fact, he'd been lucky that he'd survived all these years. After all, she'd had to come to his rescue when she was only five and six and seven years old.

She asked Raffy where he thought her father might have gone into hiding after ditching the Lexus SUV in the bay.

The Cuban bit at his soft lips. "I don't know. He always tells me, don't worry, Raffy, *mi amigo*, I'll be in touch, *vaya con dias*. If he's alive, he'll get the word to us, that I know. Meanwhile, I am myself a wanted man—"

She interrupted. "I'll talk to Dan Hart and see what he can do for you."

"Oh Annie, Annie. 'Therefore is wingéd Cupid painted blind.'" Raffy dramatically strummed an imaginary guitar. "That's the wisdom of the Swan. Love is blinding you from the fact of the matter. Which is this above all: Never trust a policeman! If there's one thing I learned from the street, because I never had the opportunity for a college education, it's the son-of-a-bitch cops will say anything to close a case and the Miami police, in particular Miami Vice, well, they are not sincere individuals."

The mournful sweetness of Raffy's dark eyes as he offered this warning about Daniel Hart rattled her. What did she really know about the man she'd just slept with? What if Hart had been using her, making a fool of her? As doubt rushed like heat through her body, she felt sick.

"Eat something." The Cuban slid a plate of toast closer. "But I'll be honest. I didn't care for your husband either."

"We'll be divorced in a week." She squeezed her neck. "No. I promised him I'd wait a month."

He asked her why she'd done that.

She rotated her neck side to side. "So Brad would lend me the plane to get to Miami to see Dad."

Raffy smiled at her. "Ah, I told you, didn't I tell you? With *familia*, you cannot take it or leave it. Not if you're human, which you definitely are." He poured milk in his coffee but it didn't seem to help the taste. "Last night at the Dorado bar, your husband gave a one-dollar tip to my cousin Juan at the piano, a man with a large family to support, one dollar. As the Bard tells us, nothing can come of nothing. Not to mention he left the place with Skippings, pardon me, forgive me, but what a *balabuster*. She always treated Chamayra like gum on her shoe—"

Annie rubbed her fingers at her temples. "Wait a minute. Back up. Did you say Brad left with Melissa Skippings?"

Rafael nodded vigorously. "Yes! *La puta* who fired my Chamayra from Golden Days. But I have to be honest, it could be your husband was only waiting with her for valet parking."

"I doubt it." Annie burst out laughing, which hurt. "Melissa Skippings. Did you know this? She was married to Dan. I'm serious. They're divorced."

"Skippings and Hart, you're making a joke!" The news stunned him. "Wait'll I tell Chamayra, if she'll stop hanging up on me. All the world's a stage, Annie, or possibly more precisely, cable television. Coffee?"

She was struck once more by how oddly restful it was, talking with Rafael Rook, despite her horrible headache. With a comforting pat of her arm, he offered her more aspirin. "What with all the whips and scorns and fardels of life, even the extra-large bottle of Tylenol from Costco is insufficient. Such a world we live in. Such a world. Grandpapa Simon Rook died for what he thought was America but it turned out to be only the same old bowties and wingtips piling their fortunes on our backs."

Annie tried to finish the piece of toast but she wasn't hungry. She had faith that her father had sunk Skippings's SUV without drowning in it. But where was he now and how would he reach them? What should they do to help him?

Pouring salsa on his scrambled eggs, Raffy danced his fork above his plate. "Look at it this way: That your papa ditched her Lexus is infinitely superior to the alternatives."

"True." She sipped slowly at her tomato juice.

"But *zindik nit*, we have to look at all rational possibilities. It's possible he was shuffled off. It's possible Diaz grabbed him and wants to trade him. Jack's enemies," sadly suggested the Cuban, "the rotten bastard sons of bitches, if you ask me how much of the milk of human kindness is in them? Not this much." He held up the heavy brown mug of coffee. "But it's also possible, and let's believe it, he just swam away."

A memory came to Annie. "I used to dunk him in the pools. At the motels where we stayed. He always said he would never drown. I didn't know this at the time, it had to do with his brother Johnny dying in the family pool. Dad said it wasn't possible to drown him. He said he could float for a hundred years."

"Like Mark Antony, dolphinlike."

They sat a while longer.

Raffy sipped his coffee, nodding in thought. "Okay, here is my plan. You go to the bank in Cuba and get the jewels with the passwords. We put the jewels back in the Queen and we trade the Queen to Diaz for your papa's debt." He looked at her sadly.

"Or maybe we trade the Queen to Diaz for your papa himself if that s.o.b. has got him for ransom."

"But if Diaz had Dad, wouldn't he call you or—"

Suddenly Raffy saw something behind her. Whatever it was made him fling loudly out of his chair, flipping it over. He ran, stumbling past crowded tables, weaving around waitresses as he headed for the kitchen doors. There he collided with an enormous bald waiter with a walrus moustache. With surprising dexterity, the waiter swung a large tray of fried eggs and hash browns out of Raffy's path. Raffy slid between the kitchen doors.

Looking around for the cause of the Cuban's abrupt flight, Annie spotted Dan Hart as he moved toward her through the crowded restaurant.

Chapter 46

The Bride Came C.O.D.

The detective made his way through the tables of noisy breakfasters. Maybe it was the blue of his cotton shirt that made Annie feel as if a wave were about to roll over her. When he took off his sunglasses, his eyes added more blue. Reaching her table, he stopped and shook his head in reproach. "You couldn't wake me up?"

"No," she told him. "Nobody could. How'd you find me?"

"Got your messages. Saw your rental car out there." He pointed toward the window with a steel courier case he held. It was the case she'd hidden under her bed when she left. "So, do you know your dad wasn't Coach Ronny Buchstabe?" he asked her. "Coach Ronny was eighty-six and married a hooker in her twenties and had a heart attack."

She was hoping he hadn't seen Raffy. "Ah. Yes. Thanks."

Dan swung the case in the direction of the kitchen doors. "Rafael Rook had another appointment all of a sudden?"

She shaded her eyes from the sun that was glinting in the big window behind him. "Rook? That was just some man hitting on me."

He righted the knocked-over chair and picked up the broken coffee mug. "Looks like you had a strong reaction." Sitting across from her, he placed the case on the seat beside him. "You're actually a pretty convincing liar. But Rafael Rook is peeking out of the kitchen doors at us right now."

She glanced behind her, and in fact Raffy was undeniably standing with his head stuck out of the doors. She said, "Hey, come on, give that poor guy a break, Dan. I told him you'd intercede for him. He just wants to help out my dad."

"Everybody just wants to help out your dad. You included. Well, I'm officially off the case." Dan blew a flamboyant good-bye kiss in Rook's direction. "So vaya con dios, Rook."

She rubbed at her temples. "Thank you."

"You're welcome. You look like you're seriously hung-over."

She nodded. "I said I wasn't much of a drinker."

He looked solemn. "Annie, there's something I've got to tell you." Her heart sped: what if he were going to say that their being together last night had been a terrible mistake? Instead he reached for her hand and kissed her fingers. Relieved and preoccupied with the feel of his lips on her fingers, she nodded. "One. You know your dad stole a car from Golden Days?"

She shrugged in an uncommitted way.

"Also." He pulled a police bulletin printout from the pocket of his jeans. "My partner just took this off the MPD feed." The gist of the police wire was that a stolen vehicle, a 2000 Lexus SUV, had been recovered from Biscayne Bay after crashing through a guardrail on the causeway. Inside the car were certain personal effects. There was no body in the car but fingerprints on the steering wheel had identified the driver as John Ingersoll Peregrine, who was currently wanted for questioning in three states, including Florida. He was presumed drowned. "You don't look surprised," Dan added.

Annie asked if the effects included her father's wallet. After glancing through a two-page document, Dan said yes, the wallet was there with Peregrine's driver license in it. She asked what the wallet looked like. The description didn't resemble the wallet her father had shown her in the hospital. "Were there old photos of me in it? Baby pictures?"

He checked the list. "Nope. No photos in there."

Annie smiled. "Then he planted the wallet and he's not dead." Odd how sure she was that he would always keep those pictures of her in his wallet.

"But there were a couple of IDs. Plus $280 in cash." Dan handed her the report.

Looking over the list, she let her eyebrow arch. "You think my dad had generic IDs in his own name? No way."

Rubbing his unshaved cheek, Dan studied her face. "You're saying he dumped the Lexus and swam off? The thought did occur to me." Grinning, he ran his fingers through his curls. "I sure hope Melissa kept up her car insurance. It was her Lexus."

Annie laughed. "I heard that rumor."

He set the metal case on the table between them. "Okay. This morning I wake up with your dog but you're nowhere to be found. So I'm taking a shower and I hear the dog bark. There's no one in the room when I get there but the door's wide open. I see this metal case lying in the middle of the floor."

"In the middle of the floor?" Her first thought was that Rafael Rook had robbed her before showing up at Rest Eternal.

"So now you're surprised." He swiveled the case onto the tabletop. "Is this where you kept *La Reina Coronada?*"

Annie spun the combination to 2506 and popped open the latches. The Queen of the Sea was no longer inside. In its place, there was a note in printed capitals on Dorado stationery that said "IOU $1,000,000."

Annie slapped the lid shut. "Goddamn it. My dad took the Queen."

Dan looked at her with skepticism. "You and your dad and Rafael Rook—who just peeked out of the kitchen again—you're in this whole scam together, aren't you? You're pulling a sting?"

She laughed. "On whom?"

"On me, for one. Don't con me."

She raised her eyebrow. "Ditto."

Dan waved for a waitress. "I'm starving." He took a piece of Annie's toast, which he ate with a grimace. "Cardboard. Also, did you know your husband checked into the Hotel Dorado last night and was there looking for you at one in the morning?"

She asked who'd told him that.

"Juan Ramirez. Relative of Rook's. He's the piano player in the bar."

"That man should have his own talk show." She felt her neck flush. "Did 'Juan' tell you Brad was in there hitting on your ex-wife?"

"Melissa would hit on a mannequin if he wore nice enough clothes. I guess your husband would too." Dan opened his arms in a comic gesture. "God's speed and God bless."

"Please stop calling him my husband," Annie sighed, rubbing her head. She was thinking that she'd been an idiot to promise Brad not to sign any divorce papers for a month; she didn't want to have to admit to Dan that she'd done so. "I've really got a hangover."

"That's no excuse. If you're not divorced, you're married." He chewed on a piece of bacon from her plate. "If they told you this was bacon, they lied. Me, I'm officially legally divorced. Trust me, Annie, you've got to pull the trigger." He tasted her scrambled eggs and made a face.

When their waitress paused at their table with a pot of stale coffee, Dan asked her if their eggs came from chickens.

She was too tired to joke. "Yeah, probably."

"Go find out where the chickens came from."

"Wise guy."

Dan pointed out the window. "Uh oh. There goes your friend Rafael. Looks like the Feds are picking him up."

Annie stood to look outside. A stolid man wearing a tropical shirt was strong-arming the disconsolate Rafael Rook through the steamy-hot asphalt parking lot while a thin man in a straw porkpie hat trotted ahead to open the side door of a white van. Dan pulled her back to her chair.

She resisted him. "I want to tell Raffy I'll get him a lawyer."

"Yeah, looks like he'll need one. Don't worry. I'll call somebody. He's safer with the FBI than with Diaz picking him up. You should know, the Feds want me to bring you in too."

"I don't think so." She watched as the FBI men placidly lowered Rafael's head into the van. His hair worked loose from his glossy black ponytail when he struggled against them. The agent in the straw hat walked over to the restaurant, tapped on the window, and gestured at Dan to come outside.

A frown narrowed Dan's eyes. It was like a fast cloud hurrying over the sky, graying the blue for an instant. "That's the agent that grilled me about your dad. If I'm not back in ten minutes, call this number. My partner." He pulled a card from his wallet. "Okay, now I need you to put on a show. Right now."

She looked at him suspiciously.

Dan turned his back to the window. "It's for your dad. I want you to act as if I'd just made you really really angry. I mean it. Slap me."

Immediately she slapped him hard in the face.

He rubbed his bright-red cheek. "Damn, you're fast."

"Don't ask for things you don't want." She raised her hand again.

He grabbed her wrist. "I'll remember that. Now wait here. Trust me." He hurried outside. "We'll get you out of this."

"Out of what?"

As she watched from the window, Dan approached the FBI agent, listened to him talk for a few minutes, then walked with him to the van and vanished inside its side door.

Ten minutes later, Annie lost patience and hurried from the log-cabin restaurant; she was crossing the parking lot toward the van when Dan hopped out of it and grabbed her by the arm, leading her away. "Hang on. I worked something out. You're going to Key West for questioning."

Annie was taken aback. "I'm not about to go to Key West!"

"This isn't an invitation you can RSVP. If you don't believe me, get in touch with your Commander Campbell in Annapolis. FBI's already talked to him." Reaching his vintage Thunderbird, he tilted his head in the direction of the white van. "Okay, keep acting. Righteous indignation. Look unhappy."

"This is not an act." She shoved hard at his chest. Old angers surged in her. "Are you lying to me? Raffy told me not to trust you!"

Dan caught her hand, holding it tight against him. She could feel his heart. They stood that way for a minute, hearing their own breath.

He looked at her fiercely. "I mean this, trust me. I just heard something from my partner. Somebody in MPD spotted your dad about an hour ago. You want him back?"

Annie stared at him, then at the van. "He got away from them?"

"Yes, but that's not going to last. They are real serious." Dan touched her shoulder softly. "And he's not well, Annie. My partner heard on the street your dad's seriously sick." Did she want to make it possible for her father not to spend the last months of his life in prison? If so, she had to trust Dan. Did she believe him?

There was nothing to go on, thought Annie, except his eyes. Clarity, careful thinking, wise decisions—these were the habits of her life. But, somehow deeper than any thought she could fashion was the beat against her palm of his heart.

Near them, a thin teenaged boy was loudly and dexterously shoving shopping carts into a silver chain. Racing them into motion, he stepped gracefully onto the back of the last cart and rode the clattering train he'd created across the asphalt, passing the white van when it pulled out of its parking spot. The boy's leg stretched out behind him like the god Mercury, flying faster and faster.

"Yes." Annie nodded. "Help me."

Dan grabbed her arms. "Okay. Here we go. I said I'd bring you in. So let's do it. Make it look like you're arguing. Fight me. But for Christ's sake, don't slug me again!"

She let him push her into his truck just as the van drove slowly past them. She saw, in the passenger seat window, a flash of Raffy's sorrowful face.

• • •

Chamayra was waiting for them in the Dorado lobby, where her tight shiny orange Capri pants and turquoise La Loca

T-shirt was in noticeable contrast to the loose taupe linens of the hotel guests.

"This is all your fault," she shouted as they walked toward her. It was hard to know whether the accusation was at Annie or at Daniel or both. "Golden Days was my best shot at not dying a waitress and now I'm out on my ass. So gracias! Plus I lose the first man I met this year not a fuckin' druggie beating up on Wife Number Four!" Chamayra did a rapid dance of rage. "So you get Raffy out of Dade County jail pronto pronto pronto!" She had begun at so intense a pitch that she had no place to go but the physical, which is where she went, jabbing Dan in the collar bone with her short strong fingers.

Snatching her hands out of the air, he pulled them together and to her shock kissed them. The surprise calmed her. "Baby," he told the quivering woman, "you take a deep breath. I didn't put Rook in jail and I can't get him out. My ass is as fired as yours. But I will *try* to get him out, if you'll just have a little faith. I will *try*." He pointed over at Annie. "Meanwhile, what about her?"

Chamayra glared. "What about her? Her daddy stole that Lexus and got me fired. And why didn't you tell me Ms. Skippings was the Melissa you've been bitchin' about for two years?"

He put his arm around Annie. "Annie just heard her dad went off the causeway into the bay in Melissa's car."

She gasped. "Shit, I saw something about that on the news! I didn't know it was Raffy's Jack."

"Well, I don't hear any sympathy. Come on, Chamayra, where's the Love sign? First things first."

The young Latina woman gave a great shuttering sigh that shook her short frame. Reaching out, she hugged Annie brusquely. "He's right! Danny, you're right. I'm out of line. Anybody's daddy checks out like that, it's primo."

Annie felt the woman's embrace, her short sturdy arms pressing against her and she realized in that moment curiously enough that she'd never before let herself feel the physical presence of other people when they touched her—to shake her hand, to kiss her cheek, to rub her shoulder. Now she let herself actually feel Chamayra's sympathy. It was as true as thought. "Thank you but I don't think my dad was in the car," she told her. "I think it's all a con."

"What else you gonna think?" the waitress said kindly. "Can I do something?"

Annie impulsively hugged her back. "Could you possibly keep my dog Malpy till tomorrow night?"

Without hesitation, Chamayra said, "Sure." She held out her hands at different distances. "How big's this dog?"

"Little," Dan assured her. "Cute. Friendly. Wait right here. We'll be right back with him." He explained that Annie had been ordered to appear at the naval base in Key West and Dan was going to drive her there.

"If they're sending you to Kuwait? Tell 'em no fuckin' way. What did I say to my brother Luis?" asked the waitress. Angrily she crossed her arms, lifting her breasts. "I go, 'Luis, don't enlist!' Now he's got one leg." She followed them to the elevator. "And Danny, soon as you find Raffy, you gonna call me, right? You got my number."

"I'm gonna call you."

"You call me."

"I'll call you."

When Annie thanked her profusely, Chamayra made her imaginary Love sign in the air.

• • •

In the hotel room, Annie quickly packed, while Dan spoke with his former partner at the police department. The Peregrine case, the detective told him, had not only been taken over by the Federal Bureau of Investigation, other government agencies were also involved now, for unknown reasons. Rafael Rook was at this moment being transferred out of Miami to Sigsbee Naval Base in Key West. Meanwhile, the partner said, word was there was a mob contract out on Rook. That Feliz Diaz's people had offered fifteen thousand dollars cash for Rook's right hand, so no doubt the musician's leaving Miami was a good thing.

As for Jack Peregrine's whereabouts, some people in MPD seemed to believe that the con man had really drowned while trying to escape from the submerged Lexus SUV. But Dan's partner had confirmed the rumor that a cop had spotted Peregrine today at a bus station. By the time this officer had called in the ID, Peregrine had given her the slip.

"His specialty," said Annie.

"Soon as the FBI hears he was spotted, there'll be a mega-search."

There was a sharp rapping on the hotel room door. Holding Malpy, Dan motioned for her to keep quiet. After a check through the peephole, he yanked the door open.

Brad Hopper stood in the hallway, carrying a soft leather briefcase with the Hopper Jet logo on it. Shocked to see not Annie but Daniel Hart standing there, Brad made a series of faces, widening his mouth, squeezing his eyelids, apparently unable to assimilate the coincidence that the anonymous, annoying businessman whom he'd flown in his jet on the Fourth of July from Emerald's Destin Airworks to St. Louis was the same man who was now standing in the doorway of his wife's Miami hotel room.

Eventually Brad stopped trying to make sense of the disjunction and simply shouldered his way into the room. "What's up, A? I've been looking all over hell and—" Thought caught up with him. "What the fuck is this guy doing in your room?"

"Brad, calm down."

Malpy flew out of Dan's arms at Brad, snarling madly.

"Get that dog away from me!"

Annie scooped up the Maltese, grabbing his muzzle. "Malpy, be quiet!"

Brad pointed a rigid arm first at Dan, then at the young woman he still thought of as legally his. "You know who this is? This is that businessman your bud D. K. made me give a ride to, back on the Fourth, the guy I flew from Emerald to St. Louis!"

Annie zipped up her packed suitcase. "Yes, I know that. Brad, I am really sorry but I can't explain it all now, there's no time. I should have called you but things are crazy, my dad's disappeared again—"

"On the local news they're saying your dad's dead! I've been worried sick about you."

"Don't believe the news." She gestured at Dan. "This man's a police officer. I tried to tell you not to come to Miami, Brad. I tried to—" She stopped talking, since nothing made much sense even to her. She came to the abrupt decision that she would simply tell Brad the truth about Dan. And that decision stopped her cold because she had to ask herself what the truth was. Bizarrely enough, what popped into her mind was the line that Claudette Colbert said near the end of *It Happened One Night* when she was about to marry a man she didn't even like and her father asked her to tell him about the Clark Gable character, the one she'd ridden with on the bus all the way from Miami. And Claudette had told her father, "I don't know very much about him…Except that I love him."

Annie recalled how earlier (was it today?) she'd said something similar to Georgette about Daniel Hart. "I don't even know him and I want to spend the rest of my life with him." What an astonishing thing that a line from a movie, and such a ridiculous line, should feel like the right answer to so much. "I love him," she blurted out. Then speechless, she looked over at Dan.

"Love who?" Red-faced, Brad set down his briefcase. "A, what's going on here? What are you talking about?"

Annie looked to Dan for help.

With a frown, he slid out his wallet, flipping it open to show a large police badge. "Mr. Hopper," he began in a professional tone. "I'm with Miami Vice. Sorry about the undercover thing but I had three warrants for major felonies on Jack Peregrine and I had a tip his daughter was meeting him in St. Louis." Dan pulled steel handcuffs from the back of his jeans. "Lt. Goode here is under arrest for aiding and abetting in the escape of a wanted criminal." He shook his head solemnly at Annie. "Love's no excuse for crime. She's implicated in Peregrine's felonies, including—just today—grand larceny and international fraud. Possible spying. That makes it treason."

Brad's mouth dropped. "Treason?"

Dan shook the cuffs. "Could be. But Lt. Goode claims that you're actually the one who sneaked her father out of St. Louis. Is that true? Because harboring a felon's a felony. 'Course, it's your constitutional right not to answer."

With a queasy nervous smile, Brad glanced from Annie to Hart and back to Annie. Then, with his eyes blinking rapidly, he swore to the Miami detective that he had never been involved in any act that might even remotely have aided or abetted Jack Peregrine.

Dan asked if Brad was accusing Annie of lying.

With a reproachful look at his not yet ex-wife, Brad advised her to cooperate with the police.

Annie picked up Brad's briefcase, shoved it at his midriff. "Will you just get out of here?"

"A, come on. If I went to jail, it could kill Mama Spring," he whispered.

"That bitch will outlive us all," Annie predicted.

Brad's face puckered. "Don't start."

"Brad, the extra month I promised you? You can forget it. We're signing those divorce papers." He looked caught between anger and a puzzled relief. She added, "I'll be in jail in a month anyhow. And I hope you go too."

Dan clicked the handcuffs on her. "I wouldn't be surprised. But Hopper here could cut a deal. 'Course he can't testify against you if you two are still married."

Brad was indignant. "I'd never testify against Annie."

"Can I cut a deal, testify against him?" Annie asked.

Brad's eyes darted everywhere, looking for an angle. He turned a solemn look on Annie. "Let's don't get personal."

She scoffed. "Don't get personal? We're married."

"Well, maybe you're right, we shouldn't wait a month." In fact, Brad said, he wasn't going to argue with Annie anymore about proceeding with the divorce. He'd sign right away. He did have to think about his responsibilities to his family and to Hopper Jets. He did have to consider the firm's reputation and—

Annie interrupted him. "Oh Brad, just shut the fuck up."

"I don't like to hear you talk that way," said the handsome pilot.

Dan laughed. "Okay, Lt. Goode, let's go. We got some cellmates waiting for you—some wino hookers, four or five skinhead bull dykes, half a dozen paranoid crackheads, you know, the regulars. Don't leave town, Hopper."

Brad's eyes squeezed shut as if he hoped to make everything go away.

At Annie's handclap, Malpy jumped into her arms. Dan picked up her duffel bag and led her out of the room.

"Annie, want me to call you a lawyer?" the handsome head of Hopper Jets shouted down the hall.

She turned back and waved good-bye. "No thanks, Brad. Just go home."

"Okay, take it easy, Annie. Want me to call Sam?"

"Just go home."

Chapter 47

Practically Yours

It was a long trip south down through the keys on US 1. Passengers in other cars waved happily at the pale green 1957 Thunderbird coupe with its white top and whitewalls. The car, said Dan, probably looked to them like some old lost innocent dream of American freedom. Dan and Annie crossed bridge after bridge, heading toward Naval Air Station, Key West, at Sigsbee Park, where they would meet at JITAF EAST (the Joint InterAgency Task Force East) with agents and officers involved in "the Peregrine matter."

From Key West, the southernmost tip of Florida, Jack Peregrine had been illegally flying in and out of Cuba in his Cessna Amphibian for years. While allegedly on "fishing trips" in the waters off the key, he had actually been smuggling goods into the country for Miami businessmen expatriated from the island. Dan's investigation had never been able to prove exactly what the goods were: propaganda material, laundered money, weapons, drugs. Possibly Jack had also been smuggling on his own into the U.S.—maybe illegal immigrants, maybe artifacts like the Queen of the Sea herself. Dan wasn't sure. He'd been focused not on Jack's smuggling but his fraud scams.

Now Cuba (represented by officials at Museo Habana in Plaza de la Revolución) was claiming that Jack had stolen their sixteenth-century statue of the Virgin Mary. While they did not appear to have known about the relic until Feliz Diaz announced he was giving it to a cathedral in Miami, they had immediately insisted that because five hundred years ago *La Reina* had sunk in Cuba's territorial waters it was therefore legally a national antiquity; to keep it would be diplomatic trouble. The FBI was in charge of getting it back for them.

Driving to Key West, Dan and Annie practiced what Annie would say in her "interview" with FBI and NAS officials at the Sigsbee meeting this evening. They also talked about their past marriages and their childhoods and their likes and dislikes. They had no trouble finding worlds to talk about.

In Islamorada, Dan suggested that Annie, exhausted, might want to nap. She insisted she wasn't tired but her eyes kept shutting, the long curve of lash closing over blue. Finally she nodded against his shoulder. Later, drifting awake, she listened to him singing along with Sarah Vaughan. "What a difference a day makes. Twenty-four little hours."

"You're a terrible singer," she mumbled drowsily.

"Awful," he agreed. "But you can't stop enjoying things just because you're bad at them."

It was a surprising point of view for Annie, who had always believed you had to be first or right or best or why bother. But then everything felt like a surprise to her now, including the realization that she'd been so often wrong. Riding in this car half-asleep, hearing the whir of the wheels, soft jazz on the radio, it all felt so surprising and yet so easy; it all felt comfortable enough for her to drift in and out of sleep, just as if she were home in Emerald. "Is everything okay?" she asked Dan.

"Fine," he promised.

She'd certainly been wrong to so dislike him, and not that long ago either, just like…like, she yawned, like Claudette Colbert in…

The car hummed over miles of bridge, island to island.

The next thing Annie knew, she was staring up at gold in the afternoon sun. Dan was ending a phone call. He pointed as they passed a sign for Key West. She stretched, yawning, feeling curiously rested. "We're in Key West? I never go to sleep like that," she said. "Are we driving straight to Sigsbee?"

"No, they just postponed. We don't meet them till 7 a.m., tomorrow."

"I thought it was urgent, that we had to be there tonight."

Dan lifted his hips to slip the phone back in his jeans pocket. "Don't ask the Feds to explain themselves. They're flying somebody named McAllister Fierson in from the State Department and he'll be there in the morning. Whatever they ask you, just keep saying you don't know a thing. We'll get you out of this and your dad too, if they ever catch him." Reassuring, he moved his hand against her cheek. "It'll be fine. I think this whole thing is about smoothing Cuba's feathers over a stolen statue before anybody gets embarrassed. Two weeks ago the FBI was negotiating with state prosecutors about your dad. Now they're just pissed he got away from them."

She smiled. "I know the feeling."

"Rafael Rook's already in Sigsbee, spilling his guts."

Instinctively she tensed. "I thought you said your lawyer friend could get Raffy out on bail?"

Dan took the Key West exit. "They wouldn't have brought him to Sigsbee from Dade County if they hadn't needed him to tell them stuff. Raffy knows how to cut his own deal. But for insurance, whatever favor they want from you, you make them ease up not just on your dad but on Rook. All they want's the Queen."

The problem was, she no longer had it. Her father had stolen it out of her hotel room and left her a million dollar IOU in its place. If he was alive, he was halfway around the world with the relic by now, having outsmarted the police and Feliz Diaz and God knows who else. She grinned. "Well, at least it was your ex-wife's SUV Dad sank."

"Melissa's car was a real gas guzzler. Serves her right."

Annie gestured out the windshield. "Are you kidding? What do you get to the gallon? This Thunderbird's got a McCulloch supercharged V8 in it. You could hit 125."

He laughed. "How do you know that?"

"I looked under the hood. That engine has speed."

He kissed her fingers. "I bought this Bird for its looks, the grille, and the tailfins. I don't want fast, I want beautiful. But, hey." He smiled at her. "I'll take both."

As they headed into Key West's Old Town, Dan got another phone call. His chief at MPD was officially reinstating him. The paperwork was already in the chute. The chief also wanted in on Dan's involvement in the Jack Peregrine case. Dan told him one sure thing was that the con man's daughter Annie knew absolutely nothing of her father's crimes.

"Not really true," Annie admitted after he'd hung up. "I've always known Dad was a crook."

Dan shrugged. "The Vapor didn't believe me anyhow."

They agreed, and she leaned to rest her hand on his leg, that they would need to stay in a hotel tonight, since they weren't wanted at Sigsbee base until morning.

They drove past the harbor of tall ships and through blocks of pastel Victorian B&Bs and converted bungalows that had once been the homes of Cuban cigar workers. Dan was looking for Duval Street. "There's a '20s place I always wanted to go. Casa Marina. Are you hungry?"

Touching the skin of his hand, his wrist, his arm, as if to memorize the unfamiliar, she thought again, oddly, of It Happened One Night, of a moment when Clark Gable was cooking breakfast for Claudette Colbert in their roadside motel cabin, how delicious the simple egg had tasted to the spoiled heiress. Annie said, "Totally starving! I hope they have key lime pie, I hope they have a pool and I hope our room faces the sea."

He pulled her closer to him. "Hope's good."

"Oh it's very good," she agreed. "I'm hoping to get in the habit of hope."

Curving westward, they were driving now into the sunset, as if they were about to step onto the top of the enormous round sun, where both of them would be able to balance for a while, like dancers on an orange circus ball. All around them the sky flung purple streamers though the clouds and the ocean brightened, red as a parade.

When they reached the hotel Dan was looking for, there happened to be available—a cancellation—a beautiful room with a balcony facing the ocean. They could see the pool from this balcony. Annie swam laps while Dan made phone calls and then they changed clothes and strolled along Duval Street through crowds of summer cruise-ship tourists. They found a pretty restaurant where they ate tuna tartare and coconut shrimps and very good key lime pie. At the meal's end, Dan noticed that his phone was no longer in his jacket.

As they walked back to the hotel to look for the phone, he suddenly stopped and asked Annie what were her plans for the future? She thought for a moment and then told him, "More of the same."

"Same what?"

She meant, doing more test flights and teaching more flying and hoping in a few years to be promoted to a senior officer, then to lieutenant commander, and then to commander and maybe some day captain...

He pulled her hand through his arm as they walked in step along the old sidewalk. No, he meant "personally." What were her plans for her personal future, after her divorce? She said she had no plans, an uncertainty that, she admitted, ought to make her more nervous than it did, because she had always made detailed plans for the future. "I guess I don't know." She stopped, turned to him.

"Sure you know." Dan leaned to her, his eyes intent on hers. "I know."

She pressed her hand against his heart, listened to its beat. They kissed for so long that a passing pack of intoxicated college boys hooted at them.

• • •

On the balcony at Casa Marina, their bare feet tangled resting on the rail. Dan kissed the inside of Annie's elbow. He pointed to the moon's white shadow on the sea.

She looked at the tilted three-quarter's moon for a while. "Let's go to Machu Picchu," she said.

Surprised, he laughed. "So I can propose to you there?"

She moved her cheek against his. "No, I'm thinking maybe I'll propose to you. Maybe I'll propose tomorrow at Sigsbee at the BOQ. I bet you've never been proposed to by a Navy pilot at the bachelor officers' quarters."

"Just shows how much you know." He walked her back into the room, fell softly with her onto the bed. He kissed the inside of her palm, the hollow of her neck "Understand that I'm prepared to say yes if you propose. I'm practically yours already." He kissed her shoulders. "Did you know Sigsbee Base was named for the captain of the *Maine*? That the *Maine* left for Cuba from there?"

"Yes, I did." She kissed along the line of his jaw.

"Right, that was dumb of me. You're a naval officer." He kept kissing her neck.

"Daniel Hart," whispered Annie. "You don't know what dumb is until you've been married to Brad."

His lips brushed the corner of her mouth. "Oh, yeah? Have you met my ex-wife?"

Annie laughed a loud long laugh. "Well, guess what? What we're doing is totally irrational and I know, I *know*, it's the smartest thing I ever did in my life."

• • •

Hours later the full moon wandered into the window and awakened her. She wrapped herself in the white robe and slipped quietly out onto the balcony where she could see the luminous globe floating down below in the hotel pool. Someone had left a towel spread over a deck chair, white as a ghost.

Back in the room, the hotel phone rang. Hurrying to the bed, where Dan was sleeping, she picked it up quickly so he wouldn't be awakened.

"There's an old movie," said her father without preamble.

"Rosalind Russell; Amelia Earhart-type character, famous woman pilot." His voice was raspy.

"Where are you, Dad? Are you okay?"

"I'm fine. Just listen. *Flight for Freedom*, I think this movie's called. It was on TV last night. Rosalind Russell tells Fred MacMurray, 'My Dad always used to say, when you're safe…you're dead.'"

How strange her father should have seen the same cable movie she'd noticed on the television screen at the Dorado hotel. Where had he been when he'd watched it?

His cough sounded tighter. "'When you're safe, you're dead.'"

His repeating the quote scared her. "Dad, are you in a hospital? Go to a hospital. Where are you? Are you here in Key West?"

"Annie, when you get to Sigsbee Park tomorrow, you call their bluff. Full immunity."

"What? How do you—"

"How about that moon?" He was swallowing his words so that they were almost hard to understand. "Your pal the moon that always came along for the ride?"

She ran out to the balcony, searched the darkness below her.

"Where's Raffy?" he asked. "Raffy can get you to our plane and into Cuba."

"Dad, forget it. Raffy's a prisoner at NAS Key West. He can't help me or you either." Below, beside the pool, she saw a slender man in the moonlight step back into shadows.

"Who told you I'm going to Sigsbee tomorrow?" she asked, trying to follow the gleam of white shirt in the shadows. He didn't answer her. "Dad? Whatever the FBI asks me to do to get your sentence reduced, I'm doing it. I want you to turn yourself in and go to the hospital."

"Full immunity. They offered me eighteen months if I'd give them what they want, and that includes Diaz and the Queen."

"Take it."

"Not eighteen days, baby." He paused a minute, coughed. "Okay, just listen. You're the only one but me who can get access to my account at Banco Centrale. So let the government send you to Havana. The FBI honestly believes it's about catching criminals and protecting sources. But this State department jerk, Fierson, is the key. He'll pretend it's all about Cuba and the Catholic church and the statue. Our picture's what he really wants. I told him the print in the bank pouch is the only print. You know it isn't. But he doesn't. Sam's got the original. There's a negative in the bank, too. Palm the negative out of the pouch. Don't give it to anybody but her. She'll be there."

"'Her'? Who's her? Sam? What do you mean?"

He spoke quickly. "Helen Clark. Tell her it's my gift. And give her the Queen. She'll have the cash. Here's all you have to remember. King, Queen, Sam. The Queen's in the plane. And you can count on Raffy. Tell Raffy to be ready to do what he always does. I've got to go. I love you, baby. Good-bye."

"Dad! Don't disappear on me again!"

"Good-bye. I'm so glad I got to see you."

"Dad!"

Her shout awakened Dan. "What's the matter?"

"It's my dad. He was just on the phone."

They dressed quickly and hurried down to the pool. It was empty. They couldn't find her father on the grounds or in any place they searched up and down the street.

But back at the pool they saw a cell phone lying silvery on the patio bar counter, like a goodbye gift. It was Dan's phone.

Annie and Dan talked late into the night. What had her father meant by "our picture" being what Fierson wanted? Why should Annie give that picture, whatever it was, to Diaz's mistress instead? Annie understood trading the Queen for cash, but how was she supposed to find either the Queen or Helen Clark? Her father had sounded so strange on the phone that maybe he didn't even really know what he was saying; mostly he was rambling on about old movies and the moon. But somehow he knew Annie was going to the base at Sigsbee in the morning; he knew the name of the State department representative, McAllister Fierson, for whom the meeting had been postponed. Dan said, "It's got to be FBI. He must have talked to some agent, about this deal he turned down."

"The only thing clear is, he wants to sell the Queen to Diaz and he needs me to make the trade." In St. Louis, the Queen had been hidden in a rear panel of the *King of the Sky*. Maybe that's what her father had meant by "The Queen is in the plane." He'd hidden it in his amphibian plane that was parked here in Key West, in a panel the way he'd hidden it in the *King*. "King Queen." But why had he added "Sam" to his list of the three words she should not forget? And why should she count on Raffy to do anything?

Dan said it sounded as if her father might have some sort of photograph that he at least thought would be of interest to the government. There was no telling what sort of blackmail goodies Jack might have hidden away in places to which he'd illegally flown the Cessna. And after all, they knew he could hang onto photos for a long time, despite his vagabond life. Hadn't he kept those baby photos of Annie?

Crouched on the bed, Annie hugged her knees. "I'm scared for him."

Dan shrugged. "He wouldn't take a deal for eighteen days, much less eighteen months. That man is not going to jail if he can help it. I don't know what he's up to but it's sure not plea-bargaining."

Annie nodded. "No, he doesn't like small spaces." She was surprised by her pride at the extensive flying her father had apparently done and flying of a dangerous kind too. "He's a flyer." She smiled.

• • •

Annie was falling asleep with Dan's phone on the pillow, in case there was another phone call from her father. She was thinking about why and when he had first wanted to fly, about all the different childhood dreams he'd reached for but failed at, or forgotten. Had there ever been a gift from his parents as key for him as the *King of the Sky* had been for her? She doubted it. Her father and Sam appeared to remember their childhoods so unhappily that they didn't want to remember them at all.

But now that Annie thought back, now that she let herself remember those seven years with Jack Peregrine on the road, what she remembered was not unhappiness but stars, poems, praise. She remembered dance and song and laughing.

She thought back to Raffy's singing to her.

> What is love? 'Tis not hereafter.
> Present mirth hath present laughter.
> What's to come is still unsure.

She remembered laughter.

part four

West

Chapter 48

Tomorrow Is Forever

Early in the morning, Georgette, about to leave for Emerald Hospital, saw Clark Goode in the front yard of Pilgrim's Rest, where he was raking up the few remaining branches from the past weekend's storm. Teddy the old Shih Tzu lay down on the leaves as soon as there were enough to make a cushion.

Georgette raised her briefcase and waved it at Clark. "Work! It's what I do instead of a life," she called. "Where's Sam?"

"Moving furniture into Jack's room."

Georgette opened her hands in an inquiring gesture. "According to Brad, Jack's either dead or disappeared."

"I wish he'd make up his mind." Hoisting the rake over his shoulder, Clark strolled across the gravel drive to her. "Want to come to 'Play It, Sam' tonight? She's showing some island movies."

"Like *Blue Lagoon?*"

"More like *L'Avventura.*"

"I'd rather take inorganic chemistry again." Georgette put down her briefcase while she searched for her car keys in her purse.

"I know you haven't heard this one. One hydrogen atom says, 'I've lost my electron.' The other one says, 'Are you sure?' First one says, 'Yes, I'm positive.'" Clark held the rake out like a vaudeville cane, slow-dancing sideways.

"You're right; I haven't heard it." She found her keys, shook them at him. "Clark, you know how I feel about voting for politicians: it only encourages them? Well, that's *one* reason why I don't laugh at your puns." She picked up her briefcase. "Brad said Sergeant Hart arrested Annie. I was feeling guilty because I didn't tell her about Ruthie, but frankly she's got enough on her plate as it is."

"Told her what?" Clark pulled leaves from the rake. "That Sam's got the idea that Ruthie's Annie's mother?"

Georgette wryly noted, "Jack's home movies of Aunt Ruthie were a lot more riveting than *L'Avventura's* going to be. Ruthie was hot."

Clark glanced across the yard at the Nickerson house. "Yes, she was." Taking off his glasses, he rubbed at his eyes. "But don't believe everything you hear."

"I don't," said Georgette, opening her car door. "I've got a patient who tells me he's Jesus Christ."

"Well," smiled the tall thin man, pulling the last leaves from the rake prongs, "Jesus did say He was coming back."

"This man also thinks cockroaches are crawling all over him."

Clark told her that when he was a POW in Hanoi, cockroaches *were* crawling all over him.

"Clark, you're getting old. Unless they watch the History Channel like me, people my age don't know Hanoi from Hamas." Georgette started her engine. "Maybe we should get some bail money together for Annie. And a lawyer who can go for an insanity plea." Annie had either suffered a radical psychotic breakdown or she was living a very romantic life of the sort Georgette had always wanted to live herself. Well, romantic except for the fact that she might soon be killed or court-martialed.

"Georgette, honey, with love, I think crazy's the only way to go." Clark stepped away from her car. "Meanwhile, you sure are on the phone with Brad a lot."

"It's not love. I'm not that nuts."

They heard something loud, crashing; the noise came from inside Pilgrim's Rest and was followed by a scream.

"That's Sam!" Clark took off running. Georgette was out of her car and caught up with him on the porch.

Bounding up the stairs, they both kept calling "Sam!" They found her on the floor of the hallway on the second floor. She was pinned beneath a heavy walnut armoire. It had fallen over on her leg. She was gray-faced and panting for breath.

"Sam, don't move," Clark instructed her.

She looked up at him, her pupils contracted, her face clammy. "Move?" She gasped. "Move? A two-ton armoire's on top of me. Plus I think I had a stroke."

"You didn't. You're okay," Georgette said.

"Get this thing off me!"

Clark grasped the foot of the armoire. "Okay, Georgette, on three, we're going to lift this end up and move it off her. Ready?"

"Go."

They slid the armoire over on its side. Sam whispered, "Much better. I thought I could tilt it through the doorway."

"Oh Jesus." Clark checked her eyes, neck, then her limbs. One leg looked seriously damaged. He ran to call 911.

Sam muttered to Georgette "How do you know I didn't have a stroke? Heart attack maybe."

Georgette asked her, "Who's the president?"

Sam panted, "Don't tell me George W. Bush, because Gore won that election."

"You're fine," Georgette told her. "Why are you wearing that big wide belt? That's a weight-lifting belt."

Sam whispered, "Who knew how much I'd need it? Don't worry Annie about this, promise me."

"Annie who?"

Sam lost consciousness just as the old blind Shih Tzu Teddy made it to the top of the stairs and began licking her face.

• • •

At Clark's urging the ambulance sped at over 80 miles per hour to Emerald Hospital where the emergency room staff set

Sam's broken femur and made her ready for surgery. An orthopedic surgeon had driven up from Charlotte to operate on her leg,
for the knee was crushed and there was possible nerve damage
in the thigh area.

Clark bent over Sam's gurney as the ER personnel bustled
around them. "Sam, it's Clark, can you hear me? You had an
accident. You're going to OR now. This doctor here's going to
do a little work on your leg."

"I'm getting a new knee, I hope?" she mumbled. "I've got the
Senior Singles Finals in October."

"Maybe next October," Clark told her, brushing his hand
over her white hair. "You know what's good about doctors?
They've got a lot of patients." Sam stared at him baffled. "That
was a pun. It's me, Clark? The mushroom tries to pick up a
woman, tells her, 'Hey, I'm a fun guy!'"

Sam groaned loopily, heavily drugged. "This not fair, can't
get 'way from him." Turning her head, she saw Georgette. "Get
me out."

"Right," Georgette agreed. "Take it from a doctor. A hospital's the last place you want to be." She left to go call Annie,
although she'd promised Sam that she wouldn't do so.

Weakly, Sam tried to talk to the surgeon, a thin red-haired
woman in her fifties. "Only other time I've been here, when my
mother stabbed me in the back."

The surgeon hung the clipboard at Sam's feet. "Is that a joke?"

Sam winced. "Not at the time."

"This is Dr. Sarah Yoelson." Clark moved to let a nurse
check the IV drip. "She'll be your surgeon today."

"Hi there, Sam," said Sarah.

Sam turned drugged eyes on her. "Yoelson. That was Al Jolson's
name. Father was Moshe Yoelson. Lithuanian rabbi."

Sarah nodded. "I hadn't heard that."

Sam grinned sleepily. "'You ain't heard nothin' yet.'"

Clark leaned over Sam to speak to the surgeon. "*The Jazz
Singer*. She loves movies." He moved to the head of the gurney,
motioning for the nurse. "Be careful with that leg, Sarah. She's

a tennis player." Clark patted Sam on the head. "I'll cancel *L'Avventura* tonight."

Sam smiled, morphine-high. "No, show it! 'What's all this crud about no movie tonight?'"

"I've heard that one!" The red-haired surgeon helped roll the gurney to the OR doors. "Wait a sec, don't tell me, I'll get it."

Clark gave his old friend a kiss. "So, Sam, maybe we should get married. What do you say?"

Sam's eyes fluttered closed. "Forget it. Few gay years left in me."

He held open the doors. "Come on, Sam, old Jill will be a distant memory."

"Old Jill *is* a distant memory. Everything distant memory." Sam bit her lips from the jolt as they pushed the gurney through the OR doors.

Sarah Yoelson leaned down to Sam's face. "*Caddy Shack*, right?"

Sam was fading. "*Mr. Roberts*. Watch out for Clark if you're a radiologist."

Clark said, "Sam, would you please just go to sleep?"

The surgeon gestured for Clark to leave the OR. "Seems like a nice guy," she told Sam, "but I'm an orthopedic surgeon and a Lesbian."

"'Nobody's perfect,'" Sam mumbled.

Outside the ER entrance, Georgette Nickerson left a message for Annie, still not knowing that her friend's cell phone was sunk in the surf of the Atlantic Ocean. "Sam doesn't want you to worry but she's in the hospital. She'll be fine. Call me back."

Her cell phone rang as she walked back toward the doors. She assumed the caller was Annie but instead it was Brad Hopper, phoning her from Atlanta. Learning that Sam was in surgery, he urged Georgette to take her to a better hospital. After all, Emerald wasn't Atlanta. Georgette assured him that Sam was in perfectly competent hands, even beyond the Atlanta city limits.

Brad thought it was a shame Annie was going through so much right now and mostly because of her dad. That detective

Hart had sounded dead serious about her going to jail. He'd practically frog-marched her in handcuffs out of the hotel. She'd be dishonorably discharged. Her whole career, down the tubes. Should he get her a lawyer?

Privately Georgette considered the chances of Dan Hart's actually arresting Annie miniscule to nil, even if he actually still had the power to make an arrest after being fired. But she didn't say that. She said that finding Annie a lawyer was not Brad's responsibility. Moreover, as Brad's friend, she felt she should advise him that as soon as Annie wasn't legally his wife, she would not be his legal liability either—whereas now, technically, until Brad signed those divorce papers, he might be implicated in who knows what crimes (Georgette left this vague) that the unprincipled detective Hart might devise against Annie, *and* against anyone connected to Annie. Georgette further suggested that there could be huge financial liability for Brad as well, civil suits from the victims of all the frauds and swindles in which Jack Peregrine had been engaged.

"I hadn't thought of that," Brad admitted. "That's something to worry about."

Brad *should* worry about it, Georgette urged. He should just sign those divorce papers immediately. Remember: his first responsibility was to his company Hopper Jets and to his mother Mama Spring and to his sister Brandy, whose husband had left her. Brad had to take care of his nephews. Annie could take care of herself.

Brad felt very calmed by Georgette's tone. He found himself wondering what she was looking like these days. He told Georgette that tomorrow he was going to fly up to Emerald to visit Sam in the hospital. He had always—and he choked up even thinking about it—loved Sam. Maybe Georgette could meet him at the hospital and go out to dinner with him.

Georgette didn't think so.

Chapter 49

The Sign of the Cross

Annie had flown in and out of Boca Chica Key any number of times; she routinely clocked fifty flight hours a month as a jet instructor and often did so off Key West waters. So she'd been more accustomed than Dan to procedures at the security checkpoint, where MPs checked them in at 07.53 hours, 07, 07, 2001, and instructed them to put their personal belongings out for inspection, including their cell phones, which were not permitted inside the facility. Such things, she advised Dan, had to be tolerated at a high-security military facility.

But Dan didn't see why he should have to pass through a scanner as if he were a grocery item. He didn't like handing over his Swiss Army knife to the military and he said so.

The MP ignored him and crisply saluted Annie. "Please follow me, ma'am."

At 7:59 a.m., in an NAS staff room, the young couple sat at a large oval rosewood conference table. They might have been waiting for any sort of business to start its meeting, except that Annie wore a white Navy uniform and Dan had a Miami Police Department badge hanging from his rumpled blazer and the business was U.S. Government business. There were twenty chairs on rollers around the table, sixteen of them still empty. Two uniformed naval officers, one senior to the other, their faces set, displayed excellent posture at the far end. After introductions, Lt. Commander Bok and Chief Warrant Officer Sims had nothing to say except "Mr. Fierson will be with us in a minute." When Dan stood to stretch, loosening his tie, both officers turned their heads, not their shoulders, to glance at him briefly, then returned to the file folders they were studying.

In the deep silence of the room the sudden noise of doors opening was a shock. First slipped in a young, bone-thin woman in a stylish black pants suit, with a white shirt; she wore a head-set, carried a clipboard. Two male civilians stepped around her and moved to the table. One was the chunky FBI agent who'd been wearing the porkpie hat when he'd arrested Rafael Rook in the parking lot near Rest Eternal in Miami. "Hi, Dan," he said.

"Hi, Willie. How's it feel? You one-up me. State one-ups you."

"We all want the same thing." The agent pulled out a chair.

"Think so?" Dan asked amiably. "Annie, this is Willie Grunberg. He's been after your dad as long as I have."

The third man to enter was older, taller, thinner, wore a much more expensive suit and had the rich slightly waved gray hair that accompanies institutional success. Indeed, his dark pinstriped suit, substantial and imposingly tailored, gave off an impression of such consequence that the suit appeared to be wearing the man inside it. He nodded affably. "Good morning, everyone. I'm McAllister Fierson. Apologies. Fog delay at Andrews. Why don't we introduce ourselves?"

No one saw any reason why they shouldn't.

Fierson took his seat at the head of the table. "Pardon me one second." His assistant handed him a page she took from her clipboard, which he initialed. The door opened again. The man who walked into the room this time was such a shock to Annie that surprise brought her to her feet. "Trevor?"

In this room and wearing a regimental tie and sports jacket with his button-down shirt and chinos, Trevor looked so out of his habitual setting that she almost didn't recognize him. "Where are Amy and Elliott?" she blurted out.

"Her cat, my dog," Trevor explained to the others in the room. "They're with a pet sitter. Good one."

The thin young woman with the clipboard laughed as if to express her amazement that they were wasting their time on cats and dogs.

Annie turned to Dan. "This is Trevor Smithwall. He lives next door. Trevor, what are you *doing* here?"

Trevor held out his hand to everybody, who had to introduce themselves all over again. He told them he was "Agent Smithwall, Justice."

"Sergeant Hart, Vice," replied Dan.

Annie was wondering if she had herself unknowingly given Trevor the means to pursue her father. How stupid not to be more suspicious of his willingness to use his FBI resources to help. "Trevor?" she said again but he seemed to think that it would be inappropriate to meet her eyes.

"Let's begin," suggested McAllister Fierson. "And I want everyone to feel comfortable. Lieutenant Goode, your father has placed us in an awkward..." He looked at Trevor.

Trevor said, "Situation."

"My dad is a con artist," Annie replied. "I don't see how his 'situation' could involve the Navy, the—"

The thin young woman suddenly cursed in a loud whisper into her headset. "No, you need to get here at 8:25!" Everyone turned. She noticed their looking at her and told the man in the expensive suit, "Sorry!"

Fierson lifted an admonishing finger in her direction then turned back to table. "So we—" he bowed slightly to the flag in the corner "we find ourselves in this, as Agent Smithwall put it, situation."

As he seemed to be speaking to Annie, she replied, "Which situation is it, sir?"

Fierson's assistant opened a folder and placed it in front of him. Glancing in it, he replied, "A serious one." There were details he would not be able to share; they were protected by the government's claim that it needed to protect them. "But shall we be candid? We all know your father has, or had, in his possession a certain artifact to which the Cuban government, specifically—" he checked his notes "—the Museo Habana in Plaza de la Revolución, is laying claim. A relic that is reputedly a quote 'national treasure.'"

Annie asked, "The Queen of the Sea?"

He nodded. "We'd like your help in solving this problem with Cuba, without further embarrassment to anyone. Your father is not yet in police custody, although charged with a number of felonies."

"Sixty-one counts," threw in Willie, the chunky FBI agent. He thrust his finger aggressively at Annie. "We want that statue back and we want the jewels that go in it. It belongs to Cuba. Your dad's got that statue or he hid it someplace and he's figuring to unload it for some real dirty money. He's a fugitive. And you know where he is!"

Fierson ignored the agent. "Lt. Goode, by protecting your father, you have made yourself vulnerable to serious charges."

"Like 10 years worth," the chunky agent couldn't stop himself from saying.

Fierson held out a palm to silence him. "If you can assist us in recovering this artifact, and arrange for your father's return, his problems, and yours, become less…urgent."

Before Annie could reply, Lt. Commander Bok assured Mr. Fierson that to serve the United States government in any way they asked was both Lieutenant Goode's duty and her privilege. Chief Warrant Officer Sims couldn't agree more.

Annie sat straighter in her seat, hands folded tensely but quietly on the table. "Mr. Fierson, should I have a lawyer present?" She glanced at Dan. "I mean, before I speak as to my knowledge of any stolen object?"

"Or the felon that stole it," growled the FBI man. "I bet you know exactly where Peregrine is."

"I think I can safely say," Fierson gestured at the officers and (sternly) at the fat agent, "I think we can safely say that a lawyer won't be necessary, since any information Lieutenant Goode may have obtained from her father—"

"Or from Rafael Rook," Dan interjected.

Fierson nodded agreeably. "She obtained without being made in any way aware of its criminal nature. And any ex post facto actions she took to relieve, comfort, or assist her father or his accomplice, she took in ignorance of the fact that they had committed felonies. There was therefore no criminal facilitation by the lieutenant."

Dan muttered, "So much for *ignorantia juris non excusat.*"

The thin young woman laughed but quickly stopped herself.

After a brief glare at them both, Fierson held up for view the Photostat of the sketch of the Queen of the Sea, the one that Raffy had already shown Annie. "Let's put our cards, all our cards, on the table," he suggested.

Annie motioned with her hands as if they were spilling those cards before him. "Yes, sir."

"Your father has somehow acquired this valuable object, a gold and jeweled Spanish Renaissance reliquary known as—" he checked the piece of paper "—*La Reina Coronada del Mar.* Sources indicate he has a buyer of some sort who intends to donate the statue to the diocese of the Catholic Church of the Sacred Heart in Miami." Again, Fierson checked his pages. "'*El siglo decimosexto reliquia dorada*' appears to have a certain religious significance. We already have in our possession a small, quite authentic silver casement alleged to have been removed from the statue, containing a so-called thorn from the crucifixion crown of Christ. Its existence strongly suggests the authenticity of the statue from which it was taken."

Willie set a small package in bubble-wrap on the table. He unwrapped a little silver box with empty prongs on its lid. "This goes straight to the Cuban government," he told them. It was the box Rafael had dug up at Hialeah racetrack.

Dan gave Annie a knowing glance. Obviously, Raffy, imprisoned somewhere here on the base, had given up the reliquary and who knows how much information about Jack Peregrine with it.

Fierson picked up the box and examined it. When he set it down, Willie grabbed it and wrapped it back into its package.

Fierson turned to Annie. "We know this box was given to Rafael Rook by your father. We know Peregrine recently traveled to St. Louis to retrieve jewels belonging to the statue."

Annie leaned around Dan. "Thanks a lot, Trevor!"

Trevor flushed. "Hang on, Annie."

She stood up. "You hang on! Were you already involved in this mess of my father's when I met you, or did you get involved after I came to you for help because you were my *friend?*"

Trevor's ears darkened. "By the book, Annie. Your motto."

Officer Sims interrupted them. "Lieutenant Goode, your mission is not to analyze. Your mission is to obtain a certain object and locate a certain person for your government. Is that not so, Mr. Fierson?"

Fierson wrinkled his mouth. "Let me assure you…Annie… that our national and strategic interests are involved here." He stopped, closed and tapped his folder. "We not only want the statue back, we understand that some of its jewels have been placed by your father in a bank account in Havana. We'd like you to go get them."

Annie scowled at Trevor. "Even if the emeralds and rubies are real and even if they're in this bank—my dad's just a crook. Why is this so important to the U.S. government?"

"That's right." Dan stood, leaning over the table at Fierson. "The U.S. didn't steal the Queen, you aren't trying to sell it and what's it worth anyhow? A few million bucks? Chump change," he growled. "So why are you here?"

Fierson turned a page in his folder. "Actually, even forgetting the national antiquity value, the emeralds and the 135-carat ruby are worth approximately forty-five million dollars. But you're correct, Mr. Hart, the question is, why should we care?"

"And the answer?"

Fierson again nodded at the flag. "We don't want Cuba to have the advantage of us in this matter."

"Right," snarled Dan. "Cuba's so big and powerful."

Dismissively Fierson swiveled from him toward Annie. "While we deeply care to see the people of Cuba once again living in freedom…all in good time. And while we know that a Communist regime will not cherish this Christian relic as a…as a relic, still there is the matter of the press this incident could cause if the Cubans were to make a public fuss about an American criminal robbing them and American law enforcement simply dropping the ball. But settling these claims—between Cuba and the Catholic Church, is not your responsibility, Annie. You produce the statue. Produce the jewels missing from it. And assist us in locating your father. You are relieved of other duties for the following two weeks in order to carry out these tasks."

Annie pivoted in her chair toward Lt. Commander Bok. "But sir, I'm already under orders to report back to Annapolis on Monday at 0600 hours! I'm scheduled to test the F-35 Lightning II at Air Systems Command."

With a glance at his superior, Chief Warrant Officer Sims answered for the Navy: They had already discussed with her base commander Dicky Campbell the scheduled test flight at ASC. That test would take place as planned but with a different pilot. In official records, however, the pilot performing the test would be Lt. Anne Peregrine Goode.

"Fake alibi," said Willie, who was ignored. He picked in disgust at a cinnamon bun he took from a wrinkled bag.

Next to Annie, Dan startled everyone with a sudden hard whack of the table. "Why fly a test? Just have the news announce she broke the record!"

Annie hushed him. "I can handle this." She turned to Commander Bok. "Sir, can't this statue thing wait till I do the test or can't somebody else go to Cuba—"

"Lieutenant!" snapped Bok.

"Sir! I have an opportunity to break a—"

"Lieutenant Goode!"

Furious, Annie bit her mouth closed.

"This is bullshit," grumbled Dan.

Fierson's voice sharpened. "Young man, we've heard enough from you. If you don't want to be removed from the room, please keep quiet." The government official turned his back on the detective. "Annie," he soothingly went on, "I admire your desire to serve your country by testing the Lightning II. But this Queen of the Sea matter involves your country as well. We might not care for the kind of nation Cuba has become, but we can't have an American con artist stealing its historic treasures. Can we?"

Annie looked at him for a moment. "No, sir."

"If the statue is returned, quickly and intact, there would probably be very little reason—" he glanced with some disdain at the chunky FBI agent's gnawing on the bun—"to call attention to its theft. Do you see my point, Lieutenant Goode?"

Annie twisted her neck side to side, trying to ease the stabs of pain. "Yes, sir, I do see it."

"Good," smiled Fierson. "We agree that such a treasure belongs either in a museum or...a church. Not to your father?"

"Yes, we agree."

Dan blew a loud breath into the room but said nothing.

Fierson motioned to his aide, the young bone-thin woman, who checked through her clipboard and showed him a page of it. "All right then, to specifics. Access to the account at the branch of Banco Centrale in Havana depends upon a visual identification and knowledge of certain codes. Has your father confided these codes and the contents of a bank drawer to you?"

Annie scowled at Trevor. "Is there anything you didn't tell them?" She turned to Fierson. "With respect, sir, what my father may have confided seems to me a personal matter."

Fierson smoothed his tanned and manicured fingers across his lips. "I assure you it is not, or I wouldn't be here. I would be fishing on Jupiter Island with my grandson."

Flipping to the next page, the thin young woman placed her clipboard in his line of vision and pointed at something. He paused with a questioning look to her. She handed him a manila envelope.

Dan flung out his arms. "Are we ever going to say the name Feliz Diaz here today?"

There was puzzlement from the naval officers, a brief uncomfortable silence from the others.

Annie asked, "I think Diaz tried to have my father killed for reneging on the sale of the Queen. I won't do anything that will jeopardize my father's safety."

McAllister Fierson bent over to whisper something to Trevor and Willie. They spoke back and forth. Then the government official told Annie, "Assuming of course the FBI has access to Jack Peregrine, they will take any necessary steps to protect him. His best protection is to stay away from dangerous people."

Annie looked up and down the row of solemn men. "I think he's trying to do that."

Embarrassed, Trevor still didn't look at her as he asked, "Do you have this statue in your possession now?"

"No, I do not." She smiled. "And I don't think you've ever known me to lie."

"No, I haven't. Do you know where the statue is?"

She shook her head.

Dan glared at Trevor. "You skeeze. She trusted you."

Annie grabbed Dan's arm. "It's okay."

Fierson interrupted. "The minute your father's in touch with you, you're in touch with us and he's brought into custody."

Annie heard her father telling her to call the bluff. She took a deep breath, her hands flat on the desk, the gold buttons gleaming on the white cuffs of her naval jacket and looked steadily around the table, from one male face to another. "With respect, sir, I won't bring my father into custody unless I have a written guarantee of his full immunity from prosecution." She looked straight at Fierson. "That's not a threat. The law's position on my father is absolutely right."

Dan leaned forward. "Bottom line, Mr. Fierson. Take it from the Miami police. She blew off every offer I made. She gave us total shit fits. And she *likes* me. She'll go to jail but she won't give him up."

Fierson studied Annie.

She added, "I understand and accept what the repercussions for me could be. But this is my father. He's dying. He has a horror of confinement. I won't help you put him in jail. It's just an absolute, sir."

The room was quiet. The well-dressed, silver-haired man contemplated for so long a moment that Commander Bok wrote a note to Officer Sims, who abruptly left the room. Fierson gestured for Trevor and they had a short, whispered conversation.

Finally Fierson said, "All right. Full immunity."

Willie spluttered his indignation but Fierson paid no attention, turning instead to his assistant. "Call Justice." He nodded at Annie, who let out her breath. "If you find your father in Havana, get him on the plane and bring him back. I hope he won't object to a brief conversation."

Annie asked, "Sir, how am I supposed to get to Cuba?"

Trevor, with flushed cheeks, pulled folders from his briefcase and passed them out. Annie would go directly from here to Boca Chica Key. Her father's Cessna Amphibian would be turned over to her. She would make a sea-landing off Puerto Esperanza in Pinar del Rio, Cuba. Accompanying her would be Sgt. Daniel Hart, who not only spoke fluent Spanish but also would be in charge of the State of Florida's prisoner, Rafael Rook. Rook was a U.S. citizen of Cuban descent who was all too familiar with illegal ways to re-enter the island. Rook would be their intermediary; he had relatives working both in harbor security and in customs in Puerto Esperanza. He had another relative at the bank branch in Havana.

Dan muttered, "True. Rook's related to half that island and a third of Miami."

Walking around the table, Trevor dropped thick packets in front of Dan and Annie. "Passports, etc.," he said. Annie kept staring at him, without effect. "We've given you both pretty deep covers. But if they get blown—" he blushed, two red circles spreading over his face "—Annie, you're stuck with who you are. You're illegal, you're Navy, but they might buy that you're desperate, you're searching for your dad and he's terminally ill. Stick to that. It's personal."

Annie's eyes were icy. "Well, Trevor, it has the coincidental virtue of being true." Finally he glanced back at her but quickly looked away.

Dan was leafing through his packet; he held up a Canadian passport. "You're kidding? I teach moral philosophy at the University of Toronto?"

Willie laughed out loud.

Fierson took a photograph of a young, muscular nondescript man from his folder. "I understand you have a very good memory, Annie." She nodded. "Can you remember this gentleman?" She glanced at the photo, nodded. "His name is Fred Owen. When you get the bank pouch, give it to him. Only to him." He removed another photograph from his blue folder, sliding it over to Annie. "Her name," Fierson checked the back of the picture, "is Helen Clark."

Annie studied the photograph of the coppery-haired woman she'd seen at Golden Days. "She may be in Havana. Do not be conned into letting her take the bank pouch from you. Your friend Detective Hart—" he gestured uninterested at Dan, "mentioned Feliz Diaz. This woman is his mistress." Fierson stood, smoothing his suit. "I'll leave the arrangements to Agents Smithwall and Greenberg."

"Grunberg," Willie muttered.

Fierson showed his handsome watch to the thin young woman who stood waiting at the door with her clipboard. He said to Annie, "Whether you succeed or not, you are in and out of Cuba within 24 hours. You fly back here to NAS with Sergeant Hart's prisoner Rafael Rook, who will be remanded into custody to stand trial."

Annie stood too. "In exchange for Rafael Rook's cooperation, shouldn't he be extended the same deal as my father?"

Willie burst out, "Absolutely not. Don't push." The agent said that considering the number and severity of the charges against Rook, an eighteen month deal was a gift. "Total gift." Besides, Rook had already accepted the deal and pled guilty.

Fierson shrugged at Annie. "But I admire your tenacity." He shook her hand. "Lieutenant. You've done a service to your country. Gentlemen, thank you." He bowed his head briefly. "I hope we've kept it comfortable. Best of luck." The assistant held open the door for him.

After the State Department official left, the other participants at the meeting quickly gathered their belongings to follow him out. Willie detoured to a sideboard of croissants. Dan moved over to talk to him.

As Trevor passed close to Annie, he leaned in to her and surprised her by whispering, "Trust Helen Clark. She's with us. She's got your back. Be careful, Annie." He moved on as if he hadn't spoken to her at all.

Commander Bok stopped Annie in the doorway. "Good luck."

"Thank you, sir. With permission, sir, a question. If I can manage to get back to Key West in time, and make it to Patuxent River for the test flight, can I fly it?" She saluted him. "I would really like the opportunity, sir."

A tiny smile escaped the edge of the commander's tightly compressed mouth. "Lieutenant Goode, if you can make it back to Sigsbee in time, the Navy will fly you to the test."

"Thank you, sir!" Annie smiled so infectiously that even Officer Sims grinned back at her.

• • •

Dan fumed about McAllister Fierson as Annie and he followed a husky MP down a long corridor to the area where Raffy was being held. Fierson's heading home to fish with his grandson on Jupiter Island struck Dan as "just right." Jupiter Island, Florida, was the most expensive zip code in the United States; there were only about two hundred households there, most of them Duponts and Fords and Harrimans and the descendents of Prescott Bush and other Yale Bonesmen. "I guess he feels 'comfortable.'"

Raffy sat crouched at the end of his cot in a neat, spare "confinement area." His fingers laced around his knees and he was talking out loud to himself. He still wore the lime-green floppy trousers and yellow shirt with dancing alligators that he'd had on days ago and he looked dirty and tired. His voice was as soft and rhythmic as a rumba.

Be not afeard; the isle is full of noises,
Sounds and sweet airs, that give delight and hurt not.

So intent was the musician on Caliban's poetry that he
seemed not to hear their approach.

Sometimes a thousand twangling instruments
Will hum about mine ears, and sometime voices
That, if I then had waked after long sleep,
Will make me sleep again…

The Cuban saw Annie and his face lightened, incandescent.
"Annie! Can you believe what I just did?" He jumped to his feet,
reached his manacled hands out to her. "I did a whole speech!
Did you hear me do that whole speech?"

She took his hands. "I did."

He was exuberant about his achievement. "It just all came
into my mind! Just the way your papa would recite it for me in
our cell. I could never do that before! I couldn't retain the words.
But now, just listen to me!

…And then, in dreaming,
The clouds methought would open and show riches
Ready to drop upon me, that when I waked,
I cried to dream again.

"A-plus, Raffy," she told him.

"You look like shit, Rook," growled Dan. "They haven't
messed with you, have they? Nothing nasty?"

Raffy pointed significantly at his ear, spun his finger at the
ceiling of the room as if to suggest there were people up there
listening. "Loneliness is the sum of my torture. As prisons go, it's
still America."

Dan asked, "Then why'd you blab your guts? You gave it all up.
I thought you were going to present that Jesus splinter to your mom
in a big prodigal son number? But you gave it up to the Feds."

The musician hunched his shoulders apologetically. "Annie, forgive me but I didn't give up more than necessary to only serve eighteen months and I ask your pardon for what I did give up but if you'd done time in Dade County, well, all I can say is, if Hamlet thought Denmark was a prison, let him go to Dade County for eighteen months. I'd prefer no months at all, and losing *la espina de la corona de Jesús Cristo* to those *s.o.b.*s that was supposed to go to my mama, that is a deep, deep pain." He sighed, his eyes large and sorrowful. "But *vivamos nuestras vidas cotidianas.*"

Annie explained to Raffy that he was about to be released into Dan's custody. "And guess what? We are going to Cuba. You were right about that." Annie told him of her deal with the government. How in exchange for her help, Jack Peregrine would be given protection and medical attention. She, Dan, and Raffy were going to fly her father's Cessna to Havana today, using Raffy's relatives to make their illegal water landing and their entry into Cuba possible. They would withdraw the contents from her father's bank drawer in the Plaza des Armas, just as Raffy had discussed with her.

Raffy's "no" was so vehement that his black ponytail bounced on his neck. "I was never in that water plane but the one time with Jack and that's the time when we landed in a very stormy sea and we almost crashed to death and my relatives were not waiting in their little boat but the Cuban police were waiting in a big boat and they caught us! That's when we went to jail together, your papa and me. The mice and rats are not so cheerful the way they are always singing and dancing in Walt Disney, let me tell you. So no, gracias, I am not flying with you to Cuba."

Annie assured him they weren't going to have bad weather and they weren't going to jail; they would just fly in, fly out. Didn't he want to go home, see his mother?

"'I dare do all that may become a man; Who dares do more is none.' I don't have the nerve for little planes, especially not on ocean waves. And Cuba? My memories are not so good. As my grandpapa Simon told my *abuela*, 'A broch tzu Columbus!'"

Dan asked, "Is that Yiddish for fuck Christopher Columbus?"

"Pretty much," admitted the small musician. He motioned Annie away from Dan, whispering, "Your papa is alive."

"I know he is. So does the FBI."

"Feliz Diaz is paying him a million dollars in cash for *La Reina*. In cash! A million dollars! Your papa is going to get that money to you. Don't trust the government. Trust your family."

Annie pulled back, ironic. "Ah, my family? When did *you* last see my 'papa'?" She wasn't sure whether they could be overheard, even whispering, so she hesitated to tell Rook any specifics about how she'd spotted her father last night at the hotel in Key West. "They don't seem to have caught him."

"Ah." Rafael held the forefingers of both hands to his soft lips, blew away all questions. "Shhh. Flights of angels."

"Flights of angels to where exactly? Has he left the country?"

The slender man lifted his shoulders rhythmically, so that the alligators danced on his yellow shirt. "I know nothing. I am only Rosencrantz and I forget the other one."

"Raffy, isn't a friend like family? Wouldn't you rather help out Jack, your best friend, than sit here alone in this cell?"

He glanced sadly around the small bare barred room. They looked at each other.

Dan said, "Do it, Rook. Annie's fought for you. You should have heard her in there fighting for you. Come on. Help her."

The Cuban sighed at the ceiling. "Ahhh, Annie...'my love's more richer than my tongue.'..." He sighed at the floor. "I'll do it."

Dan gave him both thumbs up.

Annie told the MP that they were ready to go. The young man helped Raffy to his manacled feet.

"I don't want to do this," Raffy whispered to Annie. "I really don't want to. I don't want to go back to jail in Cuba. Not without Jack."

She kissed him. "You won't," she promised. "I'm going to get you through this. And you're going to see your mother. She doesn't want to see a Thorn of the Holy Crown in a silver box. She wants to see you."

His ponytail flicked from side to side. "That's what you think."

Annie stepped back so the MP could walk him out of the room. "Everything's going to be okay. Do you believe me?"

His eyes sweetened. "I do believe you." He leaned around her to Dan. "You, you son-of-a-bitch Miami police, I don't believe. But her I do."

Dan slapped the Cuban's thin back, assuring him he'd be home with Chamayra and they'd be hanging out the Love sign in no time.

"No time would be better than eighteen months," sighed the Cuban as he shuffled down the long, overlit corridor.

• • •

Just as McAllister Fierson had pledged, the government made the arrangements. If there was one skill the government had, Dan noted, it was VIP arrangements: The government knew how to grease the wheel (in the packets Trevor had handed them there were Canadian passports and Cuban pesos and euros with which to bribe any people whom it might be appropriate to bribe). The government was good at paving the way (at the Key West airfield, Annie's father's Cessna Amphibian was already checked out, gassed up, and waiting on the ramp). They knew how to jump the queue.

Annie moved the Cessna to first position on the tarmac. Eagerly Dan pulled open a loosened panel in the fuselage of the Cessna. Annie had told him the sort of panel to look for, predicting that her father would have hidden the gold statue of the Queen of the Sea just as he'd done before in the *King of the Sky*. Why else would he have told her in his phone call last night, "The Queen's in the plane"?

Dan whistled when he pulled out of its green cloth wrapping the gold Virgin Mary in the Incan Pachamama cape, with her sunburst crown and large rectangular emeralds inserted in three of the seven gold rods. "Look at this thing! Holy Mother of God."

Carefully strapped into his seat, Raffy clutched a life jacket.

"Yes, it's the Holy Mother. Are you being funny? Don't be funny. Aren't you scared?"

Dan looked out the window at the naval crews. "I tell you what's scary. I'm in love with somebody in the U.S. military."

Cleared for take-off, Annie taxied onto the runway and turned to look down the center. "You know what, Dan? You're a whole lot better off with the military than you are with politicians. Like I keep reminding Sam, it was Eisenhower who said, 'Watch out for the military-industrial complex.' It was Admiral Leahy who said dropping the A-bomb on Japan would turn us into Dark Age barbarians. Good guys are in the military."

Raffy shouted at Annie, "Stop talking, stop talking, pay attention to what you're doing. Oh Jésus Cristo, hear my prayer!"

Dan laughed. "'Hear my prayer'? Rook, you said you weren't a believer."

Raffy checked the buckle on his guitar in the seat next to him. "'I love long life better than figs.' And Chamayra will kill me if I get myself killed!"

● ● ●

The flight was not a long one. Within the hour, they spotted the green mountains of Cuba's coast. The mountains were heartbreakingly beautiful.

Soon their small plane was approaching a quiet harbor north of Puerto Esperanza in the western province of Pinar del Rio. Right on time, they were coming in for a sea landing on the Archipiélago de los Colorados: lat 22°47' N, long 83° 43' W. Annie radioed her position as instructed back at Sigsbee. She lowered the pontoons and soon was being guided in her descent by Raffy's cousin Tico Ramirez. He'd been watching for them from his boat, just beyond the reef off the coast of the dockmaster's office in the harbor.

The sea was gray and unexpectedly rough.

Annie glanced behind her at a strange noise. Raffy was making it. "Dan, get Raffy's head down between his legs right away!"

The musician was hyperventilating in loud gasps. She called back from the cockpit. "Raffy, take it easy! This is nothing! This is just a little choppy! Hang on."

Dan cupped his hands over Rafael's nose and mouth. "Breathe slowly, *paison*. Don't fight me, you chickenshit Cubano."

"Let go, son of a bitch," panted Rafael, pulling free of Dan, his hair flying, distracted from noticing that the seaplane was gliding with a smooth straightforwardness onto the bouncing waves. "O my Savior, gracias, gracias!"

They motored toward the buoy where Raffy's cousin's boat was waiting to meet them. So far, Dan admitted, every-thing had happened as Jack had said it would. "Let them send you to Havana, he said. Fierson will pretend it's about Cuba and the church and the statue. And the FBI will really believe it. Jack's gone way up in my estimation. I don't mind having him for a father-in-law. If they double-cross us and he gets 20 years, I'm going to go visit him in prison."

They still didn't know what was in the bank pouch or what picture Jack wanted them to give Helen Clark. Or what Raffy was supposed to do that he always did.

"It will all fall pat," the Cuban promised, cheerful now that he was out of the sky.

Chapter 50

Only Angels Have Wings

Sam, in the recovery room following her surgery, felt herself float up to the ceiling away from the pain. She had wings and was flying all around the room but, like a fly or a bee in search of an exit, she couldn't find her way out and struck herself against the windows.

Annie, seven years old, stood with Clark at the foot of the hospital bed, their heads tilted back, turning to watch her aunt fly from light to light. "How come she's got wings?" Annie asked Clark. "Is she dead?"

Clark said no, that Sam was not going to die yet because she hadn't finished cleaning out the attic as she often promised to do before she died.

"Only angels have wings," Annie told her.

"Don't flyers?" he asked.

"That's true," the solemn little girl agreed. "Flyers have wings." She unpinned the tiny medal bar of wings from her jean jacket and broke it in two, fastening a wing to each of her shoulders. The wings suddenly grew to full size, sprouting out of her jacket, and, using them to fly, Annie glided up to the ceiling next to Sam, who was trying to kick open a transom window. "Come back, Aunt Sam. It's about that time." The phrase was the one Sam used nightly to let Annie know it was time for her to go to bed. Tugging on Sam's hand, Annie floated down with her in looping circles back onto the hospital bed below. Sam lay on the bed and Clark pulled up the white sheets around her.

• • •

An hour later, in the recovery room, Sam awakened from her dreams, worried that Jack hadn't received the FedEx he'd asked her to send him two nights ago to his hotel in Key West— enclosing the photograph of Jack and Annie at The Breakers Hotel in West Palm Beach that he'd left in Annie's little blue suitcase so many years ago and that Sam had framed when she'd found it. There had been something about that photograph that Jack had suddenly needed. Sam couldn't now remember if Jack had explained what the importance was and she worried that maybe she hadn't sent the FedEx correctly. Had she talked to Jack since she'd sent it?

Something had happened to her this morning; something had fallen on her. The old Worth armoire, that's it, it had been her mother's armoire. She'd been distracted, listening to news on the television from down the hall while she'd tried to drag the heavy ornate mahogany piece of furniture into Jack's room. That's right, she was fixing up Jack's old bedroom for his recuperation. The armoire had caught on the doorsill. Served her right. She'd been wearing her old leather weight-lifting belt to help strengthen her back but it hadn't helped. She was not as strong, not as fast as she once had been. Why, when she was a girl, she'd once caught a runaway horse for a neighboring farmer and she'd ridden the horse home bareback. Once she'd killed a wild pig with a bow and arrow. She'd shaken apples out of the tops of trees for her friends and rescued her brother Jack from a bull's charge.

Jack had called the teenaged Sam "the fastest woman alive." He'd boasted to D. K. of her "amazing catch" of the infant Annie when the year-old baby was crawling so fast across the porch that she headed straight off into the air over the top of the steep steps. Jack was standing not far from the steps, talking to D. K. about the *King of the Sky*. They hadn't noticed the baby. Sam had been upstairs, cleaning out the rooms that she never seemed able to empty of the collected past. She heard Annie laughing downstairs in the hall and then the door screeching open. According to Jack, Sam had flown down the stairs and through the air out onto the porch and never touched the floor before she had snatched Annie's heel with her outstretched fingers and stopped her from falling.

But then Jack always exaggerated.

Sam drifted back into a dream in which she was trying to edit together a film but at the same time she was showing that film on a projector at the Paradise, Emerald's now defunct old movie house. Sam was in a state because the film kept jamming and breaking off and unraveling, twisting like small black snakes, like a mechanical hydra, lashing the projection room. She had to keep stopping the movie, to the displeasure of the audience. They sat in the dark, chanting "Slowpoke! Slowpoke!" which is what her mother had called her when she'd "dawdled" over difficult homework.

The scenes of the movie, jumbled and disjointed, included awful memories that Sam had told no one but Jill and Clark and that she was upset to see playing out at the local cinema. In one scene, her father Judge Peregrine, austere in his black robes, spoke directly to the camera in extreme close-up. Addressing the mourners at the funeral of his two-year-old son John Ingersoll Peregrine, he told them that "candidly" he did not care for his daughter Samantha, whom he considered not particularly bright and that "frankly" he had an aversion to his son Jack, who had from his youth been defiant and volatile and beautiful and who had therefore always reminded the judge of his wife.

The camera panned rapidly left to right and ended up on the second-floor hallway of Pilgrim's Rest. Then it tracked into the bathroom where the judge was pushing the teenaged Jack down into a tub of scalding hot water, holding the boy's head under, while his wife Grandee beat him on his back.

The next shot was in a tennis court, where Sam hit dozens of serves of yellow apples to her mother, who ignored them.

Then her mother was sitting on the living room floor, bloody, with photographs of Johnny around her. The photographs burned like candles.

Then Sam ran into the St. Mark's cemetery. Her mother was there, digging a hole and jumping down into it. Sam heard her screaming from beneath the ground and she heard the deep growling bark of a dog down there. Sam pulled her mother out of the open grave, just before a massive black dog snapped her leg between his jaws. Sam's mother held to her breast the blue corpse of her first-born son, dressed in his white burial clothes.

Sam awakened to sharp pain in her leg. A young African American nurse leaned over her. "You doing okay?"

"Not really," admitted Sam.

The nurse looked at the IV drip, adjusted it, gave it a tap. Sam drifted back to sleep.

Outside, alone in the recovery room lobby, Clark sat on a vinyl couch, his long legs resting on a nearby chair. He had read a report about Sam's surgery and it looked to him as if the orthopedist Sarah Yoelson had done a fine job repairing the nerve damage, replacing the knee. There was no reason Sam wouldn't even be able to play tennis again, although it would be unlikely that she could again be a state champion. He recalled how once years ago they'd pushed a big dead oak root up out of the loosened earth. He'd wanted to quit but she hadn't let him. By strength and will, she'd kicked the last tendril loose. Sam never quit; not with him, not with Annie, not even with her awful parents.

• • •

"Tell me what Sam and Dad's parents were really like." On summer break from her first year at Annapolis, Annie had asked Clark that question one hot summer night. "Really. Tell me."

And so he had. At least the part he knew at the time.

Sam's father was a Peregrine, the youngest Superior Court judge in the state; snobbish, bright, cold, and sanctimonious.

Sam's mother had from her baby days been called Grandee Worth as an ironic comment on her petite stature and her illustrious family. She was capricious and charming, with a reputation as a great beauty. Grandee had tormented young Judge Peregrine into proposing, flirting publicly with his friends even on their wedding day. She had once confided to Clark—she was erratic and careless in her confidences—telling numbers of people that she had never liked her husband but that she had started actively hating him after the death of their son Johnny. "He killed my baby," she told Clark in her soft secretive lilt.

The toddler Johnny, while in the care of the judge, had drowned in the new swimming pool Grandee had insisted on building between Pilgrim's Rest and the Nickerson house. It was the first inground pool in the town of Emerald, and the briefest, for the whole thing was filled in with dirt within a month after the two-year-old had playfully jumped off the diving board and sunk to the bottom. The judge had possibly drifted off to sleep for only a minute in his poolside chair and had awakened too late.

Pregnant at the time with Sam, Grandee soon began—as the town put it—"acting up." But of course, they understood why, after so terrible a loss. She went out alone at night, driving recklessly on winding country roads, while her husband sat waiting for her on the porch. The town thought she was hoping to die but was unable deliberately to drive off the road because of the baby she carried, the girl she would name Samantha Anne.

Once Grandee didn't come home till dawn and that time the judge, who'd never been known to lose his composure, slapped her. He hadn't done it before and he never did it again. He was a large, thickly built man and Grandee was small-boned and slender, but her leap at his face knocked him to the floor and her bite mark on his hand didn't heal for a month.

A year later she tried to pour a pan of boiling water on his face, but only scarred his ear.

Sam knew from an early age that her parents were very

unhappy together and that nothing she did made them feel any less so. Jack learned the same lesson. Grandee gave her second son the name she'd given his dead older brother. The name but not the love. Framed baby pictures of the dead Johnny crowded the lid of the grand piano. Johnny's baby clothes crowded the drawers of the dresser inside the closet of Jack's room.

By the time Sam reached junior high school, Grandee had briefly gone twice to a hospital for "nervous disorders." When she scratched an orderly the first time, they strapped her to her bed. When she started pulling out her hair the second time, they gave her sedatives. The pills helped her through the rest of her life.

By the time Jack was a teenager, the town no longer talked much about the fact that Grandee was "troubled." They had their own troubles, almost everybody did. Those were times when half the country couldn't get along with the other half. Jack fought more and more violently with his parents, especially after "the Ruthie episode." Sam tried to repair the rifts. "Why do you care, Sam?" her younger brother would yell at her. "Stop caring. Why do you love them? They never loved you or me or each other. To hell with them."

But Sam thought there must have been love. She was always searching for photos of her mother and her father to prove it. Photos from some unknown time when they *had* loved each other. She always believed Jack was wrong, that at least far in the past her parents had been deeply in love. One day in her early teens, she'd been seized with the idea that her parents' happy pictures were hidden away somewhere, maybe inside her mother's "sitting room" on the top floor, the door of which was kept locked. Sam found the key to this hidden room and opened the door.

She was horrified by what she saw. Every piece of cloth in the room was sewn together with red yarn. A white window curtain was stitched to a blue bedspread. The spread stretched down to a throw rug on the floor and was sewn to it. A silk slip and a bath towel hung together from a curtain that was sewn to a pillow. Everything was sewn tightly, senselessly together with the blood red yarn, like sutures in some awful botched surgery.

Unable to breathe, Sam shut the door behind her. She sat on the stairs and finally she wept at the evidence of her mother's madness until she was wrung dry of tears. The twelve-year-old Jack found her, her head pressed to the stair rail and he tried to make her laugh by doing a crazy dance for her.

Clark told Annie a version of one family story that was incomplete, but he wasn't to learn that until a few years later.

He told her this much: On Sam's last Thanksgiving vacation from college she came home early. It had been a hard time for her. Her first love affair had ended with the woman's calling it quits. Jack and his parents hadn't spoken since the Ruthie episode. Ruthie had run off. Clark had returned to Vietnam. D. K. Destin had joined the Navy and been shot out of his plane into the China Sea.

The last night of her vacation, Sam drove to downtown Emerald to see a late movie with George Nickerson and his fiancée Kim. While they were inside the Paradise, a terrible storm came squalling over the hills and tore a great oak tree in the Pilgrim's Rest lawn out by its roots. It lay on its side across the yard, like a giant tangled in a net.

By the time they left the movie house, the storm was over. Sam returned home to find both Jack and her father gone and her father's car missing. She found their mother sitting on the floor of the living room. Her clothes had blood on them. The framed pictures of Johnny from atop the black grand piano were arranged around her on the floor like candles around a saint.

When Sam asked what had happened, Grandee said only, "Accident."

Sam took her upstairs, undressed her, put her in the shower, and helped her wash the blood off herself. Grandee went limp, offering no resistance. By the time Sam got her into bed and returned downstairs to call the police, she heard Jack coming in the door. His clothes were wet from the rain and he was red with mud. He told Sam to hang up the phone. She needed to sit down.

He said that a few hours earlier when a friend had dropped

him home from the local pool hall, he'd found their mother sitting there on the floor with blood on her clothes, just the way Sam had found her. But Jack had also found a note from their father propped on the hall table. Sam needed to read this note before she decided to call the police. So Sam hung up the phone and opened the envelope he handed her. The letter, on thick paper with the judge's name engraved at the top, was in her father's upright stiffly formal handwriting.

Dear Family,
    I have come to a conclusion that feels to me irrevocable. Mother and I have quarreled again. I can endure no longer the unhappiness that weighs on me. I hope that you will forgive or at least understand my decision.
    Father

The rest of his letter dealt with financial matters.

Finally Jack pulled the letter away from Sam; she just kept petting the piece of paper as if it were alive. He said he had been out all this time looking for their father's car but had been unable to find it. He figured their dad had driven the car into the river.

Sam called her friend, the new police chief, and told him she feared her father had committed suicide. When he arrived, she showed him the note. He urged her to hope; maybe they'd find her father safe and sound. He agreed that in the meanwhile there was no need to awaken Mrs. Peregrine tonight.

The Emerald police started a search for the judge.

At breakfast the next morning, Grandee appeared not to know that something had happened. She kept asking where her husband was.

The police found ruts on a high bend in River Road, three miles from the house, where the judge's large sedan had clearly gone off the road into the Aquene River. They began dredging for the car. Questioned on the local news, the chief spoke of how bad a storm there had been last night and how strong and fast a current; how, in the same storm, ten miles to the north, two men foolishly trying to scavenge debris from the river had drowned in a dinghy. He reminded the town that he'd told them for years they needed a guardrail on that curve in River Hill Road. He said the judge might have had a fatal accident.

It took a week to find and pull up the car, which had been swept half a mile down the river by the current. It took another week to find Judge Peregrine's body, which had been sucked out of the driver's seat. The police chief brought the judge's wedding ring back to his wife. The chief thought the family shouldn't view the body, which was—he told D. K.—"a god-awful mess." The town thought Mrs. Peregrine had very bad luck—first her baby son drowning in her swimming pool and then, twenty years later, her husband drowning in the river. There were a few rumors about suicide, but the rumors faded quickly to other topics.

It was this version of the story Clark told Annie on the hot summer night of her freshman year at Annapolis, when she'd asked him why Sam didn't talk about her parents. A few years later Jack confessed the truth about the judge's death to Sam and Sam confessed the truth to Clark as he was recovering from his own car accident. She told no one else.

As Clark lay in the ICU, critically injured, Sam had phoned Jack with the sad news that Clark might die. A few weeks later Jack suddenly showed up in Emerald, only a day after Annie had left to return to classes. Clark had survived and was recovering. It was then that Jack told his sister a different version of the story, a confession that he had covered up the evidence that their mother had murdered their father. He said that he'd fabricated their father's suicide in order to spare Sam the ordeal of her mother's arrest. He said that he'd found Grandee that night, sitting on the floor with the judge's bloody head in her lap, his skull broken open. He said that he'd wrapped his father in a rug and carried him to the car. He wrote the suicide note himself, forging his father's handwriting, and left it on the table in the hall.

He told Sam how, as he drove off with their father's body to the top of River Road, the car slipped sideways in the smear of mud that switchbacked along the hill above the river. Rain and wind thrashed the black trees. The car skidded onto the shoulder, scraping against scrub brush. He was almost on top of the fallen telephone pole before he spotted it and slammed his foot to the brake. The telephone pole lay tangled in live sparking wires, blocking the road at its sharpest curve above the black river.

He said it was as if the storm was telling him what to do. He pulled the body out of the sedan, rolled it out of the bloody rug and propped it up in the front seat. Then he steered the running car toward the shoulder's edge, almost sliding off the soft bank, and at the last second, jumped clear. He'd seen it done in the movies.

The roiling red current carried the car along, floating it in the churn like a raft, until he'd nearly despaired that it would ever sink. But finally the river sucked it under.

Carrying the bloody rug, he walked back to Pilgrim's Rest. The storm scudded away and sullen clouds crept into the sky.

He burned the rug and put the bloody kitchen mallet he'd pulled from his mother's hand into the dishwasher with the supper dishes.

Judge Peregrine's funeral was the biggest at St. Mark's since the funeral of his grandfather, "The Boss." The judge was buried next to his dead son Johnny. Sam sent out the invitations, cooked the food, and cleaned the house for the reception. Three hundred people attended, including the lieutenant governor.

Jack refused to come to the funeral. Instead he robbed the house and drove off in Grandee's Mercedes. Sam was left to take care of their mother. It was only after Grandee stabbed Sam in the arm with scissors that she'd been persuaded to have her mother institutionalized. But until Grandee died, Sam went daily to see her, even when, propped like a doll on her bed and fumbling with the wrappers of candy, Grandee had no idea who Sam was.

More than a year passed. One day "out of the blue," Sam would say, "like Gary Cooper in *Now and Forever*," Jack returned home with the baby Annie and the airplane he'd named the *King of the Sky*. Grandee was in the hospital at the time, having one of her "episodes," and her son did not go to see her during his month-long stay.

Years later, when he returned with the seven-year-old Annie, Sam told him their mother was dead, although he hadn't asked.

Sam took care of Annie until the girl went away to college at Annapolis. Sam tried her best to make sure that Annie had, as far as childhoods go, a happy one.

• • •

Clark was standing beside Sam's bed when she awakened. His white lab coat appeared to her to be billowing, wriggly. A black head with a white topknot peeked out and Teddy barked.

"You can't bring dogs in here," Sam mumbled.

Clark spilled Teddy onto the bed. "This is your lucky day, Sam. Your surgery was a total success. Good surgeon, that Sarah Yoelson."

"I could love that woman."

Clark advised Sam, "Go for it. As the great Bob Dylan says, 'Love and only love. It can't be denied.' Georgette says Annie's in love with that Miami cop."

"Hart. Dan Hart. He's after Jack. How's Jack?"

"Jack escaped and probably isn't even dying anyhow."

Sam smiled as she fell back asleep with Teddy snuggled beside her. "Jack always exaggerated."

Chapter 51
Under Two Flags

The drive from Puerto Esperanza to Havana was only 112 miles
and didn't take long at the speed at which Raffy's elderly uncle
Oswardo Ramirez drove his (also old) cavernous pink Cadillac coupe de ville. Round-faced, friendly, sweating, Oswardo
swerved dangerously as he pointed out landmarks of the glamorous seedy city of Havana. With his rapid speech and flurry of
hand motions it was as if he were rushing to finish a tour before
his car, spitting and groaning, gave out on him. He hurried them
past the Capitol Dome, past the monument of the revolutionary
hero José Martí, past the huge stone fortress of Castillo de los
Tres Reyes del Morro as fast as the Cadillac could maneuver in
the heavy traffic.

Holding his guitar case, Raffy sat silent in the back seat
beside Annie. He said too many memories were sweeping over
him. He hadn't driven around Havana since his early teens, for
on his one trip with Jack he'd been arrested before even reaching
land. All he'd seen of Havana had been the very small view from
a jail cell window.

By the time they rattled past the high curved sea wall of the
Malecón, Raffy was in tears.

In Habana Viejo, streets changed from asphalt to wine-red
cobbled bricks. Lanes curved away under low arches of amber
stucco. On either side of the avenues, the tall elegant pastel

colonial buildings greeted them like ruined monuments to antiquated and neglected triumphs.

Oswardo took them to the Plaza de Armas, near the hotel into which they'd been told they should register even though they would leave before nightfall. It was across the square from the bank. The long pink sedan rattled to a jiggling stop and let out Oswardo's passengers—Annie and Dan and Raffy. Annie carried the Queen of the Sea, which lay wrapped at the bottom of a paper shopping bag. The contact person would have an identical shopping bag.

Raffy left them to go look at the outside of the Ramirez jewelry store, which was only a few blocks away. He confessed he might not go inside. He wasn't quite ready to make himself known to his mother. No matter what, he'd be back at the hotel in an hour to take them to the bank. The bawdy hand of time, he said, showing them his watch, was now three hours past the prick of noon.

"You show up, *linán!*" Dan told him.

"*Pito. ¡Vaya!*" Carrying his guitar, Raffy quickly danced away into the congestion of a city that always sounded to him like music.

Annie and Dan checked into the Hotel Santa Isabel. They look like what they claimed to be—a young Toronto couple on vacation, in their white T-shirts with khaki slacks and their friendly smiles. The clerk took their Canadian passports and their euros without comment. The room was large and had the same neglected grandeur as the Cadillac. The bed was beautiful.

Later, carrying the Queen with them in the shopping bag, they walked to a late lunch at an outdoor café at a side-street corner of the square, not far from the bank where it had been arranged for Annie to meet Raffy's cousin, the assistant manager, in 2 1/2 hours, just before the bank closed. Over lunch she kept looking around the Plaza, hoping to see the coppery-haired woman, Helen Clark, at one of the other outdoor cafés. Her eagerness was curiously blended with dread.

They had finished their tapas when suddenly Dan startled her by clapping his hands together. "Got it! Your dad said 'our picture.' 'Our picture.' He meant *yours* and his. The one I saw your phone number on the back of."

Annie knew instantly what Dan meant, and knew that he was right. It was the Breakers picture of her dad and her, sitting in the banquette. "He had the copy in his wallet."

Dan rubbed his hands violently through his curls. "Damn, I wish I had that picture now!"

"I've got it." She found the old tattered photo in her purse that she'd palmed from her dad. Together they examined it in the strong sunlight but it was hard to see details. Annie said, "We need the original. On the piano at Pilgrim's Rest. It's much bigger and clearer." She would have called Sam but they'd been emphatically instructed not to make, or try to make, any phone calls from Cuba.

They studied the picture: The small birthday cake on the banquette table. Annie in her velvet dress and cowboy boots, leaning happily against her father. Jack, his perfect suit and slender tie, with his deep-tanned smiling face and his trim fair mustache, with his arms stretched out, and a cigarette in his tanned fingers. Behind them, other diners filled in the background, laughing women, other men in thin ties and perfect suits. Among them were five men seated together, smoking, smiling. They were too small to distinguish. It was these men that made the photo matter so much.

Annie and Dan found a shop in the Plaza where there was a copier. They enlarged the picture as much as possible. Dan identified two of the diners (call them A and B, he said) as two very famous men who had been notoriously prosecuted later for political bribery and racketeering. A was still in prison and B had mysteriously died in a plane crash shortly before a congressional hearing at which he'd agreed to testify. The third man was Archbishop de Uloa. Next to him was Feliz Diaz. Both were recognizable, although the photograph had been taken almost twenty years ago and their hair was black, not gray.

The fifth man would be recognizable to almost anybody. And, as Dan said, anyone with a memory (unfortunately in America, that included few citizens and almost none of the press) would remember that this powerful public figure had consistently claimed, even under oath, that he had never met A or B in his life.

Annie and Dan plotted what they would do. An hour passed. Raffy didn't return. They went back to their hotel room. In their absence the room had been—according to Dan—"tossed by pros," ransacked carefully but perceptibly and then restored to order. Whether the break-in had been carried out by the Havana police or by American undercover agents or by associates of Feliz Diaz, it was impossible to guess. Maybe the infiltrators had been looking for the Queen of the Sea, maybe for clues to Jack Peregrine's whereabouts, maybe just conducting a routine search. Dan and Annie carefully checked their belongings but nothing seemed to be missing.

Another half-hour passed with no sign of Raffy. They walked to Ramirez Gold and Silver, a once handsome if now dilapidated shop with walls blue as the sea and doors and windows of iron filigree. In the main window were displayed a gold chain and a silver bowl with tongs. The shop was closed.

They strolled around the Plaza de Armas, looking for Raffy. They returned to the café on the side street where they'd eaten lunch. Now a young hard-muscled man in black jeans and a black T-shirt with a portrait of the rock band KISS was sitting at a table. He was the man whose photograph Fierson had shown them at the Sigsbee meeting.

"Fred Owen," Annie said.

Dan was amused. "Feds. We're supposed to think he's from Moscow or what?"

Noisily the old pink coupe de ville bounced to a stop near the café. Oswardo rolled down his window and told Dan in Spanish that Raffy had been detained but that they should go as scheduled to the bank, where everything was arranged.

"Is Raffy okay?" Annie called to Oswardo but he had rolled up the window and the old Cadillac was jouncing away over the cobbled bricks.

A nearby church bell rang the hour. Dan stood up. "Let's go, Sundance."

Annie smiled tensely; she wasn't sure she liked the analogy.

Like much of Old Havana, too poor to be ruined in the '70s and '80s, the branch bank was beautiful, unrenovated, with a floor of old soft-edged cream and black marble squares; the walls were a pale-green plaster, the grillwork Spanish black iron, black ceiling fans languidly turning.

Annie and Dan waited in chairs that looked like they'd been taken from a 1950s restaurant. "I'd love to get a couple of these chairs," Dan said, bending down to check out the curved aluminum legs. "Don't look now but there's our FBI buddy Willie. He really ought to work out more. Man's a mess."

Annie glanced behind her. The chunky FBI agent was leaning against a counter by the wall, filling out a bank form. He was sweaty in the heat, even in his white Cuban shirt, open-collared, short-sleeved.

The younger muscular man wearing all black stepped inside the bank. Dan grinned. "Look at his shoes. Now look at Willie's shoes. Same. Why don't the Feds work on their shoes?"

The two agents ignored them.

The assistant manager of this small branch of the Banco Centrale appeared out of the back and introduced himself in Spanish as Teofilo Ramirez. He asked, *¿Donde esta Rafael?"*

"No clue," Dan admitted with a shrug. "Oswardo said to come ahead anyhow."

Nodding, Ramirez led Annie and Dan to a sitting area near the rail separating the lobby from offices. Slim, youthful, courteous, he apologized for any tardiness. There had been none. Ramirez wore a blue suit with a blue tie. His hair was a short neat version of his cousin Rafael Rook's glossy black ponytail. His dark eyes were far less trusting than Raffy's, in fact they were rather cynical. But he began with polite pleasantries; they lasted longer than they would have in America. To Annie's surprise he brought out a color copy of her official Navy identification photo. He showed it to her, then returned it to his pocket. He smiled. *"No soy un tonto. Soy un banquero."*

Dan nodded. "He says he's not a fool, he's a banker." The

whole conversation took place in Spanish, with Dan translating for Annie, although she had the clear notion that Ramirez could understand English perfectly well.

Raffy's cousin said they would not waste one another's time. There were certain passwords necessary to access the account. *"Démelos por favor."*

Annie spoke slowly from memory, reciting the numbers whose meaning she had figured out on a night that now seemed to have taken place a lifetime ago, during the flight to St. Louis in the *King of the Sky*. The alphanumeric stood for her birthday and her birth weight and her time of birth, for Lindbergh's plane and her father's plane: She looked directly at Teofilo Ramirez. "The passwords are 362484070N and 678STNX211. I'll repeat those."

Dan translated each number and letter slowly and carefully. With a polite compliment to Annie's memory, Señor Ramirez wrote everything down. *"Tres seis dos cuatro ocho cuatro cero siete cero N. Seis siete ocho S. T. N. X. dos uno uno."* He asked Annie to check what was written for accuracy.

She did so. "Yes, that's right. Thanks."

He nodded at her.

"Muchas gracias," said Dan and handed him discreetly, but with a courteous tilt of his head, a sealed business envelope. The envelope contained twenty thousand euros in cash. The assistant manager took it nonchalantly. He told them he would return momentarily and stepped backward, disappearing behind a door at the far end of the bank marked Privado.

Annie and Dan waited nervously on a rattan couch. They kept their hands on the shopping bag between them. Two old loud-ticking round metal clocks on opposite walls showed different times in the vicinity of 4:45 p.m.

Finally the private office door reopened. Ramirez returned, this time carrying a blue zippered pouch the size of a large book; it was embossed with the name of the bank. He told Dan in Spanish that he would now need to ask her (he referred to Annie throughout as *ella*–"she" or "her") to provide him with answers to three questions that the signatory on the account (he never mentioned the name, Jack Peregrine) had added as a security check. Annie said that she would answer the questions as best she could. "Did my father prepare the questions? *Mio padre?*" She pointed at the pouch. "Mio padre?"

The well-dressed bank manager bowed to her but didn't answer. Instead he read from the sheet of bank stationery he carried. "*Primero. El Rey del...?*"

Dan turned to her. "He's asking you for the king of something."

Immediately Annie heard her father's voice, softly like a far-away echo, when he'd called her last night and then she'd seen him shimmery in the ghost light by the pool in Key West. "King Queen Sam," he'd told her then. "King Queen Sam. King Queen Sam."

She smiled solemnly at Ramirez. "I understand. My father's first question is, 'The King of the what?' The answer is 'Sky.' The King of the Sky."

Dan said to the banker, "*El rey del cielo.*"

The slim man nodded, checking the answer against his paper. "*Sí, gracias, sí.* King of the Sky. Y, *segundo.* Y,...*del Mar?*"

"He's asking for the something of the sea," Dan said.

Annie had anticipated the question. The *King of the Sky*, the Queen of the Sea, her lost father, her lost mother. "Queen," she told Señor Ramirez. "*La Reina Coronada del Mar.* The Queen of the Sea." She looked over to the two FBI agents, who were pretending they weren't watching her. Somehow she began to think, perhaps irrationally, that her father's life, not just his jail sentence—but his *life* depended on her correctly answering these questions. She could feel her heart quickening, pulsing in her neck. Would Feliz Diaz take revenge for the poker debt, for the statue scam, by killing her dad? Would the government just let that happen? Or would the government itself get rid of him, because of his knowledge of the photograph, if Annie failed to provide what was wanted? Could she make Fierson believe there was no further threat?

"Annie," Dan urged her, "One more question to answer."

Ramirez closed his sheet of paper and smiled with an ironic shrug at her as if the third question were useless. "¿Y, pasado, cuál es el nombre de su madre?"

Annie was startled. She frowned at Dan. "Did he just ask me for the name of my mother?"

"Yes."

Heart thudding now, Annie hesitated. Was this a trick of her father's? Perhaps she was supposed to say, "Claudette Colbert." Or give one of the other false names he'd offered her? But which one? She didn't know the name of her mother. Wasn't that what this whole journey had been about? Wasn't it to find the name of her mother that she'd come after him all this way? She didn't speak.

"Annie?" asked Dan, frowning. "Your mother's name?"

"I don't know," she whispered.

"What?"

She heard her father's voice's again, "King Queen Sam. King Queen Sam."

Her father was telling her the truth.

She smiled the radiant smile she'd given Sam when she'd taken her first steps into her arms. "Sam," she told the manager, so softly that he leaned toward her inquisitively. "The name of my mother is Sam."

"Sam?" asked Dan, puzzled.

She nodded. "S-a-m. Samantha. Sam. Samantha Anne Peregrine."

Teofilo Ramirez was unable not to smile back at her. "Sam, sí. That is correct. Gracias."

Dan hugged Annie. "That's all three."

With a bow, Mr. Ramirez held out the navy-blue lettered bank pouch. When Annie didn't seem to see him, he gave it to Dan. "Gracias. Adios. Buenas vacaciones." With a surprising quickness, he walked away and vanished behind the iron rail.

"Beautiful," Dan put his arm around Annie, who was breathing hard, fighting off exasperating tears that made it hard to see. "You okay? You did great." He handed her the dark-blue pouch. "Sam, huh? I thought she was gay." He spoke in a nonchalant way, gently wiping her eyes with his fingers. "Okay, they're watching us. Take your look in the pouch. Make it easy going."

Dan kept talking casually to her until she took a deep breath and took a look inside the pouch, checking through the contents. "Got it," she said quietly. She zipped up the pouch. "Ready?"

"Yep. Now we hand the pouch over to Mr. Fred Owen as instructed."

They strolled toward the bank doors and through them and into the sun-bright street, followed by the two agents. Outside the door, Willie, breathing hard, passed by, bumping them. The younger man in the black KISS shirt slipped the pouch out from under Annie's arm and walked with it to an old white Chevrolet waiting at the curb. There he opened the pouch and Annie saw him pull out the photo, quickly identify it and slip it back inside. Willie's view had been blocked by a tall man who passed in front of him. Then Owen gestured for Willie to hurry to join him. Willie ambled across the plaza and got into the Chevrolet, which sat there parked.

"You made the switch?" Dan asked Annie.

She smiled. "Yep."

"Damn, you're quick." He hugged her affectionately. "I should take you to Las Vegas."

"That's what my dad used to say. I took the negative. But Fred Owen's got an eight-by-ten print of the photo of us in The Breakers. There were also two emeralds, three rubies, six sapphires, two diamonds. The rubies are about the size and shape of tiny eggs, but there was nothing anywhere near a 135-carat star ruby in there. And if there were supposed to be seven emeralds in the crown? There are three in the queen now and those two in the pouch makes only five. Where are the other two?"

Dan said he suspected that Jack and Raffy planned to hold back an emerald each. "Finders' fees. Well, look's like poor old Willie's out of the loop on this deal. I'm going to take him out for a drink when we get back to Miami and tell him to watch his step on those big fat flat feet of his."

Somehow, strangely, Annie knew that she would see the beautiful coppery-haired woman in the café, just at the table where she was sitting. There was a row of tiny bamboo café tables next to a row of little orange trees in wooden boxes, next to the open square. The woman wore large elegant sunglasses and thin brown linen clothes. On the pavement at her feet was a small soft brown leather suitcase and a shopping bag that looked very much like the one in which Annie now carried the Queen.

Dan kissed Annie. "I'll be down the block." He pointed in the direction of the Ramirez Gold and Silver shop and kept walking without looking back as Annie headed toward Helen Clark.

Taking a chair at the table next to the woman, Annie quietly studied the crowd of shoppers and tourists milling about in the Plaza. A waiter moved nearby and she used her little bit of Spanish to him. "*Camarero. Una botella de agua, por favor. Gracias.*" After he left, she said to the woman, "You're Helen Clark."

The woman nodded yes without looking at her.

Annie set down the old shopping bag between their tables. "But your real name is Ruthie Nickerson. You're Georgette's aunt, aren't you? I met you in Emerald once. Did you pick the name Clark from Clark Goode?"

The woman's head lifted in surprise. Now she looked over at Annie, who couldn't see her expression because of her sunglasses. Then she took the glasses off and Annie saw that her eyes were as blue as the sea. She had the lovely low voice of the woman who had made the phone call warning Annie to stay away from her father's criminal pursuits.

"Hello. It's been a long time."

Annie looked from the woman's face to her hand, which was suntanned and freckled. The hand rested on the table near the small white cup of Cuban coffee. Ruthie's fingers closed around the cup. She wore no jewelry.

"You helped me with my algebra," Annie said.

A long silence. Finally the woman spoke again. "How are Sam and Clark?" Her voice was measured. "Good friends to me."

Annie told her they were both fine. "And you were a friend of my father's?"

"I suppose friend's a word." She sipped at the dark coffee.

"I really think all he wanted to do was sell Feliz Diaz that stupid statue and leave me a lot of money. Kind of sweet and silly."

"All he wants to do is make life exciting. He almost got himself killed, not to mention me. Or you." Ruthie glanced down at Annie's shopping bag. "The statue didn't belong to him. So, that's the Queen of the Sea in there?"

Annie said that it was.

Ruthie told Annie what was in the other shopping bag and that Jack had arranged for it. "The art of the con," she smiled.

"Did you know Dad's dying?"

"Did he think he wouldn't?" Ruthie drank a sip of coffee. She spoke not unsympathetically. "But I'm sorry to hear it. He was the best dancer I ever met." Her eyes moved slowly left to right across the busy plaza. "We can't sit here long. How many gems in the bank pouch?"

Annie saw no reason not to enumerate the contents. "The real Queen's got three big emeralds in her crown already. Dad must have put them back in the crown."

"Just three?" Ruthie set down her coffee cup in a thoughtful way. "How about the 135-carat star ruby?" She moved her perfect teeth over her lower lip when Annie shook her head no. "This could be a problem. Feliz is paying Jack a great deal of money for *La Reina Coronada*. He expected more emeralds and that ruby to go back on that silver box with the Holy Thorn inside it. Now he won't have either. He's a mobster but a good Catholic. He honestly believes the Queen should go to the Church, and go looking good. I'm going to have trouble selling this...'as is' sale to Feliz."

Annie was quiet a minute, then she said, "How much did my dad, or Fierson, tell you about the photo at The Breakers? The one with your friend Feliz Diaz in it."

The woman looked baffled. "McAllister Fierson?"

"Yes. The government big shot who arranged for me to get here to Havana. My dad told me last night that what Fierson really wanted from that bank pouch was a photo." Annie described her birthday party picture and named the men who sat laughing together in the background of the restaurant. "Fierson specifically told me to stay away from you if you were in Havana. You might want to watch out for him. My dad told me that the negative to that photo was his gift to you. I've got it here."

Ruthie leaned away, thinking hard. "Well, Jack has surprised me…" She stubbed out her cigarette.

Annie said, "The negative and a print were in the pouch with the jewels. I left everything but the negative in there for this FBI agent Fred Owen."

"Fred," said Ruthie. There was a world of contempt in the word. "He's over there in that Chevy with Willie Grunberg. Willie's a good guy."

"I've got the negative under my hand."

Startled, Ruthie glanced over at Annie for a moment. Then she asked if anyone, and she meant anyone, had possibly seen her remove the negative from the pouch?

"No," Annie assured her. "I'm very fast."

Ruthie said there were now at least two men at the café and there was another man standing in the Plaza; all three were watching them right now. Before too long, Annie had to leave the negative and the Queen and walk away.

Annie said, "Dad used to give me lessons every day. Five years old, I could palm the wallet right out of your purse, study everything in it, put it back and tell you the contents to the last detail. And you'd never know your wallet had been out of your purse."

Ruthie Nickerson smiled slightly. "I recall that your dad had great hands."

The remark startled Annie. "You were lovers," she blurted out.

The woman's mouth softened. "No. Never. He said he was in love with me. I wasn't with him."

Annie was confused. "I thought you were lovers."

"We could have been. But we weren't. Those were crazy

times. Clark was going back to Vietnam. He'd reenlisted. So back he went and ended up a POW." She shook her head ruefully. "Funny. Jack couldn't talk me into loving him. I couldn't talk Clark out of leaving me. I never figured Jack would do what he did. Take you, I mean."

Annie stared a long time at her eyes. They looked familiar because they looked like her own eyes. "Are you my mother?"

The older woman looked at her, looked past her, replaced the sunglasses. "I came to the same conclusion. But only a week ago."

Annie's eyebrow arched. "In St. Louis?"

Ruthie took a cigarette from a leather purse. Annie noticed her hand was shaking slightly. "Yes, in St. Louis. Of course Jack knew all along but he kept it to himself. Unless he told Sam. But I never thought it until I saw you there in the airport. I had assumed..." She frowned. "That you were growing up happy in Ohio. The way I'd planned."

"In Barbados...Why?" Annie asked.

The older woman frowned. "...College. I talked my way into a fellowship; I wanted a career." She laughed. "Not exactly the one I have. Jack tracked me down to the island, tried to stop me, and—although I certainly didn't know about it at the time— after I left for the States, he, well, stole you." She smiled. "You're the most beautiful thing he ever stole."

Annie rubbed at the back of her neck. "You didn't think I was your baby when you visited Sam that night at Pilgrim's Rest and helped me with my algebra and she told you I was Jack's daughter?"

She shook her head. "No. I just remember thinking how lovely you were, and how lucky you were to have Sam. I figured Jack had met someone, had a baby with her. But in St. Louis, when I saw you...and I, I don't know, I just knew." She was quiet a moment. "I went to St. Louis trying to help keep that idiot Jack from getting himself killed, which is exactly what Feliz was ready to do to him. Jack was sure he could get out of his gambling mess by selling Feliz La Reina. It was another one of Jack's crazy schemes. But Feliz seemed to fall for it. Like I say, the idea of making a big gift to the Church appealed to him. I did what I could to scare you off. Back in Miami I reamed Jack out about the whole thing. I told him if he didn't back off from you I'd see to it that he was locked up for twenty years."

Annie thought about this for a while. Then she asked Ruthie if she'd ever really met Claudette Colbert.

She said that she had. "Briefly." In Barbados, during her pregnancy. The movie star had been very kind and helpful to her.

Annie felt a bitter taste. "Everything was 'briefly' with you, wasn't it?"

"No." Ruthie looked at her, then with a wry smile, added, "I say this not ruthlessly, and not without rue." Annie immediately thought back to the night in the Pilgrim's Rest kitchen, the glamorous stranger punning on the word "Jack" during the peculiarly intense Scrabble game with Sam. "I've done serious work for a quarter of a century. That's not brief. I've worked with the agency, always undercover." Ruthie called to the waiter for her check. "For years, I've been passing along to our government useful things about Feliz and his friends. To find those things out, I make Feliz trust me. That's my work." Ruthie took another cigarette from a pack on the table.

"You shouldn't smoke." Annie leaned forward as the waiter left. "Okay. The negative is in your jacket pocket now."

Ruthie nodded; the wry smile widening into a version of Annie's smile. "Good for you."

"By the way, Trevor Smithwall told me you had my back."

The woman frowned, shaking her head. "He shouldn't tell you things like that. I'm the mistress of Feliz Diaz." The waiter set down checks at both their tables. Ruthie gave him money. "And you, you train flyers on combat jets for the Navy. I heard that from Sam. I called her once, just to see how she was. She told me about you and the Navy. Of course, she's a peace freak but she's very proud of you." Her hand moved forward, brushed past Annie's.

Annie paid her own check. "Are you in danger from Diaz?"

Ruthie shook her head. "The irony is, Feliz loves me and I'm actually…fond of him." She touched her pocket into which

Annie had slid the negative of the photograph at The Breakers. "At the right time, this will help. McAllister Fierson has started to distrust me. He'll find out he was right…" She glanced around the plaza again. "We've been sitting here a little too long. You need to go. Your friend Dan Hart? In Miami, they say he's a very good cop." She smiled. "Getting fired can be a sign of a good cop. You two look fond of each other." She bent toward Annie's table, moved her hand over to hers and this time let it rest there for a little moment, her fingers moving quietly, like a heartbeat. She said in her lovely voice, "I thought the world would be different." She took off the sunglasses again and her eyes wetted to a darker blue.

Annie touched her mother's fingers. "The world *is* different. I had it easier." As she said this, she felt a clear sense that what was real between the two of them had little to do with the words they were speaking to each other, the words that made sounds in the air. But that what was real was as indefinite as water and that the meaning of it all floated somewhere between them, side by side, nearly together, as subterranean as a ship's keel in the ocean, moving unseen through the waves. And then Annie slipped her hand away.

All at once there was a loud screeching noise of horn and brakes in the street beside the café. People jumped to their feet at the other tables.

Annie saw a two-tone taxi slam to a stop. A small man in bright green trousers flopped across the cab's fender, rolling over its hood and falling to the crowded cobbled pavement.

An old woman shouted in alarm. Customers ran from their tables at the café and others rushed out of the restaurant, swarming in front of the boxed orange trees near the front row of small tables; all were trying to catch a glimpse of the accident.

In the midst of the hubbub, Annie stood up and saw a slender recognizable hand move smoothly across Ruthie Nickerson's table-top. She saw two green sparkling objects fall from tanned fingers into Ruthie's hand. Then the people behind jostled her and she lost sight of her father.

Annie squeezed quickly between the little boxed trees and raced into the plaza. She spotted Dan Hart running out of a low stucco arch toward her. Across the cobbled opening, on the other side, a little apart from the crowd, Jack Peregrine stood, thinner, frailer, in the cream silk trousers and Cuban shirt, dappled gold like Ruthie's brown leather bag that he held up to her in the sunlight. He waved the Fed Ex envelope that Sam had sent to Key West in his other hand. She started running toward him but he grabbed Dan's arm, thrust the leather bag at him and then slipped through the arch, turned, waved his hand in goodbye, and vanished.

Annie spun around to look back at the café. The small bamboo table was empty. The shopping bag with the Queen in it was gone. The white coffee cup sat there on the café table, coppery lipstick on its rim. Beneath the table the other shopping bag sat beside Ruthie's chair.

Dan and Annie took the bag back to their hotel room and unwrapped the Queen of Sea. Well, at least a modern copy of that statue, done in gold plate and without jewels in its crown. But modeled—Ruthie had told her—on the real Queen; made right here in Havana by the talented goldsmith, Maria Ramirez, Raffy's mother.

Chapter 52

The Right Stuff

Rafael Rook hugged his guitar to the dancing alligators on his shirt as the Cessna Amphibian plane moved away from its moorings and bounced across the choppy waves. "Your papa astonishes me," Raffy called up to Annie in the cockpit. "There he is, dying in Golden Days. Then *kazaam* he's stealing Skippings's car. Then he's drowned in the bay. Then *kazaam* here he is today, standing in Plaza de Armas in Havana, Cuba. All of a sudden, I hear Jack's voice. I turn around and he shoves me forward. 'Flop that taxi now, Rafael, now, do it!' And I do it, I don't think and think and think and worry. I just do it. That's how we'll be in paradise. We'll just do it the way with your dad somehow I could just…do things."

Dan sat in the plane seat beside the Cuban grifter as they motored away from the harbor rocks to where they would get take-off clearance from a Ramirez relative in the harbormaster's station. "So," Dan asked, "Raffy, you little bastard, flopping was Jack's idea?"

"Absolutely."

"Well, *kazaam* times two. I'm standing in the Plaza and there he is. 'Hi, Dan,' he says. 'Take care of her,' he says. And he shoves this damn leather bag here at me. He shows me this FedEx. It's from Sam, he says, and it's all the insurance he needs. And *poof* he's gone while we're all watching you rolling around on the hood of an old cab. Willie spots him and gives chase. But you can just imagine who won that race."

The Cuban nodded. "Jack was the wind. You never know what he'll do next." Annie heard that she was cleared for take-off. As she opened the throttle, she yelled at Raffy that he should look to see what was in the bag. "It's going to be money," she predicted to distract him.

Raffy unzipped the soft brown leather bag. He was so focused on the fact that he was staring at what would prove to be, when they counted it, a million dollars, that he forgot to be terrified that Annie was taking off into air. "*Madre Dios!*" he shouted. "Whoever saw so many dollars? We did it! Jack, we did it!"

Dan thumbed one of the stacks of bills like a deck of cards. "Yep, if you've got to be left holding the bag, this is the way to do it," he agreed.

As Annie came out of their climb and headed North by Northwest, Dan and Raffy counted up one hundred bonded stacks of one hundred hundred-dollar bills,

Annie burst out laughing. "So he did leave me a million dollars?"

Rafael's enthusiasm overwhelmed him and he had to pat his chest to calm himself. "I told you, Annie! I told you! It was never the money with Jack. See how he gives away the money. Easy as a smile. He always said, 'I'll leave Annie a million dollars.' Of course, if you could see your way to sharing say maybe a quarter, okay, a tenth, with me? That would be very kind. With Jack, it was, well, with Jack—" The small man pulled at his ponytail, try-ing to think of the right way to say it. "Jack's 'nature is subdu'd to what it works in, like the dyer's hand.' That happens to be the Bard of Avon's view on art and if the Bard tells you something, you can definitely take it to the bank." The slender Cuban put down the money and picked up his guitar. "Art. It's a little past the wit of man." He played a melody softly.

> *Los amigos me olvidaron*
> *Sólo mi madre lloraba*

A Dios pedía y rogaba
Que salvara su hijo.

While the Cuban sang, Dan told Annie that he had forced Raffy to go see his mother in the goldsmith shop and that Raffy's reunion with her had been "a calamity, more or less," that Mrs. Ramirez had called him a criminal ne'er-do-well musician and had shut the shop door in his face. In fact, on learning that Raffy would be returned to prison in Florida (which unfortunately he'd told her was absolutely true), Mrs. Ramirez had called him, in comparison with his older brother, the shame of the family name.

Slumping over his guitar, Raffy sighed to Annie that Dan was right. His mother had thrown him out of her life as a failure; for a Communist, Maria Ramirez really seemed to care only about what the Bard would call, putting money in her purse.

"You're going back to Havana right now!" Annie abruptly turned the Cessna TU206 around in a high-banked 180-degree curve.

"What are you doing?" Both Raffy and Dan were shouting at her.

Annie steered the plane back toward the coast and over the Viñales Valley, so low she could see fields of tobacco. The bumpy flight at low altitude sent the two men in the rear seats falling against each other. "I'm taking you back," she told Raffy.

"Are you crazy?" shouted Dan. "He's in my custody."

"I'm sorry," Annie told him. "Raffy's going home to Havana. Give him half of the money in that suitcase, $500,000. Come on, Dan. Do it!"

Raffy shouted, "What?" He was torn between his horror at the flight and shock that she was giving him half Jack's money.

Annie yelled, "You're going to tell your mother you made all that money playing guitar. That you're not a failure, that you're a great big success, a musical star, in America."

At first stunned, Raffy pulled himself together enough to protest vehemently. First of all, Annie couldn't re-land the plane at Puerto Esperanza! Raffy had only been able to guarantee that one tiny time when his relative was on duty at the harbor. That time was past. If they tried to land now, they'd be arrested!

Annie called back, "Then I'll fly you to a drop-point over land and you'll have to, as my dad used to say to me, 'Jump!' Put a parachute on him, Dan."

Raffy grabbed Dan by the jacket, "Save me. To tell you the truth, Annie's more like her dad than I thought. I mean, crazy. Do something."

Dan pried loose Raffy's cinnamon-colored fingers from his jacket lapels. "I don't think she's joking about this. Have you ever jumped before?"

"No! And I never will!"

Annie yelled, "Work it out fast, guys."

While she made a large loop over the mountains, Dan located the parachute. He told Raffy he was a practiced skydiver and could talk Raffy through the process. Piece of cake. Annie said she was going to circle back and put him down right over a little beachy area they'd passed. She could see a road not a mile from the beach. He could hitch a ride.

Raffy absolutely, definitely refused to put on the parachute. As much as he dreaded returning to a U.S. prison, as much as he knew a coward dies a thousand deaths, as much as he would love to see his mother's face if he showed her $500,000—Annie's offering of which, coincidentally, showed, as Shakespeare would tell her, a generous hand—as true as all these things were true, there was no way in the entire history of the infinite and eternal universe of the God of all creation that Rafael Ramirez Rook was going to jump out of an airplane in the middle of the air.

"For Christ's sake," Dan said finally, exasperated as Raffy kept slipping away from his efforts to attach the parachute. "Annie, just get us as close to the sand as you can and I'll jump out with him!"

Annie twisted her head around. "What?"

Dan said he was serious. "I'll jump out with the little bastard myself just to shut him up. Come back for me! I'll swim out to you! Can you do that?"

Dan tossed about half of the packets of hundred-dollar bills out of the suitcase onto the floor of the plane. He zipped the rest in the bag.

Annie was circling again, flying low away from the western sun, heading for a lagoon with a small sandy crescent beach. She called back, "Dan! There's a little boat moored to a buoy. See it?"

Dan looked out the plane window. "Got it."

"Swim out there. I'll pick you up!"

Dan stripped off his clothes to his boxer shorts. Then he strapped the parachute on. He thrust the bag of money hard into Rafael's arms.

Raffy was shouting that Annie couldn't seriously be planning to put him down in the middle of nowhere in Cuba?

"It's your country," she said. "There's no place like home. When we get to Key West, we're going to say you pulled a gun on us and jumped out of the plane."

"I would never do that!" the musician cried.

Dan told him, "We'll make you sound like Jimmy Cagney. They don't know what a wuss you are." He shouted up to the cockpit, "Annie, it's looking good down there. So, okay, Raffy, I'm going to count, we're going to jump, just like in the movies, right?"

"Go limp when you land, Raffy," Annie yelled. "Bend your knees. Run with the chute. Trust Dan. We'll swing by once more, get the feel, then we'll do it."

Annie was calculating just how much open sand there was, how slowly she could go, how close to the beach. Dan opened the seaplane's door.

"Noooooo!" Rafael kept shouting.

Grabbing the small Cuban to his chest, Dan yelled, "Rook, you little cocksucker, hug me!" Rafael fought back but Dan clutched him tightly. "Hug me like I was the fuckin' greatest love of your miserable life!"

"Leave me alone!"

"Think of the Love sign lady. *Ame a su familia!*"

"Leave me alone!"

Annie swung the plane back toward the beach. "On one, guys. Good luck, Raffy! Five, four, three, two, one, jump!"

"Get personal, Raffy!" Dan squeezed the Cuban tightly and leaped with him out of the airplane, above the sandy beach.

• • •

When Annie looped back over the beach, she saw Dan swimming strongly below her, closing in on the little rocking boat at the white buoy. Her main worry was that they were losing the light. Get as close to the boat as you can, she kept telling herself, but do it safely. Safely. Close. Safely. Closer. Closer.

Dan swam splashing to the old white buoy, reached, grabbed its rusted ring and raised his other arm, waving at Annie.

part five

Home

Chapter 53
Fly Away Home

At the Navy testing site in Patuxent River, Maryland, in the cockpit of the new experimental plane, Annie felt the speed flatten and shake her. She opened the throttle, faster, faster, the jet shaking, her heart too fast, the plane too fast. She made herself breathe by saying over and over, "You're going to break the record. You're going to break the record."

She shouted aloud when the odometer hit the mark that she'd been speeding toward since she was a child: 3.4567. Three and a half times the speed of sound.

• • •

After her test flight, after all the follow-up and medical examinations and debriefings and all the congratulations and photographs and film footage, Annie drove home to her condominium in Chesapeake Cove.

She found her fiancé Dan in her kitchen, cooking Asian food. Pots and pans sat out everywhere. He was chopping ginger. "Welcome home," he said to her. Her cat Amy Johnson circled his feet. "Now here's something I never thought I'd say to my future wife. How did your test flight go, baby?"

"3.4567."

"That's the record! Isn't it the record?" He lifted her, spun her in a circle.

She kissed him, smiling her incandescent smile. "Yep, it's the record! In '99, Brad did 3.4498 once. So this was faster."

"Call him and tell him. And thank him for divorcing you."

"Hey, thanks for threatening him with jail if he didn't."

She picked up her phone to call Sam and Clark. They were thrilled for her. Clark added, "Okay, honey, now you can slow down."

• • •

When Annie returned to the kitchen in her robe after a shower, Dan was stir-sautéing lobster with the ginger. He tossed a tiny bamboo steamer at her. She caught it in one hand, opened it, filled it with the dumplings he'd made.

As they ate them, side by side on her couch, overlooking the Chesapeake Bay, he handed her a wrapped present. Inside was an Afro-Cubano folk-art sculpture, a little red airplane made from old tin Coca-cola advertising signs. She loved it.

"Look inside," he told her.

In the cockpit, there was a small leather jeweler's box. Gold letters spelled

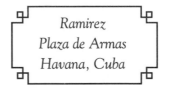

Ramirez
Plaza de Armas
Havana, Cuba

Inside the box was a beautiful, ornately worked gold ring with a blue sapphire. Dan slipped the ring on Annie's finger. It fit. "Raffy's mother made this. I bought it while you were talking to Ruthie. I had it sized in Key West. You like it?"

"Yes. The answer's yes."

"Good. I know you're marrying me for my cooking. And my singing."

"It's awful. But your marriage proposals are good."

"I'm marrying you for your cash." He followed her into the kitchen. "Your dad's cash from Feliz Diaz. Least the part of it you didn't give Raffy."

Annie tasted a piece of ginger. "That money goes in the bank for our kids."

He spooned rice into bowls. "So we are getting married? Or are we just having the kids?"

Annie took the plates of lobster back to the table. At her neatly arranged desk in a corner of her living room, her divorce papers sat. She brought them to the table and signed them.

Dan called to her. "Is that a yes? We're getting married?"

"That's a yes," she called back.

"Because, Annie, we've got to make some plans." He brought the rice to the table. "I've got to go back to Miami before they fire my butt for letting Raffy get away. So once we're married, do you move nearer Miami or do I move nearer Annapolis? We need to figure this all out. This is a major problem."

She lit the candles and poured two glasses of wine. "Oh, you're starting to sound like me. Stop planning. Everything's going to be okay."

Chapter 54

The Bride Comes Home

This time, every detail of Annie's wedding would turn out, Sam vowed, perfectly, just the way a bride's wedding should, which was just the way the bride wanted it—classic and beautiful, nothing gaudy. Oh, maybe a little cheerfulness, like the hand-painted banner that Dr. Sarah Yoelson had helped Sam hang across the porch posts of Pilgrim's Rest:

Congratulations!
Annie Goode and Daniel Hart
August 16, 2001!!!

Clark tried to persuade Sam that the banner's neon-glitter letters didn't fit in with the pale gold satin bows they'd tied on the linen tablecloths at the tables in the white tent or with the pale gold rosebuds twined with dark ivy that looped down the stair rail to the newel post and around the carved peregrine hawk. Or the garlands of small white orchids, cone flowers, and daisies on the mantels. Or his own ascot and gray cutaway.

Sam told Clark, "Love means you fit in even if you don't."

"Okay, leave your banner up, just don't start crying again."

"I never cry, Clark."

"You always cry."

Sam's surgery had been so successful that she'd been moving about on her cane and decorating the house for weeks before the wedding, without, she claimed, much discomfort at all. Despite a busy schedule, Sarah Yoelson was a big help with everything. Sarah still lived in Charlotte, where she was chief of orthopedic surgery at a hospital, but she was visiting Emerald more and more often, and Sam was visiting Charlotte, although Sam said she would never move out of Pilgrim's Rest, until Clark and Annie carried her out of the house in a box.

"Couldn't we hire an undertaker to do the heavy lifting?" asked Clark. "You've put on some L.B.s since your surgery."

"Hey, I'm fitter than you'll ever be," Sam told him.

"God knows," he agreed.

• • •

Annie finally called Brad the night before her wedding. She wanted to tell him she was marrying Dan and to ask his pardon for her part in their failed marriage. There were so many stupid things she'd said and bull-headed decisions she'd made; she'd thought she'd known everything but she hadn't known much at all.

As soon as they hung up, Brad phoned Sam and told her that Daniel Hart must have pressured Annie into marriage by threatening to send her to jail for aiding and abetting a criminal.

"I don't think so," Sam told him.

Brad claimed his heart was broken.

"He'll recover," Annie predicted to Sam.

Later that night Brad met a fashion model at the Atlanta airport. She had a gold stud on her tongue and was very sympathetic to the way Brad had been mistreated by his former wife, who was (and he choked up saying it), marrying somebody else tomorrow, even though he would have taken her back and had told her so.

"You're a prince," agreed the model.

• • •

At Pilgrim's Rest, where the wedding party gathered after the rehearsal dinner at Dina Destin's Barbecue, Sam took a stack of old sheet music from her piano bench and offered to play a few songs. But when she called for requests, she knew none of the songs that anyone under thirty wanted to hear. So, instead, Sam, rolling arpeggios up and down the keys, played a medley of "Moon River," "The Sound of Silence," and "Lara's Theme." Most of the people under thirty fled from the lush romantic music to the kitchen. But Annie sat with her aunt at the piano. As she sat there, she glanced at the tattered music cover to "Lara's Theme," where "Ruthie Nickerson" was inscribed, the looping curves under the R and the N, *con amore* in faded blue ink. She thought of the postcard with its photo of Claudette Colbert on the front and the note in the same handwriting. Maybe Ruthie had actually sent that postcard to Jack, rather than his having forged it as Annie had assumed. "Better this way," the card said. And after all, maybe it had been better.

For Annie there was no longer any surprise in thinking of Ruthie Nickerson as the young girl who'd given birth to her and then given her away. In that moment when Annie had looked a last long time into Ruthie's eyes, there in the Plaza des Armas, she'd felt a curious sense of quietly closing a door on the past; just as her father's raised hand, waving good-bye, dappled in the gold Havana sun, had made her feel so oddly peaceful.

Annie leaned over and gave a kiss to Sam's cropped white hair.

• • •

After the rehearsal guests all left, Sam announced that she was taking the plunge and throwing away the World's Biggest Jigsaw Puzzle so that Annie could have the wedding cake set out tomorrow on the round mahogany table in the bay window of the library. Besides, the family had long ago stopped even pretending they were interested in finishing that puzzle of vast rectangular cloudless blue sky. Annie herself wasn't interested, although she had once worked diligently to find parts that fit together, believing, without being able to articulate it, that to fill in the corners of the sky would be to understand something that had always waited just on the verge of meaning, like the woman on the ship in the ocean of her dream.

It was Dan who put the last pieces into the center of the puzzle, so that the sky was one huge blue square. Clark, Sam and Annie stared at it, a little disappointed. Somehow, all those years, finding the right shapes, fitting them together, they had imagined that this square would be more than it turned out to be. Bluer? Bigger? Filled with meaningful symbols? Somehow more?

Clark embraced Sam and Annie. "Well, ladies, you know how that song goes. 'It's not how you finish, it's how you start.'"

Sam said, "Clark, that's not how that song goes. Listen, I'll sing it—" She pulled away from him.

He held her fast. "Please don't go in there and play it again, Sam. Please!"

"You're a laugh riot." She scooped the pieces of the puzzle into a large plastic bag that she promised to put in the trash. But her family knew she would take the bag to the attic and save it.

• • •

Annie told Sam that the wedding was, in every way, as perfect as she could have dreamed it. Even the fact that Raffy Rook called her collect from Mexico early in the morning and told her that Jack and he weren't going to make it to the celebration. They had honestly been trying to get to Emerald for Jack to give her away but there'd been a slight problem. The two of them, Jack and himself, were fortune's fools. They'd been arrested in San Miguel de Allende for selling a Hollywood producer the last Russian Czarina's diamond broach, which wasn't exactly really Russian or exactly really diamonds either. Then they'd been robbed of all their money by the two convoy guards who were trucking them to jail. Not of course *all* their money, for Raffy still had a sizable bank account back in Miami in Chamayra's name, even after the $200,000 he'd given his mother Maria Ramirez. The good thing was, the guards had allowed Raffy to escape in exchange for everything they had on them and they promised to let Jack out in just a few days if Raffy sent them some more money, which Raffy had done.

"Is Dad dying?" Annie asked him.

"We are mortal, Annie, and, as Buddha and Christ both concluded, that sadly includes your dad. We are all dying if we take a longer look."

"Raffy! Is he dying *now?*"

The Cuban musician's voice was like his songs, soft, sweet. "Now? Oh no, not now. I have no doubt in the universe that your father will be leaving Mexico tonight at the latest. He plans to borrow a car—well, from a car lot, and I am to meet him in Vegas. Annie, your father has a terrible weakness for the four-card flush. It's his downfall."

Annie laughed. "Well, if you see him, say, well…"

Raffy sighed happily. "You love him."

"I love him."

"Didn't I tell you? 'Love bears it out even to the edge of doom.' And beyond, if you ask me. This wisdom of our human-ness was true 500 years ago when the great Swan said it. And true it will be 500 years from now, when we all of us here today are unfortunately, or not, in the earth, silent as dirt, or, let us hope, singing like angels."

• • •

Annie's long satin wedding dress, perfect for her, had arrived weeks earlier in an elegant box from a famous designer in New York. The card with the dress said only, "For Annie. From Ruth."

Down the garlanded stairs of Pilgrim's Rest, its banister hung with the pale gold roses and ivy and white silk ribbon, walked Sam. Then Dan's mother on the arm of his partner from the

Miami Police Department. Behind them came the bridesmaids in dark green and then the ring bearers and the flower girls and then Georgette, slim and pale, in the perfect dress for her auburn hair.

Everyone turned in the hallway as the string trio played Annie's favorite Mozart and Annie appeared in the beautiful dress. Everyone said the bride looked lovelier and more peaceful that she ever had looked before. She walked down the stairs of Pilgrim's Rest on Clark's arm. When she reached the hall, she paused an instant to touch the falcon carved above the words *Peregrinus sum*. Then she turned smiling and walked into the living room under an archway of roses and ribbon.

When Dan and Annie said their vows, she heard them this time, unlike at her first wedding. They said, "I do" to promises that, with love's help, they would be able to keep.

Clark and Sam and D. K. and Malpy and Teddy gave Annie away to Dan. Sam cried noisily when the minister told Dan, "You may kiss the bride." Dan said in his dinner toast in the bright noisy tent that everyone in Emerald knew that Clark and Sam and D. K. and Malpy and Teddy would never give Annie away at all.

Georgette, the maid of honor, caught the bouquet in her rose-silk Vera Wang, a dress as thin as a slip and the first dress, as she said in her maid of honor toast, that she'd ever worn that was a size eight since she and Annie were ten years old.

Georgette started the dancing in the tent, doing the cha-cha to "Baby It's You" with D. K. rolling himself backward and forward in his wheelchair, yelling, "This is a good day on the Mekong."

Georgette led Trevor through a salsa (she was taking salsa lessons) while pretending that he was leading her. They talked about the Baalbek archeological dig where Trevor had vacationed, and a trip to Luxor that they both had always wanted to take.

Malpy raced among the dancers, barking at them with enthusiasm. Teddy growled weakly in her pagoda.

Georgette ran up to Annie's room where the bride was changing clothes to leave for her honeymoon. "Annie, I'm not drunk. I'm a little drunk. I don't even drink except at your weddings. So please don't get married again. I'll get a reputation as a binge drinker."

Annie promised she wouldn't.

Georgette took a deep breath. "I just feel I have to tell you something. Maybe it's wrong. But I feel like..."

Annie asked, "This isn't about Brad again, is it? I'm sure he did hit on you. Every chance he got."

Georgette shook her head violently. "No, he's really good-looking but, I'm sorry, forgive me, he's a jerk. Besides I couldn't. We're practically, well, sisters. That's what I want to tell you. We're—"

"Cousins," Annie smiled. "We're cousins. Your aunt Ruthie's my mother. Is that what you were going to say?"

"You just have to be faster, don't you?" Georgette hugged her friend. "Yes, I did my blood work and Clark's got every test he ever ran on you. We're cousins."

Annie kissed her again, smiling. She picked up the crystal on her dresser, the wishing bell, the small neon-blue sunglasses. "Just don't do blood work on the Peregrines," she said. "Or Clark. You'll be in for a shock."

"Oh my God," said Georgette. "Just tell me Trevor's not your brother because then he'd be my cousin. And I really like him. Good-bye. Have a wonderful honeymoon. I love you. Good-bye." Georgette threw a handful of paper confetti on Annie's head.

Dan and Annie raced down the porch steps through the rainbow of confetti and ran out into the meadow between Pilgrim's Rest and the Nickerson house.

D. K.'s tethered hot-air balloon, the same one in which Annie had for the first time in her life left earth for air, floated against the blue summer sky. D. K.'s nieces held the ropes that tethered the basket. As Annie and Dan climbed inside, Clark held Malpy in a tight clasp to make sure he didn't leap in the basket too.

They fired the burner and in a whoosh the huge ruby-red and emerald-green balloon ascended with Sam's hand-painted banner of Congratulations flying out behind them, among old shoes and cans.

As Dan and Annie floated up over Pilgrim's Rest, they heard the hum of a small airplane buzzing by. It was D. K. in his Pawnee Cropduster, tipping his wing to her. Down in the field below, she could see Sam and Clark, Georgette and Trevor, all dancing. The tiny plane with its black American eagle painted on its nose vanished into clouds.

Chapter 55

Above the Clouds

On their honeymoon, fourteen thousand feet above the sea, Annie and Dan hiked steadily, pausing to rest in the thin air, trekking the steep trail that twisted through misty green mountains into Machu Picchu. They stopped to watch as dawn lined up its rays with Intipunku, the sun gate. And then, suddenly, there they stood, the two of them gazing down on the Lost City of the Incas, secret and sacred, a metropolis built half a millenium ago, when the Incan empire stretched larger than all of Europe. A city abandoned, as if overnight, who knew why?

Leaning their backs against the gray immense blocks of perfect stone that had been so long ago so precisely, patiently carved, and that now lay haphazardly toppled beside the hiking path, the young couple ate their picnic on the last weekend of their honeymoon. They had hiked in from their hotel in Cuzco, a sixteenth-century convent a few blocks from a Spanish cathedral built on top of an Inca palace. They'd spent a week with no phone calls, no television, no papers. But now Dan was looking at a Miami newspaper another guest at the hotel had given him.

News of the world, Dan told his bride. Annie was eating fruit and bread, cheese and sausage, leaning into him. Under this blue sky, in this sun, news of the world sounded ordinary: the American economy was weak, Bush's job performance rating was 51 percent negative, a consortium of major news organizations was expected on September 12 to release its findings that Al Gore had in fact won the vote recount in Florida. Israel was meeting with Palestine and the top U.S. utilities analyst had just reported that Enron Corporation was about to implode.

Dan and Annie found the local Miami stories more interesting.

On the society page, Melissa Skippings announced her engagement to local stockbroker and tarpon fisherman, Tucker Bradley. Miss Skippings, formerly chief administrator of the Golden Days Center for Active Living on Ficus Avenue in Miami, would be moving with her husband to Japan.

Danish wreck salvage divers employed by the Cuban government had made an astonishing discovery while exploring a sunken sixteenth-century Spanish galleon, a vessel sunk in a storm in 1549 while sailing in a twenty-ship fleet past the Archiapiélago de los Colorados to Havana. The divers had focused their attention on a particular cay after a local student, cleaning a conch shell on the beach there, had found inside the conch, to his astonishment, a 135-carat cut and polished star ruby.

The star ruby had been appraised at $12.6 million. Divers immediately returned to the site. There on the fourth day of diving, they uncovered beneath the seabed a few rotted ribs of the Spanish ship *La Madre del Salvador*. Over the next week, teams of divers recovered cannon balls, an astrolabe, an ivory comb, a steel mirror. Most importantly, under an enormous bronze cannon, they came upon a crushed, rusted, and barnacled iron chest bearing the escutcheon of Don Carlos de Tormes. Tormes was believed by scholars to have been traveling to Spain in *La Madre* in order to give a statue known as *La Reina Coronada del Mar*, the Queen of the Sea, to his sovereign Philip II.

Under a rusted anchor nearby, divers in fact found a crushed gold statue. But it was so smashed that it took a while to identify it as the Virgin Mary holding a baby. Salt water had seeped into the leather chest for centuries. The wood had mostly dissolved into nothing but ocean. On the other hand, the broken pieces of gold glistened as luminously as they had the day the Inca artist had fashioned them to fit the head and heart of the Mother of God.

The newspaper article said that the Cuban government was claiming ownership of the broken artifact and of the star ruby. They would be added to La Reina's relics already in the Museo Habana: the statue of the Virgin Mary (both the Cuban government and the FBI had kept very quiet about the fact that the "gold" statue was a gold-plated reproduction and the "sixteenth-century" casket allegedly containing a "Holy Thorn"—while real silver—was not sixteenth-century silver), and the very real two emeralds, three rubies, six sapphires, and two diamonds.

Museo Habana officials said the discovery raised questions about the authenticity of the so-called *Reina Coronada del Mar* "relic" that was currently on display in the Church of the Sacred Heart in Miami. Archbishop de Uloa had accepted the "relic" on behalf of his Catholic diocese when Miami business leader Feliz Diaz had so generously and with much publicity donated it and Museo officials claimed he'd either been taken for a ride or was in the driver's seat of a scam.

Rebutting the Cuban announcement, the archbishop issued a statement that the relic currently on display in the Church of the Sacred Heart was absolutely genuine, no matter what the Castro regime claimed. He even let a jeweler look at it and then testify that the gold statue was real gold and the five very large emeralds in her crown were real emeralds. More to the Catholic point, said the archbishop, was the measureless value of the holy statue as once the vessel of a silver casket (admittedly now missing) that once had held a Thorn from Christ's Crown of Thorns.

The Danish salvage company filed suit for half the profits from the sale of the star ruby found in the conch shell.

As Dan folded the paper, Annie grinned. "Dad did it. He pulled the big con!"

She said that while it was possible that back in the sixteenth century someone had removed the statue before the Spanish ship sank and that it was possible that this statue had been found by her ancestor Joseph "Boss" Peregrine and had been brought, as her dad claimed, all the way from Cuba to Emerald, North Carolina, she thought it more likely that Boss had found a few emeralds and rubies in the rubble of the monastery, or even that he had sluiced them out of the Appalachian mountains. In either case, her father had found those jewels at Pilgrim's Rest and out of them had created this whole story about a golden relic of the past that he'd somewhere read about. "Remember how Raffy kept telling us that his family had been goldsmiths and silversmiths in Havana for a hundred years? His mother made both copies of the Queen. And she made the silver casket."

"Mrs. Ramirez has a lot of talent." Dan kissed Annie's hand that wore the Ramirez engagement and wedding rings.

Annie repacked their picnic leftovers. "Dad was working with her all along. First, Raffy's mother made the fake *La Reina Coronada del Mar* for Dad to sell to Diaz. And then when they got in trouble and Ruthie cut Dad a deal with the FBI, Mrs. Ramirez made the gold-plate copy for the switch." Annie speculated that Raffy's whole sob story about how his mother had shut the door in his face had been part of the con. She grew thoughtful. "Maybe the whole setup, sending me to St. Louis and to Miami, maybe it was all part of the sting. Digging up the silver box at Hialeah was the seed; the gold statue was the payoff. I was the perfect accomplice because I was a complete skeptic. And then I fell for it. Who would doubt *me*? I said it's real. That's what Dad and Raffy planned—for me to believe it. For Ruthie to believe it. Another skeptic. They said, 'Look here!' and we looked."

"I looked too," Dan admitted. "I still want to believe."

Annie smiled. "They fooled me, you, Diaz, Ruthie, and most of all, McAllister Fierson and company. Dad and Raffy's only big con. I kind of like that."

Shouldering their backpacks, the young couple headed down into the ruins of the great lost city of the fallen Incan empire, Machu Picchu, which, on some mysterious horrible day five hundred years earlier, had been destroyed by soldiers of the Spanish empire, which had also long since fallen into ruin.

• • •

Eight months later, Sam folded Annie's satin wedding gown and carried it to the cedar closet in the attic where she would keep it, not because she thought there was a chance that Annie would ever marry anyone else but because the dress was from Ruthie and it was a reminder, a memory, of so happy a day in Annie's life that Annie's children might someday like to see it, a daughter might even want to wear it.

In the attic, Sam came across a box neatly packed with Annie's Halloween costumes; many of them, Sam herself had haphazardly made. The smallest costume she found was a little witch's outfit with a high black cone hat and a black satin cape tied with a black ribbon.

Headed back downstairs, on the second-floor landing, Sam had to sit on the step, holding the wedding dress and the child-size witch's cape, leaning her head against the stair rails, because she couldn't stop crying.

Coming home from the hospital, Clark heard her and ran quickly up the stairs from the hallway. "Sam? Sam?"

"I'm fine."

He sat beside her, his long legs bent to his chest. They sat there a while. Finally Clark said, "She'll be okay. Nothing will happen to her in Iraq."

"It's a war, Clark."

He looped his arm around his friend. "I sure did think we'd leave her a better world."

Sam kept crying.

"You know what, Sam?" Clark hugged her next to him, held up the laced satin sleeve of the wedding dress in her lap. "You know what? You're just crying because mothers in movies always cry."

"Oh Clark, stop it." She rested her head on his shoulder, her hand patting the small black cape. "Mothers cry in movies because mothers cry."

They sat at home, on the porch at Pilgrim's Rest, hoping, waiting.

January 2008

In January in North Carolina between the Piedmont and the coast, by late afternoon the sky gathers darkness and dreams of night.

The old cemetery of St. Mark's Church in Emerald had new graves this winter. The newest was the red-mounded earth where Anne Peregrine Goode-Hart now stood quietly. She wore a dark-blue winter uniform, with the badges and ribbons and insignia of a Lt. Commander of the United States Navy.

There was no tombstone yet on the new grave because Sam could not yet bring herself to choose what the marker should say. Maybe, she told Annie, they should put a pun on it. The whole idea of the final choice of what to say was going to be, Sam worried, too much of an ending for her.

Annie's six-year-old daughter, impatient, ran up and down the gravel path among the gravestones. She wore a wool Florida Marlins baseball jacket that her father had given her. Tripping on an old uneven stone, she fell, bracing her fat pink gloves in the gravel.

"Samantha, be careful."

The child ignored her. "Is it going to snow? Daddy says it's going to snow. We never get snow in Florida."

Annie studied how the clouds were rolling over the corner of the sky. "Maybe," she conceded.

"Mom!" Samantha shouted. She stood near a large bush of browned rhododendron blossoms. "Is this Grandpa Jack's grave?"

Annie walked over to her and looked at the sunken small gray marker.

JOHN INGERSOLL PEREGRINE
1946–1948
TAKEN FROM ME

Kneeling, she brushed dry leaves from the gray curve of the little carved wings. "No, that's his brother's grave. Grandpa Jack's not dead."

"Then he ought to come see us," the child solemnly said. "If he does, I'm going to thank him for all my money. Daddy said Grandpa Jack gave me a lot of money and I ought to give it to you and him when you're old. But I don't want you to get old."

"We won't for a long time." Her mother smiled but was pre-occupied, turning sadly back to the red upheaval of earth.

Her daughter ran after her, reached for her hand. "I'm sorry Uncle Clark died. He was nice."

Annie agreed that Clark was very nice.

Samantha frowned. "Aunt Sam is so sad. She says she misses Clark's stupid jokes." The little girl looked up at her mother, hoping for confirmation. "She misses her dog Teddy too. But Sam'll be okay, right?"

Annie squeezed her daughter's hand. "She'll be okay. She's got Sarah and us and the Destin family and Malpy and all her friends. Your daddy's her good friend."

The child found the large number of Sam's acquaintances consoling. "Daddy says his name is Hart because he's got a big heart. Is that true?"

"He does have a big heart."

"He says his heart hurts because you're sad about Clark. He wants Sam to take all the crap out of Pilgrim's Rest and put it in the yard and sell it. He says she should make one of her big signs that says "Crap for Sale," because you don't sell your garage when you have a 'garage sale' and you don't sell your 'yard' when you have a 'yard sale,' but Sam sure would be having a 'crap sale' if she sold all that junk in her attic." Samantha glanced quickly at Annie's face, hoping to see shock at the word 'crap.'

But all her mother said was, "Sam's not going to sell that junk. And besides you never know when you might find something you really like up in Sam's attic. Like how about that pink baseball cap Sam gave you with all the jewels on it?"

"Sam said they're really real jewels."

Annie fastened the strap on one of Samantha's gloves. "They are real."

Her daughter was distracted by the appearance of a family, a young mother and father with a little girl of about her age. They were walking up the hill to the graves. Their voices carried through the bare winter trees. They were talking about something they'd heard today on the news. The young man said, "Did you ever think they'd indict McAllister Fierson?"

The young woman said, "See, there's hope."

Annie smiled wryly. Fierson was one story of many that the news reported on, casually and with an ephemeral interest in its truth. Ruth Nickerson's part in the story would never be told.

Samantha ran down the path and stared at the other little girl from behind a large gray, pitted obelisk, the tomb of some Emerald soldier named Peregrine, long dead in some long ago American war fought for some reason or other.

"Come back here, Samantha."

Annie saw the couple noticing her Navy uniform and the braided cap she held in her hands. Instinctively she braced herself for a certain look from them, suspicious, distrustful. But instead they politely waved.

Only a month earlier she had worn this braided cap at the funeral in Arlington Cemetery of her former husband, Brad Hopper. Brad had died in a car bombing, on the road from the military airport into Baghdad. For his actions in rescuing a fellow officer, he had received posthumously the Navy Cross, accepted at the ceremony by his mother. After the service, Annie made her way to Mama Spring while Brad's sister was helping the trembling woman into the limousine. Annie said that Brad's family must be very proud of him, and rightly so. He was the hero he had always wanted to be.

Annie was thinking gratefully about Brad and the last time she'd seen him. At her request, he'd flown one of the new Hopper jets to Emerald so that she could take her uncle, Clark, up for a ride.

While they knew Clark was dying, they didn't think the cancer would take him so quickly, only six months after he'd diagnosed himself. He had hypothesized that the source of the malignancy might be the damage caused by particles of the incendiary weapon white phosphorous, used by the Army against enemy insurgents in Vietnam.

"But please don't ever mention this to Sam," he asked Annie. "It'll just drive her nuts. And smoking didn't help."

Clark waited until Annie's visit on her birthday so he could tell her face-to-face. He told her it was the last of her birthdays that they'd share, "at least on this side of the grave, which is not to be taken as a grave matter, Annie."

Inside the house, Dan and Samantha sat watching *The Wizard of Oz* with Sam. Clark sat with Annie on the porch. They watched the sun fall, reddening the river that the Indians had named Aquene, peace. He told her the news he'd confirmed only a few weeks earlier. "Now, is this fair?" he joked. "Your dad gets pretend cancer and I get the real thing?"

Annie reached to Clark's rocking chair beside her to touch his thin knobby hand. "No, it isn't fair. But isn't that always the way it is with you?" He looked at her, puzzled. She smiled at him. "You're the real thing. Cancer. The real Ruthie, the real me. At least that's what Ruthie told me in Havana six years ago. She was still mad that you went back to Vietnam, when she loved you so much."

"...Hmmm." He rocked slowly, three taps of his foot on the floor. Then he slowly smiled back at her. "Thank you for telling me that."

She held his hand.

"Well," he said, "Your dad was a real flyer and I'm sure not that."

And so at Christmas, Annie asked Brad to lend her a jet and she took Clark up for a ride from Destin Airworks. "We're going to go fast," she told him. "Faster than sound."

"Can you go faster than time?"

"I can try. Hang on."

Annie flew Clark high above Emerald, to all four corners of the sky. She flew the small light jet upside-down and then into a loop-the-loop, and then into a barrel roll and then into a long spiral. Like American flyers before her, like Bessie Coleman, like Amelia Earhart and Jacqueline Cochran, Annie was fast and sure and skilled, tipping, soaring. It was the most beautiful flying she'd ever done.

But it was not as fast as time.

Back on the runway, as Annie and D. K. helped Clark out of the plane, he laughed when D. K. told him that he looked as green as an emerald.

Clark said he wasn't surprised. "D. K., up there I was so worried I was going to die I forgot I was dying."

"Well," said D. K. "I guess that's the whole idea."

A week later, at home at Pilgrim's Rest, with Sam fallen asleep in the chair beside him, Clark quietly, slowly stopped breathing.

• • •

Standing beside his grave, Annie looked out to the horizon. Clouds roiled, black as smoke and swirled scudding across the winter sky.

• • •

Against the darkening night, small lights came on like stars in the houses of the small town, one by one. Lights came on in the churchyard where Clark was buried and beyond the Aquene River brightened the runway at Destin Airworks. Lights came on in Georgette's house.

Across America, to where Jack Peregrine caught cards in air, to where Ruthie Nickerson worked alone at a desk, lights came on.

Lights came on, steady as stars, in Pilgrim's Rest where Annie's family waited for her to bring her daughter home.

ABOUT THE AUTHOR

Michael Malone is the author of ten novels, a collection of short stories, and two works of nonfiction. Educated at Carolina and at Harvard, he is now a professor in Theater Studies at Duke University. Among his prizes are the Edgar, the O. Henry, the Writers Guild Award, and the Emmy. He lives in Hillsborough, North Carolina, with his wife.